first fallback position in which to rest if something went wrong on one of their scavenges.

Canby's mother had taught him and his brothers that it was too dangerous to recuperate and collect themselves out in the open, in some field or road or park or, God forbid, urban public sidewalk, should some form of foul fate befall them. They needed fortified protection. Thus, they had numerous and numbered hideouts all along their nightly route, each one never far from any possible current position. It was in this manner that they crept through their surroundings, seeking pay dirt: half-pound lean ground turkey packets thrown into the community dumpster behind the upscale mixed-use condominiums south of Human, Human Coffee Shop. Or the fat scraps skillfully sliced off from dozens of two-pound cuts of top sirloin. They were routinely thrown in with Gouda cheese beyond its expiration date, yet, clear to any effort of the olfactory, still prime for weeks. The packaging was mushed into the trashcan behind 23 Nyqvist, which was overflowing with a smorgasbord of rotting greens, which in their combination, smelled uncannily like dying groundhog. Or so Canby had always thought.

But at each coordinate of bounty was a danger with teeth or tires or brooms or bullets. And so, instructed as a family by their mother, they mastered swift and graceful exits. And each swift and graceful exit always led to a secure, man-made structure not far away. Such were the mechanics of human spatial organization. If a house had a ferocious dog, it might also have a shed with loose doors and open space inside in which to nap. If a strip-mall dumpster had surveillance that prompted the angry appearance of a pellet gun–armed sushi restaurant owner, then there was a pool flotation device locker on the edge of the apartment complex just thirty feet westward in which to recuperate from the startle. This was how raccoons in the city of Trams operated—with clear recovery and respite always in sight.

To get from their current location to the Ventillis' shed, the four of them would have only to sneak through a couple hundred feet of trees: Cyprus, oak, maple, birch, a few scattered dogwoods, and imported Japanese varieties thanks to overaggressive suburban landscapers before the flood of 1994 inspired conservation easements. They would then have to climb over the chain link fence and traverse a narrow stretch of grass. The exact length was unclear now because Canby had measured by watching the movement of his mother's hind leg. It was also unclear what creatures waited in the wooded area. Canby also wondered whether the houses abutting the Ventillis' had either cats or dogs. This was a problem, the unsureness. Sure, the brothers could handle a cat. They scared and became very passive-aggressive about square feet. In such case, the brothers would perform the required square-feet square dance, so to speak. But dogs, oh, the dogs. They had less awareness of their appetites. A coyote would be worst of all. An out of place coyote was what his mother had once referred to as "caput!" Canby had initially laughed at this, thinking it funny sounding, like a wet and squeaking fart. But now, caput sounded to him like the heart of doom.

So it was that the next generation of Trams city raccoons would begin to make their way through the world without their mother. Their mother's legacy and memory would carry on through the perpetuation of the lessons she taught so well and that she had learned from her mother. For the time being, the lessons would be enough. And surely the day would come when Canby and his younger brothers would encounter something that their dutiful mother never could have imagined, and the lessons would fall short. But for now, with deft effort and aside from unfortunate canine incursions, they would be safe until they needed to venture out again for food or water or until Mr. Ventilli came looking for his lawn mower.

* * *

"Saaardiiiiines!" Pollock said in a coarse, low voice, reminiscing on a fragment of a cartoon he had watched on YouTube a few weeks back. It was supposed to cheer him up. Outside, dead leaves from the previous autumn scratched their way up Nyqvist Boulevard in a hot morning gust. It sounded like a rusty manual garage door being slowly pulled open. Seated at the table in the breakfast nook, Pollock pulled the blinds open. The sunrise boiled low in the sky like a melting pack of neon crayons.

A stack of worn North American bird books sat on the windowsill. A leather case containing a pair of Bausch & Lomb binoculars hung from a nail in the window's frame. Pollock opened his laptop and yawned. He had always been a morning person but was finding waking early harder and harder as he grew older. In the summer, six-year-old Pollock had *Tom and Jerry*, helping his father shave, and then summer camp to look forward to. Ten-year-old Pollock had the construction of the putt-putt coarse in the backyard to oversee. Twenty-seven-year-old Pollock had five years of office jobs behind him. He had compaction in his neck and an unhealthy habit of drinking sherry or IPAs until he could sleep through the night.

He finished off a mouthful of the sardines he was eating for breakfast and said aloud, "Every morning I wake up and say to myself, 'It can't get any better than this. But it always does; it just keeps getting better!'" He didn't believe these words but wanted to become someone who did through their crude and continued announcement, as if teaching himself hopefulness through rote memory.

This morning and the previous three, Pollock had come to from his sleep on the couch to what seemed to be a blurry wraith, hovering, somewhere between sleep and wakefulness. Yesterday, as it sort of evaporated, he caught the image of an elderly woman with stern European features. Pulses of adrenaline, remnants of powerful dream emotions, had thundered through his chest, and he pulled his legs into his body. A tight jerk. Confounded and alert, he scanned the room. There was the wooden credenza to the left, the front bay windows ahead, and round coffee table just beneath his defensive hands. As his dream state cleared, so did his heightened concern. He had the same reaction earlier this morning, and the repetition was renewing his worry.

He selected Mingle.com from his favorites in the Google menu bar. The dating site catered to professionals in their twenties and thirties who would rather spend an evening drinking wine and watching *Mad Men* in bed while chatting with numerous potential mates matched from a questionable logarithm, than dressing and parceling out painful introductions to strangers at clubs and bars.

Despite its targeted consumer group, many older people used the site, often in a borderline predatory manner. Further, Pollock had become acquainted with a specific cross section of "daters" who introduced themselves to potential matches via a message containing carnal descriptions of the acts they pursued. His favorite had been username "fertile wet mammal 449" who had offered to trim his pubic hair and make a framed art piece out of the shavings for him to keep in exchange for a ride to a neighboring town to escape the frequent beatings of her abusive boyfriend. Pollock responded with listings of local abuse support groups. For cheer, he included a short video clip of naked elderly men unsuccessfully trying to capture seagulls with jai alai baskets on the cold winter beaches of New York.

Each morning, Pollock could expect at least two of these treats. Checking them had become part of his morning ritual. They frightened him and made life seem just a little more exhilarating. They made it a little bit more tolerable.

"I want to lubricate your toes and stick them in my asshole." Pollock giggled while plucking chunks of putrid green sardine flesh with his fork and gulping them down. That was the only message in his inbox this morning, which saddened him. Regardless, he opened the leather case and extracted the binoculars to begin the other component to his morning ritual. For the past few months, since Pollock had moved into the house, he had found the binoculars useful for surveilling the inhabitants of his new neighborhood. Surrounding breakfast, Pollock would spend fifteen minutes or so scanning Nyqvist Boulevard south to Hjelmstad and then back north and steeply upward to where Nyqvist bent east into Klum Court.

Pollock delighted in observing the diverse groups of neighbors. There was Mr. Studebaker, the tall, lean mechanic who lived just south on the opposite side of the street. He was an early riser. Pollock would often spot the middle-aged man sporting his jean jacket and heading stealthily to the detached garage for a morning cigarette, his eyes shifting, searching for any signs of detection. His motions were rife with syncopated hesitations—catlike. Through the paneled windows on the garage door, Pollock could usually make out his slender figure slouched on the wooden workbench, his head leaning back against the metal tool cabinet, sucking deep breaths of smoke and letting them slowly billow out near the cracked window, his head tilting upward in what seemed a reflex of ecstasy.

A few times, as Mr. Studebaker was enjoying his secrecy, his teenage son, Noah, was sneaking into the window on the far south side of the home, presently returned from a night out, his small dark hands pawing their way across the pale blue shingles. Once he had a female friend in tow. She was blonde with red streaks dyed in, and she wore a long white gala dress. Noah fashioned an Amish-style beard with no hair on the upper lip and often wore overalls. Corduroy, not jean. Grey. Through various interactions, Pollock had deduced that there was a Mrs. Studebaker, but he had never seen her. He imagined what secrets she had. He imagined what Studebaker family dinners were like. He wondered what was going on with them.

Next, Pollock could usually count on the emergence of the "Ne'er-do-wells," his name for a group of four middle-school children being raised by what Pollock would call *laissez-faire*-style parents. For any mishap or shenanigans that occurred on the block, they were likely its authors. The redhead, Henry, was their leader. John was next in command. He was a big-boned brunet with a large birthmark on his right cheek. Andy and Alex were both a grade younger and were on an equal footing with one another. The four little kids waddled around houses and cars like a semidemonic gaggle of ornery goslings.

They had once opened the door to the Sheffield's woodchuck station wagon and put the auto into neutral. While they sprinted away toward Klum, suppressing their exhaust-like laughs with their sticky palms, the station wagon slowly accumulated momentum until finally crunching against the concrete and brick of Danny's Bar & Grill at the corner of Nyqvist and Hjelmstad. There was a witness to the debacle. The police were involved. Some sentence of community service had been enforced on the kids. As old Ms. Nisky said, whenever referencing the period of that community service, "The street was quiet during those times!" Yet, a few months later they were back at it. On this particular morning, Pollock spotted two of the members, John and Andy, playing video games in Andy's backyard tree house. No appearance of impropriety.

Farther up Nyqvist, at the mouth of the Klum Court cul-de-sac, there were the Ventillis. The Ventillis were a newly married couple in their early thirties. Both had attended Yale University and received outstanding marks in their respective majors. Benji had focused on international studies and political science. Karen majored in microbiological engineering. She worked in a lab at Stalz Research facilities, researching cutting-edge cancer treatments. Benji worked in a management and planning capacity for two nonprofit organizations in town: Meal Source and The Face of Our Town. Each had its distinct mission statement, but in common they both focused on making food and housing available for the less fortunate, sponsoring homeless employment projects, and matching war vets with pro bono counselors and psychologists. All of this information had come to Pollock secondhand from the elderly gossiping women of Nyqvist. Basically, Ms. Nisky.

Karen was unbelievably beautiful. She had first caught Pollock's eye a few weeks back when he first saw the two having sex with the bedroom lights on and curtains open. Karen was on top, in the cowgirl position. Her caramel locks were bouncing up and then falling down and dancing around the edges of her freckled breasts. She was deliberate and forceful with her thrusts. Pollock had focused the binoculars tightly and did not waver until the couple's act had come to completion.

He felt a bit embarrassed about watching the couple for a little too long that first time, until it happened again and again. The count was in the double digits at present. It was suspicious to Pollock; how did they not know that neighbors were watching? Additionally, after Ben left for the bus in the morning, Karen would often take her time getting ready for work, walking around the bedroom and living room in the buff for upwards of an hour, occasionally sipping at a cup of tea, stroking deodorant under her arm, plucking the occasional hair from her nipple.

The couple's mere existence was a strange mockery to Pollock. They had too much going for them. He couldn't trust their presentation. It had to be a lie. They were sewing him a stuffed animal without genitals. Where was the dirty asshole of it all? Such was the state of Pollock's natural paranoia. Anyway, the curtains were closed this morning. Pollock scooped the last of the sardines and noticed that he had another message on Mingle. It was from username "wooden nickels." He clicked the envelope icon. The message read:

You seem intriguing. Would you like to meet for some coffee or drinks sometime? Ask me about my dream from last night…

This interested Pollock. He usually made the first advances. The site was set up so that the user would be notified of all those who visited one's profile. Thus, there was usually a toying game of "I viewed your profile, then you viewed mine, then I viewed yours, now lets proceed and say hello already" before the first conversation. Wooden nickels's message broke past all of that, and Pollock appreciated it. However, he navigated to her profile before crafting a response. There, he found a photograph of her with an older gentleman in a dirty cloth onesie and a younger boy with a goofy, crooked smile on his face, staring upon something astray from the camera's gaze. The girl, presumably "wooden nickels," was short and thin and plain. She had braided brown hair under a black ball cap that read "Fleetwood Mac." Underneath the picture, Pollock read her bio.

> Hi! I'm Retta. I am in nursing school. I am also Wiccan! That's right. Wicca is a discipline dedicated to the ethical use of natural forces. I do not fly on a broomstick. Ask me about it sometime. Family is very important to me. I live with my father, Remy, who is a brilliant mechanic and one-time regional bridge champion, and my little brother, Fox. Fox is a low-functioning autistic. He is brilliant at any video game and loves music and National Geographic documentaries. We just watched one about the coywolf!
>
> My hobbies include bicycling around town, visiting the local farmer's market, chain watching science fiction movies, helping sick people get better, listening to vinyl and family dinners (I am a terrific chef).

Her description painted her a little too hipster for Pollock's taste. He had grown tired of the horde of millennials sporting ironic mustaches and black zoo T-shirts. They rode fixed gear bikes, preferred vinyl to the easily accessible platforms like Spotify, YouTube, ITunes, or Pandora, and almost always had some variety of food agenda. He recalled his new coworker Sally described herself as "a green eco-captain vegan interested in improving humane treatment." She only ate at a drastically few restaurants, after a lengthy discussion with the owners about what she would be consuming in each meal.

It occurred to Pollock that this was not necessarily in any way imprudent. Pollock valued prudence, research. But, it bothered him how much it was talked about, bandied about like some fifth grader who just got her first pair of LA Light tennis shoes. Who had the time to research all of these issues and then institute some competent scheme? It made Pollock suspicious. He wanted to know where the dirty asshole was.

But he did really appreciate how she described her family, and that she was on track to becoming a nurse. He felt compelled to respond to her. After all, it had been weeks of fooling around on the site without any real prospects. And she was a blazing specimen amid the masses of perverts that had been engaging him. He ran his fingers through his straight, dirty-blond strands.

Sure, that would be nice. Have you been to Human, Human Coffee Shop?

He clicked send, snapped his laptop shut, drew the blinds and headed for the shower. Through the hallway, Pollock passed lazy stacks of cardboard boxes. The putrid green walls were lined with large wooden-framed photo collages containing colorful 35mm shots from the fifties and sixties. There was one with Pollock's father, Saul, six years old sporting aviator sunglasses and a red striped tee. Saul was hugging his aunt Anne's leg in front of a large country estate. The house was covered in strings of large colored C9 Christmas bulbs glowing in the dusk. Anne had a Schlitz and a Marlboro in her free hand, the other on Saul's shoulder. Neither was smiling.

Pollock had moved to Trams five months ago to take on a planning & development position with Trams City Zoning Department. The job had come with a steep pay increase from his previous code enforcement position in Alsbar. City planning, and zoning more specifically, was Pollock's great interest. He had tried numerous times to propose plans to the zoning and building services departments in Alsbar to no avail. The City of Trams offered him the opportunity to rile his creative energies and institute additions to the existing law. He would be working with architects, business owners, contractors, developers, and city officials, including the mayor's office and the city attorney. In an idealistic sense, Pollock saw the job as an opportunity to change the face of the city.

The decision to move to Trams was made easier because Pollock had ten years earlier inherited his great-aunt's home in an older neighborhood on the edge of downtown Trams. It had, in the interim, been rented, prefurnished, through the oversight of a property manager, Tyrese. Management of Tyrese had been one of Pollock's earliest responsibilities as a teenager and likely informed his desire to pursue a career dealing with property.

The Kripke brothers, the previous tenants, had sent notice to Pollock that they intended to vacate the premises. They had grown increasingly vicious in every interaction since Tyrese had made an ill-advised pass at the younger Kripke, Dan. There had immediately followed a fistfight between Tyrese and Dan, in the rain, on the sloping front lawn. The older Kripke, Silas, explained over the phone to Pollock that they had been looking at moving to another neighborhood for some time and now would have a reason to finally do it. The brothers Kripke also desired the liberty to furnish and decorate at their discretion. The antique woodwork and outdated color schemes throughout the home had worn on them. Pollock had already received his job offer in Trams so he took it and pursued no action against the Kripkes.

Tyrese understood and acquiesced immediately when Pollock explained he would be moving in and therefore no longer needed his services. In the years since he started as a property manager, Tyrese had acquired contracts for several large commercial lots, mostly shopping strips and apartment complexes. He had incorporated and employed a team of twelve workers. The small house on Nyqvist had become an outlier, and he was happy to be rid of it.

Upon first visiting the house, Pollock spent the afternoon looking over the objects of his great-aunt's estate: the woodworking shop in the basement, the tool-shed out back, the garage filled with odd motors, tools, and rusty metal engine parts remaining from when his great-uncle Bodey had been a machinist. A flood of memories came rushing back to Pollock and sent a spurt of cosmic energy up his spine. He had spent the summers of his youth in this house. He recalled the smell of Anne baking carrot cakes in the kitchen. The odor had merged with the strange chemical stench emanating from the basement, where Bodey was apply-ing wood finish to the birdhouses that he made and sold as a hobby. He remem-bered the knitted tapestries of Irish farmers that hung in the spare bedroom where he slept. They still hung there. Pollock had his first kiss with a girl named Callie from the next block over. It had been the last week of his visit before eighth grade.

Pollock parked his white Toyota truck near the back of the expansive park-ing area beside the Trams city facilities building. It was a monstrous brick bunker-like structure with few windows. It looked like Soviet government structures that Pollock had seen in photos. The facilities and parking lot were on the edge of town, off of the interstate in an enclave of forest. The only other business in the area was an independent coffee bean company that announced its presence in the afternoons with the smells of roasting coffee beans, which crept through the thick oaks and maples and washed over the brick bunker. Pollock stretched the remnants of morning lethargy out of his shoulders and thighs, and then headed to the front door.

Disgruntled Trams citizens seeking building permits, zoning variances, or surveyor services formed a line wrapping along the front hallway. There were twelve bays partitioned out along the front counter, but never more than three manned with employees. Thus, the numerous individuals that had planned to arrive before the facilities opened and make a quick trip of it were always there much longer than anticipated. Further, the few employees were never hesitant about allotting themselves frequent cigarette breaks. This resulted in a certain level of polite hostility that seemed to seep into the offices and create an air of defensiveness among Pollock's coworkers. Occasionally it led to strident customer invective.

Pollock shared an office area with Quentin Lovejoy. Quentin was a squat older man with fat hands and a wiry grey horseshoe that wrapped around his pockmarked head. His official title was Assistant Director of Code Development. He had explained to Pollock that the job primarily consisted of justifying his job's existence through poetics and the occasional brilliant burst of vague language he might add to a preexisting ordinance. His desk joined ends with Pollock's. A waist-high aluminum shelving unit enclosed their space in a rectangle. Ingress and egress was accomplished via a swinging gate that screeched like a miffed pterodactyl. The rectangle's shelves were stuffed with poorly maintained city code books and maps. Their pages were all frayed and torn around the edges and otherwise littered with inky fingerprints. Outside of their shared area stretched curious and sometimes maddening patterns of cubicles in every direction for a hundred feet. It was all grey and brown.

The work flow in the department was questionable, but no one questioned it. Several Tuesdays past, Quentin had argued with Sherry about classifying electric car chargers similarly to fire hydrants in the city code and specifying a stream-lined permit system through which commercial lot owners would acquire permission to install them in the areas they saw fit. Sherry thought the city should preassign acceptable locations and not classify the chargers themselves, but rather issue zoning variances similar to those for larger sheds and fences in a residential neighborhood. The argument took place around the coffee cubicle and lasted the better portion of an hour. It garnered a handful of spectators, participating to various degrees and directions of allegiance. This event was the most productive the group had been since Pollock arrived.

Mostly, the code-development cohort spent their working hours in a dusty conference room musing over the purpose and parameters of their responsibilities. Jerry would tell a few stories about how he was mistaken for the Fonz as a younger man. Of course, this was during his extensive sexual campaigns before he gained weight. The stories were frequently followed by teary-eyed rants concerning his inevitable resignation. "If I am to follow my honest logic," he whined, "then I am repeatedly led to the conclusion that, I, Jerry Zane, must resign, because my position here as part of this zoning department and the decisions that we make, which are universal and categorical among humanity, thus applying to my fellow men and women who live in my community, interfere unacceptably with the individual liberties of the citizens of the city, which must flow purely from the laws of nature as they spiral out from the source of creation, whatever that may indeed be." Eye rolling abounded. According to Sherry, he had been giving the speech, in variously drafted iterations, roughly monthly since she started her position seven years ago.

Outside of the group discussions, Quentin and Pollock would visit various parts of the city to investigate anecdotal zoning violations. These included sites of new malls, disputes among neighbors, retrofitted train stations, and a proposed gondola running through the arts district. These trips interested Pollock more than his office duties. The afternoon following the great water cooler–electric car–charger debate, the gigantic bearded zoning director, Mr. Freedman, had directly handed him his first solo assignment. The task was straightforward: Pollock would visit a dozen problem areas in the city, areas where the current zoning code was causing large numbers of disputes. After interviewing some Trams residents, consulting with experts and officials from other cities, referencing planning models, and of course conversing with the great Mr. Freedman himself, Pollock would find an underlying necessary change to propose for the zoning code. It sounded like justifying the job. He was to memorialize the proposition in a written presentation, which, if successful, would be incorporated into Mr. Freedman's annual address at city hall.

It had initially seemed so simple. Now, after numerous investigations yielding dead ends, restarts, worthless conversations, and a fair amount of uncompensated car travel, Pollock's neurons teemed with the project's glaring contradictions and impossibilities. He'd learned people disagreed, no matter what, and there was no code for that. Freedman's speech was in three weeks.

Further, fuller frustration flowed from Pollock's nemesis, Hans Flowers. Hans had transferred from the mayor's office two weeks after Pollock arrived in town, at Mr. Freedman's studied and reasoned request, and had been gunning for Pollock's position. Or rather "a new liaison between the commissioners and the planners, to oversee, communicate, and effect the new needs of our thriving city." Such a position would essentially make Pollock's irrelevant.

Hans Flowers was one year and one day younger than Pollock. He sported a neatly trimmed beard, and was always moving his circular spectacles back up his sharp nose ridge with an elegant middle-finger gesture. The kid was six foot six before his curly moussed mop and always quite dapper in his inexpensive, yet trendy, business casual attire. His appearance tended to inspire a mix of mistrust, appeal, and resentment in his fellow gentlemen. There was a constant cycle of females becoming enamored with him, and then rather quickly losing interest and usually regretting the enchantment. Or so Pollock perceived.

Pollock and Hans had been at odds since they first saw one another, in the basement restroom with the cracking yellow ceiling tiles. Hans, standing at the next urinal in his tight stretch dress pants said, smirking, "So you've been out of school for a while…are you one of those guys that stroll back to campus and fuck freshman college girls? I mean …I guess it must be fairly easy at this point, as old and wise as you clearly are." Pollock, involuntarily stink-eyed, zipped and washed his hands without response. In the mirror he met eyes with Hans, who had been watching. While shaking his hands dry into the porcelain sink, he quietly said, "Australopithecus," then turned to exit. Hans let out a wry smile; he sincerely enjoyed the insult.

From that beginning, the relationship had steadily grown more adversarial, and by now, most everyone within the building was speaking openly about the competition. Reality television at their workplace. Hans was charismatic and intelligent enough that he curried strategic allegiances.

"Good morning, Quentin," Pollock said, as he collected his neatly placed notepad and books with dexterity.

"Oh is it, now? Is it…really?" Quentin's intense eyes were opened widely.

Pollock swung a leather satchel over his left shoulder and let out a slight huff of wind. "The ventilation this morning, right?" he said, checking his right khaki pocket for the reassuring presence of his pen.

"Oh yes," Quentin said, "Disappointment with impressive precision. Let's get outta here before we get accused of…I don't know, having a job to do." He wiped sweat from his bald dome, and it speckled the top of a week old *Trams Gazette* sitting atop a dense pile of older papers next to his desk. He hopped over the shelving unit. Pollock snorted again and followed after his mentor. He had been looking forward to this visit.

Quentin stretched his palms over the air conditioning vents in the passenger side dash of Pollock's truck. They quickly merged onto the interstate and headed north. "So…" Quentin said. He glanced sideways at Pollock.

"So?"

"So…how's the fishing going?" Quentin's eyes beamed above a tight grin.

"What fishing?" said Pollock, eyes looking in the rear view mirror to see if there was a police car behind.

"The database of women. Have you snagged one yet, kiddo?"

"Oh, yeah. I mean no. I…nothing has really materialized yet. Mostly older women with foot fetishes looking to—"

"And that didn't call out to you?"

Pollock huffed with amusement. "No. They had pictures, well some of them did. You wouldn't have been interested."

"And that's it? Any correspondence? Titillating conversations?"

"Not really," Pollock said. "We'll see."

Pollock exited onto the twisting stone road leading to Willibaugh Pines, an older neighborhood in the northwest suburb of the city, called Lathe. It was built in the late 1950s, during the height of the postwar boom, with more or less uniform brick and cedar split-level ranches placed according to an imperfect grid within the remnants of a mature pine woodland. Willibaugh referred to a local war hero, Danny Willibaugh. He had been a medic and later a sniper in the European theater. He survived. Upon returning to Trams, Danny invested in residential contracting and municipal bonds. Willibaugh Pines was his first successful effort. It currently provided residence for mostly retired folks and the odd thrifty young couple.

Quentin returned from his road trip reverie concerning hiking trail mosses in northern Maine. He inhaled and said, "And the house. Have you looked into that at all yet, kiddo?" He had been aggressively, semidaily encouraging Pollock to research the history of the property upon which he now dwelled. He had put it bluntly, "How can you do this job when you don't even know where you're living, kid?" Pollock had continued to find convenient reasons to postpone such an endeavor.

"No I haven't," he said.

Pollock nestled the truck to a stop against an unruly hedgerow. A mass of house sparrows flew overhead. Pollock idled the truck, which produced only a slight vibration from the air conditioning. Through the driver's side window, from under furrowed brows, the two looked upon 1215 Riddle Avenue, where a giant wood-paneled HVAC system, painted bright orange and blue, decorated the southern side of the home in the perfect image of a hand holding up a middle finger.

"Well, here we are," Quentin said. "If it were your decision, would we start with the middle finger or the adorable little white house at which it is giving the bird?" Pollock felt safe with Quentin. He was used to his questioning, his toying with Pollock's thought processes. Quentin calmed him and challenged his propositions, his beliefs. Under normal circumstances this would feed directly into Pollock's paranoia. But Quentin's firm eyes communicated something old and sacred. Pollock cautiously played Quentin's games, seeking to soak in the wisdom emanating, goofily yet magnanimously from his toad-like father figure. Pollock saw him as some weird joker sage, the object of both his ridicule and respect.

"Well...I would have to say we should visit"—he read the name from his notepad—"Mr. Lamar Kendrick first."

"Gooood. Why?" Quentin asked.

"Well, the neighbor who called this in didn't know why, but Kendrick must have had a reason to do this. And if he had a reason, then this was revenge. Having done the deed, he will be self-satisfied and calmer, better to talk to."

"Yes, kid, I agree that the Kendrick fella will be calmer. But why would that mean we should talk to him first?"

Pollock bit the right half of his bottom lip and looked off, upward through the windshield. "I don't know, the calmer you are…the more likely to tell the truth?"

Quentin grinned. "Hah! You don't believe that. What about psychopaths?"

Pollock huffed and held out his palms. "You think Mr. Kendrick is a psychopath?"

Smiling bigger, Quentin said, "I've no idea. Do you?"

"Who do *you* think we should visit first?"

"I've no idea, kid," Quentin said, smiling bigger still, "but it is so fun watching you take this so seriously."

Pollock, annoyed more at his unsuccessful engagement rather than Quentin's ploy, turned to open the truck door and begin the investigation he had been so looking forward to. He jumped as he encountered the dark human silhouette tapping on the glass. "Fucking hell!" He took a deep breath, and then rolled down the window with the manual crank. "Hello?" he said. The woman had frizzy strawberry locks, unkempt and crawling outward from her pockmarked skin and disappearing into the blinding sun. The two Trams men squinted to make her out.

"Hi," the lady mumbled as she dropped her eyes. Pollock noticed she was wearing a tattered nighty. Quentin pushed up so he could get a view of the female's form.

"Hi." Pollock said with concern. Silence.

"Can we help you, my dear?" Quentin belted with a flirtatious eyebrow and a poor imitation of an Irish accent.

"Are you men here for me?" the lady said, grabbing at her thighs. Her face was smeared with something purplish.

"What?" asked Pollock. He looked over to Quentin, whose brow now betrayed his confusion. Pollock turned back toward the strange woman, who slowly tiptoed back from the vehicle.

"Ribbit, ribbit," she said. "Ribbit, ribbit." She then turned and ran down the block and out of sight. The two sat looking at one another, without speaking. Only the sound of the AC humming.

The radio crunched on amid a wave of static. "Only You" by Yaz filled the truck at near speaker-splitting levels. *"All I needed was the love you gave, All I needed for another day. And all I ever knew, only you!"* Quentin covered his ears, quickly pressing against the seatback. Pollock tapped the black plastic radio power button repeatedly. On the seventh tap, quiet. The two sat breathing harshly, their adrenaline drumming. Pollock checked the rearview mirror for the lady. Nothing. Rolling blacktop with an asymmetrical assortment of tin garbage cans above the road's heat mirage. "Sorry, that's been happening lately," Pollock said.

After Quentin rang the doorbell for a third time, the two men heard slow, hard footsteps. The heavy wooden door creaked open. A tall, muscular man in a black tracksuit looked out with dead eyes. In a raspy drawl, he said, "Can I help you, gentlemen?"

"Hello, Mr. Kendrick, I am Quentin and this is my understudy Pollock. We're from city zoning. We were wondering if—"

"I've been expecting you. Please come inside," the man said with a flat voice and unchanged facial expression. He jerked his thumb at the interior while holding the door ajar. The three made their way through the foyer into the living room, where they sat in plastic lawn chairs around a circular glass coffee table.

Pollock scanned the room. It was lined with stacks of old, yellowed papers. On the walls hung aerial photos of famous battle sites taken immediately after combat. In one, bodies lay along a river. A man's head bowed, his neck caught on a barbed wire fence. Frozen blood adorned a snow-covered meadow. "That was the Battle of the Bulge," Kendrick said, the bottom half of his face covered in sunlight spewing into the room from behind Pollock and Quentin.

"Interesting," replied Pollock, his eyes now back on the man who was acquiring growing gravity.

"My father was there," Kendrick droned. "More accurately, my father lost his life there. A tremendous man. A tremendous generation."

Quentin, noticing Pollock's interest and trying to avoid any lengthy delay in their mission, began right in saying, "So we've received a call about the new vents on your south wall. We had some questions for you if you would indulge us." He paused. A boiling pot could be heard around the corner, the contents spilling over onto the burner and sizzling. "You see, we're not—"

"Before you ask questions, you need to get a sense of the fiendish neighbor I have been living next to."

"Please, tell us," Quentin said.

"I have been living here for eight years. She was here, Mrs. Odes was here when I moved in. I had just lost my wife and retired from work as a contractor. She wasn't exactly welcoming." He pulled out a corncob pipe, filled to the brim with shaggy dark tobacco, lit the top with the clack of a metal zippo, and took a deep toke. "As I was saying, she wasn't exactly welcoming at all. The first thing she informed me of was the two outside security cameras pointed directly toward my back yard. She said she had had troubles with people breaking into her four-seasons room and stealing her porch furniture, some…I believe a whole set she said. Anyway, she had hoped that I would eventually put in cameras of my own. I didn't think too much about that. Fine by me. Might help in the long run. But then I quickly realized she kept floodlights on at night. They shown through my bedroom curtains and kept me up some nights. I sleep light. Anyway, I confronted her, and I may have been a little direct about the whole thing." Mr. Kendrick paused and did an upward half circle with his eyes, as if searching for a memory. Quentin and Pollock had become somewhat seduced by the cadence and diction of the man's explanation. The boiling and sizzling continued.

He eventually said, "She notified me that she was in charge of the neighborhood watch, and that they had decided that flood lights at night would help prevent crime in the area." He took another long toke. Pollock wrote notes in his pad, feeling the sun beat onto his neck. Quentin nodded. The sound of boiling water continued from around the corner. Kendrick exhaled to the side, and sat the pipe down on the glass table next to a neatly folded newspaper. Quentin made out a half-completed crossword section.

"I put up thicker curtains. Anyway, they were already in my closet and I'm not interested in petty disputes. I just wanted to peacefully spend my retirement reading and doing puzzles." He tapped his right knuckles down on the paper three times, as a great ape might. "Well, my son had been having a hard time since the economic flux, and I invited him to move in to help him for a while until he got back on his feet. He's a beautiful musician. He owns many instruments and a fair amount of recording gear. He's played shows around town, even went on a couple regional tours. Anyway, I offered to build a shed in the backyard with sound-proofing that he could use as a studio. He could make some extra money charging fifteen dollars an hour to record albums for high school kids from the suburbs, you know their parents' money and all. Point in fact, helped out a local kid who is now big…Rob Durci, that's his name. He's national. Really strange arrangements. Anyway, I thought building the studio would give me a project to work on." He leaned back against the lawn chair, its plastic frame squeaking under his weight.

"So I went to the zoning office, got the required permits, began building the thing. Two days later, after the thing was half finished, I awake to the doorbell. I robe myself and find a mob at my door. The crazy lady, who is somehow also the head of the home owners' association, had summoned a dozen or so of its membership to come berate me before I'd had morning coffee." He paused, jerking forward, rubbing his scruffy chin chaotically. "Apparently there is some sixty-year-old covenant in our plats where none of the lots shall construct any structure in the back yard that isn't for housing an automobile unless approved by a majority of the home owners." He paused again, looking off through the front windows, then down at his hands.

Passing clouds cut out the sunlight and the room grew dark. Pollock felt relief come over his neck, but the silence had grown uncomfortable for him, along with the sound of water splashing and sizzling around the corner. He said, "So they prevented you from building the studio?"

Kendrick's focus snapped back to the present. Quentin leaned his elbows forward, propping his lips on his intertwined knuckles. "Yes. She threatened to get lawyers involved. I think she mentioned that her son is a lawyer." He grunted, pursing his lips. "Anyway, I yielded. I could have tried to rally some of the other neighbors. But I'm new and I've mostly kept to myself. Besides, I didn't want a petty argument. I didn't want any of this business here. So, that was that. For a time. It was hard telling Kelly, that's uh my son, Kelly. I don't know why, maybe even harder than telling him about his mother. He is a beautiful man, Kelly, and he's had a very rough go of it the past couple of years." His eyes grew fierce and alive under taught brows. Pollock and Quentin gave each other a look of curiosity. Knocking sounds had begun in the kitchen, as the pot rocked over the stovetop from the high boil. Pollock wondered if Kendrick could hear that.

"Anyway, that's what I think did it. The pile of shit, of pure stinking shit, and my beautiful Kelly. And this crazy lady…I think she was molested or something as a child, did I mention that? Huh, I mean why else?" He looked at Pollock, imploringly, his fierceness giving way to a soft madness in his eyes. "Anyway, she had no interest in Kelly's studio. No interest at all. Just power hungry, like a petty toddler in the sandbox, wants to run her games over the neighborhood, bully the others. Well, you know, it set me over. Just set me right over. So I said to hell with it and decided to put a permanent fuck you in the side of my house! And there is that. The *disappointment!*" Breathing hard he sat stiffly, with good posture, pushing his chest out, then stood, toppling the lawn chair onto its side, and strode heavily into the kitchen.

From the living room, Pollock and Quentin heard the pot being poured into the sink, followed by a cacophony of clanks and dings. As Pollock wrote furiously in his pad, taking down the details from Mr. Kendrick's monologue, Quentin called out, "Mr. Kendrick, may I ask you—"

"That will be all for today, gentlemen," Kendrick called out from the kitchen. "If you would be so kind as to let yourselves out through the front. You may leave your business card on the table if you would like. Thank you." Pollock looked to Quentin for direction, who pulled out a card, placed it on the table, and nodded to Pollock.

Once outside, Quentin hesitated for a moment. Pollock noticed and asked, "Should we just head back?"

After a prolonged sigh, Quentin said, "Since we are here, we might as well see what Mrs. Odes has to say on the matter." He extended his arm, showing the way to the adjacent house. Pollock huffed. "So much for him being the calmer of the two."

Quentin smiled enormously as the two started next door. "Experience confounds, kiddo."

The house was yellow and purple, with numerous hanging plant baskets lining the front porch. An assortment of flowerpots, garden gnomes, lawn orbs, and garden fairies in bedded planters adorned the concrete landing beneath the front door. Pollock knocked on the glass door. It was reinforced with black steel rods. He noticed similar rods in all of the first level windows wrapping around the house. Above the door, on the wooden porch ceiling, there was a dark glass dome that Pollock recognized concealed a camera. Beneath his feet, a tweed doormat read, "I got this doormat for my husband. It was a good trade." He pointed at it, and looked at Quentin. The two smiled. But Pollock noticed a growing anger within himself.

Brown eyeballs appeared through the chink to the side of the doorframe, darting to take in the scene. After the sounds of multiple locks being undone, the door cracked ajar just enough for Pollock to spot the same wild eyes. "Yes?" came in a quick whisper.

"Mrs. Odes, hi ma'am," Pollock said. "We are city officials and were wondering if we could talk to you a bit about the vents on the side of your neighbor, Mr. Kendrick's, house?"

The eyes continued in their chaotic patterns, seemingly expecting some dangerous surprise. "I have no appointments for today; I double-checked this morning," she whispered. Quentin stepped around Pollock, getting close to the door. The wild eyes grew in a flash of horror.

"Hello ma'am. I am Quentin and this is Pollock. You are quite correct; we did not make an appointment with you. We have just spoken with Mr. Kendrick about the situation and would like to hear your side of events." The eyes narrowed. "Okay, but I will need to see some identification."

Having scrutinized both city ID cards, Mrs. Odes gracefully slipped out onto the concrete landing. She wore a beige dress with a brown stitched tree outline in the middle. It reminded Pollock of a sweater his third grade teacher, Mrs. Steed, had often worn. Mrs. Odes stood on her barefoot toes, squirming, similar to how a young girl who needed to urinate might. She said, "Okay, so what did that old bear tell you? Let me guess; he gave you some sob story about his son, huh?"

"Mr. Kendrick told us that you two haven't had the most pleasant of interactions," Quentin said.

Pollock said, "He did kind of concede that he lost it a little with the vents, but also that you kind of…put him in a… position that…" He made spherical gestures with his hands, struggling to conjure the right description.

Mrs. Odes jumped back inside. "Look, I am responsible to the members of the neighborhood to keep things in the right condition around here. You see, it starts with modified sheds, and then someone wants to add an office on the side of their home. Then someone is running a flower business out of a garage, and the aesthetic, the shape of the area has changed from what brought us here in the first place. Mr. Kendrick agreed to the same terms as the rest of us. Why should he be special?"

"That is a very valid point," Quentin said.

Pollock was a bit unsatisfied with her answer. It seemed to him that she had ulterior motives. Her speech was rehearsed, polished; it wasn't what she actually wanted to say. He said, "There wasn't anything else between you two that lead to this?"

She looked at him directly for the first time, pausing with a hurt face. "It's that son of his. He is trouble. He speaks of him like he is some innocent angel that the world keeps bullying. The boy is troubled. Wonder why he can't keep a job or a girlfriend? And why would he show up in my backyard, crying in the middle of the night? You know, I have a daughter of my own with troubles. And his son had no right to get involved with her. Heck, most of us here have children, and most of them have problems and—"

"Perhaps that's who we had our little run in with," Quentin said, turning to Pollock.

"Run in? What run in?" Mrs. Odes said, leaning forward and touching his chest with her palm.

Quentin looked down at her hand, and then said, "Yes, she snuck up on us as we were pulling up and nearly expedited my afternoon constitutional, pardon my language. Wily lady in a nighty?"

Mrs. Odes pushed quickly back through the doorway, between the two, and sprinted on her toes down the concrete walkway. She stopped, looking about vigorously, then said over her shoulder, "She was out here just now?"

"About fifteen minutes ago," Pollock said. He and Quentin exchanged confused glances.

Mrs. Odes tore back past them, loudly whispering, "Deary, me!" She slammed the door behind her. The garage door opened and a car screeched out from behind the house. The two stood, dumbfounded.

"Well, shall we?" asked Quentin.

"Please. Let's get the hell out of this neighborhood."

There was an accident on the interstate, so Pollock took a detour onto Cook Road, a long, winding country road. His idea was not novel. They sat with the engine idling, waiting for the long line of other detourees to make their way through the stoplight a quarter mile ahead at Duessel Graveyards. "More public transit, please," Quentin mumbled, throwing a look of disgust at the license plate on the Land Rover ahead of them. It read WARBLER 3.

Pollock took his hands from the wheel and gently rubbed his temples with his middle fingers. A quagmire of questions troubled him. He felt a bit guilty, and quite sad for both of the people they had just met. He had sided so easily with Mr. Kendrick at first. But, after their brief interaction with Mrs. Odes, he wondered how much they had both left out, how much more was really going on between the two households, and why there were so many parents with troubled children in that neighborhood. He reassured himself that it was prudent to be untrusting, to maintain suspicion. Because there was always a deeper truth hidden. Yes, some system in the murky underpants of people's lives. The dirty asshole. He needed to get to that system, to inspect the machinery, the cogs and programming, the oiled joints. Pollock needed to wrestle with the antiquated furnace powering the city and then fix it. He began to feel a bit embarrassed at himself for the growing hubris of his thoughts.

"This might be an apt time to tell you the story of the Titius Rombathians," Quentin said, glancing from the stone Duessel Graveyards sign back to WARBLER 3 applying bright pink eye shadow in a fold out mirror.

"What the hell are those?"

Quentin took a heavy breath and turned to look at Pollock. "Titius Rombathe was a man. He was a leader and a...well, we'll get to that part a little later. For now, know that this is a long story that begins in a graveyard. It begins a long time before that even, but that is where we would have to start the story." He raised his eyebrows, angling his head forward and holding out a hand as if asking for permission to begin.

The AC rumbled with the uneven idle. Pollock felt sweat spreading out over his lower back, wetting his undershirt. The last story Quentin told Pollock involved matricide, self-mutilation, and drug mules. However, it had, in its own way, explained a fair deal about local politics, and thus, after some muddled parsing and stretching of metaphors, Pollock had filed his own revised version of that story under the title of "useful knowledge." And so, Pollock reticently said, "Yeah, go ahead, we're stuck here for a bit anyway." Quentin cleared his throat and began.

Chapter Two

The day had been warm enough to melt the snow, which froze into a sheet of ice overtop the grass during the cold, clear evening and added difficulty to Maximilian's dig. The metal shovel clinked and rang out in low, humming reverberations as it bit into the rocky soil. Max tried to keep it as quiet as possible, looking left and right between each strike. Without the lantern fire, only the moonlight lit the excursion, casting a blue hue across the granite tombstones. He had done this enough times to know to pace himself. He paused, putting his knees into the earth and his hands in the pocket of his jacket. Two more feet to go. He grabbed a nearby twig and pushed a glob of mud from the edge of shovel blade. He rested the shovel against the rim of the rectangular hole.

Without the digging noise, the graveyard was quiet as a void. It was a windless night. Max, still breathing heavy, lit a cigarette, glanced up at the waxing gibbous moon, and then began scanning the area for signs of movement. His earlobes burned from the cold, but his body was wet from the work. He thought again of Ethyl, her freckled neck. He remembered how her skin felt against him. His teeth clenched through habit. He pulled his hands from his pockets, replaced his gloves, and, standing quickly, reached for the shovel handle.

"Looney ass!" The gruff voice rang across the graveyard.

"Shhhh!"

Max froze and darted his eyes toward the perimeter. Nothing. He hunched down, balancing on his knees so that only his eyes and head were above the edge of his hole. The cigarette hissed against the cold earth as he pushed it out and placed it in his chest pocket. The smoke swirled for a moment and then mixed into the air with a waft of Max's right hand. He scanned the edges of the yard along the four-foot high crumbling ruins of stone walls.

Max had almost been caught a few cities over the previous week. It was his first real scare. One of the groundsmen tackled him as he was setting up. They wrestled for a bit, and eventually Max broke free and sprinted into a nearby thicket. He still had scrapes on his neck from the struggle. Since then, he had become much more precautious: check the perimeter every five minutes, damp out the lantern, only one trip per night.

On the far end of the yard, he eventually made out two figures skulking low along a row of headstones. One of the figures was much larger than the other. The two stopped near a particularly regal stone. Max could not make out their conversation, only indistinct whispers. The smaller man was pointing his finger at the headstone, and the larger man was demonstrating something complex with both arms. They each dropped a dark satchel. The larger man grabbed a hand held digger out of his and began, slowly and quietly, clawing into the ground while the smaller man kept watch.

Max didn't know if they were here for valuables or a body. He couldn't see well enough to determine how new the site they were excavating was. The digging man was making quick progress. However, he was quite large, and, judging by their precise movements, the two had some experience at this. The main decision Max would have to make was whether to abandon now and sneak out or wait the fellas out with the hope that their experience had taught them similar lessons about the need for brevity with these kinds of activities.

Maximilian thought of Ethyl. Pure, smart Ethyl. He remembered her dancing awkwardly with her long legs wrapped in Maris's quilt, laughing on the drafting table in front of the fireplace. She made mock tentacle movements with her arms, looming tall over Max. After a near fall, she blew him a kiss and winked. He stood from the rocker, mounted the table. Ethyl gave him a death stare, grinning widely. He grabbed her in his arms and nuzzled her cheek with his unshaved chin. In that moment, he had forgotten all about the print and the Randalls. He had made a home. He had made a series of correct decisions, aided by the most fortunate luck. Then and there in that small room, for those small hours, the two of them, Ethyl and Maximilian, were the envy of all of the world. And they knew it. *He* knew it. The thought warmed him and he shivered in his hole. He would wait them out. This was far too important to be impeded by what were likely drunken thieves.

Max hunkered down against the wall of his hole where he could still see them. The ground was cold, and he hugged himself as his sweat cooled and chilled his body. The smaller man now dug as the larger man leaned against the tombstone, smoking and jerking his head back and forth with every noise of settling ground or bending branch.

"Psst!" The smaller man signaled his partner. The two grabbed a curved bar from the larger man's bag, then positioned themselves shoulder to shoulder and began pulling up. *Snap!* Wood slivers burst around them, and the two men fell, their backs against the hole. Max was surprised by the noise, so loudly had it shattered the silence that had prevailed up to that point. The thieves froze for a moment, then returned to work.

After another moment, the two stopped and began a frantic conversation. Perhaps they had found something unexpected. Again, Max could only make out indistinct whispers. The larger of the two poked the other's chest. The smaller man threw his hands in the air, exasperated. Max was shaking in the cold; he had expected to be digging and then running. The cold had become a mean presence. He was growing tired. His mind leapt back to Mrs. Randall. The look on her face made his gut ache, the deploring and pleading eyes hurling her pain out into the world. He remembered the flurry of black chickens in their sandy, fenced-in back-yard, tussling and bawking, as if heralding the end of an era: the premonition of hopelessness. And those despairing eyes, targeting Max. He clenched his fists and stretched his eyes wide, forcing out the tired.

A noise caused Max to jerk his head in the opposite direction of the men. A flame shone inside a lantern hung from the arm of a lean black-coated man stand-ing next to four other similarly dressed men. They stood still, unnoticed by the robbers in the grave. Max's heart punched like a steam engine, pushing up into his throat. Quickly and calmly, he grabbed his bag, slowly placing the strap over his should with his right hand. He looked at his shovel realizing that it would have to be left behind. The ground crunched under his weight as Max hobbled his way with bent knees and sloped shoulders to the far end of his hole. He poked his eyes up over the edge.

There, in the adjacent corner of the graveyard, fifty paces or so to the right, stood another three men in black. Instead of a torch, they had two large hounds that were just then released. "Goooaa!" yelled one from the group, and the other men sprinted after the dogs, headed directly for the robbers in the grave. Those in the other corner followed suit, led by the man with the lantern, holding it out-stretched as he trotted forward. The ground was alive with thumps. The two thieves hopped out of their hole and ran in separate directions, the larger headed for Max's hole.

Max fell to his side and covered his head, hoping the man would be caught before reaching his tomb, allowing Max to remain undiscovered. Muffled strug-gles found their way to his covered ears, scattered footsteps thumping. He remem-bered Ethyl chasing him through the alleyway beside the press, holding her arm high overhead as if clasping a harpoon, ready to toss. Max had made grunting, guttural noises, emulating a great sea beast. They weaved out across Acklund Avenue and into the market, where Ethyl snagged the corner of the wooden walk with her newly purchased boots.

The two sat on stools outside Norris General, Max brushing the dirt from Ethyl's Sunday dress. She gave him a stern look, a question of sorts. They were supposed to have made it to church but, by then it was too late, and they were already coconspirators in their latest secret escape constructed of their collective imagination and desire to be anywhere other than where they were. More often than not, the escapes took them into the imagination of Jules Verne, where they fantasized about exploring space or the deep waters of the oceans of the world. Ethyl's parents would be very upset.

Maximilian spent his days apprenticing in the paper press for Mr. Overmeyer. The press doubled as Mr. Overmeyer's private bookstore. Overmeyer Papers received copies of newly published works from around the country and from Europe before anyone else in town. Max, and Ethyl, after hours, had unlimited access to hundreds of novels, several fashion magazines, news articles about Africa and the Orient, and advertisements for futuristic grooming products that seemed to defy reason. They spent their time immersed in literature from the world, together escaping the frigid New England winter, their minds in sync and their bodies addicted to one another's.

The thumping from above subsided. Max uncovered his head. A mustached man popped his head over the hole's edge and looked down at him curiously. Max's eyes widened and he took a defensive posture with his hands. He knew that in a split second he would likely be required to fight his hardest. Penalties for crimes such as this were quite brutal. Max could recall a bedtime story his father had told him involving some such punishment. It had accounted for many sleepless nights.

The man shouted out, "There is another over here, boys!" Max's heart sank. He was good at hand-to-hand battles, but against a group he knew he stood no chance, and so he began thinking in terms of persuasion.

Two more heads quickly appeared next to the mustached man's. "Well, well," one said.

"Don't just stare, grab 'em, hoist 'em up, and get 'em in ties!" shouted a voice from behind. They pulled Max out of the hole, shoved him to his knees, and bound his wrists together with twine that cut into his skin causing a great discomfort. He stared at the other two men who were bound in the same fashion a few feet away. The larger man had a scar across his forehead. His nose was round and he had raging brown eyes. His cheeks were hidden under an unkempt red beard. The smaller man's blue eyes darted ceaselessly, as if following the trajectory of a moth about. His face was sharp and cleanly shaved.

The group of captors hovered around the leader, now holding the lantern at the end of his relaxed arm. He shushed his fellows and stepped firmly in his high leather boots to place the flame atop a small headstone between the others and Max. The man, arched his back in a bow with his left hand clasping his right, and cracked his vertebrae, much like a cat might. He let out an extended exhale with closed eyes underneath his circular spectacles. Light from the flame shone upward upon his face, making strange shadows of his features.

"Have you ever found out a truth about yourself that is certain but unfortunate? And, the certainty of that truth treats you better than you know the fortune would have?" The leader's voice was high pitched and percussive. It reminded Max of pig sounds. The others looked at Max and back up at the man. The group of captors was silent, standing in a semicircle a few yards away. "That was not rhetorical," the man oinked.

"Well, I suppose that *is* fortunate," the larger of the captives responded with a defiant sneer.

"And yet, here you are robbing graves!" the captor oink-shouted, stepping forward and rewarding the sass with a backhand to the head. The larger captive toppled over onto the ground. The pig-sounding man quickly grabbed his shoulders and jerked him back to his knees. He trotted back to his position between his men. The dogs sat obediently, panting.

"What kind of witless fiend makes his way in this world by violating the resting place of his fellows? How can he, having just carried himself as a demon haunting the heads of young innocents, then hang his hat and sleep with anything resembling peace? Why should he? And who are we, we who have named ourselves the keepers of order and nobility? I say, who are we, if we do not seek out and destroy every trace of such vermin from our midst as a rat carrying deep and mischievous illness? Hmm?" He leaned down far, looking at Max from behind spectacles ablaze with dancing reflections of the lantern's flame. Max met the man's gaze.

"This town, this state, this country has no place for you vermin. Under ordinary circumstances, I would take out my hunting knife, splay you gutless fiends, leave you in a pile of mess. I'd let the foxes and coyotes decide exactly how you'd be scattered," he took in a deep, harsh breath, curling his upper lip in disgust. "However, these are not ordinary circumstances. Thus, I must, at present, suppress my righteous anger. I must grit my teeth at you unconscionable fiends and take refuge in the knowledge that I have a higher duty. A duty that calls for more of me as a man."

Max's hands were numb from the cold and the tightness of the twine. But his chest grew hot with violence. The man knew nothing of his plight. Max knew he was no "gutless fiend," and he did not belong lumped in with these other men. Who was this man to question Maximilian's honor? He knew absolutely nothing of it! The rage in his chest surged up into his throat and came out in a roar of words. "Sir, with all due respect you have absolutely no semblance of what you're talking about! I am no fiend, I am—"

The man bent his knee high in the air and thrust his boot down hard on Max's head. Darkness.

Chapter Three

The sun hung low in the sky above Trams. Pollock felt feverish as he hovered absentmindedly over his finished bowl of pork stir-fry. His thoughts trotted. Then they galloped and changed directions without warning. They switched to a sort of slow dance, and then a sickening swirl, faster and faster, closing in on something that was very slippery and elusive. Its presence vanished and menaced him with the mystery of its identity. The afternoon had passed in a snap of the fingers. Pollock had gone through it with limited participation. The last hour at work was always an awkward and insincere act, with its actors rummaging among mimicked motions, already having mentally left work and begun engaging in their workout routines, cooking dinner, and doing hot yoga with Bruce. The majority of the Trams Facility inhabitants spent the better part of the two hour period between 3:00 p.m. and 5:00 p.m. checking their Facebook pages, their personal emails, Flickr, tumbler, Buzzfeed, Cracked.com, and numerous other sites on the internet that provided lowbrow entertainment while providing the user with the outward appearance of dutiful adherence to their professional agenda. Jerry would spend forty-five minutes organizing papers atop his second and third desks. There was such a beauty to crisp stacks. Sherry watered and trimmed the dozen potted plants within her cubicle. She fantasized about a house in Spain with indoor-outdoor living spaces. Multiterraced adobe slabs with breeze-agitated white cotton curtains.

Quentin had long ago discovered that a certain door on the third floor was adorned with an inaccurate metal sign that read "Alarm Will Sound" and could be opened and closed at will without consequence and without locking. He would slyly head toward the stairway leading down to the basement restrooms, but instead head upward, pipe and tobacco pouch in his pocket. He would sit on the roof, smoking and musing over the parking patterns of the workers without assigned spots. "Hmmm, Pollock always parks as far away as possible. What happened to that kid?" he had once uttered in curious admiration. He would remain atop of Trams Facilities, smoking and thinking to himself, for anywhere from thirty minutes to two and a half hours, on which days he would observe his peers leaving the building and getting in their vehicles, except for Sherry, who always walked from work to yoga. Hot yoga, with Bruce.

Quentin had disclosed this ritual to Pollock. That was the other side of their relationship. Quentin saw in Pollock a comrade, a fellow outsider, a proper asshole, someone who could understand the magnanimous sanctities of certain solo peripheral remedies, and also someone who could keep their mouth shut. Pollock, to Quentin, was ruined. He was a kid far too authentic to ever make a successful go of it. Quentin on the other hand, he had just enough flair for politics, those social nuances and niceties that, fairly or not, usually propelled otherwise lesser individuals ahead of the Pollocks of the world, who were intelligent enough, but caught in a current that kept them at arms length from others. Quentin thought Pollock was too paranoid, too pessimistic. A while after first meeting Pollock, Quentin announced he had made it his personal mission to lighten the kid up, who was, in Quentin's estimation, tighter and tenser than was warranted from Pollock's experiences.

The musky tobacco scent from Quentin's pipe would often greet Pollock on his way to his car, and he would turn and look up, spotting a billow of charcoal disseminating from behind the brick and concrete balustrade at the top of the roof.

He would smile to himself, or scowl and shake his head, depending upon the mood and events of the day.

This afternoon, as Pollock was leaving for the day, he had crossed paths with two of the younger "counter girls," Teresa and Mary, on a smoke break talking about a house party they were heading to that evening. Teresa invited him along, in her touch-tone voice. She annunciated all of her syllables clearly and affectionately, as if she were speaking to a dear friend that was much younger, perhaps even a lesser species. Pollock had accepted the invitation, perhaps out of loneliness—he hadn't made many friends in Trams—or perhaps out of boredom. Perhaps he accepted without thinking about it at all. So, after pork stir-fry, as he finally came back from his aimless reverie staring out at the early evening, he looked at his watch, and the true horror of the idea set in. He explored the repercussions of not showing up. He slapped the back of his head with gusto. Of course he would have to go. Once he admitted the possibility of being a coward, the choice was made.

It was a blue three-story carriage house in a seedy section downtown nicknamed Pip Town. The streets were split in two with long grassy courtyards full of weeping willows. Pollock recalled riding along in a minivan with two of his supervisors his first week in Trams while they explained the politics of this region of town. "Basically, the queers have marked this area with a giant x. It has become a mass exodus of sorts. And the locals that have lived here for years, mostly low-income black families, aren't taking it well. They can't afford the increasing rents and taxes. Gentrification 101. This is the Israel of the city. A lot of hate crimes, home invasions, beatings. Going both ways," spat Tom, another zoning official.

Quentin said, "A lot of same sex couples realized the economics of the area and took advantage. The identity of the neighborhood is changing."

The party was afoot. The house was dark and filled with music and dancing bodies. A strobe light clapped out flashes among the crowd in front of a two foot tall wooden stage in the corner of the main living room. On the stage stood six dark shadows with instruments pushing out some strange flavor of, perhaps, acid funk. It sounded like a mixture of Talking Heads and Debussy, in slow motion, with tribal percussion and sassy Freddy Mercury–style vocals. Pollock didn't mind it. It sounded like breaking the walls of one's self. He noticed a cardboard sign with green glow-in-the-dark spray paint that read "Peabody's Resurrection!"

Pollock squeezed his way through the sweaty dance crowd, into the white tiled kitchen and located a keg in the rear. He pumped the handle and poured frothy brew into a red Solo cup he removed from a stack on the counter. For a few songs, he hovered there, stranded, listening in to various conversations. He wandered through the crowd for a bit and then into a mazelike section with hallways and two ancillary kitchens, both full of people. He wandered out back onto a long wooden deck looking over a grassy slope that lead down, seemingly forever, to what sounded like a waterfall emanating from the darkness below. There was an assortment of hip kids smoking j's, a hefty couple making out, and a quintet of cardplayers at a wicker table near the far corner. He took a long swig, finishing his beer, turned and reentered the house.

"Hey, Pollock!" he heard from behind in one of the maze section's hallways. He flipped around and saw Teresa, tripping over an unstrapped sandal, floundering against the wall, and juggling a bottle of Ketel One vodka. It bounced off the tiled floor and spun wildly until settling against Pollock's left shoe. He picked it up and approached Teresa. "Sorry, I have been such a bad girl tonight. Oh my gawwd! I am going to be dead in the water tomorrow. Why on earth did you make me come to this awful party? This was a mistake! Suuuch a mistake," she said hoarsely as she launched upward and wrapped her arms around his neck, pulling with all her weight.

"I didn't bring you here," Pollock said, struggling physically, and, in his mind, with the implications of Teresa's words. "Would you like some water?"

"No, mister! I need to find Thomas! Now! Where is that boy?" She began walking the two of them back into the second kitchen. They bumped into numerous folks en route, some who responded with happy looks and others with impromptu dance moves.

Eventually they found their way back out onto the deck and she let out a celebratory, "Yay, there he is. There is my little Thomas." They approached a tall man in a grey hoody hunched over the railing, looking down into the blackness. She pulled hard, and they slammed against his back. He quickly turned and pushed them back, the two falling mostly because Teresa had her paws on Pollock's shoulders. Thomas instantly bent down and grabbed Teresa. He placed her gently against the railing, Teresa giggling and shuffling in drunken ecstasy. Then he placed one hand around Pollock's neck and another on his right bicep, and shoved him against the back of the house. His shoulder blades hit bricks with a muffled thump that knocked most of the wind from his lungs.

"Did you just fuck her, man?" Thomas said. "Just tell me if you did. Just tell me man!" His eyes were bloodshot, and his breath was foul.

"I didn't do anything with her. Relax!" Thomas looked over his shoulder at Teresa, then back at Pollock. Pollock shoved Thomas off of him and stood. "Look, I was just helping her look for you. She invited me here, which was clearly a mistake. You need to get your jealousy under control, mate." And with that he turned and wended his way back through the maze of the house and out the front door.

Once home, Pollock poured himself four fingers of sherry into a coffee mug and sat back on the couch trying to calm down. The ordeal at the party had piqued his adrenaline, and he wished that he would have bashed that Thomas fella in the face. But, he knew it was better that he had not. Regardless, the sound of Teresa giggling stirred frustration and resentment. Regretting that he had bothered to show up, he took a long draw of sherry. The Kripke brothers had left several bottles in the kitchen pantry.

A loud, clicking rattle came from upstairs. Pollock tightened his posture and listened. A moment of silence followed, then a bang and the creaking of a door opening. He placed the coffee mug on the table and moved toward the stairs. He walked up with slow, deliberate steps. His nerves played with him a little, reminiscent of so many childhood ascents after covertly screening horror films downstairs after his parents went to bed. He pulled out the pen from his pant pocket, smirking at himself a little while doing so, but confident in his decision nonetheless. Half way up the stairs he called out, "Hello? Who's there? I have a weapon on me and am calling the police unless you reveal yourself right now!" He felt in his left pant pocket—his cellphone was not there. He pictured it sitting on the kitchen counter. No one answered him.

Atop the stairs, Pollock saw the guest bedroom door was ajar. He slowly opened it fully, threw on the lights inside and scoped the room, grasping his pen tightly, raised by his side. Nothing out of place, though his adrenaline had been fully rekindled. He repeated the same procedure for the other two rooms, the closet, and the bathroom. No one was there. He told himself it was a draft or the house adjusting to the heat. He stood for a moment in the hallway and stretched, arching his back, taut in the middle and pushing his elbows upward. Above him, he saw the ceiling door to the attic. It was also slightly ajar.

With all three one hundred–watt light bulbs on and dangling from the slanted ceiling riddled with the pointy ends of roofing nails, the attic room appeared very small. The heat from the day still clung tight, the dizzying effect of which was furthered by the humidity rising from damp, fiberglass pillows covering the floorboards. They were oily to the touch and made Pollock queasy. All that occupied the room was a small green metal chest abutting the brick of the chimney. Pollock knelt in front it, minding the crossbeams above.

The metal clasps at the front were rusty and resisted opening at first. After some struggle, Pollock sifted through neatly folded woolen skirts, silk blouses, and hound's-tooth scarves. At the bottom of the chest, underneath the stack of clothing, Pollock's fingers crossed a hard rectangular object an inch or so thick. He pulled out a leather bound book with the initials M.R.S. imprinted at the top middle. He repositioned himself on his bottom, crossed his legs and slowly opened the book. Inside, he found pages and pages of dated journal entries penned in pristine blue cursive. The first date was 10-7-76. He flipped to the last entry, about twenty pages from the back. It was dated 4-14-77. He opened to a page at random. 12-23-76. Before he began reading, he pieced together Mary Roberta Shewecker. It was his great–aunt's journal.

Today turned out to be a triumph for me. For the first time in a long time I had hope. I do think this to be hope. The race was dull and I've only cut back to six or seven drinks a day. But, today Richard stopped by and convinced me to go on a walk with him. The temp. was mid-teens, and I was bitterly cold. But, the sun came out and it glistened on the snow in Echoes Park. We talked for a while about the old holiday get-togethers, how much has changed. We are the grand-parent generation now. Saul turns 34 tomorrow. Richard invited me along to their home for a party (provided I say goodbye before leaving, wink wink...). It was nice to catch up. I made him a toddy and sent him along warm.

Somewhere along the way I realized that I hadn't thought of Homer for most of the day. So, I went into his workshop in the basement and thought about him. I became quite sentimental being around his woodworking tools. They are still as he left them. I am still as he left me. He was very confused in those last days. But he was somehow sweeter, kinder. I remember it made me, well irritated. But, maybe he saw something or knew something. I'm not sure. It is odd to think on, and I must admit it is a little scary to me. Challenging thoughts for a frigid atheist to wrestle with. Anyway, it is nice to have people that care and check in. I look forward to seeing more family tomorrow. Answers to come. Tonight, I try to cut it back to five drinks.

The words stirred wonder and guilt in Pollock. He snapped the book shut, pulled the three light strings and stepped down into the cool, air-conditioned house. The spring-loaded ceiling door pulled shut with a loud rap. He walked to the front window in the master bedroom. Outside, he saw two young raccoons quickly scurrying across Nyqvist. The journal was still in his hand. He tossed it onto the floor next to the window.

Maybe the house was getting to Pollock. Every sound carried the hint of serious mystery and ominous threat. Loose floorboards and such. Warped vintage ventilation ducts. Every object still inside it held a possible memory. The dozens of unfinished birdhouses in the basement workshop. The masterful finished product in the backyard, a three storied chalet on a pole, had various tiers for multiple types of feed to support a community of species. On the occasions when he gazed out back, or when he had to take the garbage out to the alley behind the back fence, the sight never failed to amaze. A flirtatious cornucopia of twirling wings, dancing to and from the birdhouse landings, quickly pecking small multicolored grains. It was a divine sight. In the evenings, the raccoon family would come and make their claim, climbing up the pole like cat burglars. Pollock's great uncle had left enough bird feed in the basement to last the decade. All of it was stored in airtight rubber tubs, stacked neatly on one of a few industrial metal shelving units lining the back wall behind the workbench. Pollock had been refilling the birdhouse tiers every few days.

Pollock needed more kinship; he needed more intimacy. He needed to be less reflective. But when he went out to the social spots nearby where twentysomethings, having looked forward to it throughout the work week, could be found doing what was popular and accepted and exciting, it didn't encourage intimacy in him, rather, despondency and withdrawal. Perhaps it was the triviality of it all, against the grand cosmic scale. Maybe Pollock was a brutally boring person. Boredom often motivated him. Either way, what had happened earlier that night at the party was only the youngest of a lineage of disappointments. And with each new iteration they grew more pronounced. This had trained Pollock to divert his hopes and dependence away from others. And the more he did so, the greater the longing for others grew. He poured four more fingers and opened his laptop.

Wooden nickels had responded to his message.

Hey You! I have not been to Human, Human but I've heard good things. They have coffee and beer there, right? Meet there at 8pm tomorrow night? Ok. I still have to tell you about my dream from the other night. I am going to wear wearing a new black dress. Night!

Pollock couldn't decide if her message was too desperate or too confident. It perplexed him for the briefest of moments until he found himself typing.

Yes, coffee and beer. I will see you there at 8.

That was it. He exited the internet window and shut his laptop. It was going on midnight. He laid on his sleeping couch on the cool first floor, listening to an old Beach Boys playlist from his cellphone. The music mixed with the cracking and popping floorboards, the air-conditioning unit, and the old fridge's rattling and humming. It was a sleep-inducing grey noise. Together with the sherry, it was putting him out. But just as his awareness was fading into oblivion, he caught another glimpse of the elderly female wraith wearing a gown. She had tired, concerned eyes that pierced into him. The sight brought him troubled dreams.

His childhood dog, Lorie, had a deep, gushing wound in her side while she lay panting heavily on linoleum while legless woodchucks crawled toward her. The groundhogs had satanic smirks and wads of crisp money in their paws. They crawled ever more quickly toward her, smearing their entrails along the way. The first arrived and began stuffing the money into Lorie's wound as the others formed an assembly line and passed their wads forward. The sharp edges of the new bills scraped the inside of Lorie's wound, and she yelped from deep in her gut with displeasure. Panic and deep reverence washed over Pollock; these woodchucks had to sacrifice their legs for his mistakes. As soon as this thought crossed his liquored mind, the chief chuck turned with bloodshot eyes, pulled a match and cigar from some unknown location in his side fur, lit the cigar, and then tossed it atop Lorie, all the while keeping his direct and malignant gaze on Pollock. Pollock's arms were tied against the wall with many thick and wet strands of dark orange orangutan hairs that crept up into his face. Lorie caught fire instantly, burning in a blue fury while her limbs kicked to cries of agony. All the while, Pollock choked on wet orangutan hair.

Pollock shot awake. His cellphone was in his left hand. He had a new text. It was from a number he didn't recognize.

Hey Bud. It's Cabe. I know. It has been forever. I saw you live in Trams now. I'll be there next weekend for a new job, hopefully. How would you feel about me crashing at your place for a couple of nights, drinks on me?

Pollock's freshman year at VU was one of heroes and villains. There was a simple symmetry in everything. Yin and yang. This was before the conceptual framework had grown into, or perhaps rather been revealed to be, a labyrinthine patchwork of slippery architecture requiring agile footing and ibuprofen. There was an "us" and "them" that lent itself to tossing one's being blindly into what a friend of Pollock's once called "noble cries." These were the instinctual yelps heard from a group of brethren heavily invested in unity of purpose. That year, it seemed that potent cosmic forces were in play.

His dorm room was on the first floor of Oyster Hall, an ancient stone church refitted for college students, which sat on the south green at the bottom of two notorious hills. The room was a quad, 1023 Oyster Hall. There were four roommates. Tyler was a charismatic liar who was good at seducing females, karate, and acquiring drug connections instead of listening to lectures. He made friends with everyone quickly and was on academic and disciplinary probation early on. He was likable enough and charitable in his victories, but it was clear there wasn't much depth to him. He often seemed to Pollock a good-spirited child, innocent and irresponsible. But he loved, and was loved in return. And he always had projects in the works.

Then there was Jay, a short Korean kid obsessed with guns, airplanes, and social hierarchies. He was very unsure of himself and wanted to be accepted. He had an insincere laugh, which occurred at any moment he believed was strategic. He didn't have his own sense of humor or, rather, he did but was embarrassed of it, so it went into hibernation, only to come out after hours with the trusted. He would many times give Pollock a very concerned look and then proceed to ask if he thought this or that quality of his was bad. But mostly he had a cheerful disposition and would gladly follow along in unwise shenanigans. He had six handguns in his closet.

The fourth member was Cabe. Pollock grew to respect Cabe very much. He was short and built, with a swollen chest like a tree frog. He incessantly chewed tobacco. He loved "hippie" music and dirt bikes. He was quiet until inebriated, when he would make up for previous silences with long, winding rants about what he perceived to be character weaknesses in others present. He had a chip on his shoulder and would start a fight with anyone. He was angry, and he needed to have something earned. But he also would consume too much and slouch in his pajamas on the couch and beg Pollock, half jokingly, half seriously, to comfort him. "I'm in a shit mood, bud. Give me compliments. Stoke my ego! Be my family!" The spectrum was wide with that one. He also had the unusual ability to always look unwashed and unkempt despite how clean he was.

After four months, only Pollock and Cabe remained. Jay had been "administratively removed"—kicked out—for "noise violations." He had been using the abandoned sixth-floor hallway as a shooting range, with old chemistry textbooks as targets. Tyler was caught cutting cocaine with ephedrine in the shared restroom, blaring the Temptations from an iPod speaker port, wearing nothing but an American flag and a Confederate soldier's hat. It took four campus security to best him physically. Later that evening, he broke an actual police officer's nose and escaped custody for a day or so. He was later caught and put on a pilot reform path by Student Services, and the next time Pollock saw Tyler, he was wearing a suit, sprinting through the local grocer with a wire cage containing panicked chinchillas. "Good to see yah, buddy" he said, running into the meat section with two large gentlemen in overalls in tow.

One Saturday before they were gone, late in the afternoon, in early autumn, Pollock decided it would be interesting to build a hot tub in the dorm room. He and Cabe ordered a two-and-a-half-foot deep inflatable pool on Amazon and, after some quick-paced reorganizing, placed it along the edge of the room. They then obtained a submersible water heater. Lastly, Cabe nabbed a hose courtesy of university grounds keeping. While inebriated, jokes were later made about the reasons for tuition increases.

Their room was directly across from the janitor's closet, which had a sink with a threaded faucet. Pollock, Cabe, and Jay would take turns running the hose from the closet, through the hallway and to the pool to fill it up. If anyone asked, an assured response flew out. "We are filling up our large humidifier." Once finished for the evening, with prune-like fingers, they would put the hose out their back window, which overlooked a grassy slope littered with ramshackle shrubs, and siphon the hose to drain the dirtied pool water. If anyone asked, they would respond, "We are draining our large dehumidifier." This happened most nights for a month or so. Why the air in the dorm room was so damned moist or dry, nobody ever wondered, at least not strongly enough to pursue answers despite the many times these rote responses were given by one of the boys wearing nothing but swimming trunks. The janitor, Tomlin, knew. But, perhaps identifying too heavily with a certain character from *The Breakfast Club*, he stored the information away in the filing cabinet of his memory, to be used only for some future noble cause. Such a cause never showed its face during the time Pollock and Cabe remained at Oyster Hall.

Many friends would seek out their hot tub parties, and Pollock and Cabe would charge for drinks and use of the hot tub, and on any given night, there would be upward of twenty people in their little room, all heavily intoxicated in bathing suits or panties or saran wrap, celebrating with absolute abandon what they perceived, quite correctly, to be a truly rare moment in their lives, a very localized and illusively idiosyncratic victory of youth. Tyler, before he was gone, would put on Luis Armstrong and wave his arms and hum loudly. Folks would join in, and there was unity in the motion, tight brotherly and sisterly hugs and kisses, and shouts, with unknown and never repeated sounds flying loose.

The cute girl Jenna from the fourth floor would flirt with Pollock and he would love the tease, the craft of the conversation keeping it hanging barely above the obvious sexual subtext. Cabe would light a cigar and sit on the windowsill and scream out into the dark autumn air. They had Christmas lights and Tyler's piss-poor cut cocaine. It was a giant exhilarating stupor, long weeks of ten- and twelve-hour parties followed by short sleeps and intense studying so that they could maintain their educational cover, the front for their true college purpose.

Through the commotion, the bodies of college buddies rocking and jumping, through the smoke, and the joyous howls, Pollock would catch Cabe's eye and Cabe would point at Pollock and squint. And Pollock would bow slowly, grace-fully, a master artist acknowledging the greatness of his works, and then return the squint. Cabe would return the bow and grin. And then and there, they knew they had become legends of sorts. They had left the mired lowlands of human commonness and flown to envied heights. Upperclassmen were routinely visiting them; a local actress, who had been in a dozen independent films, spent a week-end crashing on their futon. Pollock was pleased with himself that first quarter of college at UV. His grades were good. The parties were even better. He had forged a community, a family of his own, and his own niche therein as the idea guy. Things were progressing.

And, things only heightened further as the year passed along. By the end of winter, most nights would conclude with demolition. Cabe and Pollock would take any glass containers they could find, sometimes raiding industrial recycling bins behind the mess hall for them, and raise them above their heads and smash them against the concrete floor in the corner of their room opposite the pool. They would just heave them at the floor or even the dorm room walls. The late-night crashes mirrored the vigor in their hearts. It left piles of shards that they shoveled away into trash bags once they accumulated to knee height.

Their lifestyle was exhausting. Cram for seven hours straight on Adderall and nab an A on a political science project, then come back to the dorm and drink twelve beers, six shots of rum, and a bottle of wine, smoke two packs of cigarettes and three or four bowls of pot, and do a few lines of cocaine. Then, pass out at some odd hour and awake to a headache-addled five-mile run around town on the lower slopes of the hills that made the town of Valia a valley. Those runs were more of a therapy session. Pollock punishing himself, Cabe punishing himself more. He would pull away from Pollock, who would work to try and catch up. They would sometimes fall into a sort of fluid, Zen-like state, absent of their bodies and the environment, contented in the absence. And the two seldom slowed outside those runs. They were always the pure joy of young group energy and substances and freedom and naïve visions, day after day after day. In hindsight, Pollock would have had a hard time tracking his thinking during that time period. There was no time to actually think. He was absolutely immersed in each moment, living nearly perfectly the motto "be in the here and now," his intuitive logic proving fruitful at every turn, enough that reflection and analysis never became prudent.

The stairs were cold under his feet. Pollock stared out at the streaks of grey morning mist lying low above Pollock's backyard. He couldn't see the bird feeder, his great uncle's masterpiece. He peered a little harder to make out the yard with more clarity. The birdfeeder was not there.

It had rained during the night, and the humid air was confronting. Pollock snarled as the soft wet grass tickled his bare feet, oozing brown muck between his toes. He looked over at the patio. Little raccoon prints made designs over the marble tabletop. Back in front of him, where the birdhouse had been, there was merely a hole in the ground, about three inches in diameter. He knew raccoons couldn't have run off with it. It was early still, and the back alley was quiet. He clicked open the back fence gate and stepped onto the gravel roadway. Across the lane, he noticed an object lying a few feet in front of a white garage belonging to a house facing Lamet Road.

Pollock had not met these neighbors. In fact, because he had not seen anyone coming either to or fro in a few weeks, he suspected that the residence was temporarily empty. Perhaps the owners were on vacation, or the house was between tenants, as Pollock's had been in the weeks leading up to his move. However, every night many lights were on inside, often accompanied by sounds of conversation, laughter, even music. Pollock thought of the cardboard cutout scene from *Home Alone*. If the pattern continued without any visual confirmation of the inhabitants for much longer, Pollock would institute further investigative measures to satisfy his curiosity. He noticed the raccoon prints leading under the white garage door.

He pulled a thick twig out of the brush pile he had amassed next to the city-supplied garbage bin and ambled toward the object. Once in close, Pollock saw it was a dirty machete. Its blade stretched two feet long, with an eight-inch rubber-gripped handle. There was a leather tassel tied onto a ring on the metal pommel. Bending far forward, elbows on knees and toes pressing into the gravel, Pollock noticed the initials S.T.R. expertly engraved on the middle of the orb. He looked around, suspiciously. Pollock wondered if this machete had anything to do with his missing birdfeeder. Regardless, he felt exposed kneeling in the alley next to a discarded weapon behind his neighbor's. He pushed the twig through the handle loop and carried the machete back inside.

The machete sat on the kitchen counter beside the sink while Pollock sat eating sardines, drinking tea, and mapping out the trajectory of the day ahead. But he was distracted by the morning's events. His thoughts landed on the Ne'er Do Wells. He knew those kids would find this hilarious. He imagined the sound of the group laughing and became agitated. He then pictured the birdhouse stashed in the boys' clubhouse, next to stolen mail, dog toys, and perhaps nudie magazines from the local mart. This made Pollock even more angry. "Shenanigans, fucking hell!" he belted out, picking up the binoculars and scanning Nyquist. But he found no action this morning. He went for his morning shower.

There were nine members of the Jalisco Neighborhood Board. Eight were female. Pollock thought they looked like ostriches as they flocked noisily around Mrs. Hayden, the obvious leader. She maintained a severe expression, which communicated a cache of painful experience from under her red curly fro. It was apparent to Pollock that she was involved in a sort of sad tussle with aging. Skinny jeans, black, stuck to her thin legs. She wore a trendy grey shirt with a very low V neck, exposing her otherwise saggy, wrinkly breasts, taught in a yellow push up. The shirt read "Caffeine, Nicotine, Alcohol." She tapped her nails on the conference table throughout the meeting.

Pollock had been welcomed warmly enough, although perhaps dismissively. He clearly held no consequence to anyone present. Each member smiled and gave their last names. Mrs. Hayden directed him to an office chair against the wall in the corner. The meeting bumped along from one subject to another, each ending in a resolution approved with final words from Hayden after a challenge by Mr. Ferris that was always shot dead by some insult invoking the widespread belief that males were inferior dunces, dawdling through existence by the grace and allowance of wise women. Ferris would redden in the face and look at Pollock beseechingly, hopeful that the unusual presence of another penis might aid in his quest to rectify the effects of the gender imbalance. Pollock offered no such assistance.

Perhaps he would have aided Mr. Ferris if he had not been so inwardly adrift. After the opening procedures, Pollock's mind retreated again to thoughts of college. He remembered how it ended with Cabe. He remembered sitting on a paper-covered examining table at the doctor's office after injuring his fist on Cabe's cheek. They had never mended things. That was six years ago. However long ago it was, the wounds were still open, for whatever reason. The text had made their relative freshness apparent. He could feel it there in his guts, like an assortment of odd burning sensations. It bothered him that Cabe, like an entitled prick, expected him to accommodate out of the blue just like that. Yet still he wanted to explore this. He pulled out his phone and texted:

I'll be around. You can sleep here. Let me know when you get in.

He felt relieved but lost, as if he had no grounding. He wondered whether he should have aided Mr. Ferris after all.

"Fucking cunt!" yelled Mr. Ferris as he stood in excitement and snapped Pollock's attention back to the room in which he sat. The ladies all smiled and cheered.

"Woo-hoo!" Hayden said, in her raspy voice. "There he is, the real Mr. Ferris! There's the vengeful weasel we all know and love."

"Poor, poor Mrs. Ferris," one of the Ostriches said, to the laughter of the rest.

Mr. Ferris pointed his finger at the gaggle, sneering, and said, "Leave my wife the fuck out of this. You like power too much. You don't listen. I know, I have a dick so my opinion doesn't count, that's what you're saying right?"

Hayden responded quickly. "Hey, technically, you said it, not me." The ostriches roared, self-satisfied.

Mr. Ferris waved his hands dismissively. It appeared in Pollock's imagination that he was watching a lone chimpanzee confront a gaggle of ostriches. He felt sorry for the man, for the chimp.

"Look my boy," Hayden said, holding her arms out wide and engendering silence from her acolytes, "we all care about this as much as you. Cheryl had her mailbox taken two weeks ago." One of the birds nodded. "Becky's kid's playpen in late winter. My own garage was raided in March. They took my lawnmower. That damned thing set me back four hundred dollars. The warranty had run. I am lucky that the Luis boy at Gardy's respects my feminine charm." She smiled big, visualizing her cherished sexual rendezvous–lawnmower exchange with an eighteen-year-old foreign student. She came back quickly, as he had.

"So you see, we have all been touched by this. But running around like little chickens with our heads cut off will only increase the mayhem. This is not the end of the world, my boy. We have a group of bandits on our hands. Teenagers…likely boys abusing the area for juvenile entertainment. They are not intelligent, and they are not dangerous. They are little puke-brained brats, and I want justice as much as you. That's why I've decided we should have everyone take turns patrolling the neighborhood in groups of four. We will have a sign up sheet at the clubhouse, and everyone can find times that work for them. I will put in time everyday, as I'm sure my ladies will as well." She tilted her head left to right as each ostrich nodded one by one. Hayden looked at Ferris. "We will have our bandits by next week. Or they'll relent due to the oversight."

Mr. Ferris sat, letting the tension in his body fade. "Yes, you see, that's what I wanted to hear. Thank you!" he shot his right hand in the air, signaling his exasperation.

Hayden said, "That's right, let mama handle this." Ferris rolled his eyes and nodded with tired, dismissive agreement. "Oh, and Ferris….I've seen you at the pool. You can't call that little pistachio between your legs a dick!" The ostriches exploded into ecstatic convulsions. Hayden took her rounds of high fives and celebratory shoulder slaps.

Ferris immediately took to his feet. "God dammit, Hayden! Why? Just…why?" he said.

Pollock had forgotten entirely the purpose of his attendance. He glanced down at his notepad. He saw a note from Quentin that read, "Find out how Jalisco resolves its power line easement issue." He wasn't sure that had even come up. The mention of missing items had piqued his interest and, because the neighborhood was completely across town from his own, certainly exonerated the Ne'er Do Wells for the birdhouse if the thefts were related. If not, there were too many coincidences lately.

However, the war of the sexes that had erupted in front of him was a bore and a nuisance. He slowly tiptoed out through the open door unnoticed. As he picked up his stride down the hallway, he heard Mr. Ferris speaking. "There are too many pretty boys nowadays. Why doesn't anyone want to look like a man anymore? I will tell you why! Its because of vindictive, self-righteous women drumming the…" His voice faded out of earshot and Pollock smirked, curious about where Mr. Ferris's futile efforts were headed.

Human, Human Coffee Shop sat at the northwest corner of the steep intersection of Alma Street and Belgrave Alley. The establishment was housed in what used to be a garage and auto repair shop. The structure had been retrofitted with modern amenities but still retained its industrial feel, sporting concrete slab floors, large metal garage doors, and refurbished oil and auto parts signs scattered about the walls. A seemingly out of place, white wooden cottage-style porch wrapped around the majority of the coffee shop and spread out into a large deck area in the back, with holes sawed out of the floor boards to accommodate the mighty maple and oak tree trunks whose leafy branches provided cover, predominantly for smokers.

Belgrave Alley split a field into two empty lots and Human, Human patrons, responding to the general lack of parking options within the city core, began trying their luck by leaving their cars there. The lots belonged to the city as part of their land bank, but no efforts had been made to address the ad hoc parking, which had been steadily growing over the past year to the point that Human, Human now situated an employee at the lots to oversee orderly spatial organization of the autos. It was usually Tomato Tom, the chubby Asian cross-dresser, sitting on a wooden stool playing Tetris on his old color Game Boy, oblivious to his surroundings until he intuitively detected a driver making final placement decisions that offended his three-dimensional sensibilities and would run over to the car and politely provide notes.

Pollock sat in his truck watching the orange clock lights blink in the console. He had arrived ten minutes early. The area was alive, crawling with beings, shoes scuffling, insects buzzing overhead, combustion engines whizzing by—loud cars owned by townsfolk who spent muffler repair money on too many eleven-dollar Moscow mule drinks. Distant laughter, gasps and faint chatter carried through the winds. A haunted city. It was that late supper time of day where mood became apparent and accompanied the transition into evening.

Pollock had found it best to maintain motion throughout such "hinges." He took a stroll around the block. He returned to Human, Human precisely ten minutes later and entered, ordered an iced tea, and chose a seat by the door to the back porch. The AC was either broken, or management had decided it was cool enough outside to only run two overhead fans. This, in conjunction with small slits left open in the sliding glass doors, provided no relief. The espresso machines, dishwashers, grills, and fire lit cauldrons shot hot smog to the ceiling, where it twirled about, lingered, grabbed hold of itself, sank, and made even a T-shirt an entirely inappropriate wardrobe decision.

Pollock savored his iced tea. An awful pop song, the lyrical content of which dealt with a protagonist whose decision to marry his wife merited sympathy because she was rude, subtly overtook the hum of the coffee shop conversations. Listening to the dreck made him entertain the notion of leaving. Then a hand appeared palm out on the table next to his iced tea. Pollock shot his head up, surprised, screeching his chair legs backward. Wooden nickels stood laughing and covering her mouth with her hand. His alarm had amused her.

Reaching out and caressing Pollock's shoulder she said, "I'm so sorry, I didn't mean to scare you. It's just, well…I've just like been working on sneaking up on people. You know, like you've been eating a certain brand of toast for a decade, in that same yellow and white wrapping, and finally some cloudy Saturday morning a friend asks you why, and like a crazy rush of confusion, you can't remember why. It just sort of snuck up on you, or at least maybe that's how it seems when you're remembering. You know? Like, you have to recover the reason why? Like, you have to rediscover it? Almost like a test to see if you can remember, or come to the same conclusion about it? She chuckled nervously and dropped her voice an octave. "Scared true."

Pollock gave deep thought to what had just been said. "So, are you saying that you expect us to be together ten years from now, or that if you didn't sneak up on something, it would preclude a ten-year tenure? Or…are you saying that….well wait, if that's how the person remembers the beginning of them eating that type of toast or bread, then why is it important to actually sneak up on someone when its that later memory that really counts? How do you even predict something like that? Wouldn't the actual sneaking up make it more likely to be remembered? Or you just like seeing someone come to consistent conclusions? Or, people can't be true without the start? You believe that? You can't believe that. Do you?" The grinning girl in front of him still had her hand on his shoulder. He liked it.

Wooden nickels jerkily sat herself at the table across from him. "It was just a thought, so I decided to startle you. I guess it's not really important anymore why…I'm sorry. Like, can we start out differently? Start this again?" She raised her eyebrows in pathetic puppy dog fashion. This was a gesture that would usually fill Pollock with indignation, but for some reason it worked well, here, tonight, now. He smiled long, rubbing the sweat from his temples, and wiping it on his khakis. Wooden nickels smiled.

"Yes, yes of course we should. Um, hi, I'm Pollock," he said, unsure of whether she was being sincere or mocking.

"Hi, I'm Retta, it's nice to meet you." A long pause followed, filled with background chatter and the orchestra of the bistro machinery. Retta awkwardly laughed while setting her phone on the table. Pollock noticed Retta's brown curls, her black dress. Retta wondered why Pollock was sweating so much. He looked exasperated. There was a hard internal agony between the two newly acquainted people.

"So….about this dream…" Pollock said, heartily trying to push the encounter into shape.

"Oh yes, yes!" Retta said. "It starts in the jungle. It's rainy and very hot. There's steam everywhere, kind of like this place." She gestured a circle above her head. "I am wearing, like, a loin cloth and bra wrap, something that Eve would be wearing in a Bible film from the fifties. And there's this weird bass riff echoing off from the distance…boom, boom, boom, bah, boom-buh-boom. It's really deep and melodic. Anyway, you know how sometimes in dreams you just know certain things, like who someone is even though you've never seen them before, or like your longtime friend is there but you know, in the dream, like, they are a serial killer?" she paused.

"Yes." Pollock nodded, further wetting his khakis.

"Ok, well there's a muscular older man with face paint, like elaborate black and white war paint, hunching behind a tree with me. And he is my older brother. And he's explaining to me that our village is going to be invaded by the El Bareebo people, led by their savage leader, Tampa."

Unbeknownst to him, Pollock had begun to lean in with interest. Retta spoke with fire in her eyes. She was lit up. Her dimples flared with each sentence-ending smile. Her pale fingers, gesturing wildly in front of her, drew each word, each idea for her listener. The story was coming to life in Pollock's imagination.

"Well anyway, he tells me about this war brewing and how the El Bareebo need our lands because it borders along the Fish River, which the El Bareebo need to transport their main export, which I guess is a mineral, or a rock called Pait that they mine from the ground in the hills outside their villages. Anyway, it's a drug that's snorted; it gives you visions that I guess are important for religious ceremonies celebrated all throughout the lands. And my father was our people's leader, the leader of our village, and he was a reformer who defied the temple. Our people were skeptics, and so he instituted a policy of no Pait transport. He believed that it made the mind weak. People became addicted, and then whoever controlled its distribution ruled. That's how he felt about Tampa and his council—that they were evil, well, like power hungry. So, like, our village enforced a policy disallowing Tampa to use our ports.

"Well, my brother said that Tampa was going to use force, to invade and take over our village. Apparently, my brother, I can't remember his name in the dream, but...apparently he was the leader of our village's defenses and was going around recruiting soldiers for the inevitable battle. And, like, he was recruiting me but in a different way."

She took a deep breath and crossed her ankles in the opposite fashion, starring inquiringly at her listener. Pollock took a long draw through his iced tea straw. The cold liquid pooled at the back of his mouth before he swallowed and sent a chill through his throat and chest. He said nothing.

Retta noticed Pollock's stern facial expression and wondered if he was another of those cynical people she had been meeting lately, too disheartened by shortcomings to allow for the possibility of newness, of wonder in the world. Because, that is what she was looking for; joy in this world. That was what she needed. She felt there were enough critical realists beaten by life, left with nothing but a condescending shell of a person, eager to goad and glory in another's failures or mistakes. She hoped for better.

"So anyway, in the dream I have a heart condition. My heart was growing too big for my heart cavity. Like, at some point it would grow so big that my chest cavity would essentially be choked and I would die. And apparently Pait helped with the condition. Contrary to my father's economic policy, he had been smuggling Pait into our village and putting it into my meals everyday. My brother told me this. And with the war coming, and the future of our people at risk, my brother asked me to leave the village, go into the mountains where elders go to pass away."

Pollock's felt horror at the proposition. "Wow, that is wild!" he said. Retta smiled, delighted with the effect of her telling.

"Yea, I was very emotional. It was like my family was betraying me. But it also somehow made sense. You know, like if Tampa found out about my use, then they would have an amazing argument against my father's policy. If our people knew, they would likely claim that our family was hoarding Pait for ourselves and depriving the rest of our village, selfishly. We'd be hypocrites. They would revolt. And that would like be the end of the reforms. So I was being asked to sacrifice myself."

A hairy arm abruptly slammed a frosted glass mug on the table between the two. A gentleman in a pink tank top looked down through his narrow slits and roughly shouted, "Frozen strawberry Daiquiri for the lady. Enjoy!" then turned quickly to return to the counter where Retta and Pollock, startled back into awareness of the shop, saw there was now a line out the door.

"I guess we came at the right time." Retta said, nodding behind her toward the crowd of customers.

"Yes. Apparently." said Pollock in agreement. He pointed to the stout mug, noticing with particular lust the cloudy chunks of ice sliding down its sides. "That looks pretty amazing, I should have ordered something frozen."

"Well anyway, it sounded good." Retta said, leaning forward and taking an extended sample of the product with a slurp. She closed her eyes. "Mmmm." Opening one eye in a sort of inadvertent wink, she asked, "Want some?" and wondered if that was too forward.

"Absolutely," Pollock said, grabbing the cold mug handle and sliding the drink underneath his chin. He took a small sip from the side. The taste didn't impress him. He slid it back with a reserved nod.

"So what happened, did you leave?" asked Pollock, finally, casually, slicing the silence.

"Yea, I did." She felt guilty, as if the story had garnered enough attention and now needed a swift ending. Pollock would have listened for hours. "The last image I have was my chest split open and my bloody hands holding my heart, then I died. And then I woke up."

"Wait. So you ripped it out?" Retta nodded. "What does it mean to you?" Pollock asked.

Retta continued to nod, thinking. "Well there's a bit more to it. Okay, when I was eight, that summer my father had to take down an ash tree in the backyard that was decaying from bores. A friend of his from work, Chris Clark, came over to help him out. They had been working all morning, clearing shrubs and then chain sawing off the limbs before getting to the big trunk. The phone rang and it was Mrs. Clark. She sounded hurried and shouted that she needed to speak with her husband. I hollered and he came in. Anyway, he dropped the phone and sprinted out of the front door. My dad later found out his son had died in his sleep that morning. Hypertrophic cardiomyopathy."

"What is that?"

"Its when your heart is too big for your chest, so it stops. Their son was twenty-four when this happened. He was perfectly healthy, had just moved out west and got a job as a journalist out of college. That was the last time Mr. Clark ever came around. He soon after quit his job. My dad told me years later that he ended up a divorced alcoholic with numerous DUIs. Like, ever since then, I've been really scared of my own heart. I have recurring dreams where I tear it out of my chest or dreams where I wake while I'm cutting myself open with knives and hatchets and, for whatever reason, I just continue, I see it through, like out of momentum or something. Like I know it's inevitable. Anyway, that was my dream. And that's my fear...I am afraid of pulling my heart out during my sleep because I am afraid that it's too big for my chest cavity. So, like, now it's your turn to share something about you."

"Well, I am fairly certain that my house is haunted," Pollock blurted out, shrugging his shoulders and sipping his tea.

"Really? I love hauntings! What is going on? What have you seen?"

Pollock smiled and said, "I should begin by telling you that I am skeptical. I don't believe in spirits, ghosts, and the afterlife. Any of that. I'm not religious—you know, what's beyond is...beyond; it is unknown. But I am also open to new data. And lately, I keep waking up and I swear there's an old lady watching me. I only catch her for a few seconds, only take in a faint glimpse, and then she just, well...is gone. It began when I moved in a few months back. You see, it was my great-aunt's house. She passed on when I was younger, and, well, I think it may be her I am seeing. I am not sure why. It's probably some projection from my memory, er, I don't know." Pollock carefully ran through his recent string of "astral projections." Retta sipped her strawberry Daiquiri and smiled.

The conversation strode on, gaining momentum and, helped by the alcoholic ciders they switched to, reached a dashing pace. The back and forth became rapid fire and increased in volume as they covered general topics concerning their upbringing and education. The evening air outside cooled, the crowd thinned out with a smattering of "goodbyes," "later mans," "bye girls," and "drive safes." The two made their way out to a table on the back porch. Cicadas leeched out their primal song and joined the faraway howls of the freeway and the squeals from the trains. The metal patio table wobbled and rocked under each clumsy replacement of their drinks. Those customers that remained mirrored Retta and Pollock's inebriated ecstasy.

"So what's the story with you being Wiccan? What is Wicca, even?" Pollock asked with a smirk and an arm raised toward the sky.

Retta had prepared a mental outline of her speech on the subject but couldn't presently recall it, which made her embarrassed and afraid. "Okay, like, Wicca is essentially a religion aimed at understanding and using the forces found in nature. It's traditionally ditheistic. There is a moon goddess and a horned god. But my coven doesn't really believe in the gods, or any "other" realms really. Like, we see them more as expressions of subconscious archetypes, reflections of the cosmos's functions. We're more akin to animists, who see everything as being comprised of the same "soul material," but its all the same material, its nature, its forces, yin and yang. Everything is comprised of the same energy and of the same materials. We, as Wiccan, seek to get in tune. Like, we tune in to our surroundings, with the universe, and so are seeking the truth. We emulate the shapes of the truth. Sing the right songs. Anyway, there is one moral component. It's the Wiccan Rede. It goes 'An it harm none, do what ye will.' It means if you harm no one, then you may do as you wish. It's basically Jesus's golden rule and maybe somewhat like Kant's categorical moral imperative. It makes sense when you see everything as one. It's almost, weirdly, like self-interest." She took a breath and a big gulp of cider.

Pollock was intrigued. This explanation was surprisingly close to his views. Still, he quickly revived his suspicion. "Hmm...so do you work on spells and such?"

Retta observed the condescension; it was common. "No, we don't mix herbs and animal parts in a cauldron and try to put an ugly curse on our foes! That would violate the Rede anyway." Pollock recognized his trespass and made a nodding apologetic gesture. "We do have rituals. Mostly for the solstices but other ones as well. And yes, we do have what we call 'spells,' but they are not how you would think of them. We speak words and try to all focus on raising energy, usually healing of some form. We try to explain our intentions and see them come to fruition. Then we say our thanks for the season, for the past year, for each other. Like, it also provides community. Good people that I've known my whole life who keep me accountable and who support me, though I've not been that involved lately."

"And when you perform these rituals," Pollock said, "I suppose that you are all naked?"

Retta opened her eyes wide in a charming imitation of horror. "Yesss! And snake blood smeared on our breasts!" She leaned forward and pushed Pollock's shoulder in affection and mock offense. They laughed for some time, then they grew quiet. The sound of a folk singer covering Bob Dylan in a nearby tavern came into focus.

"You say 'like' too much," Pollock said.

Retta blushed. "I know. I know I do. You're not one of those critical people that live to tear things apart are you? Like, with a stick up their ass?"

"I'm critical, yes."

Retta squinted and bit her lip. "But, you're not one of those people who act like someone stole their lunch. You know, walking around trying to avenge some past wrong, and when you're around them, you are the one that gets the blame?"

Pollock rubbed his eyes in a circular motion a few full revolutions. "Maybe. I mean that's just how things become when you get to thinking. It's painful. It's a knife. But the other side of it is that there's always something more, something better. Progress, I suppose. Yes, progress. I mean, I'm critical of myself most of all. I'm not blaming anyone; its all our fault. We need to be better than we've been. And nothing goes anywhere without that criticism, that negativity, actual negativity, the questioning. Everything worthwhile is painful. And the painfulness can make you unhappy."

Retta became very stern-faced. She was aflame with intrigue, with passion, with cider. "But don't you find it bottomless? I mean, like, doesn't that process keep going and going, pushing everything away, breaking everything down? Like there's no bottom, no foundation? How do you build anything like that?"

" I give things up...I...let certainties go to see if there's anything else. Then the thoughts get complicated; I feel confused, er, not confused. I separate myself. I lose trust in the interface..."

"The interface?"

Pollock tilted his head in an effort to retrieve the proper words. "The, uh, membrane between people, everything that is assumed, subtext perhaps. I see too many possibilities, so that everything becomes a potential problem." He rested his words, unsatisfied with their clumsy configuration.

"Stop thinking so damned much," Retta said, wryly smiling.

Pollock smiled back, embarrassed that he had rambled on so vaguely.

The conversation went on, becoming less coherent and more emotional as the evening stretched on. They parted ways a little after midnight. Retta had made

Pollock promise her that she could come over to help investigate the haunting and the missing birdhouse. They agreed to meet at the farmer's market that weekend.

* * *

"Pollock, my young comrade, come chat with an old man," Quentin said, waving him over. Pollock tiptoed his rolling chair to the space between their desks. Quentin tipped his forehead down in an interrogatory manner and gave an ornery leer. Pollock smiled involuntarily. These sorts of odd interactions were part of Quentin's charm and appeal for Pollock. Others routinely found such oddball antics, ill-placed pauses, and unusual facial expressions troubling, even mocking. Many reacted to Quentin from a place of fear, intuitively recognizing his unique wisdom and sincerity, which conflicted with any form of lazy status-quo human behavior such as verbalized clichés. People saw Quentin as a menace and perhaps a bit of a rascal, but one with merit and wit. Less thoughtful or playful patrons of Trams Facilities maintained their distances.

"How is life with Pollock?" he asked, easing up on his leer.

Pollock didn't enjoy revealing personal information in their work rectangle, where all passersby could overhear. But such feeling was always overcome by the usefulness of Quentin's thoughts. He took in a deep breath, physically ushering in honesty and answered, "Well things are even, I suppose. I'm....well this project is really giving me trouble. I'm behind where I should be at this point, and no clear solution has presented itself. Really, I think what I'm finding is that the disputes are much deeper than the zoning code. Its just...people."

"'It's just people.' Aha-ha-ha! That is great, 'it's just people!'" Quentin held his belly with one hand, and pulled his T-shirt away from his throat as if it was attacking him. Pollock looked up from his concentration. He was being scolded.

Quentin continued, "We should have that as a department motto: 'Trams Zoning—It's just people.' Ha-ha. Or if we can't come up with a fix for competing uses of land, we'll just exclaim, 'It's just people!'" He convulsed with laughter. Counter clerks looked over, alarmed at the raucous outbreak. Quentin wiped his sweaty dome and forced himself to recover from the hilarity.

Pollock, unfazed by the customary episode, said, "Well, it is. You of all people understand what I am saying. People are incapable of living together. It's emotional and gets really specific, really particular. And I don't know which parties are right. And as soon as you try to make the dispute fair, someone loses. The zoning code just decides which friends it would like." Pollock searched for his words, at a loss for how to make himself clear. He had failed Quentin. A warm hopelessness filled Pollock.

Quentin, now fully composed, detected as much and so focused on the perceptive kernel within Pollock's statements. "Peace is unfair, right?" Quentin said. "Most of us either aim to be martyred, because we followed some code regardless of the others, or we idolize some predator animal and live by the idea that we peril or profit from our skills. Peace disrupts that natural order. It's a tension against the universe. I mean, how can you tell someone that they are not entitled to their answer, their revenge? That there is this arbitrary cutoff in the way of their vengeance, and it's called peace? Why wasn't there peace before that which necessitated their vengeance? Who determined the timeliness? It's a tough notion to hold, even harder still to actually put into practice. On a small scale, localized with willing participants, maybe. Broadly institutionalizing it, I think would be insanity. And, I don't want you to go insane. So, by way of advice, I would suggest that you start your project with a taxonomy of options and outcomes. Take each case and propose, say five possible zoning or variance solutions that we *could* implement. Then project what effect that would have on the parties, and what problems might arise. That in itself would undoubtedly provide valuable insight."

Quentin stopped speaking and raised his eyebrows in question. He loved to watch Pollock think.

Pollock nodded as he explored the suggestion. "And so a different solution for each instance may be right," he muttered.

Quentin mulled that over for a moment then responded, "I'm willing to bet that a pattern will emerge, if not themes at least." Now both of them were tilting their heads forward, engaging in some heavy noodling, chasing tangents to far corners as diverse as Japanese existentialism, astronomy, oil drilling, and dietary preparations for oral sex. Their nods synched to a common rhythm. One of the counter clerks noticed them and believed they were sharing iPhone earphones to listen to a song.

Quentin finished, "Once you've done that for all of your cases and feel confident in your options and results, bring them to me and we can go over them together, okay?"

Pollock, resupplied with some hope, acceded. "Sounds good, Quentin. Thank you." He smiled amicably.

"Don't ever smile at me like that, you fiend," Quentin said. Pollock snorted. "Now let me continue telling you about the Titius Rombathians."

Chapter Four

Maximilian's thawing nose burned. His fuzzy sight revealed a tall burning candle atop a wooden table over which he was hunched, his hands bound to ribbed rungs of a bench built into the wall behind him. The room was a small pub filled with hot air and the smell of pine and stale ale. The rope binds were rough and tight, rubbing his wrists raw.

Adjacent to the table, there was a bar with an assortment of liquor bottles containing amber and crystal spirits, neatly rowed, with stools below. The other captured men sat opposite Max in similar fashion, their heads hanging down, unconscious. The snow on their legs had melted into a pool on the floor, which combined with Max's own. Through the log walls, Max could hear muffled sounds of music and laughter. It sounded like children were running around in clogs playing tag.

Solid, heavier footsteps approached, growing increasingly pronounced until an alarming thud swung the heavy copper door open, slamming it against the logs behind it, testing the steel hinges with a shrill squeak, waking up Max's fellow prisoners, and jangling the liquor bottles. A suited gentleman with a beer mug in one hand and an axe in the other stepped quickly forward and scanned the room.

The tall fellow from the graveyard slithered in behind him, arms folded. The man in the suit pulled out a stool from the bar, slowly scraping its legs against the uneven flooring and sat himself upon it, smiling slightly. He leaned the axe against the legs. He took an extended swig of ale, finishing the glass with emphasis, and handed it backward to the tall man, who took it in both of his hands carefully and placed it on the counter-top directly next to the suited man. The other captives stretched their faces and straightened out their posture, acclimating to their present predicament.

A high, rough voice rang out from behind fat lips. "Before we begin our discussion, its important that the four of you understand that, by rights, I could kill you right here." He pointed downward with vigor several times. "I would be justified. Appreciate that." The man made eye contact with each captive. A wave of dread came over Max. He was tired of feeling awful for so long. The rope threads had now cut into his wrists and sharp pains ran up his forearms and into his neck. His ribs were sore.

"I am Titius Rombathe," he belted out with dramatic sweeping gestures, as if delivering a rehearsed thespian's monologue on stage. "You are currently in the drinking room in my winter quarters. In addition to heading several interstate going concerns, I privately own and oversee the operation and maintenance of Rowe's Charnal House and God's Acre Cemetery, where you were introduced to my compatriot, Mr. DeBeers." Titius gestured to Mr. DeBeers, who had poured a mixture of beer and whiskey into the empty mug and was returning it to Titius's left hand. "My right hand man, so to speak." Titius chuckled, then sat the mug down, grabbed DeBeers by both cheeks, stood on tiptoe, and kissed DeBeers on his long, greasy nose. DeBeers waved it off, an inconsequential remark from a nag.

Titius returned to his audience. "The income from these cemeteries is minimal and mostly revolves back into general maintenance, employment expenses, et cetera. The true value lies in providing a final resting place befitting the noble character of the local community in which I have spent a lifetime. Community.

Community is what gives us our authenticity. Our community leaders should be mirrors and examples."

Max glanced over at the other two men, who were squirming in various contorted states of discomfort, their expressions falling somewhere between smelling someone else's wet fart and beholding the beauty of a sunset for the first time. Max wondered to what extent his circumstances would change if he could explain that he was separate from these other men, but decided it wouldn't matter because his crime was the same.

"So what are you going to do with us?" the larger of the two captives spit out through sloppy lips, holding an intent stare. Titius stood and approached the man, bending at the waist and tilting his head as a curious dog might. He was amazed at the audacity of the fat wretch. DeBeers took a step forward and pulled a leather object from his inside coat pocket, ready to move.

"What is your name, fiend?" Titius asked.

"Clayton Morris." The man flashed his teeth in a defiant grin. He foolishly felt that he could defeat his captor with spite.

"Clay-ton Mor-ris," Titius sounded out. "Well, Clayton, you're clearly not a very perceptive man. You see, if you were in fact perceptive, you would have taken note of several important things in this particular scenario. First, that you have no leverage to be asking questions. More, that you have no bargaining power whatsoever. All advantage is ours," he gently placed his palms on his chest. "But, more important than any of this, is another fact that has evaded your perception. It is…crucial." He stopped speaking and stepped back a little. Clayton relaxed his face, searching the room in growing fear as the import of Titius's words grew.

"It was DeBeers that chased you across the river behind the Charnal House two weeks ago. He recognized your face." Titius pointed at the smaller man and then looked back at DeBeers who nodded in affirmation. "And what is your name?" The smaller man's face grew red and his eyes enlarged. Clayton quickly said, "He's mute. His name is Ben." Titius squinted his eyes at Ben, then back at Clayton for longer. After a silent moment, he continued.

"That was a trying night for me…After that night, we increased our watch of both cemeteries. This was required, necessary, especially in light of other growing problems in this part of my country. So to say, you were doomed the moment you arrived in God's Acre tonight. You," Titius turned and pointed at Max, "we had to let work awhile in hope that your associates here would turn up. And sure enough, my instincts were correct."

"Sir, these are not my associates," Max said with conviction. His and Titius's eyes locked. There was an intensity in Max that Titius recognized.

Titius asked earnestly, "So they've yet to arrive?" DeBeers shot a worried glance, experiencing a moment of panic at the thought of failing in his job duties.

"No, sir," Max said. "I have no associates. Nor have I ever seen either of these men before. I…" Max stopped himself, keen on limiting the information he would disperse. Titius and DeBeers exchanged glances in what appeared to Max to be wordless communication. In his mind, DeBeers was asking if they should believe the new information. Titius silently understood, as men who have been close for many years will, and communicated back that it wasn't as important as the current proceedings. And, anyway, he was inclined to believe the kid, for whatever reason.

"Yes, fine. You'll have your turn. Your go of it," he said, turning from Max back to Clayton and Ben. "When I introduced myself to you, I gave you my last name, Rombathe. R-O-M-B-A-T-H-E. Doesn't that name mean anything to you?" He scanned back and forth between the two with raised eyebrows, his growing frustration and disgust visible. Clayton decided Titius wanted his ego fed, which angered him, but he truly hadn't ever heard such a name. He'd be smart to start humoring the man, but he remained silent. DeBeers gripped his leather tool tightly.

Titius leaned down, placing a hand on each man's knee. He put his mouth right next to Clayton's ear and screeched, "Rombathe!" Clayton recoiled in pain, jerking his neck away and clenching his eyes shut. Titius took a deep breath and asked Clayton, "He's not also deaf, correct?" He then repeated his scream, "Rooombaaathe!" into Ben's right ear, who whimpered and curled up onto the bench as much as the binds would allow. Max thought he looked like a beaten dog.

"No?…Nothing? Either of you fiends?" Titius swept his short curls back into styled position, pulled out a white silk square and wiped his face. He exhaled hard, closing his eyes. Max's ribs and lungs burned with a desperate urgency. Titius stepped away from the duo and walked back over to the bar. DeBeers relaxed his stance and loosened his grip on blackjack. Titius took a long, hard swig from his mug, finishing its contents once again with an exaggerated stretch of his shoulders.

Max began entertaining thoughts of dying and found it hard to draw conclusions from premises. He wondered if dying was the only way to find Ethyl. The thought of her eased his discomfort a good measure. He closed his eyes. They were reopened by the slam of Titius's mug on the solid counter.

"We found some interesting items in your bag," Titius said while wiping excess spirits from his mouth. He nodded to DeBeers, who pulled his free hand from his other jacket pocket to produce a small bracelet onto the table of thieves. Titius continued, "I had figured that, most assuredly, you would have capitalized on your bounty by now. Though, maybe you have a…routine. The opossums hang around the same spots at harvest. Ah, bah!" He sat upon the stool, placing his palms in his eye sockets, pushing them up his forehead in a frenzy of trembling fingers. "I remember her mother picking that bracelet out for her," he said to Max.

Chapter Five

A cacophony of birdsong seeped into Pollock's dreamworld and he had images of feathers in his head when he woke up at 10:38 on Saturday morning. Rays of sunshine lasered into the living room, illuminating lazy, midair twirls of dust. Shadows from darting bunches of house sparrows outside danced across the floorboards like sped up weather radar patterns. The couch was cool underneath him as he stretched his arms and yawned. He was excited for the day in front of him.

Pollock tried a can of sardines in mustard, instead of spring water as usual. There had been a sale in which the mustard sardines were six cents cheaper per ounce. He'd figured it while in a contorted position on the grocery's floor. He was wary of the purchase because there were so many different kinds of mustard. "What kind is it?" he said aloud in the international aisle at Bud's, having returned to an upright posture. If it was spicy brown mustard, well that'd be alright. But he wondered how horseradish mustard or classic yellow would jibe with sardines. That might be worse than olive oil. He laboriously scrutinized the label for more information. He asked the overdressed cashier gentleman, who, with a dour expression replied, "Ew, no. Who eats sardines?"

Thus, he purchased one can and decided to investigate further before committing to the sale price for his full provisions. It turned out there was merely a yellowish, chunky substance littered throughout the can, without any noticeable mustard-like flavor. This confused Pollock because they could have just been named Yellow Sardines. He would have to buy another to compare and contrast in case this can was a dud. This project required more effort than he had first realized. "Oh well, at least I get to enjoy regular tasting sardines."

A number of users had viewed his profile since he last checked in. There was only one message. He opened it.

> Hi there.... My boyfriend and I think you're cute. We are looking for a submissive third who likes to please. We prefer hairless but are open to some hair (no bushes, please – Also, no burning…the smell stays longer than you think). Also, you must be at least 5 foot 10, well endowed and able to prove it before meeting up. Let us know if this is you and if you are interested. -Channi and Mike

Pollock scoffed and exited the site. He opened the *Trams City Gazette* website and began scrolling through the headlines. Nothing of interest popped out to him. There was an article highlighting the features of the farmer's market. He closed the laptop and grabbed the binoculars. He scanned Nyqvist. Quickly, he spotted the Ne'er Do Wells rocketing single file through the Epsteins' back yard and under their back deck with shovels and trowels in hand. He rested his gaze there. After a brief moment, bunches of sand came flinging out from the edge of the deck in regular intervals.

Further up Nyqvist the young Ventilli couple sat in their front room playing chess. This was a new development and only added to Pollock's suspicion. Hopefully this would be a foolish and short-lived flight of fancy for them. Otherwise, how would he live with the assault that such concentration of success and talent would have on his self worth in comparison. Where was the dirty asshole of it all? He surveyed the remainder of the visible neighborhood and found nothing of interest. It was a fairly uneventful late morning in the suburbs of Trams.

Bastien Ebersold noticed his reflection in the glass covering his latest work of art. Violently green eyes shaped like pistachios jumping from the darkness. It was a three foot by four foot charcoal drawing within an ornate, brass frame that added about eight inches to the matting. It hung on the wall at Bastien's eye level in the basement underneath Ebersold Family Clocks. He was satisfied with the finished product because it made him feel terrible. The drawing depicted a man sitting naked on large rocks near crashing ocean spray. On his left outer thigh were piano keys comprised of bone and flesh, tattooed black for the minor keys. A cloaked man crouched beside, stealthily pressing the keys. On the lower back of the naked man there was a circular region of enlarged pores, roughly the size of dimes. Out from the pores shot gusts of wind, much like a speaker. The wind was accompanied by puss, bile, and crawling insects including ants, centipedes, and spiders. The man held his head skyward, mouth open, yelping in agony.

Bastien mused on the smell of the speaker. He wondered what the pain and terror of having a piano running through one's body would feel like. A strange tension grew in his upper abdomen. It felt almost as if someone had put their little hand up his midsection and began tickling the bottom of his heart. He thought about his father and his nostrils flared wide. Bastien stepped back and his reflection faded. He let out an exhale of transition, then turned and headed for the spiral staircase to the shop above. He took short, choppy steps that moved his entire body side to side in a wobbling fashion. He was older, with shaggy grey hair. He matched his hair with a buttoned grey cardigan abutting loose black slacks. His spectacles hung on their chain, bouncing off of his chest with each step.

Ebersold Family Clocks sat at the end of Ferris Street, which dead-ended into Trams Square. The square itself consisted of a two acre mowed lawn with a white gazebo adorning its center, where horny teenage boys would convince their girlfriends to give them hand jobs under leather jackets on weekend evenings. Stretches of wild brush progressing into thick forest edged the lawn on its road-less sides. Beginning a little before 6:00 a.m., all sorts of folks began arriving for the weekly Trams farmer's market. The event was one of the few highlights listed on Trams's Commerce Office website, along with their annual pumpkin festival and January sled-building contest.

By the time Pollock walked up, the entire lawn was covered in tight-knit rows of vendor tables serviced by predominantly by men in dirty, tight cotton shirts spread over big bellies, leaving skinny runways full of townsfolk squeezing through with their bags of produce, bric-a-brac, and knickknacks. All varieties of fruits, vegetables, grain, meats, cheeses, bottles of locally grown wines and meads, tobaccos, comic books, antiques, quilts, photographs, oil paintings, vintage maps and magazine advertisements sat in varying formations of stacks, piles, columns of crates, boxes, jars, bowls, and vials on top, below and beside a varied collection of tables.

It was pushing noon. The heat bit and stung like some omnipresent invisible insect. The freshly laid blacktop from Ferris was emanating sickening odors. The wave of human noise crashed upon Pollock: laughing and crying children, smartass teenagers back talking their clearly ignorant guardians, vendors hollering about the quality of their goods and the inferiority of their competitors', old men letting inappropriate sexual innuendos slide toward thirtysomething females with supple bodies unbeknownst to their hubbies who were focused on their price haggling over something that would eventually make its way to the corner of the garage to collect dust and cobwebs for years until their future child and his playmates uncovered it in a fit of boredom. This place was lively.

Pollock pulled out his cellphone with his sweaty hand. Cabe had responded.

Great to hear, bud. I get in Thursday night at 7:18. Ill grab an uber to your place. Could you send me the addy?

Pollock sent the address and put the phone away. He had arrived early and so he navigated his way to an open picnic table on the edge of the market square and texted Retta his coordinates. He reflected on their previous date, which he felt had gone quite well. But now there was a dark anxiety that it had all been a one-off, composed mostly of the alcohol or otherwise illusory. It was also daytime now, which added an entirely different element to the ordeal. Shadows, for example. Large dread loomed.

He wondered about the wisdom of spending time on a person, investing in them. He didn't like the feeling of depending upon someone else. It reminded him of group projects in classes growing up. Pollock would always elect to be the recorder or writer, so that he could have the least involvement with decision-making. This was not because he didn't like making decisions but rather because he loathed the decision-making process with others. Whenever the choice of recorder was unavailable, he would take initiative and delegate tasks to his project mates. Otherwise, he would wait for his task to be assigned.

Retta hopped abruptly into a cross-legged crouch atop the table opposite Pollock, her brown curls bouncing and flopping in the wind. She smiled and her cheeks pushed up on the bottoms of her yellow circular sunglasses. Pollock, who had begun to slouch in his growing fatigue, straightened and asked, "No jolt of surprise from behind this time?"

Retta made a stern face. "Well, we saw how well that worked out last time, mister." She tipped her head, allowing her sunglasses to slide down the ridge of her nose and expose her playful eyes. Her black dress emitted a faint floral aura

that vaguely reminded Pollock of his great-aunt. He chuckled in sheepish conces-
sion, gathering his concentration back from the daydreaming he was so accustomed to on these hot weekend afternoons.

Retta said, "I'm actually really glad you agreed to go to the market with me.
It's one of my favorite things to do in Trams. Like, I find some new esoteric treasure each time."

Pollock, realizing that his previous apprehension was ill-founded, warmed
quickly. "It should be interesting, to say the least. Off we go!" He jumped to his
feet, holding his finger to the sky and skipped around the table. He offered his
arm to Retta, who accepted with oomph and an adamant head nod, and they
skipped off toward the vendor tables. Pollock recognized his burst of enthusiasm
as a Quentinism. It made him smile to himself. A rush of optimism swept through
him.

Retta and Pollock joined forces to haggle with an older gentleman who had
CD collections of animal mating songs. Retta explained it was something with
which her younger brother was obsessed. While the bearded man spit globs of
chewed tobacco into an empty green beans can, Pollock explained that they could
check out similar sound collections from the library for free. Retta seconded the
notion, saying that she had done so in the past and was only interested in the CDs
in question on a whim. The man went through a poetic spiel on how his recordings were the extensive PBS and Discovery Channel collections, which exceeded
the local libraries. "Mint condition," he muttered uneasily.

Under her breathe, Retta dryly commented, "Well, then it's a shame you
didn't decide to donate it to them," to which Pollock let out a gust of air. The man
gave them the stink eye and came down a bit on the price. Happy with their minor
success, Pollock and Retta nodded and ended up purchasing four CDs. Pollock
wondered what a Reeves's muntjac was.

After hours of looking, touching, inquiring, standing, bending, and laughing; inhaling astringent fumes, mildew odors, and dust; painfully bending their necks toward the tables and grass; and pushing and sliding their way past and around bodies of all types of grotesque and appealing forms, the two were exhausted and ambled from the square back over onto Ferris. Pollock had acquired a bag of morel mushrooms, freshly picked by a child from a local river valley, and a plastic box full of artichokes. Retta, aside from the CDs for her brother, left with a jar of organic strawberry jam. Retta's legs hurt something awful and so she proposed they get ice cream cones from ART. Pollock agreed, enthused, as he needed badly to cool off. He could feel droplets streaming down his sides underneath his tee.

The low, late afternoon sun formed long extending shadows to the east of structures, and the wooden bench that ran along the side of ART Ice Cream on Ferris was cool against Pollock's back. He extended his legs and crossed his ankles, stretching the tight calves and hamstrings in semipleasing pain. Retta finished her gumball cone, cricking and twisting her neck as she licked. Neither spoke. They just sat, watching the groups of townsfolk going to and fro, some filtering into various street shops and restaurants. A midday drunk stumbled out of Portico's Pub, half singing, "And get my vacuum sweeper, can't drink those legs, vacuum sweeping *baaaby*…with those vacuum sweeping *leeeggs*…drink and sweep up...until she sweeps up all of my *gawd damned sweetness*…" The song faded around a corner into the alleyway. Pollock and Retta met eyes, bursting into a roar of laughter. Then they grew quiet again for some time.

"So, like I don't know if you have plans tonight, but we are having dinner at six if you would like to meet my family," Retta said. "Sorry, was that too forward?"

Pollock looked seriously at her. He was bewildered by the coincidence of thought. "It wasn't," he said. "Actually, I was absolutely going to ask you on another date, anyway. And I didn't foresee that going badly. Thus, I anticipated many potential future dates. Which, would inevitably lead to meeting your father and brother. So, it might as well be tonight, right? Yes, actually that sounds good. Although, you know you haven't really told me much about either of them. They were all over your profile."

Retta's gut tickled with delight. "I'll fill you in on the way." After a moment, she grew somewhat ashamed and embarrassed that she hadn't said more about her family. She prided herself on her relationship with Remy and Fox. She felt to good to have somewhere to be where she didn't have to think of them, though. She was having a lot of fun.

As they were tossing away the remnants of their cold treats into the city garbage bin at the edge of the sidewalk, Pollock looked up and took notice of Ebersold Family Clocks. It was a sleek modern building, with steel beams lining clean glass plates. Along the right-most window, painted black letters in a simple font listed the goods and services to be found inside. Third down, Pollock spotted 'Birdhouses & Bird feeders.'

Retta put her hand on Pollock's shoulder. "What's up?," she asked. Her hand felt good on his shoulder. It sent chills through his back. "Would you mind if we stopped in to that clock shop real quick? I think my great uncle used to work there." Retta glanced over at the shop front, then up at Pollock's face, which appeared somewhat discombobulated to her, then down at her cellphone clock. "Sure, we have plenty of time. I just need to get home by 5:30 to help with the cooking."

The store was stuffy and quiet, filled with a strange anticipation. It reminded Retta of an art museum. White Berber carpeting lay underneath intermittent rectangular black-slate columns, bearing cuckoo clocks on all four sides. Some of the clocks were inside of clear plastic cases. Others lined the bottom of the wall, lying on their sides. Each clock was outfitted with a card containing the title, year made, and where it came from. All of the prices were negotiable. On the far end of the single large room sat a tiered shelving unit with birdhouses, house clocks, carved wooden tree ornaments, and an assortment other cutesy trinkets.

Orchestral music softly played from behind a shiny steel service counter at the back of the shop. Retta and Pollock naturally moved toward it and, as they neared it, Bastien popped up from behind, a stack of magazines in his arms. Retta jumped back, gasping in surprise. Pollock ducked slightly, and Bastien dropped what he was carrying. After catching his breathe, Bastien extended his arms in invitation. "Oh my dear, what a fright! I hadn't realized that we had customers. My sincere apologies. Please, come have a seat." He waved his arm toward a break in the counter leading into a back room.

After exchanging quizzical looks with Retta, Pollock lead the way into a tiled dining area containing a single circular mahogany table with a hanging lamp above adorned in fake green leaves. The two sat themselves and surveyed the back room. "I am Bastien Ebersold. I am the owner of Ebersold Family Clocks. I'll be with you two in just one moment. Can I you bring either of you any coffee? Tea? Water?"

"No thanks," the two responded in unison.

After quickly reassembling the pile of magazines, Bastien returned and sat himself opposite Pollock and Retta. He breathed in deeply, exhaling into a gigantic smile. His eyes grew and made contact with both of theirs as his nostrils flared. Retta was receiving strange vibes from Bastien, as from the store. She felt something was off with him. There were two men's voices coming from another room. They seemed to be arguing.

"And now how may I be of service to you today? Bastien quietly asked, adjusting his posture into rigid form, his right hand placed gently over his left wrist on the table in front of him.

"This may be out of left field, but I think you knew my great-uncle before he passed on," Pollock said. "Homer Shewecker?"

Bastien's nostrils flared, and he turned red at the mention of the name. He kept a straight face as a rush of thoughts flew through his skull. His heart fluttered, but he didn't believe Pollock knew. "I apologize, the name doesn't ring any bells. But, you must understand that we have had business with many, many individuals over the years. Do you know, would he have been a buyer or seller?" Pollock saw instantly that Bastien was holding back, heightening his curiosity. Retta continued quietly in her awkward discomfort, paying close attention to the interaction unfolding in front of her.

"From what I understand, he was a close friend. He made birdhouses…and cuckoo clocks. My grandmother said he sold through Ebersold," Pollock said with an air of accusation, which added to Retta's discomfort.

Bastien remained calm whilst deciding his best route of evasion. He said, "Pardon my further inquiry. Would these have been utility or ornamental birdhouses?" He tilted his head upward and to the side in a motion of effeminate defiance. Pollock felt as if there was something occurring to which he was not privy, some mysterious subtext.

Leaning forward and speaking aggressively he said, "He made very ornate houses. Fifties diners, chalets, famous skyscrapers, even mailboxes feeders. Different every time. They all had excellent woodwork. I think a few people even commissioned him at one point." He emphasized this last sentence. The conversation had become a passive aggressive battle.

Bastien turned his eyes to Retta, but directed his words at Pollock. "That's very fascinating. Were there any pieces remaining in his estate?" Retta found the question to be a tad indelicate, and looked over at Pollock in anticipation of his response.

Pollock did not honor the slight. He calmly answered, "There were numerous half-completed projects remaining. Only one that was finished. But, it's kind of odd; it was recently stolen out of my back yard."

Bastien smiled, sensing an opportunity to veer away from the testy back and forth. "Stolen from your backyard! There has been a lot of that going around. I assume you've heard about the marauders?"

Pollock snorted. "Marauders?"

Bastien continued, confident in his deflation of the emotional friction. "So you haven't heard. Well, there was a story about it in the Gazette a little while back. Things are being stolen at a much higher rate than usual. All sorts of objects from yards, garages, cars, even from inside some homes. No one has been caught in the process. The thefts focus on certain neighborhoods for an evening and then, after a few days of radio silence, a neighborhood on the opposite end of town will get hit. There is no apparent pattern, either in who's being targeted, or what is being taken. Just because of the sheer volume of stolen objects, rumors began that there was a gang, or that it was some organization, a roving group of marauders living off of the grid."

Pollock and Retta looked at each other in wonder and suspicion. "Pirates," Retta said. "Trams has pirates!" Pollock wondered whether he was being played with, as a toy. He decided that he would search for the news article later on.

On the way out, Bastien handed Pollock a business card and promised to be in contact if he found any records concerning his great-uncle. As they walked up Ferris, away from Ebersold Family Clocks, Bastien watched them and felt wistful. There had been a few times where he wondered at any of Ambrog's family or friends visiting. Such was a routine musing after utilizing the Sargus. But he had never entertained such thoughts far enough to arrive at a plan of action.. He had been unprepared. He stood in a panic, rubbing the edge of his hanging spectacles nervously, searching for comfort. It felt great to feel this bad.

Pollock thought he had responded to quickly to Retta's dinner invitation. Now, sitting in his truck parked outside of the address she had texted, his insides buzzed with nervous energy as his mind prepared for the oncoming trial of paternal judgment. A forceful breeze had manifested and was tormenting the long branches extending from the gargantuan maples lining the winding Hiedl Drive. The houses were newer on this side of town, late eighties maybe, covered in stucco earth tones and light blue shingles. But the developers had been careful to keep a great deal of the mature forest weaved throughout. Retta stepped out of her Corolla and waved Pollock over.

The two entered into the kitchen through the garage. Pollock sat at the bar at the edge of a large two-story living room with television and fireplace. Retta marched around between the fridge and the counter, chopping vegetables, grinding spices, oiling glass pans, and eventually stirring sauces and flipping baking chicken breasts. Pollock offered to help several times, but Retta insisted he not and opened a beer for him.

Pollock enjoyed watching Retta concentrate. He also enjoyed watching her body move around. Retta felt Pollock's eyes on her and would glance over occasionally with glee. Pollock's thoughts became sexual, then guilty. He felt uneasy about drinking a beer while watching a female cook him dinner. Just then, the door to the garage shook as the outer garage door buzzed and rattled open. "They're home. Great timing, the chicken is almost done!" Retta said. Pollock tensed.

The door flung open and inside jumped Fox. He was a very thin child with straight light-brown hair. He wore a plain blue T-shirt and jeans. "All of the static from all of the televisions in the world!" he yelled in a high pitched voice, putting him out of breathe.

Retta continued stirring the pasta sauce. "Hi Fox. Dinner will be ready in a minute. My friend is joining us. His name is Pollock. Say hello to him." Retta was worried about how Pollock would interact with Fox. Over the years of her friends and potential suitors meeting Fox, the common pattern had been veiled panic and avoidance.

Fox turned and noticed Pollock. Pollock smiled and said, "Hi Fox. I'm really happy to meet you." Fox took a step back toward the open vestibule in surprise. His lips quivered. After a brief lapse, the child began repetitively banging his rigid right palm against his forehead in a saluting motion that looked painful to Pollock. Fox blurted out, "He's not *my* mighty captain but he's definitely a mighty captain! I am the captain, I am the captain!" And with that, he began laughing and ran across the kitchen, disappearing into the dark hallway that stretched out between the kitchen and living room.

"He likes you," Retta said earnestly. Pollock let a burst of air through his nostrils. He was a little unnerved by the interaction but also entertained.

But then Pollock's thoughts sunk, dragging him into a quagmire of sad pondering. He wondered what motivations had brought him here. He put it down to programming. He was here for a family. He was here for a younger brother. He was here for sex. He was here because he was afraid to die alone. He wondered what he would get from this evening. He knew that he would never fit in with a family, with a community. He felt once they knew him, they would turn on him. That's why he had to keep them at manageable distance.

Retta finally assigned Pollock the task of setting the table while she went out into the garage to retrieve Remy for dinner. While setting, Pollock took note of the scarcity of home decor. There was little on the walls, a few Georgia O'Keeffe flower paintings in the living room and a plain black circular clock hanging above the fireplace mantle. There was no real trace of a family here. Not much separated it from a generic hotel-room aesthetic. Pollock found it alienating. A nondescript cookie cutter suburban home without any trace of personality. It seemed contradictory to Retta's colorfulness.

Retta returned downcast and apologetic. She informed Pollock that Remy had experienced some turmoil at work and needed the evening to unwind. "He won't be joining us for dinner." Further, Fox declined to come to the table because he needed to eat on the living room floor watching a documentary titled "The Future of The Buffalo." So Retta and Pollock quietly eyed one another while catching bits of narration from the film. They opened a bottle of wine. Time flew with sturdy wings. Retta invited Pollock to stay the night so they could watch B movie–horror flicks. They started with *Re-Animator* and then *The Burbs*. Fox would occasionally make bird sounds, high pitched squawking and chirping, which could be heard from his bedroom long after he left Retta and Pollock's quasi-company.

Remy never materialized from outside. It was not until the following morning, when Pollock awoke on the couch where Retta had left him to sleep, that he saw Remy. Or rather the top of his head as it bobbed past the window over the kitchen sink.

Regardless of the mystery surrounding Remy and his bad Saturday at the garage, Pollock did not know if he should stay or leave. He went back and forth several times before deciding he didn't want to awkwardly cross paths with Remy in his house, especially because, if he had stayed out all night, how would he know Pollock was still there. "Bah," Pollock said aloud, in sincere physical aversion to such a meeting. He sent a short explanatory text to Retta and hurriedly jaunted out of the front door into a cloudy Sunday morning in Trams.

Pollock spent the remainder of Sunday working on his zoning project in the fashion that Quentin had instructed. Some progress had been made, despite recurring nagging thoughts that the task was pointless, futile. It scared Pollock to think that, because he could not come to a conclusion about a specific zoning dispute, there was something missing within himself. It had occurred to him that there were only two weeks left and he still had to make one last visit. By 11:00 p.m., Pollock pushed his notes to the far side of his kitchen table and poured himself four fingers of sherry. He stared at the machete, still lying in the same spot on the tiled counter.

The neighborhood was quiet. Only the steady wind rustled about. Sunday nights always hung heavy over Pollock, like a bittersweet last serenade to the youthfulness of weekends. His thoughts traced back to Cabe, then to Retta. He thought about Hans and how, if he did not knock this project out of the park, Mr. Freedman would surely see his way to replacing him. Pollock decided Hans, the ass kisser, was a smug fucking bastard, the dirty asshole of it all. "Bah!" he shouted and kicked his left foot. It took hours for his anger to step aside and allow for sleep.

A loud thrashing from behind the house thrust Pollock into consciousness on the couch during the early a.m. He scanned the room, darting his head back and forth, trying to identify the exact direction of its origin. The sound ceased almost immediately and he wondered if it had been real at all or carry-over from a now-forgotten dream. He sat still for a moment, tuning in to all of the most minute creaks and cracks throughout the aged and uneven house. Just as he was reaching assurance that he'd been mistaken, the lights flashed on for a mere second, blinding Pollock with their twinkling. From the darkness, an elderly woman in a dazzling glow leaped out from a moving rocking chair and reached for Pollock's face. In terror, he impulsively jumped aside and onto the floor, rolled, and reached up hitting the light switch. Nothing. He jerked his head about in all directions. Nothing.

His heart racing like a Triple Crown winner, he focused on the memory of the woman. Grey hair pinned up in a bun, white floral sweater hanging over a dress. Different clothes, but it was her, again. Pollock stretched out his long, sweaty fingers with his palms up, grasping at something familiar and concrete to ground him in reality. A muffled crash resounded from the back yard.

Dexterously snagging the machete en route, Pollock launched out the back door to find two adolescent raccoons just above eye level, hanging from the house's rear gutter, a third desperately grabbing onto their outstretched arms, sporadically kicking his lower limbs to regain position on the roof. Pollock lowered the machete. The sight was so cute and so harmless that it instantly charmed Pollock. The raccoon found traction and climbed over the other two, who followed out of sight. The pitter-patter of their little paws dissipated above.

Monday morning was a hell-awful, soul-sucking kind of morning for Pollock. Hans was waiting for Pollock when he showed up to work, wearing a pastel blue suit with yellow plaid shirt. He sat on the edge of Pollock's desk with his arms folded, holding a confident sneer. The posture struck Pollock as that of a model in a trendy catalog like American Apparel. Pollock opened the gate and stepped past Hans. Hans turned, looking down at Pollock as he sat himself and unpacked his notebooks and pen from his bag. Pollock's blood boiled and churned in his veins but he held a steady face. He fantasized about excuses to punch Hans in the face.

Hans extended his thin wrist out and pointed to his shiny watch. "Nine thirty-seven. Not exactly the best start to the week."

"Just decided to take my time and enjoy the morning."

Hans stood. "Speaking of taking your time, Mr. Freedman sent me over to see if you needed any help with your presentation. He said you might be in over your head on this. So, how is it coming?" Hans's smile deepened and moved into his eyes.

Pollock wondered if Hans knew he was struggling or was just fishing. "Things are going swimmingly," he said. "Thanks though." And with that, Pollock smiled curtly, then opened up his journal and began writing notes in preparation for his last visit.

Hans leaned in. "Okay, Polly. Just remember that we're counting on you." He reached out and patted Pollock on his shoulder as a father would a child.

Pollock looked up and broke his cool, spreading his lips like an angered dog. "Good day!" He huffed more than spoke. Hans held his hands up in exasperation, swiveled, and exited the cubicle. Pollock watched him strolling away leisurely and felt that Hans got the better of that exchange and it drove a wedge into him. He wished Quentin had been there. He turned his nose upward and caught the faintest smell of Turkish shag leaking downward through the poorly aligned ceiling tiles. "Of course," he said.

The office was quiet, as it usually was on Monday mornings. Most employees were confronting the onslaught of leftover problems they flung aside with abandon in the face of last weekend's impending arrival. The rest were working up the resolve to do so, organizing their workspace or shopping for new matching curtains, or perusing Groupon for that trending Caribbean getaway package for only $799. Underneath it all was the slow, sleepy hum of the building's electricity. Upon completion of his solitary time, Quentin sauntered down and greeted Pollock, "We're going to need a lot of toilet paper to get through the day…" They discussed Pollock's slight progress and his interaction with Hans.

"Freedman is just playing him against you, hedging his bets," Quentin said in a reassuring tone. "He wants a good presentation and probably thinks he'll get it if you have a competitor breathing down your neck. It's sadistic, but it is also probably prudent. Look at the fire under your ass now." He, locked his hands at the back of his dome, leaning far back in his swivel chair.

"My cats are fighting again," Quentin said, tilting his head down.

"I thought you said they had sorted it all out."

"Well, I thought they had. But Houdini is unsatisfied. And he's a little shit of a cat. God, what a shit. He follows Stanton around, and once Stanton has found something that appeals to him—yesterday it was the rubber ball, which is *his* toy—Houdini jumps in and takes the thing and doesn't relinquish it until Stanton hurts him. He damn near bit Houdini's ear off for that. Animals! Foul beasts!" Quentin let out a gust of air in exasperation.

"And Stanton can always fend him off?" asked Pollock, beginning to truly focus on the problem, refreshed at turning attention to Quentin for a change.

"Oh certainly. Stanton is the much stronger animal. He's older. And Houdini knows this. It doesn't stop him. And here's the thing. Stanton acts like it annoys him so much, Houdini always tormenting him, reaching for his toy or whatever he has at the time, or waking him up from naps. And he probably truly does dislike it. Maybe. But when it gets to the point that battle becomes necessary, he turns into something else. A lever flips, and he attacks. He wants to fight, and he absolutely terrorizes Houdini. Then I'm left wondering if Stanton wasn't plotting the whole time, just waiting for Houdini to go too far. And that's another thing. When Houdini is getting dominated by Stanton, it almost seems like he likes that. So there's this whole complex dynamic afoot that was never explained to me six months ago when I took them. It may even be a sexual chemistry, though I've yet to see it escalate that far." Quentin let out another gust.

"It sounds like you need to get out more." Pollock said, shooting a playful grin at Quentin.

"Did you have a suggestion in mind?"

Pollock laughed, warmed to have Quentin at a disadvantage, when a flash of the lady cut through his mind's eye like lightning. He dropped the laugh and said, "What do you know about outdated electrical wiring in early twentieth-century houses?" Quentin slowly returned to an upright position and squinted.

"Would this happen to be your house?" Pollock nodded. "So you tell me I need to get out of the house more, and your suggestion is to come help you with the electric wiring in yours?" Quentin fell to mocking laughter. Pollock smiled, thinking himself that the proposition was indeed amusing. Yet, he needed some-one to come over and gauge the recent electrical phenomena. He didn't know any electricians and didn't want to dish out what would inevitably amount to a rip-off, looking foolish in front of a stranger in his own home, while merely trying to prove himself sane. He bit his lip and decided to explain his recent encounters.

After some skeptical questioning, Quentin agreed to come investigate. In fact, he was excited to do so. Pollock had been spot-on in his assessment of Quentin's social isolation. And the older man loved any problem involving infra-structure, especially if outdated or unmaintained. It gave him an opportunity to fully employ his puzzle-attracted intellect and use his vast collection of tools. The more he thought about it, the more excited he became.

Being around Pollock made Quentin regretful of his decision not to have children. He looked at him as he would his own son. He played at this fantasy, thinking how he would have handled various situations with his own son. But then, the crushing reality that he would never have a child brought on agonies that scattered through parts of his emotional identity previously unknown. For, how could he logistically hope for children? He would be in his early eighties by the time his progeny approached Pollock's age. Quentin was realistic in his hopes. Thus, he confined his musings to a sort of painful half-life, never fully encourag-ing them but never damning them either.

And in this manner, Quentin perhaps both loved and resented Pollock. But he never allowed this to sour their rapport. He quietly suffered, knowing that he had made his own decisions in life. He had had opportunities to marry, to grow a family. Instead he had been selfish, glorifying some ideal of prolonged bachelor-hood. He had throughout his prime, his twenties and thirties, believed that, to enter into a relationship, a true companionship that would lead to a home proper, he would have to sacrifice aspirations and activities for which he would never fully forgive himself. He was beguiled by solitude.

So, he saw his close friends and acquaintances grow more and more distant as they got married, had children, had grandchildren, and he aged alone, becoming more and more of a pariah. The older single man. He noticed how his friends' wives didn't like him coming around. It was as if he reminded them of a dormant vitality within their husbands, which could be reignited with the proper kindling. And they had put in great care to extinguish these. Now, he mused over the relevance of his existence without any biological legacy. He would die alone, without any proper conduit for his memory.

Thus, Quentin developed hobbies, he joined bowling leagues, spent more time absorbed in his professional life, and eventually owned two cats, of whom he spoke often and with a parallel affection a paterfamilias might speak of his off-spring. And, inevitably, when Pollock, with similar circumstances as his younger self, was assigned under him, he had found in the youth someone on which to project his conflict. Regardless of blood, Pollock was family. It had happened quickly.

The wiring throughout Pollock's basement was a marvel of unorganized ingenuity and baffling incongruity. There was no logic. The insulating material was miserably behind code and illustrated the evolution of electrical covering throughout the past century. Wires dead-ended into grounding poles. There were numerous ill-placed and incomprehensibly complex soldering jobs forming the twisted joints of conjoined circuits. All of this weaving and snaking throughout a structurally confounding basement skeleton composed of various patterns of oak beams mounted upon layers of bricks between concrete blocks, some at alarming tilts and others in very unorthodox measurements. All of this beneath a gratuitous coating of dirt and cobwebs.

The entire scene made Quentin sick with disdain but also exuberant with a focused passion for improvement. He made growling sounds around the flashlight sticking out of his mouth, trying to point out various discoveries to Pollock, who was comfortably looking on from his great-uncle's workbench. "Woo-ouuuihshjheeeee" translated to "What the fuck happened with this?" in Pollock's mind. The stepladder below Quentin wobbled with his investigative jerks. It had been nearly an hour, and it began to occur to Pollock that Quentin had no traction on an explanation for the lighting issues. He was merely chasing the curiosities of it all.

But, it didn't bother Pollock. He found the activity to be very humorous. And, besides, he had a delicious cold beer to enjoy. Quentin had brought over a six-pack of Hi-Res IPA. It tasted like pine and oranges going down, and it stung the throat a little bit with its aggressive effervescence. Pollock wondered how many men before Quentin had attempted the very same investigation and contributed to the discontinuity. He chuckled and raised the bottle for a long, cool gulp.

Pfffft. The basement went black, aside from a wild drizzle of sparks illuminating Quentin's portly silhouette. "Goddamn it son of a bitch!" Quentin howled.

"Are you alright?" asked Pollock, standing as the sparks disappeared with a fading sizzle on the dirty floor.

Quentin shined his flashlight at Pollock, "The snakes bit me, but I'm still standing. I believe I may have just added to your current quandary."

After flirting with the fuse box to no avail, Quentin and Pollock marched upstairs and onto the front porch to discover that whole block had lost power. Only stars and cars, with the nectarine sunset low on the horizon. Quentin examined the rows of houses, each coming alive with candles and flashlights. A sting of embarrassment hit him. "There's no way I could have done all of this," he said. He froze in place, retracing his knowledge of community electrical grids, transformers, et cetera, searching for an honest exoneration. Meanwhile, Pollock used his phone and checked the Trams Electric website. Sure enough a transformer had been damaged by a car crash.

"It wasn't you at all," Pollock said with an air of amusement. Quentin was relieved.

Having stood around for a few moments asserting surprise and their lack of ability to change the circumstances, utilizing many different clichéd phrases, Quentin and Pollock decided to finish their drinking on the porch with candles. The night was humid and stagnant. The air felt like a hot exhale to the face. The beers became invaluable. Quentin's six-pack of IPA and four leftover stouts from Pollock's fridge all sat loose in the melting slush within the cooler beside the porch table. Conversation was minimal.

* * *

Retta had seen her father change. His pupils had contracted over the years. His back bowed outward. He had weathered from the hopeful, silly man of Retta's youth. It saddened her to think that Fox would never know that Remy. He would only know the serious, withdrawn father. The quiet, stressed man who arranged rides and spread bills out over the kitchen table, rubbing his brow with consternation. But mostly, the absentee chain smoker. No more was the man who would wake up early on Saturdays to cook French toast in his tighty whities while quoting his favorite films. "I get no respect!" he would exclaim in his best Rodney Dangerfield impression. Nowadays Retta did most of the cooking, and Remy spent weekend mornings in the garage or out back chain-smoking, pondering something large and seductive.

She respected Remy deeply. And he was still there, but only in sparse dim patches that he never allowed to blossom. Sarah had been the fertilizer. She was his excitement, his ecstasy. Without her, he was only a shadow of himself. But Fox always had rides and clean clothes. He and Retta were always provided for and always had help with homework. As far as metrics for single parents go, Remy wasn't the worst. And yet Retta wished for more and felt ashamed for it. She lamented her additional responsibilities.

Pollock reminded her somewhat of Remy. She remembered her friend, Stacey, in seventh or eighth grade, had explained to her that women usually end up choosing mates based on some perceived similarity with their father. She had found the notion interesting, if a little alarming, even sickening. But then, years later, she thought further and realized that fathers often do appear to be the most impressive men to their adolescent children. It was only later, she felt, that they lowered their estimation of their fathers, but by then it was too late. The earlier picture always stuck in the mind, comparing, lessening. Dad had been lessened.

That Monday evening, Remy and Fox were in their weekly counseling session discussing his school progress. Retta had been lying on her bed, studying for her upcoming MSN examination on anesthesia administration but she was losing focus, feeling her eyes pulled toward the bedroom window. New Order spun from the suitcase record player on the floor next to her bed. Thoughts of her mother made her lonely. She thought about checking Facebook, but decided against it after realizing it would only add to the loneliness. She didn't feel like being around anyone, so she laced up her Chucks and went for a bike ride around town.

She pedaled up Monroe Hill to the edge of the newer condominium developments still being built and past them onto the wide, newly paved suburban roads. Pink string grids marked out future plots in long, grassy fields. She gained speed, pedaling harder, picturing her mother on the bright yellow and orange flower–patterned porch glider. Sarah had loved that glider, reading for long hours with the cats.

She looped back down Monroe Hill, accumulating great momentum and enjoying the wind against her cheeks. She skidded to a stop at the bottom of the hill next to the remnants of her old elementary school. Piles of bricks and mortar were strewn about near unmanned caterpillars. The building hadn't been used in a decade and was being demolished for a future mall and movie theater. She wanted to get out of Trams, but a sense of duty pained her at the idea of leaving Remy and Fox. From time to time, an aching need to escape crept up on her and challenged her values, her priorities. This was just another of countless iterations. She never did anything about it. She knew she wouldn't now.

Her phone buzzed in her pocket. Pollock had texted her.

> Hey Retta. Sorry again about the quick departure yesterday. The power in my neighborhood is out. My boss and I are having a few drinks on my porch. You're welcome to come join us if you're not getting into anything.

Retta sped through a few more neighborhoods, exercising her nervous energies, before responding in the affirmative and heading in his direction. She stopped at a Speedway and bought a pack of hard apple cider. The cashier, a middle-aged man with a long ponytail, commented that it was a wise purchase. "The lady has distinguished taste."

As she pulled up to Pollock's and hopped off of her bike, the Ne'er Do Wells ran out from the side yard, trotted single file across the street, and disappeared into the darkness beyond the opposite sidewalk. They gave her a startle. Quentin called out from the porch, "Don't mind them. Every neighborhood has their bunch of rapscallions, scamps, scoundrels and miscreants." He wobbled drunkenly down the concrete steps and extended his hand. "You must be Retta. I've heard a lot about you. Quentin Lovejoy."

Retta, slightly reticent, extended her hand and the two shook, smiling awkwardly for longer than the occasion merited. Quentin, eager to make a good impression, grabbed the bike's frame and began carrying it up the stairs. As they arrived at the porch landing, Pollock emerged from the house with his great-aunt's diary. "Retta, hey! Did you find it okay?" he asked, his sweat-drenched V neck clinging to the outlines of his musculature.

"Yeah, it was actually a nice ride. Like, the porch candles helped with navigation," she responded pointing out to Nyqvist. Pollock looked out and took note of all of the porches adorned with flashlights, battery-powered lanterns, and multiple candles. His own had numerous large candles, burning at full intensity, generously lighting the entire front of his house and dripping wax onto the plates under them.

Fireflies came out in swaths that seemed much more concentrated than usual. Quentin spent fifteen minutes or so questioning Retta about her life. She explained how she was attending nursing school and that her goal was to become a certified nurse anesthetist. Retta returned the interest and asked about Quentin, who was happy to, in poetic fashion, describe his ascent to his current professional position from his humble beginning in rural Maine. He briefly mentioned time in Vietnam. He was drafted. His focus had turned to city and regional planning after seeing so many buildings, villages, and cities destroyed. Creation became appealing to him. Pollock remained mostly quiet, calmly enjoying having a group of people at his house that he cared for who appeared to care for him. It felt almost like an abbreviated family. With the candles and the fireflies, it was almost romantic. Pollock was surprised by his contentment.

Conversation soon reverted back to where it was headed before Retta's arrival. Quentin cracked the last IPA and said, "Well, I was about to explain to Pollock how my uncle was arrested when I was in high school." He took a long swig of beer. "Well, he had a long affair with a woman whose husband ran a phenomenally successful farm a few counties over. This is the mid sixties. My aunt had passed on when I was still in grade school. She and my uncle had a small ranch that did well enough. My uncle was also an attorney, and he supplemented earnings with occasional probate work. He met the woman—gee I can't for the life of me remember her name. Big blonde curls. Barb maybe? No, Bonnie?" He trailed off, looking downward, concentrating hard to remember the name.

Retta and Pollock laughed. "Anyway..." Pollock said.

"Whatever her name, she had hired my uncle to help her and her husband acquire additional property to build new stables. And, apparently they hit it off right off the bat. So they had been sneaking around for months. I'm sure a fair number of people knew about it. One thing my uncle was not was tight lipped. Don't get me wrong. He had a number of impressive qualities, but keeping secrets was not one of them. One night, he gets a phone call. It's her husband. Says he knows what's been going on and is going to beat the living hell out of her while he leaves the phone off of the hook so that my uncle can listen."

Quentin turned sideways and looked at Retta, instilling the gravity of the story. He continued, "My uncle had been drinking pretty heavily that night. He threw down the phone, grabbed his handgun, tucked it in his satchel, and hopped on his best horse, Thunderclap. And he rode off to save his companion. Well, in those times where I grew up in Maine, it wasn't entirely uncommon for farmers to get drunk and mount their horses in the late hours, seeking some vague mission of vainglory. My uncle made it about halfway there before he was arrested for drunk riding. He explained the circumstances, and so the police visited the woman's farm. Everything was in order, no beatings. Her husband wasn't even there. A few weeks later my uncle's buddy Druey admitted to the crank call over a game of poker. Well, my uncle gave him a braining to remember."

Pollock took a giant gulp of stout and reached for another. Retta continued to sip on her cider. "Well he never saw that lady after that. And later that year I was drafted for the war." Quentin pursed his lips and shook his head. "It was a pretty pitiful sight when I had to go bail my uncle out. He went on and on about how he missed my aunt, expressed some very depressing, very dour sentiments. Things that, at the time, I remember wishing I had never heard. It changed how I looked at him, you know? I mean I had enough experience with alcoholics by that time, but…Anyhoo, I thought about that night a lot during the war. But that's another story, one we don't have enough alcohol to get into tonight." He took a long swig of IPA.

The fireflies continued to thicken until they were almost competing with the candlelight, if only in flashes. The heat subsided slightly, and the sweat over Pollock's body began to usher waves of cool relief. The three were quiet for a bit. Slowly, the lights from neighboring porches extinguished or moved indoors and the block became much darker, accentuating the fireflies, the abundance of which now seemed undeniably freakish to Pollock.

Retta noticed that Pollock had been holding the journal on his knees for some time, occasionally tapping it against his knee to an invisible rhythm. "What's that that you've been clutching onto?" she said.

Pollock, having momentarily forgotten all about his previously intended inquiry, abruptly returned from his comforting reverie. "Well, it's a journal. It was my great-aunt's journal." He paused and tried to read Retta and Quentin's faces, feeling as if he had admitted something.

Quentin grunted in displeasure. "And what are you doing with it?" Retta furrowed her brow and shook her head in agreement with Quentin's sentiment.

"It sort of fell into my hands," Pollock said. "And it may sound naive but I think there is something in here that I am supposed to know about. Or...eh...I don't know. If anything, I'd learn something about my family history. And I don't think she would mind. She might even want it."

"A journal is by its very nature meant to be private. To go into that area un-invited, that seems like some kind of violence to me, some kind of trespass. That being said, you would know much better than I the purity of your permission, whether overt or implied."

Pollock took a swig. Retta followed suit, then asked, "Like what do you think it is that you'll learn in there?"

"Well, I never knew her very well..." The three became quiet again. Mosquito slaps and cicadas occupied the sonic foreground.

The three of them eventually chatted on about movies and music and a little about local politics. Retta made it to her third cider. Pollock checked the city website a few more times without any additional information regarding the power outage. Quentin provided a few more anecdotes involving Houdini and Stanton. The night finally began to cool off, and the majority of the candles and flashlights from the block extinguished completely, coinciding with a deep quiet aside from the insects and distant train squeals.

Retta heard it first. It was a sort of rough, repetitive scraping noise from off in the dark street. Then there were a few coughs and throat clearing. That was when Quentin noticed. Finally, shoe scuffs and heavy breathing became apparent. Pollock leaned forward, squinting across the street. There, the darkness gradually gave way to two men hunched over an unintelligible object, pulling it backward, together, out toward the sidewalk. The men were wearing beanies, one of which had a panda bear atop, with panda ears sticking out of either side. They were hoisting a granite statute of a winged harpist.

The thought of the beanies, worn in the current climate, perplexed and offended Pollock. Quentin stood and stepped forward to confront the thieves but Retta jumped up and grabbed his arm. "We should follow them," she said. Upon hearing her say this, Pollock spent a brief moment appreciating how attracted to her he was, her curls glistening in the candlelight, as she boldly proposed adventures to his boss. The alcohol had done its job. His thoughts were soft on the edges and merged into one another, and in the end, he wanted to follow these thieves.

Quentin was surprised by Retta's actions. But then, he sifted through his memory and retrieved the recent news article describing the bandits that had been plaguing neighborhoods throughout Trams. "Brilliant! Yes, trace it back to the source." He slowly sat back in the wicker chair and turned to Pollock. "Your female friend is a good influence. She's a keeper." It was loud enough for Retta to hear and she involuntarily smiled. Pollock felt a bit embarrassed, but nodded in assent.

The three of them used makeshift sign language to communicate quietly as the two thieves dragged the statue through the neighbors' lawns heading north toward Klum Court. They kneeled down behind Pollock's porch rail, leaving only their eyes and heads exposed to monitor the thieves' movements. Once the men passed the Ventillis', Pollock crawled over to the table and blew out two dwindling candles. Quentin took care of another on the railing while Retta collected the empty bottles and cans, placing them into the open cooler and fitting its lid back in place.

After locking the front door, Pollock ran to catch up with Retta and Quentin, who were already on the edge of the court heading into the Kades' side yard. His heart pounded. His legs felt like Jell-O. As he crossed the blacktop in the cul de sac, bottle rockets shot into the sky, exploded, and wilted into wide spears of color above him. They lit the way. He wondered if it were the Ne'er-do-wells, and whether some of their labors contained merit after all.

Behind Klum Court were miles of forested area surrounding Rhatze River, which separated the edges of the residential neighborhood from a largely abandoned section of industrial buildings. The factories and warehouses formed a line that paralleled a dual set of train tracks leading out of town toward Helms and Pinebrook. During the industrial era, before the outsourcing that occurred in Trams beginning in the early 1970s, these plants had supplied the majority of Trams citizens with employment.

The key concern during Trams industrial heyday was an American-owned bulldozer manufacturer that was eventually parceled out as a subsidiary of a Japanese company. This, along with the other dilapidated and decaying buildings had sat unused for decades. At one point, the city council had tossed around ideas about turning the area into a mixed-use housing development targeting twenty to thirtysomethings. At another point in time, Trams tried to entice the current landowners to lease the property for mall space. No plans ever garnered any proper traction, and the weeds held dominion.

After the bulldozer plant closed in the mid-1980s, unemployment became a prevalent feature of Trams. This lead to alcoholism and domestic violence. Foreclosures abounded. The situation in Trams mirrored conditions throughout the region where manufacturing was central. It was endemic to business in that era. In fact, it wasn't until the early 1990s when tech companies and fast food headquarters relocated into Trams attracted by large tax abatements, that the local economy gained any semblance of vigor. Since then, Trams had experienced almost two decades of exponential growth.

Now, the area was a sort of unacknowledged sore in a seldom-frequented corner of town. All of the subsequent residential and commercial growth had spread in the opposite direction, and mostly to the south, leaving the once-central industrial park now on the edge of wilderness at the county border. Local college students would occasionally break in and test out theories of hauntings while the park grew closer and closer to resembling ancient ruins.

Upon reaching the rickety wooden bridge over the Rhatze River, the two men took a cigarette break from hauling the statue. They squatted, looking at one another without speaking. All Pollock could make out was their hazy exhaust and the outline of their weather-inappropriate beanies. The three pursuers knelt behind a thick patch of ferns, curiously looking on.

The fireworks continued sporadically above the evergreen canopy. "It's pretty," Retta whispered. She was thinking of Fourths of July from her childhood. laying on warm blankets in the cool summer night, getting whiffs of her mother's hairspray. She meditated for the briefest of moments on their old station wagon, the way its leather seats stuck to her thighs and made farting sounds.

The men tossed their butts and resumed slowly dragging the statute onward. Pollock, Quentin, and Retta watched as they made their way over the bridge and through a long stretch of grass. They entered into the main yard of one of the warehouses and began following a worn earthen path that went through a hole in the chain link fence and toward a door on the side of the huge ivy-covered con-crete structure. Quentin noticed shadows moving around inside of the building. He scanned its facade, lending attention to each window. Their sills were all adorned with shattered shards of glass, and through the openings, he detected that the entire warehouse was crawling with activity. "Well...what is *this?*" he said, rising to his feet.

Retta and Pollock followed suit and the three of them stood quietly for a moment, perplexed, scrutinizing the abandoned warehouse full of people into which the duo of thieves had just pulled their stolen bounty. The inside of the warehouse was dark enough that the crowds within were merely shadows. Orange flickers from fires kissed the walls.

Pollock quickly stepped forward with conviction, making his way onto the bridge before Quentin said, "Oye!" Pollock stopped in his tracks and turned. Quentin asked, "Are you planning on going in there?"

"Well, yeah. Why wouldn't we?" He extended his arm out to Retta questioningly.

She said, "I think we should check it out. Like, we've come this far, and like, aren't you curious what's going on? Like, is that some secret party?" Pollock swung his hands up in agreement, wobbling a bit from the inebriation.

"Look, I agree," Quentin said. "This is strange. But we should come back when we are less inebriated, in the light of day. We should formulate a plan of action. There are clearly a fair number of folks within those walls. Who knows who they are. They could be homeless or teenagers on drugs. They could be hostile. I've not the temperament for a fight just now."

Retta was just delighted by the entire situation. She craved newness, novelty. Days of routine had been troubling her like a finger on a pressure point. "So, like, there is a gang of thieves squatting. Pollock! The clock man was right."

The thought of "the clock man" put a bad taste in Pollock's mouth. Nonetheless, Mr. Ebersold had been right. "It's the roving gang of marauders!" Pollock said.

Quentin looked up with a reserved smile. "That's right! They've been plaguing the city for months. Bob, Mr. Freedman to you, lost the icebox in his garage. Shit, this is big. Oh man its big." He began pacing back and forth, the bridge's brittle wooden planks creaking under his stubby steps. Retta watched Quentin and laughed. "Shifts, we'll take shifts," he said. "Yes, that's what we'll do. We will have to take shifts!" Pollock joined Retta, laughing in earnest at Quentin's excitement.

The three decided to return in daylight. Quentin parted ways with the young couple, returning to his recline-o-lounger covered in cat hair where he watched a few reruns of Cheers. At about the same time he fell asleep, Pollock and Retta fell asleep on Pollock's bed, for a change. They were fully clothed, listening to Sam Cooke through Retta's iPhone. When Pollock awoke at 5:37 a.m., the electricity had returned. He pushed his thumb into Retta's chalky thigh, leaving a red print just under the lip of her dress. She twisted her neck slightly but continued to sleep peacefully. He watched the red impression of his thumb fade back to her skin color.

Pollock spent the morning giving attention to his project. He had grouped his cases into folders, stacked them on the edge of his desk and, one by one, added his current, most completed considerations. One of his previous cases involved a couple that had chickens in a coup in their backyard. They also had a dozen ducks. Surrounding neighbors complained about the smells and the noises. An older gentleman was afraid that his dog, Nigel, who escaped frequently, would end up eating some of them because their fence was only a two-feet-high wire mesh stretched taught around several trees. The dog was an Australian labradoodle that didn't like children.

The chicken and duck owners used the chickens for eggs. They also bred with a friend's rooster and periodically ate the offspring. It was a money saver. When Pollock interviewed them, they mentioned "local food security" and "network of local agri-intelligent citizens." It made him curious about why, with those sentiments, they weren't more concerned about their outward image, their negative impact on their neighbors.

Several homeowners nearby saw it as an urban farm. The couple were well into their thirties. Art, the husband, had a black beard and ponytail. Julia had long braided hair down to her waist. They often would lie on their backs on blankets in their back yard, smoking pot and humming something akin to a song or a mantra, laughing intermittently, spitting out swathes of reefer from behind their thrift store sunglasses. The chickens and ducks would meander about the yard all the while.

So it boiled down to what Pollock had realized was a common tension in zoning; the desires of the neighborhood butted against the rights of the homeowners. The zoning code was routinely vague. And it was likely do to oversight. Art and Julia's neighborhood was not zoned for agricultural use. However, agricultural use did not explicitly extend to harboring ducks and chickens in the code. But, it was Pollock's understanding that the drafters had clearly intended for such animals to be included within the agricultural use application, and thus forbidden in such a zone as Art and Julia's.

So it was up to Pollock to decide if the vagueness of the section was acceptable, and this was an issue to be resolved among the members of the community on an individual-case basis through their own effort and time, or that he should propose an amendment to the zoning code. Urban farming and gardening were trending upward. The economic downturn and the rise of an emphasis on locally grown and raised food conspired to convert hundreds of houses throughout town into some scale of agricultural or farming operation. Many of which also had solar panels, rain collection apparatuses, and businesses within. But, Pollock didn't want to get ahead of himself. These all presented issues of their own.

Another option, and one that Pollock leaned toward, having followed Quentin's decision making process, involved an amendment that allowed for these animals in residential zones but required certain containment and safety precautions to appease surrounding residents. He understood these lots weren't intended for these purposes, but it was nice to see novel uses. He considered booting the problem to the county health board, but that would be shirking his responsibilities. Everyone else around seemed to operate that way, though. Quentin's laughter echoed around in his skull, and Pollock looked over again to take note of his mentor's absence. It was nearly lunch. Pollock wondered if Quentin was hung over or taking the morning to investigate the warehouse without him.

Loud belly laughs swept into his right ear and sliced through his hungover brain. He turned and spotted Hans and Mr. Freedman shaking hands and nodding their heads. Hans gently cupped his hand around Mr. Freedman's shoulder. "Fucking puke punk," Pollock muttered to himself and stomped his right heel in anger.

He directed his attention back to the file on his desk and jotted down "safety & containment features—confer w/ other city depts" on the corner of the county auditor's bio page of Art and Julia's house. Then he slammed the folder shut, frustrated with the notion that Hans may surpass him in his career solely on the quality of his glad-handing. "Meritocracy, indeed," he said, stomping again. Then he thought about the fact that he was closing his folder, interrupting work that, if done correctly and with deep care, could rout Hans's glad-handing, bountiful as it may be.

At 2:30 p.m., having found out through the work grapevine that Quentin had called in sick, Pollock decided to leave work for the day and investigate the warehouse further. He quickly tidied up his workspace and then hopped over the vestibule gate as Quentin had done so many times. Hans spotted Pollock leaving with his bag and car keys in hand. "Early day," he said quite loudly. He was in high spirits, seeing the shady work ethic of his competition. He found Pollock sort of pathetic. It fed into his self worth, especially so at the sight of Pollock taking abbreviated workdays. Pollock was that sad sucker who never picked up on the value of social economy. He was maladjusted for either business or politics, which city zoning was exactly both. Hans's recent proposal for the so-called university corridor proved that.

Shelia Barnes, the wife of Conrad Barnes, Trams's fire chief, headed the university zoning commission. Shelia had been Mr. Freedman's girlfriend for two years in college before being won over by Conrad who was Freedman's physical and mental superior. Conrad was an enthusiastic leader, who played situations straight and earned the respect of those for whom nobility and honor ranked high in their evaluative criteria. Such was the case with Shelia. Freedman, on the other hand, was a political individual who understood compromise and opportunity. The story went that, although the relationship between Shelia and Freedman ended harshly, the desire had never died for Freedman. Hans, having done his research, mainly through flirting with every employee, male or female, at the clerk of courts and city hall, had become privy to this ancient triangle.

Now, Shelia had been gunning for development of the so-called university corridor. She had made several proposals that all failed for lack of either private funding or city partnership. Thus, as Hans figured, if he could find interested developers and propose it to Freedman, who had relationships with city hall, it could become a reality. And Freedman would be on board if it meant bringing Shelia's vision to life. He would be her hero, of sorts.

Hans had explained his ideas for new multi-use development near the university area, and the proposal had gone as Hans had hoped. Freedman was visibly floored. The brother of the manager of the pizza store where Hans once worked, an accountant and founding partner with Layne Inc., a midsized local developer, had, as a favor to Hans's mother, run the numbers and found several partnerships that would make the corridor project monetarily successful, not to mention garner a prestigious conquest for his relatively new company. Freedman respected the designs that Hans was managing. They reminded him of how he himself functioned.

And this was how Hans worked. So, it made him a little confused why someone like Pollock would actually be sitting down sweating over theory of property rights and the language within city codes when things were actually handled, actually accomplished, much differently. He smiled sadly to himself and headed on his way, content in his belief that his fitness for the position exceeded Pollock's.

As Pollock got in his truck, he received a call from Quentin. "Pollock, you need to leave work and come meet me, my boy!"

"Yeah, I'm actually leaving right now. Where are you?"

Quentin cleared his throat. "I needed the morning to arrange my thinking properly. Once I had, it became pressing that we investigate last night's discovery further. If my assumptions are correct, it may help with your project."

Chapter Six

It was a blur of white. It was all encompassing. Then the whiteness clarified and displayed twirling objects, which eventually slowed to a stop to reveal the outline of shapes. The shapes blossomed with colors until Max could make out his surroundings. He was lying underneath a heavy down blanket. Next to the bed, a window let in daylight. DeBeers sat on a rocking chair in the corner, watching Max without expression. Max noted the prints of horses on the linen.

His mouth was dry. His ribs and neck still hurt. He propped himself on his elbow and realized that his clothes had been stripped and he was in a new outfit, a clean cotton shirt and pants. On the bedside table Max saw a glass of water and clasped it with his free arm and chugged. Sitting up, he refilled it from the pitcher beside it and once again emptied its contents. DeBeers kept watch, remaining expressionless.

It all came rushing back to him: the graveyard, the other robbers, the capture, and the grandiose monologue from Titius. It seemed as though Max had been asleep for ages. It was as if the events he had slowly remembered occurred years ago, decades even. It was only the glaringly present injuries to his midsection that made the recentness of it all so clear.

"Your things are on the floor," DeBeers said as he stood and frowned, pointing to a neatly folded pile of Max's washed clothes and bag. "I'll be just outside in the hallway. Why don't you get dressed and meet me there? Mr. Rombathe would like to speak with you more. But take your time…I am aware of your…pains." He smiled slightly, turned, and closed the door behind him as he left the room.

Max imagined his escape for a few moments. He made his way to his feet and peered through the window. Though it was quite blurry, he could make out that he was on the third or fourth story. Either way it was quite high above what appeared to be a snowy stone porch below. He tried to push the window upward, against the protests of his bruises. Despite his valiant effort, the window was frozen into place.

He followed instructions, dressing himself very delicately, and opened the door to the hallway. DeBeers rose from a chair and raised his left eyebrow as Max approached him. The two were uncomfortably close in the narrow hallway as they sidled like crabs down the long hallway, bedroom door past bedroom door.

The hallway ended in a spiral staircase. "Up we go," said DeBeers, punctuating each word with his index finger. Max looked up through the vertical passageway, seeing that there were still several levels above them. He paused for a moment to analyze the situation in his now more-lucid state. They had given him a bed, food, water, new clothes. They wanted something. They would have punished him by now if they intended to, or tossed him outside to freeze to death. And with that, Max, and DeBeers following, hobbled to the uppermost level and into a rotunda of a room overlooking the entire expanse of the sprawling estate.

DeBeers pushed Max forward and then down into a deep leather lounger. It smelled of astringent chemicals. They burned the insides of his winter-dry nostrils with each deep breath as he collected himself from the exertion of the climb. DeBeers leaned over and whispered into Max's ear, "He'll see ya in a few minutes. If ya need anything, I'll be right outside." And with that he slammed the door behind him, leaving only the sound of the frigid winter gusts squealing against the circular windows rounding the room.

Besides the large desk, the only other object of note within the room was an enormous fabric scroll hanging from the ceiling. Its bottom reached the floor and sprawled another two feet or so. The scroll must have been eight feet wide. As Max focused, it became clear that the print on the canvass consisted of lists of names, with lines connecting them, fingering out from one name at the top. All of the names were far too small for Max to make any of them out.

The scroll jolted Max's mind back to Ethyl. She used to make fun of her relatives who were, "all so very involved with tracing the history of our families." Max had been in awe of the art of tracing lineages. It fascinated him, seeing the people that lead up to him drawn as a shape like a tree, as if the whole of the history existed at once, as if he were a fiction and the whole of the tree was actually real. He remembered telling Ethyl as much. "What a pretty concept," she'd said. "If that's what my relatives were thinking whilst making such trees, then I suspect I'd have no problem whatsoever. But that's not why they do it, Max. They did it too feel important. It is as if they are drawing a stage or a podium made of their forbearers. And that podium, that stage, says 'I am so very special and important.'" She smiled widely, glibly, and kissed him. Max remembered thinking maybe that idea wasn't such a bad thing.

And now, looking at the largest, most majestic family tree he could have ever dreamt up, it seemed somehow terrorizing and foul. He wondered what Ethyl would think of it. They had always had a way of circling around each other's thoughts, antagonizing the other. One of them would be attracted to an idea and advocate for it wholeheartedly. The other would push back and play devil's advocate, only to eventually become the one that was truly seduced by the idea, its original proponent turning under the reasoning of the naysayer. And thusly, they danced with their minds, playfully and whimsically, with whatever new notions popped into their heads.

To Max, it was as if they truly crawled through each other. He explored the cupboards and caverns in her head, as she did his. And they found secrets and surprises, mined them, processed them, and then presented them back to each other as if they were their own. And each knew and recognized the procedure, until it seemed as though the division between them had blurred. And there was only one idea space, playful and innocent. This, to Max and, he suspected, to Ethyl as well, was even more connective than their physical intimacy. It was a strong cocoon, protecting them from dark mental parasites, like paranoia, jealousy, and alienation.

Their relationship, as it unfolded, as sharp as it kept their active minds, did not prepare them for any of the hardships that would eventually come their way. Perhaps this is why it was so hard for Max. A thing so pure, so pretty, cannot last but only later demonstrates the horribleness of its inevitable absence. Max was tired of feeling that horribleness. But he had set out to find her. He owed her that. He owed himself. "Once I find her, I can move on, I can work on a new way. But I have to find her first. I have to. I promised," he had said out loud, times beyond counting, convincing himself.

Flashes of bloodied torsos raced through his eyes. His pulse picked up, as if to the beat of a maddened drummer. He clinched his fists and forgot the pain within his sides. "I must find her. Then I can start on a new way!" he said, loudly.

"Who is she that you're looking for her?" Titius said from behind Max, stepping forward and plopping himself down into his cushioned seat behind the desk opposite Max. Max did not answer.

"I've been struggling with hope, lately," Titius then said, rising to his feet and looking out one of the curving windows. He clasped his forearms behind his back. "It's a pattern for me, this time of year. February. There is so much darkness for so long. And there is so much cold. It seeps into the bones and down into even the spirit, it seems. It wrests me and I begin to feel as if there can be no return. I am plunged, ever downward and beset by despair. When the warm days start stacking up in late March and into April, and there is steady groundwork, it still takes me weeks to accept it. I've been buried and must dig myself out." He continued peering out through the window, surveying the land surrounding his large house.

Max thought about how Titius had lost his daughter. He remembered the angry tirade from the previous evening. A forceful woe crept over him, and he felt compelled to confess to this man, this hopeless, wealthy man who had captured him. He felt that, In a sense, they were in the same place. Max opened his mouth to speak but no words came. Nervous flutters churned in him. He tried again. "I would…never have stolen your daughter's bracelet…from her body. I wouldn't even have—"

"My men said they found you neck deep in someone's long-filled grave. If not for depraved purposes, then why were you there?" He turned to face Max with a simple honesty in his face that wanted a sincere answer.

"I'm looking for my wife," Max said, dropping his eyes to picture Ethyl's face.

The answer surprised Titius less than he expected. He could see the emotional agony on Max's face, and it occurred to him, as it had to Max, that they shared some qualities. Still, questions persisted.

"You were looking for your wife in the grave of another?" Titius asked, squinting his eyes half in scrutiny and half in curiosity. Max looked up. "I have to, it's…it is where we are now…" Again he couldn't find the proper words, half bemused with the thought of his own plight. He pictured himself from afar telling this man his story. He thought of it as if it were told in a storybook and wondered what Ethyl would think of that story, and his character in particular. Then it occurred to him that he must be transparent with this man.

"My wife, Ethyl, she was…She was taken from me. That's not true. I left her. God, I did. I…had to. But I returned and she had been taken. She…" He looked into Titius's dark eyes. "I've received information that she had been buried in the—in your cemetery. In another's grave." Max pictured Larren, the young soldier who had told him this.

"And it was only by coincidence that you ran into our other friends last night?" Titius said with an inflection somewhere between question and command. He resumed his position looking out the window with his arms locked behind him. Flurries gusted against the stone walls dissecting the long area below the planting fields. Contemplating this sad traveler with such a sad tale of a lost wife, he began sinking back into the remorse that the late winter had exacerbated. "I take it that you aren't from around these parts. No…no, I would probably recognize you. What did you say your birth name was?"

"Max."

Titius turned and nodded, noting Max's mistrust. He recognized its legitimacy. Titius watched the changing patterns of snowdrift for another moment, casting the room back into silence, aside from the winds faintly rattling the joints of the house.

"The war tore this country apart," Titius said. "Too many casualties. Not just soldiers; but normal life in these parts was torn asunder. It's hard to pick back up from something so brutal. Brother against brother, as they say. Families split down the middle. Towns ruined, men ruined. Children slaughtered. I was fortunate to even have a home to return to." He raised his right hand and tapped the glass, drawing Max's attention outside to the expanse of fields.

"But that's the thing. Of those of us that made it out, most were too different. The change, it was too much. Here, in my town, most grown men cry frequently, others mess themselves. Many, too many, have ended it by their own hand. It was too much. And the wives, the women, the spared children, expecting their fathers, sons, brothers, and uncles to come home. Well, they were greeted by something else." Titius took in a deep breath and slowly exhaled as if trying to expel his worries.

Max listened intently, the sentiments and experience of Titius's words mirroring his own. He could have been strolling through Max's brain, excavating his wounds. Now that it was apparent Titius had fought, a new warmth and respect flourished within Max. And he now looked upon his captor as a commanding officer, as most men of his age had been for Max. And he found it odd that he needed to look upon the world as if a battle were still raging, with steadfast vigilance and a keen understanding of command hierarchy.

Titius said, "I understand the toll. I've even had episodes myself. Dark things...but even darker on the horizon." He stopped abruptly, turned, and retook his seat quickly, looking squarely upon Max, whose posture had tightened with anxiety. "You want to find your wife and you believe she is buried in my cemetery. Under someone else's tombstone, or...It doesn't matter. I don't completely understand...but...I understand, you see. We will have time for details. You may have all of the time you need in my cemetery. I'll even let you borrow a few hands to assist you. And we'll see if we can...put your wife, Ethyl, to rest." He held his hands out, palms up in offering. Max nodded and exhaled, sinking back into a slight slouch.

"But first, I need something from you. Call it recompense for your trespass and board here."

Max sorted through his thoughts. The man had been straightforward with him. A favor for Ethyl. He could not refuse. "What is it?" he asked.

His quick and accepting response pleased Titius. It seemed fate had sent just the soldier he needed.

Max stared out at the sprawling, snow-covered fields. Short corn stalk bases poked up through the snow like blond stubble on skin. He pulled his coat tight over his new clothes, keeping his body warm in the frosty air. The walk had taken him most of the day. His cheeks burned from the constant winds, but his ears were warm under a toboggan cap. "One more task," he said, speaking to Ethyl. "Soon...soon."

He scanned the ridge to the south and spotted dark smoke rising from the forested area beyond. "There it is," he said, consulting a hand drawn map, the contents of which agreed with what he saw in front of him. He folded the map and pushed it into his coat pocket. After pulling his right glove off with his teeth, he retrieved a cigarette, lit it, and regloved. He was going to have one more peaceful smoke by himself before he became a spy. And so he sat himself on a tree stump and watched the slowly changing clouds, occasionally taking long drags from stale tobacco.

At some point he would have to confront the fact that he was no longer truly living. Or he could die after all. The comfort of Titius's closeness, his familiarity, had shed with the distance he had walked since setting out from the opulent estate. And now he only felt the cold. It was dark on the horizon indeed, just as Titius had said.

Ethyl had been the reason. To have something so brilliantly best in all of everything, tucked away beside him by deliberate choice, her choice, that was what all seek. And here at the other side of its scarcity, Max pondered what next whim reaching from outside could possibly sweep in and deliver a parallel, rapturous zenith unless it was death, the last final whim. His life was an epilogue. "Struggling with hope," he said aloud between tokes. "Struggling with hope," he said again in monotone, like he once read with Ethyl in some book that monks on the other side of Earth read to find peace.

He ungloved and pulled the folded map back out from his pocket. With the pencil that DeBeers had handed him sternly, he wrote down at the bottom "hope." And he looked at it for a long moment with clear determination to find a way back, or out, or up, or even down, to find a way to revive what was naturally good. Because that surely was the only route for hope. One had to shed the quagmire deathtrap, the mangled wiry carcass of thoughts. To explode the trauma into pieces so they could melt and evaporate. He replaced the map and glove. And as the sunset faded over the dormant crops slumbering beneath February snow, he rose to his feet and began his mission, certain that it would either be his death or the revival of hope, putting full trust in a man that had been a stranger just yesterday. "To find what is naturally good."

Chapter Seven

Coy Creek eagerly trickled over the smooth landings of sandstone, shale, and granite heading west, through the long, narrow ravine. It then spilled into Rhatze River, which would receive the cold crystal waters and carry them slowly south of the city through Elder Industrial Park. There, in the summertime, middle schoolers would ride their bikes over the flat grassy banks en route to the "the dunes," a large limestone deposit that had been carefully molded into a BMX race course by fifteen years of young hands with nothing but free days to wander while their parents went to work. The scene was elaborate, with semicircular grooved lanes leading to dozens of various weather-beaten ramps, pipes, and breakneck turns, pretzeling through sparse white birch trees.

Echoes Park made a large rectangle, running two miles in length along a portion of the western side of the ravine. There was a steeply sloping gravel walking path beside the meandering creek, lined with early twentieth-century kerosene streetlamps maintaining a constant yellow hue in the evening, which lent an otherworldliness to the slender public corridor. A maple leaf canopy kept the park cool and dark during the day.

Cabe had sent Pollock another text. It arrived as he was angrily wrestling a T-shirt over his head and hitting his funny bone on the closet molding. The message was rather troubling, and it was on his mind when he met with Quentin where they had parted ways the previous evening.

Looking forward to catching up and talking like we used to. It has been far too long, old friend. Hopefully we can avoid letting those bad parts interfere. I've missed you bud. Hoping for good results!

Cabe had always tended toward the melodramatic. Pollock had been fairly certain he was bipolar. He would sleep until 3:00 or 4:00 p.m. and swear off the world as an inevitable pile of sludge sliding into pointless oblivion. Then he'd make rounds of apologies via text, emails, and phone calls for things of which no one had a damn inkling. Then he would party for days, cajoling and corralling the group, squealing with pure joy leaking through his clown-like smile. There were things in him that he could not control. Big, swinging things of tumult. Pollock had known and accepted this early on. He had tempered it with his own sturdy steadiness. They evened each other out.

The message evoked something Pollock had not wanted to think about despite knowing it was inevitable that he would. And it made him feel powerless because of his repulsion at the thought of finally discussing with Cabe the betrayal that had occurred years ago and Pollock's weary acceptance that it was necessary. He pushed these taxing considerations to the corner of his mind as he and Quentin approached the old plant into which the thieves had disappeared.

"Oye!" Quentin whispered loudly and grabbed the back of Pollock's collar. He pointed forward, and Pollock saw a person exit the doorless entryway and slowly walk toward them. Once the man reached the perimeter of the fenced-in yard, he noticed the two and froze in his tracks. Pollock looked over at Quentin, who hesitantly waved his hand and began to speak. "Good day, we're—" But the man turned and sprinted swiftly back into the building, his bare feet pitter-patter-ing on the concrete. Pollock and Quentin looked at one another, and Quentin proceeded to walk forward. Pollock hesitated for a moment, still slightly languishing over Cabe's texted "old friend." He checked himself and caught up.

Pollock followed Quentin through the doorway up wide, crumbling concrete stairs that turned onto a landing and there it was. They looked out at the giant first floor of the old factory. It was as big as an airplane hangar. But instead of machinery, tents, fashioned from all sorts of materials, lined the floor in meandering rows. Some were modern camping tents, others were huts constructed from delivery pallets and tarps strung together by twine and supported with sticks and chairs. Others still were cubes of scrap metal and fencing, PVC piping, and folded cardboard. Each had its own personality. Some were assembled haphazardly, while others with apparent construction acumen. In front of many of the tents and huts were porches made from wood and wiring, carpeting and mats. They were adorned with mailboxes, lawn ornaments, clotheslines, and various flags and flowers and other decorations.

Throughout the scene, people were walking about, whistling on their porches, chatting, and carrying on as though it was just a normal day in their village, oblivious to the intruders' presence. The collective noise rattled and echoed throughout the giant room, sounding like the largest cafeteria imaginable, carrying upward to where the pale sun rays pierced inward through slender bay windows, illuminating dust in the air above the town.

To the far right end of the tents, there was an open common area. In the middle, circles of benches lined an earthen stage. There were gardens and animals in small pens. A group of men, women, and children stood laughing and singing. The whole vista shocked and elated Pollock. It was as if he had passed through a portal into a bizarre alternate reality or some future postapocalypse environment. There appeared to be a whole complex ecosystem humming within this building, the minute details of which were too much to take in all at once, but which Pollock continued to notice as he and Quentin stood there dumbfounded.

From the immensity of information in front of his eyes, Pollock picked out a small man about thirty feet ahead, between two huts, staring at him with a subtle smirk. He had kind brown eyes and wore a Yankees hat. The smirk grew as the two locked eyes and, while doing so, a hush fell across the great hall. The villagers now turned their attention to Pollock and Quentin, gathering closer to them with quiet suspicion.

The man walked forward, his flip-flops smacking against the concrete. The others seemed to regard him with some deference. They followed his physical queues, measuring his intent. Quentin put his palm on Pollock's chest and stood forward a bit. Once he was only a pace away from Pollock and Quentin, the man, who now seemed very short, smiled a friendly smile with his big brown face. The other inhabitants remained rather silent and inquisitive behind him. He extended his hand and said softly, "I am Martin Danburry. Welcome to my home."

* * *

Martin's earliest memories were of his hands in red dirt. He would dig and search for things, like tin cans, with the other children around the compound. They would do this until their mothers and fathers returned from the fields for the day. He also remembered building forts, using blankets and tying them to the edges of bunks in the adobe boarding houses. And the other kids would always take orders from him because it was clear that he always had a vision of ornate forts. He saw how to accomplish his vision and he was very energetic and convincing in communicating it.

This natural leadership often got him into trouble once puberty began, forceful drives rushing through a not yet fully formed prefrontal cortex. His ever-present, if transient, followers always in tow as coconspirators. And thus, Martin, by age fourteen, had become what most would call a "bad influence." Martin began stealing vehicles and going on joyrides and getting adults to get him alcohol. He even grew a few pot plants underground for a while. But this was all after Wicker Home.

Martin's mother, Aurelia, was a migrant worker. His father had always been a question, and remained so, mostly. Aurelia and Martin followed a migratory path that crossed two-thirds of the continental United States from orchards to farms to vineyards, always planning to arrive at the right season, the right weekend, and sometimes earning the right to stay on at one place longer than others so long as work continued. It was a cycle that landed them in the same locations, crossing paths with familiar families making a living in the same manner.

And so Martin had only part-time and seasonal friendships. Familiar faces would come and go and grow semirecognizable as they do in late adolescence and young adulthood. There was a shorthand introduction among experienced children. "Jersey by Florida. Macon's, yeah, I been there. Two month. Jerk son…"

His education was limited, as that of most of the children whose families ran the migratory pattern. There were day classes at some of the boarding homes, and at others there were books and movies. Martin had been taught to read, write, and do basic math. His mother was vigilant in that regard. But this was the common extent of formal knowledge among him and his fellows.

He had many liberties that children often dream of having from within the constraints of their structured and sheltered childhoods. These liberties provided their own kind of education for Martin. For example, when he was seven, Martin realized that, no matter what age, a bully only responded to strength. And a noble showing of strength could only be accomplished through mustering one's courage. And so he grew to recognize those moments in which his nobility was necessary.

Martin's sex drive and general sexual abilities had blossomed very early on. He had lost his virginity when he was eight. Katy, the fifteen-year-old daughter of the New Jersey apple farmer Burrows, had lured Martin into the bed of one of the regular worker's trucks at dusk, using her sunburned cleavage as bait. They lay side by side between two layers of packing blankets, playing truth or dare until Katy dared Martin to undress completely. From there, natural inclinations took over. The ordeal ended with them awkwardly dressing without eye contact, not dissimilar to stoned late evenings Martin would share with teenagers years later.

At the time, Martin wasn't old enough to ejaculate yet, nor was he experienced enough to ask if she had had an orgasm. He only asked meekly and sincerely, "Did you like that?"

Wrinkling her nose, she said, "Did you?" and he responded yes. From then on, they formed a ritual that was repeated numerous times at dusk, until Martin could aptly identify what her various sounds and movements meant in terms of sensations and demands. The time period for the act also dramatically increased.

Some years later, a very frustrated and awful old woman tried to convince Martin that he had been sexually abused because he was too young and couldn't have consented to these acts. "You was taken advantage of." Martin shrugged this off as clear nonsense. His eight-year-old self was very aware of what was happening and felt lucky to have had the experience. It was thrilling. It made him popular with kids four, five, and six years older then him.

He was regretful that he didn't take the initiative to say goodbye to Katy when Aurelia and he packed up and hitched to Massachusetts. Much later, he realized he'd probably saved both of them an unnecessary and fabricated production.

They were merely bodies for each other to explore for the benefit of later, truer companions. No more.

In fact, for all the time the two spent together, Martin didn't know much about her—what her school was like, who her friends were, what she wanted to be when she grew up. Only that she loved horror films and Elvis Presley. But he had known how her body odor smelled, along with her breath. He knew what she felt like inside, the color of the birthmark on her right thigh. He knew she loved to be tickled under her chin and, when he tickled her there, he knew how her toes quivered. He knew that she was ashamed of the scar from her cleft palate surgery. And he also knew that she wished her breasts were bigger, but he couldn't at all imagine how that was possible, let alone how it could be a good thing.

When Martin was ten, he realized that he wanted to become a filmmaker. His knack for tents and forts transformed into a knack for creating scenes for a film, and dialogue lines to be acted out by those whom he could turn into enthusiastic participants. Martin and Aurelia did not have nearly enough money for a video camera, which was something Martin never bothered his mother over. He had great respect for her position and had no desire to trouble her. He would have felt too guilty. So, acquiring a video camera involved enlisting the aid of a sixteen-year-old troublemaker named Tommy, who was painting stables on a peach farm in Georgia as community service for breaking into the gymnasium of his high school baseball team's rival and spray-painting penises on the walls.

Tommy had been accompanied by more than ten other boys from the baseball team, but had taken sole blame in a heroic gesture of misguided leadership. Martin reveled in this upon Tommy's telling during their first meeting one hot Georgia afternoon at the drinking hose. Martin explained the film idea to Tommy minutes after hearing his story. It involved a murderer that stole weapons used in

unsolved murder cases from the police evidence locker and killed the unjustly exonerated offenders. "In this way, the killer stalked the countryside seeking out
homicides to make right, the ones where the system failed," Martin said.

"That's so cool," Tommy said. How old are you?" An instant camaraderie
formed. They mimicked each other's squinting, scheming eyes.

Despite the previous trouble and his current punishment, Tommy was more
than willing to go into his own high school's gym equipment locker and steal the
video camera, which was shared among all of the sports teams for recording their
matches. He figured they'd never suspect him. And so the theft would double as
ammunition for future attacks from other students, to keep the rivalry hot, which
Tommy saw as part of his job being one of the captains of the team.

The heist and filming went well enough. Tommy, Martin, and an assortment
of other children who didn't speak much snuck out the night after its completion
to watch the final product on one of the portable audiovisual consoles at Hill Oaks
High School. This was when it dawned on Martin how many things one could acquire from government funds if you made yourself an institution with a credible
mission. High Schools seemed to have everything, and they only taught what
could be learned elsewhere. That thought captured his mind and kept him from
truly enjoying the feature presentation. He realized he would only ever be inside
of a high school by sneaking and fraudulent means.

It was around that time that Martin began to wonder what it was he would
do with his life. It was also around that time that he began to see how limited his
and his mother's lifestyle truly was. He would turn twelve and begin working as
well. If he was lucky, he would land a stationary job. He was charismatic and
competent enough. So then he would be a steady farm hand. If luck continued,
he'd rent a place in rural America and then perhaps marry. But he wondered if
that was all there was.

Martin began to long for the life of a middle-class suburban teenager. He wanted a girlfriend and a car. He wanted to go to high school where he could read and play an instrument in band. He wanted friends that stuck around longer than the next holiday. This longing infiltrated Martin and overflowed from him. Despite his best efforts to keep it from Aurelia, she saw it. And if she weren't so continuously exhausted from the trying manual labor, she would be filled with rage at the thought of Martin's father and what he had done.

Aurelia had spent her life escaping. Escaping an abusive father. Escaping an alcoholic lover. Then escaping many more alcoholic lovers. Megalomaniacal bosses. Domineering suitors. Local law enforcement. All of which had been men. This steered her inevitably to some approximately accurate misandry. And it made her very distrustful of power. And so, after a couple of decades of escapes, some with close calls and others resulting in injuries, external and internal, she found herself in her midthirties with a teenage son, traveling and hoping each trip that it would not be another escape but prepared for it in any instant.

She had seen that many women who had been beaten or betrayed began to blame themselves, to internalize the angry language and the violence, to assign it deep within themselves and so eventually become what the transgressors had instituted. Her sister Mary had done this. Aurelia had not. She saw early on that low self-esteem, where a person claims as truth all the negative evaluations made of them, was what made those powerful men so angry to begin with. They had been told they weren't as strong as their heroes, or that they would always be outsmarted by their nemesis, or that the female object of their affections would never succumb because she measured another higher in her estimations.

The men, her father, her lovers, her bosses, countless men who traveled with her from farm to orchard season after season, this was predominantly how they lived; they all suffered one small loss at a time. They were constantly failing to be something they secretly knew they needed to. And the men would take it out on one another usually after drinks. Often in wry conversational jabs masked as healthy competitive banter. But it was always very real and potent to Aurelia. Because, at any time, a man could begin to blame a woman. That, in her experience, was what usually happened.

After drinks, or some real or perceived failure, the man would find the resentment, the self-hatred too much to keep, and he would look around and realize that it wasn't his fault at all. It was her fault. Yes, it was always her fault. Because he loved her too much, or because she should have known that she was supposed to preemptively relieve his burdens, or because she was talking with some other guy, or simply because she was there. And so it became her fault, which mandated some punishment. It was often physical abuse, sexual abuse, or public humiliation. It was often emotional violence. And the man would feel a little better, believing, if only for moments, that the blame had honestly transferred. It was gone and he could spend a few hours watching his favorite fantasy dimly materialize.

But the blame would return tenfold and it would be unbearable. And now the man could blame the women because it didn't work. Why didn't it work? That's what the woman was there for, wasn't it? And so, much like an addict, the man would double down on the humiliation, the beatings, the rough sex. The traumas would increase and increase to an intensity that would inevitably either kill the woman or the man. Or, if luck applied, someone else would interfere. And that could work any number of ways because there are men who bury their disappointments in some savior complex, which often lead to them blaming the woman because they didn't feel any better having saved her from the previously abusive and awful situation. She was appreciative, but shouldn't that have been his duty in the first place? Why the extra reward? It shouldn't have been necessary, and the sav-ior knew this was true and could only return to meditation on the disappointments. Oh those lonely, violent saviors!

And so, at some point, in the heightening of abuses, there would come the point where Aurelia would begin to consider that maybe it was her fault. Maybe she was responsible for the men—her father, her boyfriend, the crew lead—and their frustrations. Maybe it was her position to alleviate that male aggression, to be a sort of salve on masculinity and its brutal travails. Perhaps that was the kind of tool she, as many others, was intended to be.

But, thankfully for Aurelia and Martin, she would always see the other side of that proposition. For, internalizing such a way of things would only continue it further. It was something that wanted to travel. And if she internalized the brutal-ity, where would it go from there? It would either come out on someone else's children or her friends, or it would surely destroy her, eating away at her from the inside one bite at a time until she was nothing but someone's piece of property, serving their desired purpose. She decided she would not become this. She de-cided she was not rotwood.

The defiance in this realization left two clear options to Aurelia: confronta-tion or escape. She had first chosen confrontation with her father. This only lead to more beltings, more housework. He turned his physical affections to Mary, instead. She was younger and more compliant. So Aurelia decided to leave, to es-cape. Many of the migrant workers came through town and ate at their house, played games at the local cantina. She was familiar with the kind of work they did. One night, she grabbed Mary and, each with one bag under their arm, hopped into the back of a pickup and rode 450 miles away from the only home they'd ever had.

And since then, many more escapes had been necessary. Many men had been taken with her dark, smooth skin, her luring brown eyes. Many men had felt

entitled to her intimacy. And numerous other men had felt entitled to salvation
through saving her from other men. And so, many parts along the routes had to be
avoided, and the landscape was always growing smaller. Aurelia had become accustomed to observing all male humans as members of another species. Sure, she
had encountered some who kept their word and had been true and good to her.
But the potential was always there, menacing in its possibilities, stirring memories
of Aurelia's that were too important in their lessons to ever be forgotten.

Martin was a difficulty for Aurelia. He was created from the ugliest of male
behavior, and early on, it had been hard for her not to look at him with disgust and
hostility. But as time went along and Martin turned into his own person, one
guided by the proper sentiments on Aurelia's part, she realized how much of a delight he could be. And eventually, he was no longer a source of sourness or
lamentations or rages. Martin would tell her jokes, and stories that he had thought
up. And she would laugh and critique them. And for a long while, despite minor
inevitable ripples, the two of them were happy in their lives. He was her son, full
of possibility and wonder. And she made sure that young Martin respected and
was awed by women. She made sure that he knew they were life givers, caretakers, leaders, and great creatures to be treated with sincerity and delicacy.

Martin and Aurelia formed a bond stronger than most mother and sons have.
And they never spoke of Martin's father and what he had done, despite the continuous curiosity in Martin's mind. He never fully pressed the issue because he could
see the pain it brought to her face. But he dreamed about these things, almost at
the expense of all else. He began to wonder about his father, and Martin's temperament toward his mother, despite his earlier intentions, began to show unease and
antipathy. Martin became bitter and angry.

Shit-bad happenstance decided it wanted one final tussle with Aurelia. After
several weeks of calmly but sternly refusing sexual advances from Drew Kincaid,

a pretty blond field hand on a multifruit orchard in Florida, he decided she needed more barbaric encouragement. He pushed her down on the crab grass and rubbed his hands heavily against her breasts and shoulders, pinning her. She unsheathed a knife from her pants and thrust it into his crotch. He panicked at the pain and the blood, which allowed Aurelia to make it to her feet and gain a few yards before Drew, regaining his composure, caught up with her. He repeatedly bashed her skull with a baseball-sized granite chunk, using all of his strength.

Thus, Aurelia finally could not escape. Her body was found the following evening, floating face down in a lazy eddy at a bend in the Orchard River. The death put Martin into a dazed shock. The wound was too deep to be acknowledged. When anyone spoke to him, he would only nod nervously in their general direction. This gave all those around him the notion that he was either a dullard or shocked into some borderline catatonic state.

He was passed through the hands of various childcare workers and police officers and eventually was plopped down, with a black JanSport backpack with some clothes and a few personal items, on the front porch of Wicker Home, a rural orphanage run by Ms. Corin, and it would become, for Martin, hell itself. His entire life would be divided into two sections: before and after he met Ms. Corin. And his experience at Wicker Home would shape the trajectory of the rest of his life.

Wicker Home was structured around the belief that children who ended up there were in need of punishment. Punishment was the business of Wicker Home. Above Ms. Corin's rocking chair, in her office, was a framed sampler she had stitched which read, "Now the end is upon you, and I will send my anger upon you; I will judge you according to your ways, and I will punish you for all your abominations.—Ezekiel 7:3"

Ms. Corin flashed Martin an aggressive sneer from behind her circular spectacles during their introduction as she continued knitting. In Martin, the action registered as something flirtatious, even sexual. And he welcomed her direct nature; it contrasted with the ambivalent or neutral manner that everyone used with him since his mother passed. She noticed his reticent interest, and filed it away to be later retrieved and manipulated at the correct moment.

Within the time it took Martin to say hello and look around the room, Ms. Corin had determined that Martin was a sexual pervert and thought far too little about his actions before partaking in them. She raised an eyebrow as she measured him up. He was dressed in dark blue jeans and a plain white T-shirt that was yellowed in the pits and around the neck. He was too quiet. Martin was still a bit startled by how little his mother's death had torn him up. It had been so quick. He knew he would never see her face again and wondered why he couldn't feel her loss.

There were seventeen children at Wicker Home, seven girls and ten boys, all the victims of relatively bad circumstances. Martin wondered about all of the tragedies that had landed them in this place. And that made him think of Aurelia. Quietly brooding and surrounded by complaining children, he grew increasingly haunted by her murder and the suddenness of it.

The home consisted of two main structures. First, was a long rectangular hall with bunks lining both walls. There was a restroom at each end, male and female. A thick curtain on rollers separated the boys' and girls' halves of the room at night. The second building was a proper house, with a room where school lessons were given by Ms. Corin's assistant, Miss Jemmy, and the kitchen where meals were served. The second floor of the house included Jemmy's quarters and Ms. Corin's office. It was off limits unless one was summoned. This was an honor and horror no one sought.

Martin learned very little about his compatriots, and thought too much about himself. The lesson plans by Jemmy were rudimentary spelling, grammar, writing and basic math. Most of the other children struggled, with the exception of Sarah, who was older, maybe fifteen, and as bored with the schooling as Martin. It became apparent that Aurelia had been successful in her home lessons. Martin received A's regularly on his examinations. Occasionally he would get a B in math, which he didn't favor.

Weeks passed, and months. The routine was dull. There was playtime, but mostly Martin kept to himself, reading books from the small library in their sleeping hall. He made it his goal to read every book that was in the limited library. There were forty-two books, neatly rowed on a three-level red shelf. The collection was haphazard, and how they came to be there interested Martin almost as much as the books themselves. He asked Jemmy, who told him they were donations from local churches and a few from the Amish.

There were about a dozen or so Bible-related books, which he was pushing off until later in the exercise. He began with a picture book of famous billboard signs and product advertisements. It read fast. He spent a few weeks reading *To Kill a Mocking Bird* and a collection of poems by Ralph Waldo Emerson. Jemmy would frequently question him on his progress, and he would indulge her with elaborate summations of the contents. She posed poignant questions and encouraged Martin. He returned the favor by fantasizing about her nude. He liked to think of her stubby legs covered in bubbles of soap. But he felt guilty about it, sometimes. It seemed like he was betraying his dead mother.

He also fantasized about Sarah. She was skinny and plain but kind. Again, he experienced guilt in his fantasies, like he was trespassing. And the feeling bothered him, festering from time to time. But then he would wonder how it was possible to trespass in his own mind. He told himself it was natural to want to have sex with Jemmy and Sarah. Still, these naggings niggled him into riddles. He had never felt bad about his desires before and wondered why he did now.

It eventually occurred to him that it was because of Ms. Corin. Though the reading material was diverse, and their physical liberties on the grounds were great, Ms. Corin descended from her office each evening to bestow upon the residents of Wicker Home a very rigid and unforgiving criteria of behavior in sermon form. She would perch on a stool in the hall while the children lay in their beds, and read passages from the Old Testament. She would mix in personal anecdotes and private wisdoms. And she would twist into the readings her personal convictions about their subject matter.

The message, though the stories and lessons varied, always centered on one idea: there was something wrong within each person, some evil, unstable sin. And it made repentance and punishment necessary, especially if the sin involved sex. Because sex was the province of the dinosaurs and of the devil, who himself was a bird of a dinosaur, according to Ms. Corin. She often said, "Satan was a bird from before there were birds. A great flying wretched beast. And he would soar across the sky, looking to descend and copulate with the unwilling."

The sermons always seemed oddly pointed toward Martin, as if they were mocking him. When he looked up from his bed, he found menace in the shadow of her bunned hair clinging to the separation curtain. The fabric would gently blow from the old ceiling fan above and make it appear as if her shadow itself was breathing. And he would lie back again and picture vividly in his imagination what she described:

"Satan, was punished because he loved God most, even after God commended Satan to favor other humans and not slight them for their meekness. But Satan believed he knew better, better than God! So God fell him to earth, back in time, and banished him into the body of a bird dinosaur named Eskus. And in this carcass he suffered the life of animal drives and worldly baseness, until Satan appreciated humanity. Because humans have a choice. Though they are born as an Eskus, they also have angels guiding them. It is each our own decision how we live. If we choose the righteous life, the first steps are repentance and punishment.

You must know what is wrong and why, lest you end up time traveling into a dinosaur! Now, children, think about God's love, and find why you are wrong. Goodnight all."

And with that she would gently tiptoe out of the hall, half of the children already nearly writhing in fear. But this troubled Martin differently. He saw no way any reasonable person could ever believe such a story. It was dumb, unless merely some metaphor. He knew humans could be like animals, with maybe the potential to be more, and wondered why she didn't just say so. He decided she just wanted to scare the tar out of the children.

Martin found something inherently wrong with the notion of original sin. Or rather, he thought sin might be an appropriate way to describe the situation of humans, but it should not be considered their fault if it was already too late to do anything about it. Martin didn't want to have to apologize for the rest of his life. And he didn't respect a God who essentially started his children out in a trap. He became alienated and restless as time went on, and the sermons at Wicker Home increased in their intensity.

As winter came and turned into spring, then summer into autumn, Martin finished all of the books from the library, and the loneliness and boredom steadily grew. Ms. Corin became more of an authority. In the back of the recess yard, there sat a large tractor tire, the bottom of which was half buried in the ground. It was a hang out spot of sorts, especially for the younger kids, with whom Martin rarely interacted.

Jemmy found Michael and Rachel touching each other's crotches inside the tire during late afternoon and was obligated, by contract, to inform Ms. Corin of the incident. Michael and Rachel weren't seen again for several days, and served three months of playtime sitting indoors transcribing the entire Old Testament into journals. Martin wondered how, if they hadn't taken the initiative to explore each other's bodies, they were supposed to ever learn about them and grew angry with Jemmy and Ms. Corin and the world, for that matter.

Shortly after the tire incident, Martin began waking up in the night to find Ms. Corin sitting on her stool, in its usual position on the other side of the divider drapes. He would steady his breathing and move stealthily, trying to make sure his waking state went unnoticed. The shadow always made it appear that she was watching young Martin. He never said anything but would lie still and think of pleasant things until he was able to regain sleep. These episodes continued on, intermittently, for quite some time, long after Michael and Rachel returned to the play yard and had forgotten about their transcription punishment.

The image of Ms. Corin's silhouette steadily wedged into Martin's head, until it was a powerful reminder that someone was watching, someone was listening in. He didn't like how this felt. He enjoyed and missed the sprawling liberties of life on the farms and orchards, putting troves of migrant children to tasks of the imagination, unbridled and uncoerced by religious figures. There was no guilt, no concern for being wrong. Things flowed simply. Children formed order and knew when they were wrong; all else was whatever they wanted. Martin finally realized that Ms. Corin was really the warden of a prison, from which he needed to escape.

A whole year passed. The world and even his own mind grew unfriendly. It became a chore to get out of bed. Martin's aspirations dissipated. He had occasional good series. He did eventually become close with Jemmy and with Sarah. But Ms. Corin's surveillance never relented. Quite the opposite. Her night visits became steadily more frequent until one night Martin noticed she was sitting on his side of the divider, knitting but with her eyes fixed on him.

Martin began to remember all of the things that were so great about his mother. She would play with his hair while he told stories about the friends he had made. He would fill her in on all of the things he had learned about snakes. And fish. He loved fish and the idea of the sea. Exploring the deep riveted him. But he also had learned, from a fat freckled kid in North Carolina named Chad, that any-one who favored the ocean secretly craved to return to his mother's womb. It seemed strange to Martin that he had ever been in Aurelia's womb. But he did like her playing with his hair.

It was around this time, when Martin had lost all of his previous motiva-tions, that Ms. Corin invited him to accompany her on a trip into Amish country for pleasure one Saturday. The plan was to purchase some meats and cheeses, for which the community was known. She had done this often throughout Martin's tenure at Wicker Home, but had never sought companionship on these trips. Her Oldsmobile would rev up with some excess smoke, early in the morning, and the kids would hear her return late in the evening, their hearts sinking. Jemmy was al-ways in charge while Ms. Corin was away, and it relaxed Martin, as it did the oth-ers.

Ms. Corin explained to Martin that she could tell he was in a rut. "Come along with me to the Amish market, the fresh air will revive your spirit." Martin, with the implicit understanding that this was actually a command, quietly acqui-esced and stood, clean and dressed at 6:30 a.m., next to the cream Cutlass Su-preme. Ms. Corin flashed him a beguiling leer as she opened the door with a sinis-ter creak and sat herself. Martin followed suit, and no words were spoken for a good two hours in transit along a single pot-holed country road.

The afternoon spent market shopping went by very quickly and the intrigue of the Amish culture excited Martin. It was a welcome distraction. He had seen Amish people in film and in passing but never this close. They were such a quiet people, all of them in like clothing. Some of them were helping in some facet of the harvesting and selling of that which they had grown on their land. Others were making candles or dresses or tools to be sold. Hundreds of non-Amish had driven great distances to come purchase their quality crops and goods. Many of these customers were middle-class families from suburbia USA. These were the same people Martin had once wished to be counted among. He never felt further away from them.

After a few hours perusing the items haggling with a few Amish Ms. Corin had dealt with for years, she and Martin took a long respite at a picnic table by one of the farmhouses. Martin was spent from carrying crates of sausage, Gouda, and beets from the market tables and placing them into the trunk and back seat of the Oldsmobile. The two of them watched the commotion of commerce, occasionally meeting eyes. It was cool and crisp out. Ms. Corin slipped off her flats and scrunched her hose-covered toes in the grass. Martin found the action peculiar.

"They have their own way of doing everything," Ms. Corin said. "This whole community functions on its own. You see, all of this land is common land. They all share in it together. And so they are all owners." She pointed around, watching Martin peer from one adolescent Amish to the next. "That means a lot of sacrifice, though. They start work young, your age. And they all depend upon one another to work hard. And everyone does, according to his or her ability, and then they all share in the rewards. They all decide together how to use their funds. But they don't spend frivolously, either. No cable subscriptions here, no cruise ship vacations." She leaned back against the picnic table, allowing the sun to spread over her pale face.

Martin examined the scene, mulling over what Ms. Corin had explained to him. It was a revelation. He had spent his childhood on farms where everyone who performed the work only received food and board. The wages were slight. He liked that the workers could be owners because he thought they were really the ones running the whole thing. He watched a handful of preteen girls cooperating to carry a wooden jug across the gravel roadway and into the main farmhouse where the heart of the market bustled.

"I don't like that they all have to wear the same thing. Why do they do that?" Martin asked, directing his gaze back to a group of men. They were all wearing similar solid-colored, buttoned shirts and broadcloth pants underneath their straw and leather hats. "They dress only for their practical purposes. It keeps them from becoming prideful and materialistic. Their focus is elsewhere. And its also for modesty. The women respect their bodies. The men respect the women." Martin found himself deeply immersed in her explanations, which bothered him a little. It was all interwoven with her overwrought religiousness.

Ms. Corin, for all her desire to punish Martin, couldn't help but admire his curiosity and wondered if she had really brought him along for herself rather than to tend to his depressions as she had explained. She didn't think Martin very bright, but guessed he might be a bit perceptive.

Martin and Ms. Corin drove back, again mostly in silence. Daydreams of a future Amish Martin spiraled through his mind. Ms. Corin had explained how each member of the community was afforded a summer in their teen years when they are permitted to go out in the world and live as non-Amish did. "Then it is truly their decision whether they want to stay Amish. That's why it works, because most of them chose this life on their own. It was their choice. "

The trip had illuminated Ms. Corin completely differently. Martin saw new designs behind her behavior and a potential reservoir of mysterious knowledge. Sure, he still had issues, drastic issues, with her religious punishment scheme. But something, some obstinate shield that always armored her, had been tossed aside, and now her frequent surveillance of Martin's psyche was warmer, friendlier. She was more ambiguous, perhaps even an ally.

She had gone inside after slowly pulling the Oldsmobile to a stop in the fading heat of the autumn evening. Martin was terribly aware of the children in the hall who would be listening and watching through the upper window, wondering about his adventure with the Wicker Home mistress. He felt exuberance in his special situation, and it helped as he loaded the day's purchases into the kitchen as he had been instructed. He had not, however, been instructed on what to do with the keys to the car. So he locked it and left the keys on the kitchen table next to a bowl of pine cones whose odor wafted into his nostrils. The gesture was a token and an emblem of the day, which had been so surprising and rewarding for him.

After quietly shutting the house's giant wooden door, he pondered the notion of it often being left unlocked. He glanced up and saw that both Ms. Corin's and Jemmy's room lights were out. He looked across the play yard, barely lit under the brittle star light, and felt as though he were in a situation that he wasn't meant to be. Perhaps it was a misstep of Ms. Corin's to leave him to close up and find his way to bed without taking advantage of this freedom. Then he thought that perhaps it was a trust and he felt guilty, noticing her influence once again within him. He wondered if it was a test.

The guilt and the stars and the freedom made him wonder about his mother. It occurred to him that she no longer existed anywhere. He had been handed a cardboard box, inside of which was a thick plastic bag containing the ash remnants of Aurelia. This box was being stored in a safe in the basement of the house, along with his yo-yo and a whole host of other objects that had more or less been confiscated from the other Wicker Home inhabitants.

The idea was daunting, that people ceased. And there was nothing on the other side of death. To Martin, it didn't seem as though there could be. And anything said about it required dying to find out if it were true. It was a dreadfully haunting thought that caused feelings of anxiety in Martin. And it made him less judgmental of Ms. Corin, Jemmy, and the others who believed all of those preposterous tales of heaven that they continually read from the Bible. It felt better to have a story, something sturdy to hold on to. Martin clearly saw and understood the appeal.

But, though the appeal of Ms. Corin's teachings was real in its origins and purpose, it seemed that any solution to this particular problem was false. "No one will ever know," he said aloud, ambling toward the small stone steps leading up to the side door of the hall. And this conclusion made his mother's death seem much more drastic, as if there were a great unknown obstacle between him and her. It wasn't distance or even any kind of material that hung like gauze between them, as he had previously envisioned, but rather there was an empty and crushing finality. The paragraph ended midway. Aurelia was nothing more than what he thought of her, and even that wasn't her. It was his need for her.

Death didn't feel as warm and inviting in this view. It was not how he had felt of it days earlier when it seemed to be a welcome remedy for the boredom and the sadness on which he was focusing. He sat on the bottom stone step, his knees up under his chin. He desired to be alone and out of sight of the prying eyes of the cohort who, without doubt, were inside waiting to lob various suggestive insults at Martin, for surely he was to be viewed as a sort of teacher's pet from this point forward. He rubbed the prickly bristles of dark hair protruding from his kneecaps with his slender fingers and wished that Aurelia were there so that he could share his new Amish revelations while she played with his hair.

The door opened and Sarah eased herself down on the step above Martin. He felt her long warm breaths on his neck. "You know she is manipulating you," Sarah said. They sat quiet for a moment.

"How?" Martin asked.

Sarah let out a single percussive chuckle, then pulled out a cigarette and lit it with a violent swipe of a match against the wall of the building. The hot smoke spilled over Martin's shoulders. "You're usually the first person to sleep," she said. Martin waited for further explanation, but none came. He tilted his head up and watched the smoke circles rise and dissipate.

"And?" he asked.

"And now here you are up after everyone staring into the sky. You know how vicious she is. You honestly think she's trying to be your friend? Why? Why now?" The point was troubling and, as yet, unconsidered by Martin. He turned and gave her a long look. She raised an eyebrow and exhaled sideways from a narrow vent in her otherwise pursed lips. Martin thought she looked like a feral animal. Strands of her straight amber hair wandered wildly outward from her skull in magnificent crisscrosses caught by the light winds. Her brown eyes contained an oblique force in their scrutiny.

Martin felt oddly protective of Ms. Corin, and he noted a weird desire to defend her from Sarah. But then he thought over the previous year and the continuous emotional harassment that Ms. Corin had heaped upon him and his peers with monstrous abundance and, at times, the appearance of sick enjoyment. He turned back away from Sarah and mulled this discord over in his mind.

He was divided and felt foolish. It was now unclear who his allies were. Sarah, was the noble older sister with a chip on her shoulder. She spoke plainly and laid bare the obvious criminality behind Ms. Corin's religious enterprise. But then Ms. Corin had demonstrated a peculiar knowledge, which, as obscure as it still was in his mind, pulled convincingly at Martin.

Sarah sensed Martin's inner gymnastics. She placed the shrinking Marlboro between her tight lips, leaned forward, and rubbed his shoulders and neck with her thumbs. Relief flushed along Martin's sides and allowed him to cease flexing his thigh muscles, which he hadn't realized he was doing until then.

The two maintained this activity for some odd moments in the insect filled evening, interrupted only occasionally by Sarah smacking mosquitos to death on her tan thighs, which jutted savagely from her jean cutoffs and were adorned with blood. "Ah. Fuckers!" she said in a tone muffled by the act of keeping the burning cigarette balanced in her mouth. It made Martin smile. He thought she was an animal.

The end of the cigarette came, and Sarah rubbed it methodically against the dirt with her sandaled foot. She made sure to rub the dirt over the ash evidence and capture the butt to be later flushed down the toilet in the girls' restroom. She opened the door and pointing the way inside. Martin was depressed. He had wanted to remain outside for hours more, quiet and only every so often talking with Sarah. She was comforting, like a dog. "Big sister," he said, looking at her, about two inches taller than he, with both admiration and scorn. She smirked coldly and rubbed his head as she followed him inside.

While lying in his bed that night, he felt sick to his stomach. He knew that answers were necessary. But he now felt much less alone in this place. A community of sorts was forming around him at Wicker Home. That community was full of contradictions, sick landmines, potentially manipulative sadists, but also older sisters who gave shoulder massages. He relived the joy.

Martin often wondered how Sarah acquired her cigarettes. She constantly had one hung on her lip, fuming chalky white swirls. It was so often that it became almost an extension of her physical attributes like her small nose and ratty brown eyes. She would always slink to a faraway location. Her favorite spot was within the plum tree circle, which formed a sort of sad grove in the southeast corner of the play yard. Another was on the far side of Ms. Corin's house next to the garage and Oldsmobile, which always remained parked outside despite ample space within the garage. And yet, her activities were continually visible. And it wasn't clear to Martin that her smoking habits were disallowed, however incongruent they seemed to be with the strictures of Wicker Home.

She only smoked Marlboros, always a red soft pack that she nervously handled in her right palm with a roughness that made Martin curious about her leg-shaving mannerisms. She had often, beginning early on in Martin's stay at Wicker, massaged his back and shoulders during their now irreplaceable chats, and Martin now realized that this action was probably more to relieve her anxiety and quell the viciousness in her hands than aimed at providing Martin comfort. Still, it did provide him comfort, and he believed that such a by-product, however unintentional, was not lost on Sarah.

Deliveries to the home were routine and quite isolated from the children. A blue Toyota would pull up once or twice a week in the night and park on the gravel behind the Oldsmobile or out along the interstate, and an enormous man with a squinting face would smile and murmur at Jemmy while he methodically and quickly unloaded crates of supplies. Martin never saw Sarah approach the man, nor any special meetings between her and Jemmy or Ms. Corin, yet she was always viciously crumpling fresh packs of Marlboro reds, and Martin found it mysterious in a charming way. He decided that he didn't want to know how she acquired them. He envisioned late night rendezvous with strange older men in the fields halfway to town. He would look at her shoes in the mornings, checking for any indication of travel. None was ever present. It made him smirk, and he imagined her turning into a rodent after a certain hour and scavenging them from people's houses.

The other kids were much younger than either Martin or Sarah, so most of his interactions with them were in a supervisory role. They had much more energy and were constantly running about and getting into tangles and tussling with toys in immature skirmishes. Aside from his heart-to-hearts with Sarah, he continued keeping mostly to himself throughout the rest of his first year. Jemmy continued to goad him into engagement in classes, and Ms. Corin began taking Martin with her to the Amish market as part of the regular routine. And in this manner, Wicker Home's ritual pivots and swings took over and replaced the longing for the adventurous days on the migrant path with Aurelia.

Ms. Corin noticed Martin and Sarah's growing closeness. "I see that the two of you have been conspiring lately," she rasped as Martin clicked the Oldsmobile door closed at the conclusion of unloading late on a Saturday evening. She was staring off at Sarah, who sat cross-legged on the front steps huffing on a Marlboro.

"Um, yeah. She's nice to talk to," Martin said, alarmed at the severity of Ms. Corin's tone, her eyes more tense than their usual steady kindliness.

Ms. Corin smiled curtly and said, "Be careful with that one, Martin. She is deeply troubled. It's turned her insides sour. She has sour guts, Martin."

Reciprocal character stabs such as these were repetitively flung back and forth between Sarah and Ms. Corin, with Martin being the messenger while growing increasingly interested and attracted to both women in different ways. Sarah's attraction was familial and warm. She motivated him to analyze his thoughts and search for what he believed. She was direct and pointed in her frequent criticisms, and Martin, despite her harsh affronts, knew she had his interests at heart. Ms. Corin's attraction was lustful. Despite her age and conservative manner, Martin had admitted to himself how sexually drawn to her he was. She was a powerful lady, who spoke in elusive and seductive terms that appealed to his sense of intrigue.

The fact that the two of them spoke to each other, through Martin, in such territorial and threatened terms only heightened his dual attraction. He sometimes felt like a small tool in a much larger game between the females that began long ago, the beginning to which he was not privy but sure the content of which involved sinister primordial forces. Sarah would not speak about what lead her to Wicker Home. He had asked her before breakfast on a Tuesday. "No Marty, we're not playing that game now." She often spoke in these ways, not dissimilar to how Martin spoke to the other younger residents, but more glibly, almost sardonically. This would always make him happy because it was an inside joke. She didn't think of him as much younger than herself.

"Your call, Sis." It was an offer for more intimacy, knowing full well they were going at her pace.

From afar, as Martin watched Sarah in what an onlooker might categorize as a creepy way, he saw, or imagined, some vague and serious trauma. It manifested in how her smile ended, not naturally but, for a moment in mid-decline, forming an "I smell shit and can't honestly pretend not to anymore" grimace. It reminded him of a group of monks he had learnt of who had all come together after great tragedies in their respective lives and decided to walk past their sadness. They would walk all hours of the day, together, focusing on moving beyond the horrors of their pasts.

It seemed to Martin that after so much walking, day in and day out, their bodies would reach a level of fitness and health that would prompt them to feel better naturally. But on Sarah, it was as if she wasn't walking quite fast enough, and her sadness would catch up with her and punch itself through to recognizable form in her face.

Martin couldn't tell what it was, exactly, this sadness of hers, but it sometimes dissuaded Martin from attempting to make her happy. He favored, instead, interacting with her when she was on a more even keel. He knew that she had a notebook, which she kept shoved underneath her mattress and sometimes read from at night while sniffling. It was a brown cardboard notebook with the name "Mason" sloppily written on the cover in permanent marker.

From conversation, Martin knew that Mason was her older brother by three or four years, who had moved to California with his boyfriend. She had referenced him in growing bits and pieces as she and Martin spoke more often and more candidly. It started with phrases such as "Yeah, Mason really loved C.S. Lewis too" and "Mason and his friends used to make little movies with their 8 mm camera" or, perhaps most revealing, "Mason used to eat fast like that. You two are both slobs. Keep eating like that and you'll never get invited into anyone important's home!"

She had numerous memories of her brother, but the one full recounting that she relayed to Martin involved Mason's departure. He was shirtless, waving ecstatically from the back of a brown van, the rear open. His penne hair frolicking about, matching the tabor of his waving arms, as he sat cross-legged and smiled earnestly from ear to ear. The memory had troubled her. It had been worn in for a few years now, and some of the details had grown surprisingly uncertain. But one detail never altered in the slightest. Mason's goofy smile.

Ms. Corin's late night sermons grew in severity over the autumn months and it scared the younger children half to death, Miles in particular, who would crawl into Martin's bed and bury his head against Martin side, the slobber and hot breath creeping through his nightshirt. She had begun a fascination with reptiles, cats, and birds. Through them, she believed that God was presenting her with signs. It began a week before Halloween, when Jemmy ran over a common garter snake with the lawnmower. Ms. Corin nailed the two halves of the carcass to one of the old plum trees, the split ends ruptured from the mower blade hanging downward. The purple guts lazily sagged downward as decomposition began.

She went out twice a day, with her old leather-bound Bible in hand, and read and spoke and listened to something that was apparently floating clockwise through the air just feet above her. The children noticed with pangs of horror and curiosity. Upon seeing anyone watching Ms. Corin's ritual, Jemmy would shoo them back into unburdened play or chores, depending upon the time of day. Ms. Corin's rituals always occurred while the children were outside and could view the strange spectacle. Jemmy was quite bothered as well. However, it wasn't her place to question Ms. Corin, and she had been saving up good money at this job. So she just made a habit of trying to block the children's view. But Miles saw.

Miles was a frail six year old with bright blond hair and blue eyes whose predominant passions included Legos, questions about how to best stay safe, and habitual folding and refolding of clothes and sheets. He had been left at Wicker Home during winter. It was his first home. And he was terrified of it, always walking on eggshells around the others, never speaking. He spent a lot of energy being strategic about where he placed himself within a room. And once he had planted himself in that place, if he had to go to the restroom, he would hold it until there was a clear path to it, free of people. Then, upon reentering the room, he would be equally careful about replanting himself. There was always a burning terror in his chest. His neck and shoulders were always tight, ready for flight or whatever awful outburst was constantly almost about to happen. He slept deeply.

The young boy was also adorable, and Ms. Corin knew it. He had a chance of being adopted. However, his socially averse personality had found a way to kill the opportunity whenever interested parties visited. He was nervous and would completely shut down, holding his hands over his ears so that the couple looking to adopt would think he had mental issues. He would hum and rock, even in the face of the embarrassed chastisement of Ms. Corin.

And so, Ms. Corin had begun, starting around his fifth birthday, placing ground-up prescription pain medication in Miles's breakfast on the days when visitors were scheduled. The meds would make him dopey and calm, and he smiled far more often, but not often enough to alarm anyone. Nobody knew this was happening, including Miles. But he would always sleep much deeper those nights after visits, and the fits of animal contortions and silent shutdowns subsided. And in those deep sleeps he would fart and the other children would hear and laugh. Young Brin gave him the nickname "Crotch Whistle."

And so, occasionally, when someone felt like being mean or they were threatened or had been admonished by Jemmy or Ms. Corin, they would commonly take it out on the easiest of targets, Miles, by yelling "Hey Crotch Whistle, Crotch Whistle!" all the while laughing and pointing as others usually gathered in what they saw as harmless merriment. Sarah would occasionally shush them or smack Brin over the back of the head, and that would end the episode, because all of the younger Wicker residents respected and feared Sarah.

Martin had followed Sarah's example, naturally. He had always had a proclivity to favor those who were bullied. Martin paid attention to how power was
managed, which is why, Ms. Corin, for him, began to pass from curiously, seduc-
tively attractive to wretchedly vile with an alarming velocity. If the snake incident
hadn't frightened Miles enough, the cat that followed seemed to do the trick.
Miles first saw it after morning lessons while secretly transporting his half-completed erecter-set project underneath his shirt from the house to the sleeping hall.
He stopped midstride and dropped his contraption.

"I pet that cat," Miles uttered in exasperation, his lisp exaggerated, as Martin carried him to his bed to lie down and recuperate after the sighting. "It liked
me. It was my friend. We were friends. It was nice to me. We were friends."
Miles curled on top of his grey bedding and held Martin's forearm with force
enough to effect the blood flow to his hand, creating tingling sensations. It was
uncomfortable but emblematic of growing tensions and fears at Wicker Home.
Martin sat on the edge of Miles's bed while the boy lay curled for nearly an hour
before falling asleep.

That evening was the first of the heightened sermons. It was clear from the
start that Ms. Corin was in a distracted state because she did not notice that, upon
the instant of her entrance, Miles shot like a surprised rat across the length of the
hall, nine beds, and scrambled over the wooden frame and shoved his cold, snotty
nose against Martin's neck. Ms. Corin just paced right by and slowly lowered herself into her rocking chair. Her old creaking bones mirrored the sound of the old
creaking wood. If she had been in a normal state, she would have scolded Miles
and told Martin that he knew better than to encourage such behavior.

She remained seated, quietly for five or six minutes, the room full of children waiting in tantalizing anticipation, looking around at each other's faces, hoping that one of the expressions would suggest an explanation for the silence. None
did. Sarah and Martin stared at one another in a similar manner. Ms. Corin had

not drawn the divider closed. And so, the whole long wide hall was open to all, which allowed the sermon to have more of an effect by making visible the faces and torments of the lot. With the hall undivided, Martin thought it resembled the sleeping halls on southern orchards. But that seemed as though it had happened ages ago, and perhaps to someone else. Martin was living in someone else's remembered dream.

No one spoke during the waiting but merely sped up their looking around until necks were pivoting like a group of house sparrows. Then Ms. Corbin opened her mouth. "I...um..." She cleared her throat with an awful hacking of mucous. "I know that keeping the right path is difficult. I do." She spoke lower than usual and, with her chin pressed downward, looked up in a sinister way that dredged up visuals of vampires and beasts of prey for the children. "When you are younger, it is not clear how difficult it is. I've...I've done terrible, terrible things. I have." She grasped tightly to the arms of the rocker. Miles similarly grasped at Martin's shoulders, and Martin looked at Sarah. Her face had hardened with resolve. The other children shivered and pulled blankets and pillows to positions of comfort.

"It's *your* fault," she said, smiling. "You are all here because someone found you too difficult. They were the lazy ones, the wrong ones, the ones...who worshipped shortcuts. And you are the evidence! Each one of you is a little demon. Yes,"—she began croaking in laughter between her words, her chest heaving and convulsing, her hands tightly gripping the arms of the chair—"you're all demon children. You were born dirtier than intoxicated heathens! And it was my task to clean you, to bring you from Eskus's clutches. Make your backs straight. But how? Oh, how? With faith that I cannot see anymore? I've made sacrifices for you heathens, you demon children!" She jumped to her feet, faster and with more agility than any of the residents had seen her move. She continued with ever-rising volume and enthusiasm. "I've made sacrifices! And still it is unclear how I can make clean what has been born so filthy! Filthy little pups…"

Miles clung and squeezed tighter and tighter, truly hurting Martin, who squirmed and contorted himself to make it as comfortable as possible. He wouldn't break Miles's grasp because there was something sacred in it. He had gained a sacred position with Miles. He was his protector now. Martin looked at Sarah and wondered where Jemmy was. Then he caught sight of Drayton, who was crying in terror two beds down the row. His eyes were also aimed at Sarah, pleading with her, seeking some reason for this ridiculous torture.

"The devil, Satan, has claws and a beak! His beak is sharper than any eagle or falcon. And his eyesight is better too. Like scurrying rodents are seen by the eagle and the falcon, so too all of you heathens, you demon children, are seen by the devil, and he is just waiting to dive and consume you all up completely!" She began pointing at each of the children, one by one, slowly stepping to the end of each bed as she did so. She began with the girls, who responded with howls and yelps, except for Sarah, who just stared dead-eyed at Ms. Corin, as usual. She acted as if the sermon was no different than Ms. Corin's usual behavior, as if this was the status quo. It impressed and confused Martin.

By the time she made her way to the boys' side of the hall, she was screaming their names as she pointed to them. "Marcus! You demon, the devil is diving for you!" Still slowly pacing, her eyes mad with excitement, her grey bun of hair a little askew from shaking her head with emphasis on certain words such as "devil" and "demon" and "you." Spittle was spraying from her lips. Then it was Drayton's turn. He was completely hidden underneath his blanket, crying loudly with visible heaves.

"And you, dirty Drayton! Filthy heathen demon! The devil is spreading his wings, licking his beak, and opening his talons as he descends downward faster than anything you could imagine, and he is going to—"

"Alright, that's enough Ms. C.," said Sarah, matter-of-factly, standing. All of the children turned to look at Sarah. Ms. Corin slowly spun around and meet Sarah's eyes with her own, still crazed with spiritual frenzy. Martin experienced a sour dread in his belly. He wondered if he would have to get involved. He was ready, if he did, although Miles's fingernails were digging so deeply into his side and arm that, if such involvement became necessary, Miles would likely have to travel along with him.

Ms. Corin's eyes relaxed to their usual enigmatic state, and she stepped up to Sarah. Toe to toe, they stood in what Martin perceived to be a game of chicken. Sarah's pulse quickened and banged against her throat. She hadn't really thought out the consequences of her actions but rather acted instinctively, as she usually did.

Ms. Corin spit in Sarah's face. Viscous slobber dripped off her nose and oozed downward to her chin. All of the children stopped breathing. Martin stood up, Miles curled around his side in midair.

"Poor child," Ms. Corin said calmly, lovingly, as she petted the top of Sarah's head from front to back. She cupped the back of her head before repeating the motion once, twice, three times, four times. Sarah's implacable expression melted and betrayed surprise and fear, which spread a higher level of anxiety across the room. Martin was conflicted about his obligations.

Ms. Corin turned, picked her Bible up from the base of the rocking chair, and casually walked to the door. "Good night, children," she half-whispered. Then she was gone. The room she left was emotionally spent. No one knew exactly how to respond to what had just occurred, and so they were all looking around for someone who did. And thus the house sparrows returned.

Sleep for most of the Wicker Home residents came with great difficulty and only after concentration exercises worthy of a veteran Buddhist. For a few, however, the shocking jolt from the sermon was exactly what they needed to obtain deep sleep, and these few woke up the next morning feeling refreshed and hopeful. Sarah slept as usual and awoke earlier than the others. The spitting of Ms. Corin bothered her. It was insulting and degrading. But Sarah didn't view Ms. Corin as her equal. Sure, she was smart and capable. But she was like a gorilla in a giant zooscape, fiddling around with twigs as if they were spiritual totems. If a gorilla had spit at her, she wouldn't feel slighted, but merely reflect on the advanced perceptions that further evolution had afforded her, and ultimately pity the trapped animal. She thought about whether she pitied Ms. Corin, and then she remembered the brown leather couch in Mason's apartment.

She remembered sleeping on it and waking up with her cheek sticking to it. It sat directly below a street-level window next to the bakery. The odors of browning flour dough and vanilla icing sifted in through the porous sill and found their way to Sarah's nose before she woke. And they would provoke dreams of edible houses and furniture, reminiscent of Willy Wonka, which Mason had taken her to see in a seedy theater in a bad part of town. So, when she confronted the sticky hot brown leather, pulling her cheek up, it took a moment to realize it wasn't a fresh apple fritter or cream-filled Johnny.

She had spent week's worth of nights sleeping on that couch instead of at home with her mother and stepfather, Tim, who resided in Sarah and Mason's childhood home twenty minutes northeast in the suburbs where Sarah went to high school. Though she didn't have a car, it was easy to find a ride to the city for the weekend. It involved a few key steps. First, she would explain that she was going to be sleeping over at one of her friends' houses, Tina or Bethany. She would plan on having a second one lined up for the next night. Sarah had maintained a group of friends who had continued to routinely have two night sleepovers at alternating houses since they were in grade school. Thus, by the time Sarah was in high school, there was no suspicion on her mother's part. No real trouble had ever resulted, so nothing like check up phone calls or visits would occur. Of this Sarah could be sure. Tim would occasionally shoot Sarah a sideways look from the kitchen table during her explanations to her mother, but she knew that, after beer three or four, all hesitations on his part would recede and turn into his usual brew of self-aggrandizing rants and general horniness.

The second step involved a forty-five minute bus ride avoiding making eye contact with any of the other passengers, two thirds of whose personal hygiene never failed to make Sarah gag. She began spraying perfume on her purse so she could hold it to her chest and sniff it instead of the musty stomach bile and dehydrated excrement smells that wafted to her from unknown locations on the bus. She would find a window seat and watch the tan, stucco-walled four-bedroom houses with half-acre green lawns turn into red brick two-bedroom tenements with small grills chained to railings atop concrete slab front porches. The vibration of the massive engine below heightened the anticipation of adventure and escape. She liked to think that the mood and events of the bus ride were indications for what discoveries and situations awaited throughout the weekend.

Upon exiting the bus at one of any number of Spring Street stops in the university district, she would take a relieving bowel movement at a fast food or laundry mat restroom and then step outside and acknowledge to herself that freedom for forty-eight hours was available. The last step merely involved sliding the spare key to Mason's out from under the stone in the wall of the bar around the corner and plopping herself on the couch in Mason's subterranean studio apartment. It was always late evening by then. Mason was always out late on the weekends, drinking. Mason was a happy drunk. He would stumble in and, with great merriment, celebrate Sarah's arrival. That is, he would do this until it became routine.

Because she babysat for three different Catholic families in the neighborhood, and had since she was twelve, Sarah always had twenty to forty dollars in five-dollar bills neatly folded and resting between her bra and the bottom of her smaller left breast. She usually spent most of the money on movie tickets and bountiful snacks at the Old Tomahawk Theater Plex, which had three screens and showed a mixture of new releases and foreign films, mostly French New Wave, from previous decades. She would often see three or four films in a row. Their latest showings on the weekends were routinely 1:45 a.m. After her initial appraisal that they were quite boring and bland, she grew to appreciate the French films for showing real people talking about things that mattered to them. But she loved the newer big action films most. Steven Spielberg made all of her favorite movies, with the Star Wars trilogy being close behind.

All of the employees who worked at the Old Tomahawk were university students, who were required by Tomahawk policy to dress as any variety of recognizable film characters throughout their shift. It amused Sarah to no end. She had developed a formidable crush on a second year English major named Perry, who dressed as Marty McFly every weekend. They grew to know each other well enough that they developed a back-and-forth of witty remarks and inside jokes. Perry was short, had fragile features, and did look a little bit like Michael J. Fox. He was always smiling and everything he said was funny in a friendly "I'm here to cheer you up, kiddo" way. She was far from her default, sternly isolated and impenetrable "I'm not buying any bullshit from anyone, mister!" persona with him. She got to know him by lying and presenting herself as a freshman studying astronomy.

Sarah had always loved the stars. The cosmos thrilled her as she pondered the possibilities of black holes, at nine years old in her bed, up late on a school night staring through the glass window at the patterns of light sprawling across the night sky, stretching far back to the point of some inevitable question mark. She wondered if the universe ended or if there was always more. Sarah found it hard to picture something outside of everything but even harder to picture nothing outside. She decided the answer was beyond her imagination, and that someone would have to go there, eventually. She loved these scary questions and the passion she felt thinking about them. They kept her up until the whole house had been quiet for hours, except for the insect-like humming of the refrigerator. It made her groggy and distracted at school. The fact that questions like these existed at all times and were serious and frightening, made the present moment, full of all of its own wonders, seem somehow diminished and less deserving. Sarah was shadowed.

The shadow was heavy, and though they wouldn't say they saw it, most people saw it. And this kept many people at arm's length from Sarah. But that was partly because of how she carried herself, almost defeated but unapologetic. When she looked at a person's face, her eyes would first scan their features but then slowly refocus and scale back to recognize the monstrous abstraction present just in front of the face, which required and deserved more attention and reverence than the face itself. Sarah hadn't identified these abstractions with any certainty or specificity. They were vague matters. However, they mattered. Life in Sarah's company rewarded investment elsewhere. Many, like her mother and, secretly, her closest friends, found her arrogant.

Sarah was good at saving money. She rarely found something to spend any of it on. That is until her high school weekends in the city alone at the theater. So, when her friends received their allowances or their pay from part-time jobs, they always gleefully gathered for a shopping visit to Lake Land Center, the mall two blocks from their high school. There they could splurge on magazines like Vogue and Rolling Stone, acquire scarves, jeans, and records, and either watch, in guarded longing, the ever-present carloads of high school jocks parked out front like rows of peacocks and roosters in automobiles, or laugh in disdainful amusement at the skateboarders and wasters who cavorted and mingled in the back alleyway.

The good cheer and natural health of young female enthusiasm motivated Sarah to come along, but she never bought much. Sure, she would notice the nuances of current fashion motifs and those, in particular, which seemed to curry attention from handsome boys. But she never felt compelled to spend her own money on the rampant upkeep because, every August and May, Sarah would receive approximately seventy-five dollars from her mother to apply as she saw fit toward keeping her wardrobe current.

Thus, she took her pleasures more from people watching and making fun of skateboarding. She hated skateboards. They made the worst combinations of scraping, crunching, and clapping sounds. And they ruined perfectly good property. Curbs, sidewalks, benches, brick walls on the corners of the public library, all good places she enjoyed, were corroding and crumbling under the supposed "frolic" of hormonal teenagers with greasy hair and no ambitions. Sarah didn't think it was cool. And the skaters were always getting hurt. Broken ankles, sprained wrists, road burn. Plus, the skater crowd was tightly linked with other crowds presenting wildly abhorrent behaviors. One such group was that of the teenagers that played at "urban art" aka tagging. They carried cans of spray paint around branding surfaces much like a dog running free of its fenced-in yard tends to pee on any large object it encounters. Other groups included druggies, whores, junkies, thieves, and juvies. Sarah wondered why skateboarding was so closely associated with all of the foul ones. These were as close to pirates as the suburbs had.

But soaking in such disdain for too long made her feel aged and cynical, like an old cat lady who betrayed her opportunities in life for any real happiness. So she forced herself to find some appeal in the art of the activity itself. There was an art form in there, in the mechanics and grace of performing the tricks well. It somewhat resembled karate or juggling. There was definitely a feral energy to it that rewarded the kind of body mastery that majestic animals develop. She noticed these muscular faculties most in Jeremy Dillard. Jeremy was tall and thin, with long, curly black locks spewing out from the back of the battered "Ford" ball cap he wore daily. Jeremy took art classes, and Sarah had spotted his observational drawings of local public buildings. They were good.

But this was all before Mason left, and her mom started working nights. Before she was alone with a drunk and fated to lock herself into her bedroom and listen to music or else leave the house. So she left the house and made her way to the theater and to Mason's damp subterranean apartment for the weekends.

And now here she was, two years later at Wicker Home suffering the spit mongrel, the cunning and hyperreligious zealot, Ms. Corin. Here she was, the oldest of the cohort of a dozen children looking to her expectantly as the de facto leader among a tribe of misplaced little humans, defeated and thirsting for any semblance of affection and belonging.

Ms. Corin, in some way, reminded her of those skateboarders, of Jeremy. She had some attributes which Sarah saw were of use. She was a good director, very organized, and even better at reading people's personalities. That was one thing that Sarah never much excelled at: seeing and understanding others' motives, except for Ms. Corin's own. And this lack provided Ms. Corin additional power over her. But Sarah had seen clearly what Ms. Corin was doing with Martin, the way she took him into her favor and leveraged his natural abundance of curiosity. It maddened her but also made her wonder why, in his case, that her maneuverings were shed bare and made absolutely apparent to her. It was perhaps a blessing, so to speak, that it had happened this way because, up until Ms. Corin's favoritism of young Martin, Sarah was unsure of how much her impression of the woman was based on how sinister and manipulative the old spinster was and how much was just her suspicion and general displeasure with Wicker Home.

The incident recurred in some fashion every week or so for several months until most of the children had come to expect it. But it was still infrequent enough that Ms. Corin retained the power of surprise. The atmosphere created an unease that could be sensed by visitors, and Jemmy sensed it too. It also could be smelled, mostly because it made the kids sweat more. Further, bile and acid rose from their nervously churning bellies and evaporated into foul breath. As a whole, they talked less and began to laugh less. Wicker Home became an even more serious place than it had been beforehand.

Martin's growing closeness with Sarah lent a veiled reservation that he employed whenever in Ms. Corin's presence. But she still was quite kind and thoughtful in her treatment of Martin whenever they were alone together. That November, she knitted him a green scarf and bestowed it upon him, seated in her rocker, as one might deliver a carefully crafted or legendary sword to a knight. He wore it and saw kindness in Ms. Corin, and almost giddy glee at his sincere and grateful acceptance. He smiled. These was something Aurelia would have done for him. It felt right.

But he was ashamed to wear it around the others. It was almost a token of his betraying them, his earnest and private associations with the wild monster that kept captive and tortured, spiritually and emotionally, the children of Wicker Home. He resolved to hide it under his mattress, similarly to how Sarah hid Mason's journal. And this divide of allegiance festered within Martin's troubled mind. Sarah noticed the trouble and added it as another notch on the stick of Ms. Corin's transgressions. It angered her perhaps the most of all the many notches that had been added.

"Where would you go if you left?" Martin asked Sarah, stoking his fantasy of running off, once spring arrived, into the midwestern fields at night, befriended only by the moonlight overhead. Sarah smirked sideways at Martin.

"The Palomar Observatory." She watched the confusion grow on Martin's face, wrinkling his brow and lips. "It's in California. That's where the Hale telescope is. It's the largest in the world." She looked upward, as if on cue. The setting sun cast jagged bars across the contours of her face. He was taken with his sister and thought she was something special.

"It has a two-hundred-inch mirror that lets you see pulsars and quasars. You can use infrared to see the heat from the very beginning of our whole universe, the very first moments." Her speech sped up with the heat of her interest. "All of that energy is still here, out there. Oh, and the gas in super massive black holes, you can see that too, and...well, actually...if I could really go anywhere, that's where I would go, inside of a black hole. I need to know what is there." She stared off, smiling to herself.

"You wouldn't go find Mason?" Martin asked sincerely, looking up at her face sticking out in front of her bent knees as she perched on the picnic table like a valiant winged explorer.

The unwelcome heaviness of Martin's question made the outer edges of Sarah's eyes twitch, and she jumped down from her perch, transitioning to the next thing, whatever that would be. It just had to change. Martin felt bad but not regretful. He wanted them to be comrades, but she kept her distance. He felt she kept to much from him. "Sarah, what's going to happen to us?" he asked.

Sarah, turned round to Martin, leaning down so that they were face to face. She held her yellow sweater tight to her neck with her cigarette-free hand and sternly and clearly but softly said, "I think that we've got to get ourselves out of here." Her soft brown eyes were dynamic and reflected the oranges and browns from the setting sun's light. She took one last drag, flicked the burning butt, and grabbed Martin squarely by the shoulders. "If we don't leave here, we'll end up hating ourselves forever. We need to get away from people."

Chapter Eight

"Do you remember Merick Edelston?" the man said, casually, as he switched the rifle to balance on his left arm, the barrel still pointed toward Mr. Scrivener's Neanderthal brow. With his right hand, he pulled out an old black and white photograph from his tight jean pocket and slid it across the dusty table.

"You know very well that I do," Mr. Scrivener said. "How could I ever forget that name?" He picked up the photo by the bottom edge and looked deeply into the face it showed. He leaned back in the chair, shifting all of his weight off of his feet and onto his tightened buttocks. He let out a sigh, and said, "Lord knows I have tried." The image had triggered feelings he had worked hard to quarantine from his consciousness. Now they rose anew to create a pressure that tugged at his throat and pushed behind his eyes.

"We all have," the man said. "There's no use in all that. It has stained us, like a tattoo that will remain until our last day on this giant ball of dust. Lucky for you, that is today. Therefore, honestly, you should be very thankful for my visit." The man pushed his chair back, scraping the unfinished floor, and stood quickly. He gently placed the rifle on the table, still pointed at Mr. Scrivener, turned, and stepped to the window overlooking a sloping meadow. The daylight cast a sharp, warped shadow of the window frame across his face and along the kitchen floor. Mr. Scrivener glared at the man's back in thought.

"Jasper, I…" Mr. Scrivener leaned forward and put the photo on the tabletop. "Jay, the last thing I ever meant to do was harm you. There may be no stopping what you have waiting for me, and I have an idea that there isn't, but you must know that it was never my intention for you to get hurt so badly. I…it was…the job," he said, and looked off into space. He was searching for the words, for sense in the past that he had never found, trying to tease out a reason for reprieve. A long moment filled with silence hung between the gentlemen.

"I saw Maggie a few days ago. She has three sons. She got fat," Jasper said, placing his palms on his hips and leaning backward. He rocked, twisting from side to side, still looking outside.

"It's hard to picture Maggie fat," Scrivener said, relieved at the return of conversation. "But I heard she got married some years ago, didn't realize about the boys, though," Then a nagging darkness crept into his mind. "Wait, what were you doing visiting Maggie?" Jasper turned to reveal his raised left eyebrow. In that instant, Mr. Scrivener knew the answer to his question.

"Those should have been *my* sons," Jasper said. "It's all that I could think of when I saw them. My sons that never were. Perhaps I should have let hers be, but it was all just too much and…I couldn't control myself. Honestly, at this point, it's just another item on a hefty list of things I will have to atone for when my day in the, uh, well, when my day comes." He let out a sigh and turned back to viewing the meadow.

The horror of the statement set in for Mr. Scrivener with a tickling chill that ran down his neck and spine and out through the bottom edges of his fat thighs. He pictured Maggie's face. She had brown hair and freckles. Mocha skin. He remembered peering through the hole, in a door in which the knob had long ago been knocked out of, upon two figures heaving against one another by candlelight. It was Jay, violently humping Maggie atop the large tan cowskin rug next to the desk in Ms. Corin's office, the forbidden room. Ms. Corin had been taking many day trips that summer, which supplied the lovers with a room in the house for privacy. But the house was old and creaked easily. The noise had brought several young voyeurs to that perfect peephole. Then Mr. Scrivener thought about how his own son would be home from school soon, and anger rose within him. He looked at the rifle on the table and made a few estimations. He said, "You shouldn't have done that, Jay. Maggie had nothing to do with it and you know it, let alone her children."

"You all were there, each one of you decided! She decided, the same as you, Roger!" Jasper said, his voice raised sharply as he banged his palms against the edges of the window frame, knocking dust into a wild storm in the rays of sunshine.

Scrivener began to feel his heart beating, as if thudding rocks were slamming against the walls of the small wooden cottage. It kicked like a hysterical piston. His eyes found their way back to the rifle lying on the table. Jasper looked back and took note of Roger's intentions. Their eyes met. Scrivener slowly leaned back into his chair.

Jasper returned his gaze to the outdoors and caught sight of a school bus coming over a far hill. It stopped at the end of the drive, alongside a line of rusted wire fencing. After a moment, a light tan silhouette popped out and moved quickly along the lengthy driveway. The bus resumed its journey. Roger, through his periphery, saw it and felt deep loss. He knew it had to be done before the boy reached the house and became involved. His heart punched in his chest.

Roger flexed his quadriceps tightly and pressed against the creaking floor as he extended his right hand toward the rifle, twisting it perpendicular to his chest. The two men's hands grasped the barrel at the same instant, Roger's just outside of Jasper's, and they pulled with their might, from their back and legs, the opposing forces causing the rifle to rise straight up over the table and wag back and forth. The matter had not been decided with quickness, and now it would come down to strength and grit. Jasper began to shove back and forth, trying to throw Roger off balance and gain an advantage. The two jerked back and forth, grunting, and Roger flung his right knee outward, knocking the table over and into the front wall with a loud crash, which his son, now thirty feet from the house, heard. It alarmed the child. He ceased his forward motion and listened intently. Roger thrust his body upward, overcoming the ability of Jasper's arms, his elbows falling back against the wall, the rifle pushing against his neck.

The barrel pressed into Jasper's windpipe, cutting off the oxygen flow through his throat. Roger had spread his legs into a more sturdy stance with his knees against Jasper's, who, pinned to the wall and without leeway, squirmed mightily. Jasper's face grew red and his eyes narrowed. Roger took note of the desperation in Jasper's face and thrust the barrel harder against Jasper's throat. He knew he had to end this now.

Jasper released his grip from the barrel, its metal thrusting even deeper into his throat, and grabbed Roger's crotch with both hands. He could feel the broad landscape of his penis and testicles, and so he squeezed as hard as he could, feeling the soft lozenges of the testicles collapsing inward. Roger howled out in great agony, a breathy scream, and released his hold on the gun, which fell to the floor. He clenched Jaspers wrists and pried, trying urgently to peel them from their grasp.

Roger, unable to displace Jasper's grip, and with unbearable pangs growing throughout his crotch and rising into his stomach, flung his head forward and cracked Jasper's face with such velocity and surprise that Jasper stutter stepped backward, letting go of Roger's testicles, and haphazardly reached for his eyes. His legs were weak and he struggled with his balance. Momentarily blinded, he held out his hands in a defensive position, palms and forearms bared outward.

Roger, noting the success of the move and negotiating the pain of his ruined testes, hunched down and grabbed the rifle handle. Jasper heard the motion and understood its import. Without being able to see, he dove down with his arms outstretched and landed upon Roger's back, who had cocked the rifle and held it now in a shooter's fashion. Jasper reached over Roger's shoulders and grabbed the barrel, with his legs wrapping around Roger's hips.

Jasper's weight pushed Roger to his right side, Jasper following, attached to his back. Both men were badly winded, breathing in percussive grunts, their lungs straining. The two rolled around on the squeaking floorboards, seeking to discover some final advantage. Jasper noticed tears rolling down his cheeks, some indication of the exasperation of the moment. The adrenaline of the struggle had mostly dissipated with the onset of exhaustion and now only lingered as sick swimming sensations in his abdomen and calves.

Roger, for his part, felt weakness seeping into his shoulders that were keeping tension between Jasper's chest and his own grip on the gun. He began to experience a Jell-O feeling that reminded him of the ending to a flexed arm hang competition. His strength and perseverance were beginning to fail him. Jasper also felt his resolve to keep grasp of the gun barrel fading. The two men, rapt in the middle of a death spar, searched pleadingly, erratically for one final move, one final blow to end the physical pain.

Young Junior Scrivener continued to hear thuds and bangs emitting from his home as he stood in the dirt road, uncertain and afraid to enter. He kept still, and watched the house with wide eyes. The knocking and clanging sounds slowly quieted into dull bumps and then, for a while, noises that sounded almost like a rocking chair gently heaving back and forth, back and forth. But that too eventually dissipated and then there was silence for a while. The sounds of squirrels and birds dominated Junior's ears. And the silence from the house beamed outward, louder than even the birds and the gusts of wind spreading thin layers of dirt over his tennis shoes.

"Pa?" he called out, much too quietly for anyone inside to hear. Nothing. "Pa, are you in there?" he asked more loudly. Nothing. The silence continued, and Junior feared the worst. He remembered what his father had told him: "Some day someone may show up. And they will have come to hurt us for things that happened a long time ago and weren't either of our faults. But it is our lot to resolve it,. Even though we didn't do anything wrong, we are...involved."

The speech had always remained quite vague and his father never laid out any definite facts about who was coming or why. "What happened, Pa?" Junior would ask, routinely, upon each repetition of the anecdotal warning.

"Just be wary, Junior. Remember the steps. What are the steps? Repeat them to me." And Junior would repeat the steps from rote memory, vacillating between believing his father truly didn't know who was coming and was merely being proactive in case of any unforeseen danger, and that he knew a great deal and wouldn't share any of the details.

But now, standing outside his house hearing what was unmistakably a fight concluding inside, and with no answers to the calls to his father, Junior's interest in the mystery disappeared and he was thankful to have remembered the steps. "The steps," he whispered under his breath. In the same moment, one rifle shot rang out, with the wooden guts flying outward from a fist sized hole in the front house wall just below where the kitchen tabletop would be. Junior turned and hopped into full gallop toward the garage, his loose white Adidas tennis shoes flapping loudly against the beaten earth under his stride.

As he approached the garage door, his legs gave out. He found himself lying prone in the dirt. The fall stole his breath. He pulled his hand up from his belly and saw red fluid coating his palm and wrist. He'd been shot. The realization ushered in a wave of pain. He pulled his knees up to his chest and angled onto his right shoulder, a position in which his aunt had once informed him he used to sleep as a young child.

Junior heard the bang of the front door flinging open and slamming against the metal hinge rail. He heard the slow crunching footsteps approaching. He tried to push himself up, but he needed to keep his right arm over the wound, and the pain was too great. He couldn't extend his torso to stand. A metallic flavor flushed over his tongue. The bullet had punctured his abdomen and blood spilled out so rapidly through his fingers that he started to panic. The unseen foe approached, presumably to finish the bullet's task.

"Please, no...Please, just st—just stop. Stop." It occurred to him that he may have been hit by the shot accidentally, the ultimate path of the bullet unknown inside the house. "Dad?" he said with a momentary surge of hopeful foolishness. The footsteps continued their pace, without response. That hope quickly died. The crunch of each step grew louder and more pronounced until they stopped next to Junior's head. A leather boot slid under his torso, lifted his unwounded side, and tipped Junior over onto his back.

Lying supine, Junior squinted to see the silhouette hovering over him. The glare from the sun was blocked by the shoulders of the stranger enough for Junior to make out two green eyes. Junior's tongue communicated the metallic taste again, this time more severe. The green-eyed man produced a long black object and pointed it at Junior's head. He looked into the small circular tube and then back into the green eyes as fire loudly expelled from the end of the tube.

Jasper had two pounds of raw sirloin wrapped tightly in wax deli paper. It sat on the desk next to the eleven-inch television screen, which currently displayed images of skinny female hands rubbing and pointing to a vegetable dicing mechanism that was available for purchase in five different colors. The fingers of the female hands were well tanned but wrinkled, and underneath the orange glow was a tangle of blue lines. Jasper took notice of this intently. It irked him so that the creators of the Multi-Tiered Dice-O-Deer! three-in-one dicing mechanism infomercial had found it acceptable to use an old woman's hands in the close up shots of the product.

It reminded him of old person smells. Like harsh and somehow spicy aftershave, which was almost always too strong. And floral scents for the females that bordered on mildewy. And coffee breath that had accumulated its severity through coffee drinking rituals spanning five, six, seven decades, and then some dull crotch smell that was sulfuric. But, Jasper couldn't bring himself to watch either *Three's Company* or *Magnum P.I.* reruns. So his steel Airstream travel trailer was filled with flashes of blues and oranges from the absurdly inhuman planes of the kitchen in the background of the infomercial. Jasper was waiting to see if the elderly hands disappeared before he began.

They didn't. So it would be a frustrating session. He placed his glass of milk next to the sirloin and a container of Jeb's Cajun Spices. He unbuckled his jeans and pulled them and his cotton speedos down to his ankles. The plastic of the chair was cold on his rump. He spit into his right hand grabbed his flaccid penis. He began stroking savagely hard, almost angry at it for existing, for requiring him to service it in this manner that always ended in lonely shame. His penis filled with blood, and the friction began to supply a surge of pleasure with each stroke.

He did his best to avoid looking at the hands on the TV but, in the end, failed. And so he imagined some aged wealthy mistress whose body had retained its youthfulness. What he imagined was essentially a twenty-year-old with the head and hands of an old woman. And so he turned his focus from those to the breasts and the curves of the buttocks. The pleasure heightened and spiked. He quickly nabbed the Kleenex from the desktop behind him. Semen shot out and formed pool on the tissue. His mind went blank for a moment, and when he returned, he felt healthy and fresh. Then the shame came.

Jasper tossed the tissue into the open brown paper bag that lay at the foot of the desk and served as his trash receptacle. With the shame had come hunger, which he had avoided until he could finish his ritual. He tore open the deli package and clumsily splayed out all of the thinly sliced morsels of red steak. He messily sprinkled Cajun spice all over the pieces, most of it landing on the bare desk in between the steaks. Then he chewed the raw meat, one piece at a time. Most were too large to swallow in one piece, so he grabbed an end with his front teeth and pulled the other end, ripping the piece in half like a feral cat might. Jasper thought about all of the bacteria that he could be ingesting only for the briefest of moments.

Once finished, he blew the remaining spices off of the desk. Red clouds of pepper, salt, and some proprietary mix of tangy flavor erupted and slowly fell down behind the desk and into the lower cracks and crevices of the trailer to join the remnants of thousands of other midnight meals that were consumed equally savagely by a heavily intoxicated Jasper. He crushed the deli paper into a tight ball and tossed it into the paper bag. Some blood stained the folded rim of the bag.

The ceiling fan pleased him as he lay on his back on the bed, watching the infomercial and sipping on his bourbon. The paper had forecasted rain for the next few days. That meant he would, for the most part, be confined to his trailer. This brought dread. He didn't like his television, and he was running low on money. He still had a lot of work to do. There were still six names. He would run out of cash in two nights if he continued to visit the Tustler and see Providence. And he surely would visit, either tomorrow night or the next. He had to space out his shame. And the three channels that he got on his eleven-inch TV rarely provided adequate visual stimuli for the ritual. So he would likely need enough cash to get his room in the back of the Tustler. Providence worked seven to two on Wednesdays.

He had thought about bringing her back to his trailer when she was off. But that would have required cleaning. And the semifilthy state of his trailer was one of the enjoyable indulgences he allowed himself. But it would surely scare off Providence. Besides he had a good routine going with her. If he asked her, and she declined an outside meeting, he would likely have damaged their professional relationship and he'd have to find a new club. That would be a major loss for Jasper. He had become very familiar with the Tustler. And the staff there were accustomed to him, to his tics and preferences. He had broken the place in and could now enter and acquire precisely what he sought in a very competent manner. Without conversation or questions. But there were still six names. And he would soon need more cash.

The infomercial ended, and with it the elderly hands. Now there was a late-night call-in show for people with relationship problems. Jasper had seen it before. It was sadly entertaining. Average lonely people with defeats numerous and great would call in and use generically familiar archetypes of situations to help come to terms with the dread of knowing that their fantasies had died and all of life's victories were growing smaller by the day. But life went on and one must still put the coffee on, as someone once told Jasper. Or he overheard it. He couldn't remember. Either way, there were six more names and he would soon need more cash.

* * *

Retta was dismayed. It usually started and ended with her commute. Though she had a reliable car, she took the public buses to and from school. A monthly pass was less than a parking permit, especially when gas was taken into consideration. But she also preferred the idea of utilizing public transit, of leaving the door with nothing but her person. Doing so felt somehow adventurous. It had designs of mystery, the unknowable. She would be forced to speak with strangers, to overhear unusual conversations, and perhaps experience appealing chance encounters.

But this also meant she would have to be among humans. Most humans were nasty. Everyone seemed so mean and cynical to her, so sure that the rest were dumber and baser than themselves. She imagined them smirking quietly, inwardly, hoping to death that there was worth to their own experiences. And yet, she thought the same thing in her own way. It was disheartening to Retta that she was guilty of all that she witnessed. So she justified the routine by focusing on the unknowable, that possibility that some grand surprise was just about to occur. Retta longed to be surprised.

And so, with such pregnant expectation, Retta was constantly disappointed. This, she would never admit to anyone, barely acknowledging it to herself. And the longer the disappointments accumulated, the clearer it became how vapid and unformed the hope for the extraordinary was. She would perform thought experiments. She would imagine meeting a wealthy stranger who needed her for a secret job. But then she'd think that the job would probably be disappointing. And the wealthy person might be too. No answer pleased her once it was imagined.

Retta would then picture her father taking a job in a different city, and thus Fox had to go with him. So then it was just her in Trams, in her own apartment, without an autistic brother to take care of. Sure, the feeling of adventure somewhat lingered, but once the scenario was envisioned, the real weight of desire was lost. And this occurred with any scenario, any turn of events that she put in her head. Once it was nailed down, poof, the longing disappeared and it was only a matter of analyzing the pros and cons in comparison to her current situation.

In this manner, Retta came to see that the unknowability of the thing was its greatest appeal. And, as such, anything would initially and automatically be a let down per se. It was like with horror flicks. All growing up, Retta loved horror films throughout the first and second acts, before the reveal of the ghosts or monsters occurred. The wondering about it was so rewarding, it stoked so much interest within her. The actual visual reveal in the third act always fell short. She had stopped watching horror films.

That Monday evening, Retta sat at the dining room table with an expanse of opened and unfolded bills fanned out in a large semicircle in front of her. She hunched over them, shoulders slumping with stress. Fox sat Indian style in front of the television set at the adjacent end of the dimly lit living room. He pecked at the screen with his pointer fingers and made bird noises. "Caauuck!" "Cewwaoook!" The sounds drilled into Retta's head as she tried to organize the bills by due date, and it tested her sworn patience for her younger brother's condition.

Remy was visible through the window over the kitchen sink, a fresh cloud of cigarette smoke hovering over his head. Just months ago, Retta would have reached out to him for help with scheduling the payments and balancing the checkbook. But now she had access to the online savings and banking account, and made all of the payments online. She had set up extended plans for the cellphones, gas, her nursing class payments, and Fox's Helping Hands daycare.

The clock by the fireplace ticked away. It was only ever noticeable as she sat with the bills. She recalled her parents sitting over bills. Now it was her turn, and she felt that perhaps it came too early. But she was old enough. But she was also generally responsible for keeping track of and feeding Fox. And she had to study for her classes, and the garage wasn't making as much money as it used to.

And the back porch was wobbling when you walked on it, and it was getting worse and worse. And it seemed dangerous. And Remy stomped over it every time he went out back.

Retta didn't even know if she wanted to be a nurse anesthetist anymore. Sometimes she did, but she had too many moods, and they were too powerful. They overshadowed her thoughts and the room right in front of her until they became difficult to manage. The bike rides had helped. The record collection helped. And it had been very nice hanging out with Pollock. But the fact remained that her life, for the most part, was in an unsustainable state. With the mortgage, the school expenses, the credit card interest, healthcare, food, and utilities, they, as a household, were taking in less than what they needed and subsisting by putting off payments, paying of one credit card with another. Likely, she was handling the finances in a less than prudent manner but only because there wasn't time to sit down and Retta couldn't really get Remy to sit down and talk it out. It was always on to class, to Fox's therapy, to the garage, the grocery store, back.

And she had felt wrong for taking time to spend with Pollock. She felt wrong for going on long bike rides. And she felt wrong for feeling sorry for herself and thinking, under these circumstances, she might as well have been a single mother of an autistic child. Retta bent her neck left to right and popped her vertebrae. This was a customary response to stress, one which she had done for years. It somehow convinced her something had been done about the situation. But the Visa bill still wasn't paid.

She had texted Pollock twice without response. It had been all morning, afternoon, and now evening. She didn't want to appear needy, so she decided not to pursue conversation further until at least tomorrow, Tuesday. But his lack of a reply ticked her off. That anger added to her stress. She felt entitled to a response from him. After what they had come across the previous evening, it seemed odd that Pollock's excited fervor had dissipated. She hoped that he just had work to catch up on, like her, and left it at that, switching out of messages and into the Trams Gas online payment portal.

"Drink your tea, dr-i-i-i-i-nk your tea! That's what the eastern towhee says, Retta, drink your tea!" Fox screamed from the television set, fingers and eyes still on the screen, but now he was doing short jerking squats up and down in excitement. "Squeeesh, squeeesh!" And the clock ticked. And Retta could hear Remy's steel toed boots clonking on the rotting back porch. And, though she didn't realize it, she had been shaking her right leg up and down, quickly vibrating the dining room chair underneath her as she sat with the semicircle of bills fanned out on the table.

Retta began again to fantasize about getting out of Trams. Starting over somewhere new. Australia was where she thought to go. It was a preposterously childish notion. She had no idea about which nursing degrees they recognized or whether there were additional certifications necessary, and anyway, she would have to finish her program first. Then there were the financial considerations. She wondered how much a plane ticket to Australia cost and imagined it was more than a thousand dollars. Retta only had $2,200 in her bank account. She had an credit card with a credit limit of $3,500 and a balance of $3,209. She'd have to pick a city, find an apartment, and decide whether to interview first or arrive and plan to be financially independent until she found a job. Maybe she would have to work at a service industry job until she got situated.

All of this was preliminary and far overshadowed by the moral and familial considerations. Once again she realized that she could never leave Remy and Fox. The house would fall apart, literally and otherwise. If Retta wasn't around, there would have to be a replacement to fulfill all of the duties for which she was responsible, bill paying being one. But Remy and Fox would both surely feel abandoned. And as little as Remy was hanging on, her departure would likely be crushing. Caretakers, babysitters, or who knows who would inevitably raise Fox. Retta didn't want to think about the scary consequences of such a scenario.

But as much as she blurred out the darkest realities and turned back to her perpetual mood of fortitude in surrender, she knew that she had already admitted to herself that leaving, getting far away and starting fresh, was what she desired most of all. It occurred to her that maybe her happy fantasy was blurred as well. She wondered if she would find the same dissatisfactions and shortcomings in Australia and end up no better off. She felt caged, trapped and cornered. Events had conspired to paralyze her and she felt gloomy and antsy. "Drink your tea," Fox carried on. The clock ticked. Remy's boots shuffled and clomped. Retta refocused her sight on the span of opened bills fanned out on the table. "Drink your tea!"

It was beyond her why she had decided on Australia. But she had been thinking of it almost daily for months, maybe even past year or two. It occurred to her that perhaps it was much better that she remained in Trams for other reasons. The ocean, a major point of appeal there, is filled with some of the world's most scary creatures. Octopi, jellyfish, and sea cucumbers, not to mention deadly fish and sharks. She recalled a nature documentary creating a taxonomy of all the animals there that can cause a horrible death. It hadn't phased her until now, for some reason.

There were no poisonous creatures in Trams other than some spider species, and probably one or two snakes. But they weren't prevalent and they especially weren't lying in wait along her routine path. Retta wasn't sure if she would go into the ocean that often if she lived in Australia. She wondered if it was something Australian's actually did, and whether the ocean became something very dull and pedestrian when it was always nearby, always available. She thought of Pollock and wondered if the same thing happens in romantic relationships.

She did some fanciful and speculative fast-forwarding on their involvement, their possible future together, and pictured them playing intramural sports, picnicking, riding bikes, and taking road trips. There were long morning breakfasts in bed on sunny Sundays, bonfires, concerts, and book reading while lying over one another. Then the events evolved into a different kind of montage. Agitated arguments about miniscule matters, dissipation of sex drives, increases in weight, growing desires to be intimate with strangers, a blossoming awareness that the longer she was with Pollock, the more apparent the inevitable and cruel fact that she would always be alone and unhappy became. The romance would fade, and Pollock would become pedestrian and dull.

"Drink yourrr teeea!" Fox repeated with even more gusto, squatting up and down and now smacking the screen with his flat palms. "Drink…your…tea!" The ticking of the clock continued. Remy's boots scuffled about. Retta closed her eyes and took a deep breath. She had lost all resolve to tackle the bills. "Not today," she whispered.

* * *

The map sat on his lap. Jasper thought about the uncertainty that waited for him after the last six names on the list. This looming uncertainty scared him shitless. He couldn't see what it was, his life—*a* life. He had never had a life but merely lived on the periphery of a mission that had been bestowed upon him when he was younger than he could remember. "You're a Narduccian!" as his father used to tell him, even when he was four years old. He was still a Narduccian. Jasper Narducci. "Narrr-dooch-eee," as the young librarian, Janessa, in Urxil Library always sounded out, flirtatiously. She pronounced it with smooth seduction, rolling the "r," every time Jasper came in. Jasper visited the library nearly daily for a span of eight months. And he was quite taken with Janessa. She was plain but had the eyes of trouble. And she posed herself leaning on her elbows against the counter. It was girlish, innocent, and contradicted her eyes. For Jasper, it was an advertisement billboard.

But Jasper was there for something far too important, sacred even. And so he never fully engaged with this willing girl and worthy potential conquest. He would put her out of his mind the best that he could and focus on his studies. But, her image, and her posture in particular, would seep back into his thoughts and cover over any serious thinking. So he often rushed into the third-floor restroom to jerk off as quickly as possible while holding his breath in a toilet stall.

Unfortunately, the force that sashayed her image into his mind was quite frequent and mighty. Thus, he was going to the bathroom every forty-five minutes or so. And he was also furiously scrubbing his hands clean with generic orange detergent afterward. The process resulted in quite tortured, brittle skin on his hands and penis. In fact, he often would develop sores on his penis that would re-open upon subsequent thrashings and therefore fester sometimes for several weeks in continually changing states of healing. This never bothered Jasper. He viewed it as a necessary consequence. It was necessary for him to do his work. He never tried to figure out a more physically forgiving way of going about it. He just sidelined the pain and the itching.

It had seemed strange that Jasper's father had always said "Narduccians" instead of "Narduccis." But he had not seen his father since he was young. And so he never had the opportunity to question him about its significance. It had also occurred to him that he was misremembering what his father had said. Either way, Jasper now had a soft spot for the term "Narduccian." It was a sort of true name for him, despite what his birth certificate or any other state or federal ID may indicate. He was a Narduccian, like his father.

The future used to exist. He could see it. But then he spent eight months researching and reading on the third floor of Urxil Library. The research stint was prompted by what Jasper had hazily identified as a mental break from his previous life. And now he couldn't see the future, or the future that he had seen before. And so he functioned on the premise that he was living a crisis and would end upon its resolution. He would have to break again and forget this. That's what he was afraid of, that he knew he couldn't live with this. So either his life would have to end or there was no future.

The fact that he recognized his inability to live with what he was doing brought him some excitement, for it meant he might be beyond his task. And if he was, then maybe it meant that he wasn't fully committed in the first place. Maybe that signaled a need for more commitment, that he hadn't fully broken. And that idea was very scary to Jasper because, if his prior break hadn't fully shut everything out, then perhaps neither would his next one. He feared all of this unimaginably brutal killing might seep through the next break and muddy the next chapter.

If that were possible, then Jasper knew that *this* would have to be the last chapter of his. There would be no future. And so the fear that came from this understanding urged him to put all of himself into his task. He needed to quit the bourbon and needed to stop drinking clear and stop visiting The Tustler. He wondered why he had been sharing his feelings with Providence. That girl washed off semen from fifteen other subhumans with calamitous consciences who came in to spin some tale of inner goodness and dignity, so they could feel just clean enough to be looked at as potentially desirable. Or, at least that was what Jasper did.

With his tanned middle finger, he traced the black line of a highway along the folded rectangle of map. It led to a red line, a state road, which led to a blue line, a county road. His finger continued along the county road until it came to an orange dotted line. He tapped his finger on that orange dotted line. Next to it read, "Brack River." His finger tapped thrice more, quickly. That bend in the river was a mile and a half from Wicker Home. He decided to set up there.

And with that, he folded the rectangle into another smaller rectangle and slipped the map between the passenger sun visor and truck ceiling. Light raindrops pinged on the rooftop. Jasper returned his attention to the gas station across the street. He was curious if the rain would continue through the night. He liked that idea. If it grew a little stronger, the rain would potentially mask the sounds of him breaking in. His stomach was bothering him again, but he was trying his best to ignore it.

He had botched his last attempt because he had drunk too much Star Bourbon beforehand. Though, in his defense, the back door of the last gas station had very weak hinges that snapped when he pried it open, leaving the heavy metal door to loudly crash into the corner of a dumpster. There it teetered for a moment before crashing onto the uneven concrete with a deafening clap. Perhaps if he hadn't been drinking bourbon, his reaction time would have been just good enough to catch the door and gently lean it against the back wall. Either way, it caused him to abandon the burglary altogether, and that was why he was currently low on cash. Again, he thought about quitting the bourbon.

This case had been much more intricate, and it involved much less bourbon. He had only had three or four swigs since breakfast, which, in fairness, was well past 2:00 p.m. because of the amount of bourbon consumed the previous evening. But he wasn't going to enter that evening. He thought it was better to wait and return after the name was off of the list. Then he could ride off of the momentum of the job and the adrenaline would keep his senses clear and alert. There would be no need for bourbon until after the name and the grab. And his stomach would be eased. After that, he planned to visit Providence. But then he remembered he'd decided he was done with that.

He questioned whether this plan was that grand after all, since the last name had gone so badly. The last name had been so personal for Jasper. There were a few moments when he thought that it would not end in his favor. There were a few blurry moments when he said his goodbyes. He couldn't have that again. And then there was the kid. He told himself he had to do it. The kid might have glimpsed him. He would have run off and described him and what had happened. Then detectives would be looking for a murderer. Jasper thought it would have been even worse if the boy was left to plot vengeance on him.

But the kid was the first one who was not on the list. It wasn't surprising at all to Jasper. Each name had gone worse than the previous. Each high of adrenaline and sharp sense of ultimate duty being fulfilled grew greater in intensity, as did the let down and resulting phase of aimless drunkenness. And then he would be compelled to make a veiled confession to Providence, the stripper. He disgusted himself. Each bottom was getting longer, each bottle of bourbon disappearing faster than the last. He was literally crash-landing into his trailer. Chips of the fiberglass entryway were missing where he had miscalculated his approach. He was too heartsick to even cook his meals. "I'll just fuckin' eat 'em raw," he would slur, not caring that he must look like a savage monster, willing to play the role as he sloppily stroked his scabbed dick with spit, alone in his trailer, in between his monstrosities.

That wasn't going to happen anymore. The drinking was going to lessen. The focus was going to increase. These last six names would go like the first few. Jasper was sure of this because he had come to terms with the task. He was over his sullen sulking. He had been hardened enough now, beaten himself enough now. He had admitted that this was the last chapter. He couldn't let these things squeak through. His identity couldn't swing back and forth between such contradictory judgments. He needed unity of purpose, and had, this day, resolved to recommit to the task. "My name is Jasper Narducci and I am a Narduccian!" he yelled. The statement provoked flames within him that rose and felt good. His flexed arms felt strong. He repeated, louder, "I am Jasper Narducci and I am the last Narduccian!"

The old truck engine rumbled and the seat vibrated underneath him. He squeezed the metal steering wheel and spotted himself in the rear view mirror. His skin was tan and leathery. The layer of soft dirt covering his cheeks was streaked by trails of tears. "What a hysterical bitch," Jasper said. And he was happy that he was killing that person in the mirror.

Chapter Nine

Jemmy stood at the head of the breakfast table in the house and announced to all of the Wicker Home residents that Ms. Corin's son was going to pay them a visit and would be staying with them for a few weeks. Sarah's and Martin's eyes met as this news was delivered. The general thought, not only among Sarah and Martin but among most in Wicker Home, was that the arrival of young Corin would provide a break from the menacing midnight sermons that had been terrorizing the children the past few weeks.

Sarah's thinking went a little further, however. She wondered what would happen if her son took after her. The thought made the fuzz on her back stand up. And with the recent downward turn of her luck, she thought the odds favored just this scenario. She pulled on her Marlboro at the steps after breakfast. She had sour guts. It was going to be a cold time. She didn't like it. And she was tired of having these sorts of things thrown upon her. Sarah pinched her fingernails until they flushed white, highlighting the filth just under the nail tips.

Young Dale Corin had spent the first few days of his stay at Wicker Home relatively quietly, inhabiting the periphery, under secret scrutiny of the inhabitants. He would sit, hunched at the teachers' breakfast table most of the day, reading from various piles of manila folders. Jemmy would occasionally wait on him with tea or a sandwich. He would slowly and loudly push them aside with the back of his hand upon finishing. Martin would peek through the dining room window at recess to spy on him.

He slept in the guest bedroom upstairs in the house, across the hall from Jemmy. His shy ways made the children curious but reassured. Ms. Corin did in fact transfer her energies to Dale, completely abandoning her late night ritual, to the great relief of all. She was knitting him a sweater. They took long walks around the property, talking, in the evenings. Sarah would watch them from her usual front step location or from within the grove of plums. And it occurred to her that perhaps she had been wrong in her fear. But she kept her suspicions intact, however diluted by the respite from Ms. Corin's harangues.

The children were sleeping better since Dale's arrival. The hall was the quietest it had been since Martin's time there. The rest was well received, and everyone's mood picked up a bit. The whole crew was almost chipper. Drayton smiled a few times. Miles stopped sneaking into Martin's bed, allowing his ribs, bruised from the six-year-old's clenching fists, to begin to heal. But after a few days of peace and recuperation, Sarah felt her uneasiness return and explained it to Martin while the two of them watched the Corins traverse the property boundaries.

"Kiddo, I think we're going to have to leave before Dale does," Sarah said with a puff.

"Wait, why are you saying that?" Martin asked.

Sarah crookedly grinned. "Look how happy she is now, how wrapped up with him. He's keeping her preoccupied." She pointed with her cigarette hand.

Martin took note of Ms. Corin's increased hand gestures and laughter as she strolled gaily, hand over arm, with her son. It seemed picturesque, like a commercial selling candy lozenges. "But won't it be better with her...happy?" he asked.

"He's going to leave. She won't be happy anymore. And then what happens? It'll be just her and us, again. Think about it."

"Why do you think she does it?" Martin asked.

"She does it because she hates herself…and I don't even think…" Sarah tossed her butt. "Hasn't anything terrible happened to you? I mean you're here right? I know about your mom. I know about that—" She stopped herself, her eyes widening with fear, wondering if she had gone too far. Martin's own eyes got big, then his head and shoulders drooped. "Look Martin, Ms. Corin was clearly promised something she didn't get, or someone hurt her very badly. There is something chewing into her. She's been abused or something, okay?" She slid another Marlboro from the crumpled soft pack in her jean pocket and lit it. "And I think she thought she could pour herself into the Bible and do right by unfortunate children, and if she did, then maybe that weight, that chewing feeling, would go away. But I don't think it ever did for her. So she's putting it on us now. Now it's our weight. Claws in our sides…" She sat herself back down on the step and curled her back, hunching like a cat. Martin thought that Sarah liked to impress people by throwing realizations she only just made that moment in another's face as if they should have realized it themselves ages ago.

"That's not fair. We've never done anything to her," he said, more to himself, as a familiar disgust toward unfair people arose inside him.

"Yeah, well these things don't travel in straight lines," Sarah said. "They're not thought out. I guess they just reach out and, you know kind of touch whatever is around."

Martin pictured an inexperienced blind man holding his hands out, searching for something to hold onto and guide him along. "But she's been running Wicker for decades." He was thinking aloud, spiraling toward some unseen point.

"And?"

"And, first, how long ago did this mysterious bad deed occur? Second, why is it just getting worse now?"

Sarah let out a crooked smirk, one that Martin had begun to identify as her signal of resignation. She said, "I don't think wounds like these ever go away.

And for your second part...I guess you just had bad timing, kid. The dams are finally splitting open."

Martin thought again about Aurelia. The events following her death and funeral had sped by like a film reel with too few frames per second, so that they seemed like disjointed punches forward, with blank spaces between. Policemen. A politician's wife. Office overhead lights. Green metal tables with yellow paperwork. Country drive. Light speed segments of confusion, and then he had arrived here. Dragged here, really. Then Ms. Corin. Knitting, with her evil, sexual grin. He had been given no justice. It hadn't even occurred to him that he wanted it until now. Strings pulled taught his back and cheeks and rattled clunkily against the base of his skull. Anger had arrived, and it was pointed toward Ms. Corin.

"I'm not entirely sure where we could go," Sarah said. "We'd have to take the car. Corin keeps the keys on a hook atop the staircase. She'd have to be asleep. So would Jemmy; she always pays attention when you return from the market. We'd have to sneak in at night. Car in neutral, push it down the drive, quietly. I'm sure she'll contact the police. We'll have to ditch the car before long, before wake up call. Hidden. They can't find it, if they do, they'll have our trail laid out. Probably in the woods." Sarah punctuating each step with a forward jab of the Marlboro, like dabbing the imaginary painting of her scheme.

Martin painted his own version as he followed along in his mind's eye, finding the plan well thought through and a proper vehicle through which to exact the only kind of revenge available to him. "Okay, but what then?" Martin asked.

"Good, kid. I would suggest we just camp for a few nights, but I don't think that is smart. First, there isn't really any camping gear around here. It's too cold to just sleep outside. Ideally we should leave in the spring, but there's no time. Second, we need to keep moving. Even with the car hidden, they'll eventually find it, and then it will all be about how big of a radius they are searching."

"We could sleep in the car and hide it in a different spot each day."

"No, I thought about that and it's too risky. I mean, maybe if we drove at night and hide the car during the day. But still, driving at night, just passing a cop or stopping for gas, we'll stand out. We'll get caught." She took a long drag and closed her eyes tightly. "Mrs. Corin never lets me get away, I don't know what's around. If there were a building, a barn, something where we could rest. But we'd need a bunch of them. Ahhh…that's not realistic. It makes the most sense to steal another car. A car that isn't used often, or even seen." She opened her eyes and took another long drag of smoke and exhaled. "When she took you along on her Amish shopping trips…Can you think of anything, kid?"

Martin looked down and imagined the route they had driven. He couldn't picture any buildings. Just fields, one small three-intersection town and then the Amish village. "I don't know. There was a town. There might be something there, but I don't know…I mean, they were mostly homes and businesses. Maybe a farmhouse at one point in the distance, I really don't remember. It's been a while ago since I last went." He felt he was failing to carry his own weight, beginning to think that perhaps they were only dreaming, and the realities of the situation were too heavy and mature for them to actually escape. He wondered if maybe it was just smarter to wait Ms. Corin out and then live his life once he was released from Wicker Home.

Sarah bobbed her head in short nods of agreement, indicating to Martin that she had suspected he did not have any useful information to contribute in the first place. She took another extended drag, sucking the cigarette down to the filter, and exhaled with an impressive plume of smoke. It floated and sagged around Martin's head. "Where do you get your cigarettes?" he asked before realizing how smart the question truly was. Sarah's eyes lit up as she stood and flicked her butt on the lawn in front of the steps.

She began muttering to herself, piecing together a picture that was still indistinct, its pieces still blurry and slippery in her mind. "Boyfriend in Buscarawas.

Loading the trucks…loading the trucks!" She stopped talking completely and stood looking downward, crossing her arms tightly over her chest. Martin wondered if her reaction was good or bad.

Chapter Ten

Simon wore a trimmed and oiled beard of shiny red hair. His pale skin always had a sweaty sheen. Simon was always moving very briskly, with an almost feminine gait. His hips waggled. Regardless of this, he commanded respect. Bay 4 listened to everything he had to say and followed his instructions with solemn reverence. Simon was their leader. And from behind eyes marked by swirls of blue and yellow, he spoke with a grave integrity that could be heard in the timbre and inflection of his voice. And just beyond every command he gave, was an honest and friendly plea to be better. That was what inspired his followers: that he made them better. Faster, stronger, smarter, more accountable to one another, and in the end, wealthier. Wealthier in wages and in glory.

Bay 4 had, for two years, been the most efficient of twenty-eight bays in the Hoag distribution hub of the gigantic Voldovsky complex. This trend began on Simon's second day as Bay 4 manager. And since then, word had spread far and wide, so that truck drivers, grocery store stockers, logistics managers, directors, and even company presidents throughout the region knew that if they had a large cargo, or an especially delicate or time sensitive load, going through Hoag distribution hub, then they needed it to be processed through Bay 4. "Simon at four," the drivers would say in defiance at being directed to a different bay. They would sometimes wait for three hours to be next through Bay 4. The time difference would still be in their favor.

Such reputation came with job offers from bigger and better places almost weekly. More money, more time off, stock options, larger teams under his control, a day shift. Every member of Simon's team knew this. And yet, because Simon had rejected them all to remain in the glory of Bay 4, doing so just added to the respect that he commanded and thus contributed to even more glory. And though the term "glory" had originally been thrown out with humorous irony on Simon's second day on the job, it had come to be a quite accurate description of what the boys of Bay 4 held. They were a group of ruffian outcasts that came together under the need for fanatical ideology and physical exertion. And all of them were night owls and drunkards. Simon, smiling, called them fantastic bastards.

Jemmy's boyfriend, Brass Knee, worked in Bay 4. He was second in command under Simon. "Second at four," as they called him, all these drunken loaders, in unison, at roll call at 1:00 a.m. when their shift began. Brass Knee was a six-foot-seven bundle of muscle and fat that barely fit through standard doorways. He had dark, smoky eyes and a frizzy ponytail that fell to his waist. Simply because of his sheer size, no one ever questioned or contradicted Brass Knee. That would be foolish as hell. But the fact that all eighteen of the men in Bay 4 were always inebriated made this a little surprising, but Brass Knee was that physically imposing.

In addition to his intimidating stature, Brass Knee was also a mental marvel of three- and four-dimensional reasoning. "His test scores are off the chart," was an idiom often tossed around when explaining this to one of those few fellas who didn't already know. Brass Knee was the man on the floor who interacted with each loader and unloader. So he often interrupted the progress to demonstrate quicker and more proper methods of going about the work. There were competitions during down time to rank the order of the loaders by speed.

The closest anyone had ever come to beating Brass Knee in these competitions was Derek Shelby. He loaded 112 packages compared to the 267 total packages Brass Knee loaded within the same time. That's how fast Brass Knee was. He was an incredible combination of nimble mind and physical brute. His body never failed to deliver the needs of his thoughts, which in their foresight and certitude always found the best arrangements. Watching Brass Knee function was the closest thing to pornography in the warehouse. Except in the upper bay men's room where there were actual pornography magazines. Usually African American females in the Sahara. Loin clothes, et cetera.

Brass Knee was a member of Mensa. His IQ was 194. This was not a rumor. His Mensa membership card was pinned to the particleboard above the bleachers in Bay 4 where roll was taken and announcements were given. There were rumors, though. Mostly because Brass Knee so rarely spoke, and, when he did, it was usually to chide, punish, or otherwise correct. Loading methods, grammar, and general factual knowledge. He was constantly muttering under his breath, though. Usually general misanthropic, cynical remarks that the others wouldn't want to consider even if they could hear them and follow their meaning.

The main rumors, alas, the ones with most intrigue and gossip staying power, concerned Brass Knee's past, his origins, his creation, if you will. Many had heard that he was experimented on as a child, "like in a sealed-off room in some underground government hospital in Arizona." Another involved a Native American massacre. Brass Knee was Lakota. He had briefly been enrolled in university on dual scholarships. One was because of his Native American heritage and the other was from his flute playing. But the rumor claimed that he had been living on a Lakota reservation with his entire extended family, when a band of white supremacist thugs raided and murdered his family as a means of intimidating the rest of the reservation tenants to transfer tribe lands to a powerful real estate developer from Wisconsin who wanted to make an amusement park. According to others, Brass Knee was the one who did the murdering on behalf of the developer. The details of the rumors were in constant flux, but the common thread was always that he survived and caused great tragedy at an extremely young age, was brilliant, and was a truly talented flute player.

All the "boys," as they called each other, would meet at the beginning of their shift on the grease-speckled steel bleacher that sat cockeyed in front of the conveyor belt. The belt in each bay was where specialty or heavy items would be placed for those that were assigned to handle such cargo. Brass Knee handled this for Bay 4. Each man would saunter in with a bottle, remnants of a sixer, or expectations of gratuity based upon some vague memory of a previous trade. Tiesto, a small African American with a large tattoo of a hen fucking Jesus doggy style on his upper arm, would switch on the Hitachi radio and cassette player. It hung from a large, clumsily struck nail, poking out from a corner of the two-by-four frame the announcements board. The same that featured Brass Knee's Mensa card. Collective musical tastes had settled on the Rolling Stones, David Bowie, Johnny Cash, Al Green, and occasionally *Big Band Hits of the 1930s*.

Conversation would hop along, mostly regarding women and various predictable and competitive tales accompanied by descriptions of angles, hand motions, and sounds. Some of the boys would stretch, others would begin drinking immediately, the idea being that the inebriation was motivational. Conversation and stretching would last for ten to fifteen minutes on average until Brass Knee spotted Simon leaving the receiving office a few hundred feet down the corridor that lined all of the receiving bays. He would stomp his feet twice loudly on the bleacher row beneath him and shout out, "Roll!"

The boys would all assemble into an orderly array on the bleacher that was never identical but never too different. Simon would hop over the belt, and look each man in the eyes. Roll was done silently in this manner. Then he would pace back and forth a little, nervously tapping his clipboard on the side of his tan mesh trousers. With silence, all of the boys would conjure up their inspiration in anticipation of Simon's words. It was like a group of dogs salivating to the bell before eating. Then it would come. Simon would fling the clipboard hard, in the gesture of a Frisbee throw. It would catch a metal beam some feet away and fall to the bay floor.

"Boys I know you've been disappointed. *I've* been disappointed. Hell, my *whole life* is a disappointment. I'm a divorced alcoholic with a mortgage I can't afford, and the only friends I have in the world are you disgusting mongrels. I'm going to die unhappy, and we all know there is nothing after this life, nothing but empty promises waiting to disappoint us one last time…the goddamned disappointment! We have no control over this. These forces are bigger than us. We're tiny mongrels. Most of us can't even fully wipe our own asses…yeah, I smell you," He pointed to Shelby in midpace and everybody laughed. All the men followed Simon as he walked back and forth in ten-foot figure eights, their insides stoking personal existential fires.

"This life is going to take everything from us. Everything! Just peel it all back, again and again, with a ferocity beyond any fucking animal. That giant fucking fated death, the cosmos's teeth open! But here, together…we can control our destinies. We can fight back!" His words began slurring slightly with excitement, spit spraying from his animated lips.

Some of the boys unconsciously began clenching fists, others bobbed their heads in agreement. Tiesto was standing tall with his arms raised above his head, much like one might encounter in a Sunday morning Southern Baptist service. "Uh-huh!" he said. "Speak the truth, pastor, speak that truth!"

"You boys are the finest goddamned warehousemen that have ever lived. Fantastic bastards. Twenty-six months Bay 4 has been setting the standard for how it's done. We are on our way boys! In here, we are artists, scientists, and architects! There is the glory and the glory is ours, the honor, the fucking honor! We are on our way to becoming legends, boys. We may die out there with nothing, but men will be talking about our time in Bay 4 for generations to come, until they replace the whole fucking human race with machines. Even then, sentient robots will consciously program their children to sing our praise. So I need you boys to dig deep, give me everything. Go the whole way! Tonight we've got a heavy fill." He stopped in midstep, closed his eyes to remember, then turned and faced the boys. "Two hundred and twelve boats coming our way. Thirty-six of them filled with home exercise machines. One hundred nine pounds each box. So we need to dig deep, boys. Tonight we fight back, tonight we get even!" He raised his tight fists above his head and screamed so hard his lungs burned, spewing saliva out in a cloud in front of him. "Bay Four Forever!"

All of the boys jumped to their feet, raised their fists, and repeated the chant even louder. Simon smiled like a sinister cat and shouted, "Bay Four Forever!"

The men repeated it, stomping their feet and pumping their fists overhead. "BAY FOUR FOREVER!"

"Again."

"BAY FOUR FOREVER! BAY FOUR FOREVER!"

And all of the other bays throughout the warehouse took note of the absurd intensity with which bay four approached their shift, as the resounding echoes from the chant reverberated across the intricate metal-beam infrastructure, the aluminum packages slides, and the dense copper flaps above the open loading docks. They shook the place.

Brass Knee had an arrangement with one of the frequent truck drivers, Gabby Brown, who went through their warehouse. Because Bay 4 was in such high demand, Brass Knee agreed to let Gabby skip to the front of the line upon her arrival, in exchange for free cartons of cigarettes, which she had acquired in some presumably illegal fashion in lieu of gambling debts owed to her. Brass Knee would time his break with her arrival, and the two of them would stand outside chain-smoking for thirty-odd minutes while a couple of the boys, whoever were the two best performing that evening, unloaded boxes from the rear. This behavior, exhibited most by Brass Knee, was never questioned.

Gabby was a wise ass of an older woman. She'd lived as a vagabond, going from one odd job to the next throughout her entire life. In this manner she accumulated odd bits of esoteric knowledge and sewed them together into a wild tapestry of perception. Brass Knee respected this and her sense of humor, which was pretty crass and usually involved tragicomic scenarios ending in great pain because of someone's hasty oversight or foolishness. She appreciated Brass Knee because he got her in and out of the last stop before she headed home for three days off from the trucking gig, and he was her current source of esoteric knowledge, for he contributed much by way of his own innate intelligence and life experiences.

Brass Knee met Jemmy at the Amish market. Despite their respective conservative dispositions—Brass Knee was the most laid back and least enthusiastic of the boys in Bay 4—their attraction was propulsive and caused in them behavior that one would ascribe to horny teenagers. Jemmy, herself only twenty-two, was not far removed from such behavior. But Brass Knee was into his thirties and well past such foolishness. However, he had been nearly nightly, around 11:30, sneaking up the creaking steps of the main Wicker Home to thrust himself repetitively into Jemmy, who twisted and moaned with delight. Brass Knee would usually have to cover her mouth with his dirty hands to keep the room as quiet as possible. Jemmy was allowed visitors, and men too. It was a "don't ask don't tell" situation since communication between Jemmy and Ms. Corin involved the necessary tasks of running Wicker Home and not much else. But Jemmy was terrified of Ms. Corin discovering the extent of her affair, feeling that premarital sex with a

Native American would surely earn punishment. She didn't even want to think of it.

And so, when a cold-ridden Sarah one summer evening slowly slinked up the stairs in search of medicine and found the two humping hurriedly, clothes on with the door still cracked, Jemmy sought to ensure Sarah kept the information to herself. Brass Knee, in his usually perceptive way, and with genuine feelings growing for Jemmy beyond merely carnal ambitions, simply asked, "Sarah, do you smoke?" Sarah cautiously indicated in the affirmative. That night, Sarah and Jemmy followed Brass Knee out to his small Corolla parked on the street, where he pulled out five full cartons of Marlboro reds and handed them to Sarah, who folded her arms around them as one might carefully carry a swaddled baby. Thus, a pact was formed. Silence had been secured, if not any cold medicine.

From that night on, Jemmy and Sarah had learned to stay out of each other's affairs. And when Ms. Corin began to notice that Sarah was smoking more frequently and that her two packs she arrived with surely had run out long ago, Jemmy admitted to providing the cigarettes. "Ms. Corin, she came to me and requested them very politely. I didn't see anything wrong. Anything familiar from their previous lives keeps them happy, calm, better suited for their stay at Wicker Home. That Sarah has a hard head on her, add quitting the cigarettes on top of it, and she could become a real hellion." Jemmy's heart beat loudly for fear that the "autonomous decision" would cost her the teaching position there. However, Ms. Corin respected the thinking.

"It was a wise bargain," she said, patting Jemmy on the shoulder affectionately. And, if the story Jemmy had spun had been the full truth of the matter, it would have been a wise bargain because those smokes were the only things keeping Sarah manageable. But lately, that composure was slipping.

Martin grew a little tired of being excluded from Sarah's thinking, which was all taking place inside her head. Her barely audible grunts leaked out sideways around her cigarette. "Sarah, so…what?"

Sarah, still hunched on the step, elbows on knees, said, "Brass Knee. It's Jemmy's boyfriend. He has a car."

"Jemmy has a boyfriend?"

"You didn't know that?" Amused that it had actually remained a secret, she said, "I thought we had talked about that."

Martin, detecting her condescension, said, "We don't talk about anything!" And with that he looked away, pursing his lips.

Sarah grabbed his shoulders and quietly said, "You know that's not true, kid." And with that their affections had been restored. Sarah sat back down. "You spotted him one night. The big guy with the cigarettes."

"Okay, so how does he help us?" Martin asked.

Sarah smiled at the resolution. "He leaves his car down at the road when he visits Jemmy. He leaves his keys up inside the wheel well. And he has a really good reason not to report it stolen."

Martin's eyes flickered back and forth tracing the mechanics of the idea. He asked, "What reason?"

Sarah smirked, joyous at how Martin played along with her. He was a true ally, something rare in her life since Mason.

The two of them schemed for a couple hours, or nine Marlboro reds, and came up with a plan. They would have to gather supplies necessary for several days of travel. This included a blanket, food, a change of clothes, cash, and toothbrushes. They would amass these supplies little by little over a few days and store them underneath the sleeping hall's back steps in Martin's backpack until the night of the escape.

Brass Knee's visits had settled into two to three nights a week, and so they would just have to wait until a night that he came after they had amassed all of the necessary travel supplies, and then it would be go time. They would get out of Wicker Home, put Corin behind them and begin to live their lives. They didn't have any clue where they would go next but they both decided that west was the direction they would head. It was the possibility that was important, that they would have choices. And, if anything, Martin knew he was old enough to work the fields himself and remembered Aurelia remarking to him about which vine-yards and orchards didn't ask questions about previous employment. They were states away and didn't require documentation. He could blend in for a while, save money, and start back from where he and his mother had been so violently set askew.

The idea of leaving Wicker Home made Martin a little sentimental. The place had its charms. For example, Miles had become like a sibling to Martin. He would follow him around asking him questions about everything, which had at first annoyed Martin to no end, but now, it was pleasing. It was the routine, it was the family. And that was something that was beginning to really nag inside Mar-tin's head. How could they leave the others behind? It was something that was acknowledged and left unresolved by Sarah and him while planning their depar-ture. They had considered a few limiting factors. For instance, the car could only reasonably fit five people, at most, with the provisions being packed into the trunk.

Beyond that, it was clear that a group of six or seven or all of Wicker Home, for that matter, would more easily draw unwanted attention. Sarah was old enough to drive and look after younger children, so it wouldn't look that bizarre to see her driving around two or three others. But a hive, shoved like sardines into Brass Knee's Corolla would surely sound some alarms. Further, the more that came, the more supplies they would need, thus increasing the likelihood that it wouldn't all fit in the trunk but instead eat into space within the car.

It had occurred to Martin that the most likely and reasonable scenario would involve them each picking another to join. For Martin's sake, the choice was inevitable. Miles. But he wondered who Sarah would pick? Surely not Drayton. Likely Nancy. "Mustard Nancy," as the younger boys liked to call her. She and Sarah talked a lot, Martin had no idea about what. Nancy was Martin's age, but the two never spoke because Nancy never spoke to anyone but Sarah. She was a cipher, a mysterious enigma. Drayton referred to her as an "uppity strutter." Ms. Corin once angrily scolded her for being late for breakfast, saying "You need to stop thinking you are better than everyone else!" The general consensus was that she was stuck up and standoffish. She never really got under Sarah's skin as she had the others. Even Martin got a bad taste in his mouth at the thought of her. Her face always looked like she had just smelled something awful. Martin wondered how someone's sense of smell could be so displeased so frequently. But the senses relaxed around Sarah. It didn't surprise Martin. That's who Sarah was— the comforting older sibling that, despite her rightful disdain for your situation, you confide in and then trust in the resulting wisdom she spouts.

The days after deciding to leave Wicker Home moved quicker, as if time had picked up its pace. Martin was constantly nervous, with mild acid reflux. Sure, he was going through all of the usual routines: breakfast, lessons, lunch, recess, lessons, playtime, homework, talking with Sarah while she smoked, answering Miles's questions. But now he was carrying a cache of concealed intentions, which created a queasy tension in everything he did. To Martin's eye, Sarah remained cool, but within, she too was a flutter.

She knew that plans seldom unfolded without unwanted creases. And, as the elder of the group, and the plan's primary author, she shouldered the most responsibility for the tactic. To that end, she had realized that she should not depend upon the others, that she could not, but, instead, was wholly determined to carry out the maneuvers as an individual, just with the addition of three others tagging along. She also worried that there was surely something she had forgotten to consider, some unseen variable. She wondered if Ms. Corin could see what was going to happen, if she knew. "Fuck it, it's going to happen," she said aloud, garnering courage.

Mustard Nancy exploded into convulsive crying when Sarah explained the plan to her, as Martin had predicted she would. Nevertheless, it was unexpected, and it was the most emotion Nancy had ever displayed to Sarah. Then, after a few minutes of sobbing, she wiped her cheeks assuredly and returned to her stone-faced demeanor. Martin, for his part, had decided not to tell Miles at all. He knew Miles wouldn't be able to deal with it. The night of the escape, he would merely wake him up and go. If he was against it, as he would likely initially be, Martin had already decided it was in his best interest. It was something he would be okay with another doing to him if he had had a fearful disposition similar to Miles.

Over a three-day period, Sarah and Martin each took trips to the steps at night to add to the supplies within their travel repository underneath the loose second step, which they pried up from the risers. By the time Sarah added her grocery bag with a change of clothes and her toothbrush atop the pile, it was pushing up against the underside of the step, allowing a keen observer to note that it no longer flexed as it used to. The stockpile made for more uneasiness for both Sarah and Martin.

The night of the escape, Martin couldn't eat dinner. His nerves had gotten the best of him, his stomach tumbled and burned like a sailboat amid a great rocking sea storm of acid. It was broccoli-cheddar soup, anyway. It was the most common meal that Jemmy and Ms. Corin made, and it was often leftovers from the previous serving, which had been stored in the freezer in Tupperware. Reheated, it was like frostbitten mush that faintly resembled cheddar flavored regurgitation.

Martin didn't know that it was the night until he saw Brass Knee cautiously slinking across the grass toward the side door of the house to meet Jemmy. Martin was peeking through the sleeping hall window, holding the curl of drapes in his right fist. They smelled like mothballs. Now that he thought about it, the whole sleeping hall did. He would not miss that. But now, Brass Knee was closing the door behind him and, undoubtedly, quietly tiptoeing his way up to Jemmy's room, the two of them holding hands and smiling at the fun of their shared secrecy. It struck Martin that he had never noticed their trysts.

Martin stealthily crawled on all fours and poked his head around the end of the divider between the male and female sleeping halls. This was the signal that Sarah had prearranged. Then he headed for the step to begin unpacking the provisions. Everything had been put into either grocery bags or book bags taken from the kitchen drawer and library, respectively. By the time Martin had pulled them out and replaced the loose stair tread, Sarah had made her way out. She kneeled next to him and grabbed the board to assure it was secure. It was. They sat, staring at each other. The ground was cold, with clods of hardened sod glistening around the edges with the beginnings of frost. Everything was dying.

They split the supplies in half and carried them, hunched over, crunching across the lawn to Brass Knee's Corolla. From the main house they could hear the muffled tones of a healthy brewing argument. Ms. Corin was arguing with her son. Martin saw their silhouettes in the main bedroom upstairs. He froze and turned to Sarah with large questioning eyes. "Keep going," she whispered, pushing her elbow into his ribs.

They quickly made their way down the long front lawn to the road. The blue Corolla sat parked in the grass just behind the edge of the thicket of pines, where Sarah had said it would be. They had delayed their voyage so that, during Brass

Knee's last visit, Sarah could sneak out and make sure she could find the key and get the car started. The test run had gone very smoothly. The keys sat on a rusty ridge up in the front right wheel well. There was a metal-skull key chain and three keys—two smaller and the rubber-headed Toyota key. The car had started without trouble and ran smoothly and quietly.

They hunkered down beside the front car door. Sarah reached into the wheel well and felt around. A stab of panic rose in her throat. The keys were not there. She rubbed her fingers, scraping along the rough curves of oily, rusted metal. Nothing. She pushed Martin aside and tried the front passenger door. Locked. The rear. Locked. She darted around the car and tried the driver's side doors. Both locked. "Fuck!" she said, resting her forehead against the driver's window.

She took a deep breath. "Alright," she said.

Martin watched her, his own head just above the car roof. "So what now?" he asked, with his stomach sinking and fearing the inevitable aborting of the escape. "Well," she said, "we either have to go get the keys or try again next time." But both of them had individually decided that it needed to be then. There would be no more waiting. "I can get the keys," Martin said, glancing over toward the house from his side of the car. He felt a great pride and also great terror in what he was saying.

"Alright, but how?" Sarah said, furrowing her brow. Martin thought for a moment. He pictured himself crawling on the floor, searching through jeans strewn on the floor in the thralls of a passionate jaunt onto Jemmy's bed. Then he pictured Ms. Corin arguing with her son, and he wondered what it was about. They had been so serene with one another. Who knew what he would encounter up there. It was a huge risk.

"Let me try," he said, holding out his palms. "It's worth trying."

"And if you get caught?"

"We'll hide the supplies, you go back to the hall. If I get caught, then I'll say I was looking for the cough medicine and Corin will just send me back to bed...or to Jemmy. And if I find the keys, then I'll come back and get you and we can go."

Sarah stood silently with a solemn stare. The night was dead quiet, aside from the faint hums of the Corin family argument in the distance. Martin was visibly shivering in his grey sweatshirt. She finally responded, "Okay." They quickly piled their provisions between the trunks of two larger pines. "Be careful, kid," Sarah whispered loudly as their paths diverged and they headed for their respective destinations, hunched over and crunching through the lawn.

Sarah noticed that the two of them were leaving tracks in the lawn, and that it was only getting colder. She hoped he found the keys, thinking it will be obvious they had been out there. Upon reaching the sleeping hall, she went around to the back side, out of view of the main house, and lit a cigarette. The cold was getting to her, and the heat from the burning tobacco felt good in her throat and chest. She hugged herself, rocking back and forth, trying to expel her anticipation.

Martin twisted the side doorknob approximately three times slower than he had ever opened any door previously. He felt his pulse fluttering in his neck. The wooden door creaked just loudly enough to be audible above Martin's racing heart and the murmurs of argumentation directly above him in the bedroom. He tiptoed onto the woven-cotton welcome mat, stitched together by Ms. Corin herself. As he pivoted to slide the door shut behind him, his sneaker squeaked on the linoleum kitchen floor. He pivoted back and paused to listen, looking at the back staircase leading up from beside the pantry to the second floor. Jemmy's door would be to the right at the top of the landing.

He slipped off his sneakers and lined them up neatly, side by side, to the right of the door. That seemed like the right place to him, but then he thought if he got caught, he wouldn't be leaving quickly but instead getting a lecture from Corin or Jemmy. He remembered his first real good glimpse of Brass Knee, just thirty minutes earlier. He did not want to piss off someone that huge.

In his wool socks, step to step, he made his way up the stairs, exaggerating each step as a cartoon private dick might, knees high, holding his breath. With each step, the argument became more intelligible. By the sixth step, he could hear Ms. Corin say, "They've been missing for three weeks. What do you think, they just decided to take a vacation?" Another slow, exaggerated step landing on woolen tiptoes.

"They've gone on hunting trips before, Dale said. "They've already finished the harvest; let the workers go home. I'm sure they've collected some of their portions from the union already. There's nothing keeping them there." Another step up to the landing and their words were very clear, despite traveling through her bedroom door and down the entire length of the hallway.

"Don't be naive," Ms. Corin said. "If they've been gone this long, it's because they either followed the steps, or the Narduccians found them!" Her voice sounded more hoarse and menacing than usual.

Martin's woolen toes found their way onto the landing. He hunched, his palms on his thighs, and caught his breath, lost from unnecessarily holding it on the way up. Jemmy's room was on the right, a mere six feet in front of him. Across from her door was the door to the home office where Ms. Corin and Jemmy both had their desks. Further down the hall were two more doors. The one next to the office was Corin's bedroom where she and Dale were currently feuding. The door on Jemmy's side went to a room that Martin had never entered. He turned his right ear toward Jemmy's bedroom. There was complete silence inside.

He wondered how they could be so quiet but then thought about his time with the farmer's daughter in the back of the truck. He had been sore from flexing muscles he hadn't often used to stay in certain positions that caused less motion and, therefore, less sound. He knew he couldn't just barge in. His eyes followed the grain in the door down toward the floor. There was about a three-inch gap under the door.

"I've been doing this twice as long as you've been alive," Ms. Corin said. "My father, he didn't wait like I did with you. I know. It's the Narduccians. We need to follow the steps. Oh Lord, help me. I wouldn't have invited you here if I had known." Her voice cracked, hitting notes both higher and lower than her usual assured monotone.

"Gahhh! It doesn't even matter anymore, Dale said. "It was, what...over a hundred and twenty years ago? Are you telling me that this is still a thing with these people?"

"It wasn't that long ago with Jasper," Ms. Corin said.

Martin eased himself down onto his hands and knees. He extended himself slowly forward until he was on his chest, laying his left cheek lightly against the cold floor. He focused his left eye and peered through the gap between the door and floor. Inside, Brass Knee was pulling his khakis up and buckling his belt. Jemmy sat, bare breasted, with her back up against the large black headboard. Martin thought it weird that her breasts were so small, but her nipples were huge. Brass Knee put on his shirt and jean jacket. He leaned his enormous frame over Jemmy, covering Martin's line of sight but he heard kissing noises. The motion of Brass Knee's shoulder indicated some form of nuzzling.

Martin quickly but quietly crouched backward onto his heels and then stood in anticipation of Brass Knee's imminent exit. It looked like it would have to be next time. Before he turned to head for his descent down the stairs, the far door, opposite Ms. Corin's bedroom, swiftly but silently swung inward and out stepped a tall, slender man with a mustache. In his hands he held a long rifle. Martin froze, his heart rate instantaneously skipping into cardiovascular weight loss territory. Jasper turned, his eyes meeting Martin's. Martin noticed how sad and droopy they were. There was sagging skin forming several thick half circles underneath. These were Jasper's bourbon eyes.

The two of them sorted through their panic for the right next step, but before either of them arrived at one, Jemmy's door swiftly opened and Brass Knee eased his gigantic presence into the hallway, gently closing the door behind him. He turned and saw Martin, wide eyed, and because of the direction of Martin's stare, looked down the hall the other way and saw Jasper, who was still loosely grasping his rifle, the barrel pointed downward. Jasper, finally figuring that both of his sur-prisers were harmless wards of Wicker Home, and unfortunate obstacles at that, took two confident steps, raising the barrel of the rifle toward Brass Knee's head.

At that moment, Ms. Corin's door flung open and mother, followed by son, stepped out in the hallway behind Jasper. She stopped short and shrieked, crossing her hands over her chest in a defensive gesture. Dale bumped into his mother be-fore taking in the now crowded hallway.

Chapter Eleven

Pollock's mouth was dry, and it hurt to swallow, but he felt compelled to do so, repeatedly. He was lying on his back, fully clothed with shoes on, atop his bed, not the couch. His body and clothes were soaked with sweat. The air in the room was thick, and it smelled like mildew. He tilted his head backward to look up at the windows behind the headboard. Sunshine danced in kaleidoscopic blurs against the dense brown cotton curtains. His head pounded with the fury of ten hangovers. He had never drunk this badly.

A strange sense of displacement crept in to him. He was unclear whether it was a weekend, a weekday, or if maybe he had just woken up from a nap that went on too long. He occasionally did that, intended to nap for twenty minutes or so, only to wake up four hours later woozy and discombobulated from the deepness of the slumber. He had, during such naps, forgotten his age and the city he lived in, and once he forgot what he wanted to make of his life.

Out of the corner of his eye, which was still adjusting to the light, he spotted his cellphone lying on the bedside table next to the flowered lamp, which was knocked over. He reached for it with a mysteriously sore arm. The home screen notification bar indicated he had twelve text messages and three missed calls from Sherry. In the bottom corner, the screen further indicated that it was 4:15 p.m. on a Sunday.

He immediately let the cell flop back onto the table, unable to presently deal with the barrage of communications. Several ideas meandered and dissipated in Pollock's head over the next moments. But it was the pain in his head that won out for attention and prompted him to slowly, slouchingly creep down the stairs and into the kitchen, pour himself a glass of water and take four ibuprofen pills. After seating himself at the kitchen table, he realized that the house was far too warm and the AC was off.

He rose, and marched to the thermostat. Having turned the air to fifty-eight degrees on high fan, he turned and noticed the pile of belongings in the corner of the living room next to the coffee table. A sleeping bag and pillow, a large grey camping backpack, and a pair of dress shoes that had been recklessly thrown on their sides. "Cabe," he said, remembering. They had gone gambling Thursday night. Cabe was keen to see a cockfight. Pollock wondered where he was and if he had left with a girl.

Falling down onto the couch, Pollock tried to flip through his memories and piece together a coherent series of events. While doing so, tiredness swept back over him, and he began to fade into sleep. Just before doing so, he felt a lump in his left pocket. He pulled out a wad of folded bills thicker than a hockey puck. They were all twenties. There must have been five thousand dollars in his hand. This he vaguely remembered. "I won…" he said, pulling at the thread of his recollection, trying desperately to get a larger, clearer chunk. And then he was asleep, again. It was 4:36 p.m. on a Sunday.

* * *

Quentin and Pollock were both, in their own ways, quite astounded by the tale that Martin had told them about his past. Quentin had, in Pollock's eyes, taken to Martin almost instantaneously. It was as if they were kindred. Pollock was more skeptical, which, Quentin's paranoia being the greater of the two, made Pollock wonder what additional information had warmed him to their new friend.

The two of them sat on folding mesh camping stools arranged in a large circle in the middle of what used to be a managerial office overlooking the expanse of the main factory floor. The large bay windows were, surprisingly, still intact and appeared to have been recently washed clean. One of the more reserved members of Martin's household had pointed to the circle of stools and meekly said, "Where we hold councils…" as a response to the confusion on Pollock's face as the group sat themselves. There were eight of them in total, including Quentin and Pollock. Martin did the majority of speaking. The others, who remained nameless, mostly nodded in agreement after Martin had made certain points.

"We're making a space for all of those who don't have one. We make our decisions as a group, and the aim is to make use of that which has been discarded or neglected in the community. There is a village here that is self-sufficient," Martin said, sitting with his legs crossed under him. His manner reminded Pollock of a car salesman, someone with rehearsed lines readily available to persuade. "Then who owns the building?" Quentin impulsively interjected and then looked at Martin for a beat before surveying the other five group members in the circle. No one responded immediately, but Martin pursed his lips.

"Here is…where we stand right now," he said, frowning, and for the first time speaking as if his words weren't prepackaged. "We…have a few rather large political battles ahead of us. For one, the property we are on belongs to the city of Trams. It was acquired by their commercial land bank over a decade ago, I believe. However, the ownership is in dispute. Beyond all of this…we have decided to petition Trams to convey the land to us. We've written a charter to become our own city." He looked down. The other members of the circle appeared to emulate Martin's actions, even his demeanor.

Pollock reflected on how he, Retta, and Quentin had been attracted to the current locale in the first place by the roving marauders that everyone had been talking about. He turned his gaze outward through the bay windows and looked down upon the rowed shanty homes. Each unit was adorned with all of the trappings of a standard suburban household, all the way to mailboxes shaped like little houses. And they had addresses painted along their walls, fencing, kids' plastic basketball hoops, and patio tables and chairs in miniature screened-in areas with groupings of outdoor Christmas lights and cabinets with brown and clear liquor bottles filling them.

The sight brought dozens of questions fluttering through Pollock's brain, half-developed, before it landed on what became the dominant idea. He was mad. "Self-sufficient?" he said aloud, surprising himself. It broke the silence, and all eyes turned to him. Quentin recognized the suspicious turn of mind within his young colleague and decided to see what results it would produce, as opposed to quashing it with misdirection or apology. "We followed thieves here. They stole from my neighbor's yard. And there have been quite a few other thefts throughout town, lately," Pollock said, his heart beating hard, now that he understood himself to be making an accusation.

Martin instantly rose to his feet and held his palms out to the side as if to say "you got me." But, instead, he said, "That sort of thing has been finding its way over to us. Let me assure you, we…" he waved his palms over the heads of his circle-mates, "we all decided together that stealing would not be allowed. Nor anyone who stole. We don't associate with that establishment, and we certainly don't tolerate it here. So yes, there have been a few infractions and we've dealt with them. We've had to banish a number of violators," he said and smiled amicably.

"What establishment?" Quentin asked, turning his gaze sideways toward Pollock to acknowledge that the paranoia had been useful.

"The Rings," Martin said. "We don't patronize their matches, and we allow those who have done so to stay here only after signing a pledge to stop attending." Martin's smile vanished as he had begun to realize just how little his two visitors knew about this topic. He scrutinized their faces and concluded that they were entirely ignorant, their scrunched stupefaction readily apparent to all the other members of the circle as well. "There are basement cockfights on the south side of town, one facility in particular. Well…there is a large destitute population living there. Some of them raise and fight cocks. And a lot of others steal to fund their losing streaks. It's become a, uh, trend. Local pawnshops aren't that discriminating. So long as they can't prove something's stolen, they'll take it."

"Then where did you get all of this stuff?" Pollock asked.

Martin, recognized this form of aggression very well and found it impotent and somewhat charming. He smirked and said matter-of-factly, "You'd be surprised what folks toss away around here." And with that his right dimple grew deep as he slowly turned and recrossed his legs beneath him on the mesh camping stool.

The office grew quiet again, and all of the complex activities from below grew in relative volume, overcoming the great hubbub of inner conversation that both Pollock and Quentin were having with themselves. One of Martin's people, a slender woman with rosy cheeks and dark eyes said, her voice wavering, "We have an earnest vision for the future of our city. We are trying to generate goodwill with Trams so that, one day when we are sister cities, we can interact with dignity and without any hostility." She flashed a pleasant smile.

"Oye, I understand the idea of the charter," Quentin said. "Trams follows its own charter. And that's all fine and well. But what I wonder about is how are you going to…function? I mean, are you going to have electricity and water? Where will you get these. How will you pay for these things?"

"We already have an entire year of—" Martin reached his arm out and touched her on the knee. She ceased speaking, and her cheeks went red. Martin patted her on the knee. Pollock and Quentin found similar expressions of alarm on each other's face.

Martin stood again, smiling his car salesman smile and reaching his palms outward in a welcoming but out-of-place gesture. "Okay folks, it has been really nice meeting both of you. You are welcome to be guests in my home whenever you would like. Unfortunately, we have to ask you to excuse us for now. We have several meetings this afternoon and we've already spent too long boring you with our plight."

Sitting still and alone back at work, Pollock was able to see the value in a tent city popping up in Trams. It would be beneficial for those who ended up on the street or needed a different environment or support group to have a place to go, to fit in. Pollock found it strange, perhaps ironic, that he envisioned its usefulness in terms of there being a market for it. The decline of industrial employment three decades ago, compounded by the financial meltdown last decade, had made things tougher for lower income families struggling to keep basic utilities hooked up, eat well, and manage some sort of entertainment regimen, let alone afford any kind of mortgage or a better rental. Yet there were swanky mixed-use model neighborhood condominiums popping up all over in seemingly excessive quantities. The older houses and tenements were crumbling from neglect.

Pollock had wondered who was renting all these newer units. He pictured all of the credit card advertisements landing in his mailbox and email inbox almost daily, claiming he was preapproved for $1,000, $4,000. He still owed $349 a month for having gone to college. In addition to the mixed-use condominiums, the other thriving developmental progress would have to be attributed to corporate headquarters campuses. And they employed thousands for these service sector companies. But the jobs came from elsewhere and didn't correspond to the skill of those who once worked in Trams's great industrial sector. But all of that was a different question, which would inevitably lead to another separate investigation. For now, the primary focus needed to be his project for Mr. Freedman's speech. He needed to focus again, as he had after Quentin had provided his experienced guidance.

Still, the collection of disparate recent discoveries, the warehouse, Martin, and the Rings of which he spoke felt somehow vital, crucial even, but how Pollock didn't know yet. These additional wrinkles only added a sense of frustration and helplessness to his view of his project.

And Hans had something cooking. He was right there, glad handing at every corner, weaseling his way into Pollock's position, soon to surpass him. Sitting at Pollock's desk. There was a competition of styles. Hans was the slick deal man with swagger, and Pollock was the purist, stuck in reasoned reflection. At least this was how Pollock fashioned the situation for himself. Then he would recoil from the bitter egoism involved in such characterization, even if he felt it was truthful.

Regardless, Pollock wanted his job to be done the way he was doing it, even if done by someone else. That had to count for something in regard to the truthfulness. "Deep dive" was a term used by a human resources liaison person during their last quarterly presentation. Deep divers needed to be alone with the material to delve fully into the landscape of an issue, inhabit it, feel the climate and the wind patterns, and then return with a map and directions. To Pollock, these simple zoning disputes had important philosophical consequences. It was more than an arbitrary marking left over from a business deal between two free individuals in a marketplace.

Such a view always yielded to power sources. Political power. The zoning variance board and the zoning code development department both essentially paid tribute to the mayor's office and city council, which in turn paid their own tribute to whichever local businesses footed the bill for their elections and initiatives. This was simply because most of the code and variance officers wanted to move on to higher government positions. Thus, they needed the help, the connections, the social networks, and access to local fundraising and the local business community, all provided by a simple bargain: come down on the side of these contentious issues that you're asked to by the council member or mayor's office, and you'll have access. You'll be in, get invited, and get sponsored. The decisions usually served those interests.

It all irked Pollock to no end. The whole geographical arrangement of the town was being whored out to predominantly private developers by cynical and ambitious city officials at the cost of the public good, which they vowed to forward at the inception of their tenure. It put a bad taste in Pollock's mouth. But he would always then turn slightly against himself for pretending that wanting a change could make it so. He knew he wasn't that naïve. He thought about accepting it all and getting his hands dirty, as Hans was doing. Either way, it was a genuine existential corner, the solution of which was impossible so long as he was waffling on the project. He was stuck.

He thought of Retta, and their time together, and how all these stressors paled next to the good feelings which predominated during their hang outs, and were maintained so effortlessly. He pictured her sardonic grin underneath sunglasses. He pictured her mature way of handling her brother and father without betraying any sense of interrupted entitlement. His problems felt so petty and hyperbolic compared to hers. Retta had an actual existential crux. His seemed merely theoretical. Even *that* he waffled on, and as he thought it, he realized he might always be stuck in this spot. Waffling. "Pollock the Great Waffler!" he imagined some barker hollering to an assembled crowd waiting to see him like an exhibit in a freak show.

Fearing he had lost any coherent thread of reasoning, and descending into a quagmire of self-referential mockery, he decided to call Retta. The two of them, prompted by Retta's suggestion, made plans to visit a food truck "festival" during the two hours that she had free the following evening.

The conclave of food trucks and shipping containers had assembled in an unused drive-in theater, one by one, over the past several years. By the time Pollock had moved to Trams, it was a permanent vendor district. The land had been properly purchased by a coalition formed of the various food and drink business owners, and a variance issued for their use. According to Trams municipal zoning code, the variance was an inlay categorized with fairgrounds, the downtown farmer's market, parking garages, and used and new car sales lots. As of that May, there were thirteen trucks and nine shipping containers, which amounted to approximately half of the spatial capacity of the lot.

One of the only perks of the location, which was south of any populated neighborhoods and nearing "the boonies," was that the Trams light-rail train, limited as it's route was, made its last stop there. Thus, one could freely ride directly to the locale. Secondly, there was often live music. Tony, the son of Malty, who ran the Toasted Tub, which sold deep-fried homemade ice cream, orchestrated the schedule and marketing for all of the performers. There was a pavilion and stage with a weatherproofed PA system, and bands played Wednesday through Saturday, rain or shine. Each vendor added its share of local flavor.

On Tuesday evenings, Tony hosted an open mic night, playing two songs himself in between each act. There was usually a good turnout because Tuesday night was also Taco Tuesday when TacoMeter had one dollar tacos. This special had acquired citywide fame and garnered favorable reviews in all three of the major local publications. The sheer volume of customers translated into a steady stream of open mic participants. So Tony ended up playing many songs, all of which seemed to suggest that, years ago, previous to the bald head, beer gut and uneven pubic hair–like beard, he had a girlfriend who left him. Their lyrics suggested a mad cruelty to the abandonment. Tony was very charismatic and had a winning shaggy-dog type of charm that made people like him because he drank a lot of beer and knew something about having the blues.

Many college students would congregate in the conclave, drinking newly discovered craft beers and smoking American Spirit cigarettes on the matrix of wooden cafeteria style seating along the eastern edge of the lot. Because there was no fence enclosing the lot, it was technically illegal to allow open containers on the premises. However, because all of the vendors who sold booze had dutifully acquired the correct state permits, the police and everybody else of consequence or authority ignored that little technicality.

Abutting the northern side of the lot and running northward for several blocks was a mess of unused factory housing and abandoned industrial mills east of the railroad tracks and Rhatze River. Rust and spray-painted graffiti predominated. It was a call to tetanus shots. And teenagers out after curfew, with hormonal intent and no more suitable landing spot. Within the walls of those blocks of buildings, there was a cornucopia of wild beasts: raccoons, cats, dogs, coyotes, coywolfs, rabbits, field mice, rats, possums, groundhogs, rat snakes, garter snakes, hognose snakes, frogs, toads, and even, once, a middle-aged hardware-store-chain manager from Riverton who thought it would be wise, or at least marginally worthwhile, to pull up alone at night into such a shady landscape to meet a criminal pharmaceutical rep for the first time in order to purchase cocaine.

Pollock hung out at Retta's for a bit to help clean after dinner and make sure that Fox was in his pajamas and had entertainment for the evening before heading to the festival. Once again, all that could be seen of Remy was the top of his head through the window above the sink, pacing back and forth under a trail of smoke. Pollock felt Remy's absence and that of Retta's mother, and it made him wonder if he should feel guilty for leeching Retta's time. Time was clearly valuable to the barely functioning family. But he thought he was, perhaps, being helpful in providing respite, teleportation back to the enjoyable frivolities of being in your midtwenties and alive and happy with beer and good food on a weeknight when it was warm out. Besides, he didn't want to engage with her so intellectually. He needed to be back in the moment, to behave intuitively. He grew sick of all these rueful contemplations separating him from the now. But then Retta sensually grazed his wrist with her fingertips as they exited into the garage, and it jolted him present.

Retta was relieved to be leaving the house, and not alone on her bicycle. But she also had been experiencing flickers of sadness. She had once had a tight-knit group of friends. Then college came, some got married, and many moved to other towns. The keggers turned into potlucks and fires and eventually brunches and then coffee meetings until there really was no more cohesion. Each friend had crawled off into separate areas and was now building a nest filled with their respective ideologies and fantasies. Now, Retta could barely remember her friends. The grand old mirage of their collective youth had faded in her. She had her family, her nursing instructors, and Pollock. The world had shrunk down to a computer screen where she could follow all these now vague others on Facebook or Twitter or see their Instagram photos. Haunted through electricity.

And the impetus to swan out to a local pub and scrutinize potential companions one by one as they became more intoxicated and aggressive just wasn't Retta's idea of time well spent. So she had resorted to online dating as the logical echo of the other digitized parts of her human experience. It seemed to her like a cocoon of representations and nobody touching, mirrors of loneliness. The dash in Pollock's truck rattled sleepily.

Retta and Pollock had chosen Tenken Co. for their food. The red and white camouflage–painted freight container cooked up Asian fusion dishes such as truffle-covered pad Thai noodles. They also served an impressive variety of Scotch egg deserts consisting of bacon, eggs, and ham coated with some combination of sugary glaze, honey, cream, nuts, and fruits. These sweet delectables were served in folded slices of wax paper that quickly became amorphous and nearly unmanageable. There were the necessary containers of wet wipes on several picnic tables. The large -bearded lady who ran the place exhibited a frightening wobble, often invaded customers' personal space with her foul coffee breath, and managed to carry two stink eyes at all times. She reminded Retta of someone who would live in Tolkien's shire. But the food was tremendous, if messy. The astringent film from the hand wipes coated their knuckles.

The expansive dining area was full of patrons and a loud folk band with two banjos and a mandolin rang out from the pavilion stage. It took some confident and potentially offensive maneuvering to acquire seating amid the rumbling human sea. The two shared a dessert and noodle dish and afterward Pollock got pints of locally brewed IPA for them from Lake Brewing Co. while Retta defended their territory.

The night sky was full of fast moving cumulus clouds and a frenetic breeze. It was welcomed by most. The alcohol set in and alleviated Retta and Pollock's respective anxieties. They loosened their shoulders and breathed from deeper in their lungs. They began to allow vague private engagements with the metaphysical to coat the words they spoke to one another.

"Honestly, I'm just exhausted," Retta said, blankly staring off over the heads in the seating area.. "It's impossible to get ahead. Anytime I've put away a few hundred dollars and think that, hey, this will add up to a thousand dollars in a couple of months and then a year from now it could be three or four thousand, but then the air conditioning breaks and that's $1,800, or the porch starts giving out, or Russell, Fox's caretaker, raises his hourly rate. And bam, right back to square one!" She sighed and focused her sight just long enough to locate her beer and bring it to her mouth.

"Are you doing too much?" Pollock asked.

"God, yes…"

"Can I help with anything?"

Retta snapped her neck left, cracking it loudly. "I don't think there is anything to be done, you know, like I just don't have a lot of time for fun things…like *this*, so like, I guess I shouldn't spoil our date by letting it spill over…Like, I just feel like I'm always on the clock, one thing to the next. There's never any down time…you know, it's rare, and then the downtime that I do get…like, I'm stressed about all of the things I should be doing or what I need to do next, watching the time, like, you know?"

Pollock could see the battle going on inside of her, the struggle. It was hard for him to relate to not having free time; he had a lot of it. But he dug through his feelings and found an offering. "Well, I understand being stressed about what comes next. I mean, I could always be doing more…for my job, my outstanding errands…"

Retta recognized Pollock's effort to comfort her through solidarity and it was cute to her, but the actual content of his comfort was empty. It didn't help in the way it was intended and, instead, made her feel more distant from him. Pollock, for his part, just began to get more stressed out. The two of them took swigs of alcohol in unison. "We *are* getting older," Pollock added. Retta nodded in agreement as her mind wandered to Australia. The folk threesome had added a woman on bongos, which in turn raised the level of the music. The volume of conversation throughout the crowd rose.

Retta said, "I was thinking the other day, like, how I have so many memories of being in foyers or the front closets of houses so much when I was a kid.

Like, putting on and taking off coats and shoes, scarves. My mom dropping me off at a friends house for a sleepover, and me, like, being nervous about whether or not I should take my shoes off or leave them on. I never take my shoes off anymore, at least not there in the entranceway. Like, I usually kick them off later by the kitchen or in my bedroom," Retta explained, off in her own reverie and quite far from Pollock, mentally.

"That's an interesting thought," he said. "It reminds me of how Japanese families are strict about removing their shoes at the front door. I think they have slippers, sometimes, to wear inside." The thought made Pollock tired.

The separation between the two became more and more apparent to Pollock. It was as if there were some semitranslucent substance working as a divider, and each of them were flinging their internal impressions against it, but upon making contact with the substance it would morph and slip and change until they each were looking at entirely different objects obstructing their view of the other. Pollock thought drinks would help. Thus, fully in battle mode, determined not to fall further into this quagmire of virtual solitude, which threatened authentic solitude, he returned to the brewery and, this time, acquired an entire six-pack.

"I am fully aware that you have limited time," he said on his return. "That being said, I think you need at least one more beer, perhaps two." He cracked a can from the plastic six-pack ring and handed it over to her. Retta perceived his raised eyebrows as sheepishness. The can felt cold and good in her hand, and she emptied it quite urgently. It was immediately replaced by another. And the music started to seem a little more pleasant, the crowd a little less savage and annoying. Endorphins were released into Retta's neurochemistry. Pollock began speaking less from a place of consideration and more from intuited rhythms.

An hour and a half passed, with more or less successful conversation that overcame the earlier drags. Retta shared a dream she had about her feet growing quite large while she tanned at a private swimming pool located within an apartment compound somewhere in the desert. With the increase in size, her ability to maneuver them normally dissipated and she became stranded in the beach chair along the concrete berm underneath a palmetto tree. She called for help but was overcome with embarrassment and remained there, quietly in deep discomfort. Pollock laughed at the appropriate times, sincerely amused with her descriptions.

But he also recognized a subtle sadness to the dream. She was stuck somewhere she didn't want to be anymore, by conditions she couldn't control. And further, she was afraid to let anyone know. She didn't approve of her own reactions. Yet, here she was telling him about it now. He was flattered by the confidence, though he was also cognizant that she was essentially displaying her "baggage." Retta, the whole Retta package, came with a very sturdy set of circumstances that she openly resented, and she was ashamed of her resentment.

Pollock thought perhaps he was stuck in his own shameful posture. Everyday was the same stuttered failure at work, with a real and growing urgency to resolve his qualms. He shared as much with Retta over their fourth cans of beer, after having made another trip to the brewery. He also explained Martin's plans for the tent city and how it weighed into his considerations for his project.

"You'll wow your boss. Like, I just know that you will, Pollock." Pollock found this wholly unfounded, but appreciated the gesture. Retta was also completely incredulous of the tent city, playfully accusing Pollock of making up the whole thing. She pushed him in the shoulder and he nearly spilled his IPA. They laughed. They had successfully fled from their melancholy completely. At Retta's suggestion, they toasted "to alcohol!"

After a break, the band started a second set of low-key love ballads and softer, more melodic songs. They, too, were drunk. As if the dip in music quality was a signal of the inevitable decline of the evening, the crowd began to thin out until it was possible to find a seat at any picnic table.

The winds picked up until the umbrellas, which adorned every other picnic table, began rattling and tapping their hard plastic shafts against the inside of the holes in the wooden tables. Pollock and Retta's table vibrated as a result and the edges of the umbrella's wide grey sweep swung sporadically downward behind Pollock's head. Charcoal clouds sped overhead, merging, breaking, and oozing quickly into new forms, the starry sky and waning crescent moon only seen in glimpses. Retta found it eerie and attractive. The whole panorama filled her with bizarre energy, perhaps rays of recognition from the Moon Goddess, or the triple goddess of the moon and Earth and stars, communing with her.

Retta reflected on her first ritual circle to celebrate the sabbats with her mother. There was a full moon that night, and there were a dozen strangers, all holding each other's hands and staring at the same hypothetical point above the center of the circle. They hummed patiently. Her mother had whispered in explanation that they were raising energy to connect to a religious experience. It terrified and confounded young Retta, but it also provided a curious captivation with the central mystery of it all. They were approaching something that couldn't be seen and that touched all other things. She had been neglecting her religion lately, which somehow felt like a slight against her mother, and she resolved to fix it.

Pollock had begun to flirt with what it was, exactly, that he was enjoying about Retta. Earlier, after their first few dates, he had decided that he enjoyed himself more when she was around. This conclusion came from his reflections on her playfulness and earnestness. She seemed genuinely to care about his mood, his concerns, and his deeply private integrity. And so he felt less alone, and the world felt slightly less cold, less pitted against him. Retta was almost akin to some human form of analgesic or anesthetic or even neurostimulant. He saw that these attributes, which had comforted him and attracted him to her, were the byproduct of her unfortunate familial arrangement. Her deceased mother, her absentee father, and her severely autistic brother had forced her to become the primary care-taker, to be involved enough in the inner workings of Fox and Remy to hold things together, to be the responsible overseer. However, he realized that any number of people would have responded differently than Retta. This was a testament to something about her, peculiar to her character, and not her circumstances, the forces conspiring against her.

So, his thoughts traveled elsewhere, to Cabe. He would be there in two days. His heart sunk a bit as he considered the realities of the reunion. It was going to be a chore. Cabe's communications, which were almost completely out of the blue, suggested a harmonious and civil return to their glorious friendship as undergrads. Pollock knew this was an immature conceit. They would have to talk about it, discuss it. There needed to be some resolution for them to ever even imagine a reconciliation. Pollock had mixed feelings concerning his desire for any reconciliation, and he was beginning to grow mad at himself for so glibly acquiescing to Cabe's request for cohabitation. And so, darkness and isolation overtook Pollock once again, as he faded deeper into his musings and grew further and further from Retta.

Retta was now viscerally involved in recollections of her Wiccan beginnings, her childhood nightmares of the Horned God coming to push his dirty, overgrown fingernails into her abdomen and impregnate her. The horned God had been introduced to her by her mother at the extremely early age of four, before any of the other more wholesome and fundamental information related to their Wiccan practice.

Pollock's view had drifted during his musings and landed on Jerry Reinart, a thirty-seven-year-old logistics analyst and warehouse supervisor for Pelts, a company that manufactured gerbil tubing for cages and aquariums for distribution throughout the US. Jerry was sitting at a picnic table approximately twenty feet closer to the stage then Retta and Pollock, his drooped, long body clothed in jeans and a black Styx T-shirt. Jerry's lips were madly curled up at the ends, his eyes glimmering and wide. Altogether, he had the appearance of a madman who had just come to terms with the hilarity of his condition. Or so Pollock thought, which was his last thought before a man with tanned arms in a white T-shirt lowered himself onto the picnic table between Pollock and Retta, who was still gazing absently at the sparser and sparser crowd.

* * *

The music from the pavilion had become a somber ode of woe, the four musicians all closely huddled and harmonizing in Gaelic, a tale of obvious tragedy. As the tender pain resonated from the music, Jerry lowered his head and acknowledged solemnly to himself that he would not be going to work tomorrow. Instead, he would be traveling to his seldom-enjoyed nineteen acres of wild land to drive his four-wheeler. This thought powerfully contented him, and distracted him from his earlier thoughts on not having had sex for over three years. But beyond sex, his not having had a woman put her hands on his bare skin in that time.

Jerry had a renewed perspective. He was warm with the dizzy hope of breaking through the chains of repetition and boredom within his structured domestic life. He was going to survey his undeveloped land in a manner he had longed to do. Because of his excitement, he consumed six beers, two weak gin and tonics, and two Moscow mules in freezing brass mugs, and then three glasses of scotch, neat. These drinks were spread out among the food truck bay and two other bars further north in the university district, which he hadn't patronized proper in nearly a decade. He couldn't say which bars for sure, because his surroundings began to smudge together into a confusing but delightful blur of colors without depth or definition before leaving the picnic table.

At 2:47 a.m., he made it home. He flopped clumsily onto his side of the king-size mattress like a landed fish. Once his right cheek made contact with the dear pillow cover he had saved from childhood, now threadbare, he was asleep so quickly that his wife, Eddie, had no opportunity to chastise him between the time of her being awakened and him being unconscious. This made her so upset, she couldn't get back to sleep. Jerry's snoring shot gusts of breath stinking of beer and rotten fish toward her head. His stonelike incapacity meant she had to walk down to the living room couch and lie there, watching reruns of *Friends*.

The whole ordeal reinforced her until-then recently shrinking rationale for seeking divorce. "It would have to be divorce," Eddie said under her breath. "He'd never agree to dissolution. Macy is absolutely right. Never. Never in a million years. Selfish ass." She rocked her head from side to side. "Selfish fucking ass!" As white and blue flashes of light from the TV screen decorated the outline of her obese body, tucked tightly under an orange afghan, it occurred to her that this was how Lisa would likely find her in the morning. For the past year or so, Lisa, who worshiped her father, couldn't muster the decency to refrain from nasty teenage-angst-fueled complaints anytime she was around Eddie. She remembered that she had been the same way with her own mother, decades ago, so she thought Lisa would return.

Eddie realized the volume on the TV was barely audible, but the remote was atop the hutch, where Jerry habitually left it. He would stand there on the far end of the huge oak hutch, which had been a wedding gift from Eddie's grandfather, and nervously rub his fingertips against the bottom of his scalp. Eddie, Lisa, and Tom would all be seated comfortably and relaxed on the couch and love seats and there would be three or four open spots still available for seating. But Jerry would choose to stand, one shoe crossed over the other, knees locked, and rub his neck, which was cocked painfully downward and to the right to catch sight of the TV. It made the whole family anxious and hostile, except for Lisa, of course, who found this behavior endearing and quirky.

Jerry's various innate idiosyncrasies had all coalesced to ruin any possibility of peace. She was being worn down. It reminded her of the book club that she had attended briefly, eight or ten years ago, at a time before the children could construct meaningful histories of their own. The club consisted of eleven women, all "housewives" to varying degrees, but housewives nonetheless. Their meetings were held weekly at the Jennings's house down the street, with the American flag on a twenty-five-foot pole. Eddie went to seven or eight meetings before it became clear it was not a book club at all, but rather a "women's issues" club.

The housewives, unsatisfied with their lives fulfilling and reinforcing more or less clichéd feminine societal roles, met once a week to discuss what it was to be a woman and how they could be better women. Jerry would refer to the club as a "chick party," and chuckle with flirtatious glee. Regardless, the talk there often circled around to the topic of returning to college or graduate school, which most had abandoned once pregnant, as Eddie had abandoned her food science master's when Lisa's existence became evident. But one of the younger housewives, Cheryl Wycombe, had not abandoned her studies, which, not coincidentally considering she was one of the founding members of the group, was a feminist literature degree at Trams Community College.

Cheryl frequently spoke about "being defined by the men in our lives" and its negative consequences, its potential to degenerate their psyches and accommodate male chauvinist behavior. She encouraged group members to define themselves "through their own contributions." It had sounded vaguely like battle or sport to a younger Eddie. At least, it was something she didn't fear was taking place in her own experience because Jerry was fantastic, and she herself had chosen to stay home and raise Lisa, which was a vital and demanding contribution.

But now, a decade or so down the road, marooned on the old, sagging living room couch at 3:19 a.m., she wished that she had taken Cheryl's message a little more to heart. New Jerryisms coalesced in her mind's eye, adding to her dread and despair and frustration and anger and loneliness. As she admitted to herself how lonely she was, she noticed that her ankles and feet were stinging with quasi-numbness. This had been happening for some time and was growing worse the past few months. It was the type 2 diabetes, secretly thinking of it, especially in moments like these, as self-punishment for her angry failures. More Jerryisms joined, louder in her head now than the TV dialog, where Phoebe was sarcastically sounding out "Pay–lee–ohh–lith–ic. Mez–ohh–zoh–ick."

She didn't want to watch *Friends* anymore, nor did she desire to change her current position on the couch, despite her numb ankles and feet. But the frustrations of the night had made her hungry. She was always hungry, to one degree or another. She thought of the leftover shrimp and bacon Alfredo in the quart-sized Rubbermaid container on the third shelf in the refrigerator. It had been fantastic and a great comfort in an otherwise run of the mill–type day, week, even. After one minute and forty-five seconds in the microwave, it would taste almost freshly cooked.

Lisa would be clomping down the white Berber-carpeted stairs at 5:30 a.m. in her athletic shorts and neon-yellow sports bra to eat cereal before sauntering outside to begin folding and banding the pile of *Trams City Gazettes*. Eddie could always pretend to be asleep, but that would require ten to fifteen minutes of boredom, lying on her right side facing the back of the couch, paying too close attention to her breathing patterns and the intimate noises of Lisa chomping her brown sugar–sprinkled generic brand Cheerios a dozen feet away in the kitchen. This was an unacceptable scenario. So, having prepared her meal, she made her way down to the cool finished basement, out of sight.

Eddie had grown up falling asleep to television watching *Cheers, Mash, All in the Family*, and *Sanford and Sons*. They were her drowsy sirens. It seemed strange that anyone could even drift into sleep at all without the aid of the lulling TV noise and lights or at least some music. It was like having an electronic friend purring to you and gently petting your hair. Whenever forced to sleep in a quiet room, which she first encountered at childhood sleepovers, her mind would jump frantically into action, grasping at any shape passing by, and try to build upon it, add to it, and thereby craft some helpful construct. As she aged, her thoughts turned more often toward paranoid self-persecution and worry.

If someone responded to an email from her with the sign-off "Cheers!" which, since venturing onto the internet, she regularly used as her own sign-off, then she would become alarmed, question the sender's true intentions, and ultimately judge them suspect or mocking, thinking they were subtly implying that her sign-off was stupid and, therefore, that she was stupid. This example had occurred with two coworkers, her father, and even Jerry. Most people would be flattered and accept that the emailers had found merit or worth in the sign-off, and consequently mirrored its use. Not Eddie.

Self-inflicted, inward abuse in this style was as constant as her hunger, and plausibly related. Because, as her self-hatred and fear of humiliation ratcheted upward, so did the hunger. By satisfying that hunger in a self-comforting way, she had become heavy and tired. Through this process, she had become diabetic and entirely addicted to sleeping to television in order to escape from her self-abuse. She often drank to excess at the same time.. And now, with a plate of steaming pasta and a blue bottle of Riesling in her hands, she was covertly escaping from her own house and husband and children, and headed to a musty and mildew-smelling basement couch next to a nineteen-inch portable DVD player/television combo unit. And the rest of the family never really knew or asked about her traumatic self-battles. Just that she was fat and stern, unlike Jerry, who was quirky and lively. "Cheers!"

Eddie's present situation mirrored much of her childhood. Back then, she would often isolate herself in fear that her private problems were an embarrassment, and therefore, it was necessary to have a space away from others in which to ruminate on her troubles alone in terror. This place, and this process of slinking away to solely bask in her own private awfulness, was what Eddie considered the truth. This was the dark and inevitable end of things. This is where she would end up, the place that people were referring to when they said, "everyone dies alone."

It wasn't lost on her that most people felt this way. She knew, through her profession, that her situation was anything but unique. Others just never *seemed* to have these issues, except for Macy, of course, who courted her horrors openly, almost reveling in any minor misfortune. She was the kind that enjoyed the attention afforded to victims and losers. Anytime anything went remotely wrong with Eddie's life, such as the time when her father came out that he was, and had been for ages, in love with his secretary, Macy's reaction, more than anything that Eddie had conveyed, became the centerpiece of the whole tragedy. "Oh my God. My poor Eddie, your father has scandalized you," Macy had said. "Does this mean all of his travel was just cover for, errrm…sexual rendezvous?" It was this provocative stoking of tragedy and controversy that Macy thrived on.

Aside from Macy, everyone seemed to have such shiny exteriors, such shallow discontents, that is, in comparison to the deep well of self-loathing and constant self-abuse that Eddie's inner truth allowed for. The acknowledgement that the shiny exteriors of others were likely just fronts, as hers was, did not prevent her dark turn of mind from oozing out obliquely.

For example, her coworker Lindsay once said to Eddie that their boss, Dan, had made a mistake in his accounting of her travel logs for home visits. Instead of addressing him she, sneakily, included her correct versions of the logs in a separate report she handed in to him. Thus, he would see his error, correct the mistake. "Because you don't want to make the boss look bad, you know," Lindsay said. She explained her strategy, which turned out to be successful, to numerous other coworkers, who had all responded with praise for her ingenuity. She had expected the same from Eddie. But Eddie said, "What kind of person is afraid to question their boss?" and then stared emptily off into space.

The comment wasn't a jab at Lindsay, at least not in Eddie's estimation. Eddie was afraid to question Dan. It was rather, an indictment on a whole category of human nature, which she recognized she was particularly guilty of. The meek, surrendering plebeian who subsumes all her real desires in order to maintain the comfort and expectations of others was how she thought of herself, within her blank stare. Lindsay had taken it as a jab, a personal affront, and therefore shared less with Eddie after that. Eddie had this specific effect on most people. She saw and was disdainful of many common human traits. Again, they were always traits she recognized within herself, sadly or angrily. Her manner was akin to a very idiosyncratic confession. But it was always decisive. People always saw her darkness, the tremendous sadness that ignored the back-and-forth of common social niceties, and, therefore, learned to interact with Eddie only when necessary and with as little sharing as possible.

This resulted in further isolation and greater private awfulness for her. Suicidal thoughts began to appear. But every time she considered, soberly and thoroughly, the proposition of killing herself, she always found a reason not to. Sometimes, the reason came from a hope for improvement. She would decide she could change, do new things, start forming a different perspective, and do what she told her patients to do. This resolve conjured feelings of admiration and good cheer. She would spend a week learning and cooking new, healthy recipes. She would organize the kitchen desk that had previously been covered in careless mounds of bills, statements, and pension fund details. She would say nice things to Lisa, Tom, Jerry, and the coworkers nearest her cubicle. She would do all this unprovoked and "out of nowhere," so unbeknownst to her, it appeared manic and desperate. But, all the same, people responded positively. Then her mantra, "People respond in kind; they treat you as you treat them," would grow in force, echoing solidly within her psyche throughout the days.

And everything seemed to brighten. She considered the truth of her own private awfulness as being incipient; the darkness, the isolation, the truth all created a starting point, only there to provoke growth and achievement.. She could respond to it however she saw fit. And so she was finding out that she had guts. Eddie had the guts, the courage, to push past that terrible and seductive quagmire and build character. She could build a character that walked and lived without apology, in the sunlight. And with the sun shining on her face, she wouldn't be marginalized, consigned to her tunnel of forsaken self. She would melt acceptingly into the stream of happy human fantasy.

But then a weird sense would always come, after a week or two, that she could only describe as infinity. Her ability to formulate the happy fantasy, the mantra of self-improvement, somehow began to blend with the possibilities of so many versions of the mantra, the fantasy. It often happened while she was shopping for clothes for herself or for Tom and Lisa. There, standing under florescent overhead lights, atop multicolored tiles with black rubber smudges from disobedient shopping carts, on a Saturday afternoon or a Wednesday morning when she had called off work to gain advantage over her backlog of errands, she would freeze and take real notice of a rack of collared business blouses.

Each one was the same. Sure, there was the varying spectrum of sizes, and there were minor variations in how the dye had been applied to each one by the unfortunate human being performing the task, and each woman standing in front of the rack of blouses might have a thousand quite different reasons for choosing this sea-green silk business blouse. But they were all the same blouse. It reminded her, for a moment, of how she was never really sure she understood the Andy Warhol soup can paintings. She didn't know if they were art for the people or a mockery of commoditized dreams. It all lent to the notion that her happy-human weeks were not immune from the isolation, the awfulness. She was still alone, still forsaken, because though they were all the same blouse, they really weren't. Or, alas, Eddie couldn't say one way or the other.

And so it became apparent how easily fantasies of happiness could be manufactured and instituted as habit. It seemed fickle and without justification. She would lose interest in cooking. She again would notice the little smartass teenage slights that Lisa routinely employed, the transgressions of her husband Jerry. All of the Jerryisms. And so they were all inside of their own different happy-human manufactured fantasies. Flimsy and meaningless as the starting point. Thus, her reason would drop out at the seams, and she would find herself back in her private awfulness contemplating suicide again.

The other main reason for ending her thoughts of suicide, was the repercussions. She couldn't do that to her family. They would be the ones to find her, to "make arrangements," and ultimately to be negatively effected by such a tragedy. It would surely dement and deform her children in some grotesque manner. That was one of the ultimate mockeries for Eddie, that the one true escape from all this was already teasing her from the grave, molesting her children in her mind, demonstrating the utter lack of control that Eddie had over the whole damned thing. Not to mention what kind of things people would say about her, having offed herself. Ominous whispers would abound. She couldn't let them have the last word.

With both major reasons failing, she would always slide back to her default private awfulness, resolute and almost with calm acceptance. She understood that she would suffer the rest of her years in what perhaps, was the inevitable, awful truth. She was just less talented at constructing happy-human fantasy defenses or more talented at piercing through them, with their strange but gaping holes, their weaknesses. So she would walk through her days as a servant to life, occasionally allowing the misery to accumulate and propel her to an isolated area, usually after hours, to eat unhealthy food, to binge drink sugary-sweet alcohol, and to concoct a hazy coma-like barricade between her and her life.

Stowed away, alone and surrounded by her persecuting family, she would fade into warm oblivion, drunk and with belly full, comforted by the friend that always found her in her private awfulness. The one friend who truly understood her plight and endeavored, successfully, to cease the nagging, tormenting foul mouth of a consciousness gone bad. Eddie's best and only lifetime companion, the television set.

Chapter Twelve

As Max approached the edge of the forest encampment, two men with dirty faces and baggy pants stood up from oak logs around a small fire. Behind them, Max could make out a half mile or so of tents and cabins circled around additional fires and clotheslines. One of the men had a silver musket and held pointed it toward Max's legs, clicking the hammer back. Max raised his arms and continued to slowly step toward them. "All right, that's just about far enough, there," said the man without the gun. "What are you doing in these parts?"

"Yeah, whatta you here for?" the armed man said. Max remained silent for a moment, gauging the best way to proceed. His recent experience had, more or less, been a string of confrontations with gentlemen all either better armed or otherwise at some advantage over Max. His continued existence came from some combination of luck, the machinations of other, such as Titius, and his ability to quickly neuter animosity and form camaraderie.

"I heard there was work here, that's all. I could use a warm meal and a night's rest. It's been such a burden, since winter came on. And I'm a good worker…strong." Any decent man who wasn't rich could easily relate to such a sentiment. And, as Max said these words in service of a long deception, he took note of how true they really were. Titius's home had been such a respite for him. He had even forgotten how good it felt to sleep in a soft, blanketed bed, not waking up with a tight and sore lower back, to have a relaxed neck because he wasn't shivering all throughout the night's sleep. The overnight hike to this thicket of oaks and maples provided context for how good and rare it had been. It was almost a heartbreak to leave the luxurious Rombathe estate and head cross-country. Almost. Ethyl gave greater warmth and comfort than any bed or fireplace. And Ethyl was with Max, like a warm guardian, overlooking his actions.

"Who told you there was work here?" the armed man said, thrusting the barrel of the musket forward. Max's attention was stolen by two men whistling as they carried a mesh stretcher through the opening of a green tent just twenty feet along a beaten dirt path that appeared to run through the entire encampment. "Eh, you deaf boy?" The man said leaned sideways and peered into Max's eyes. He pushed the barrel further, now a mere foot from Max's knees.

"A kid who works the fields in Trenton, he said there was work here if you're not squeamish, if you're not afraid of blood and guts."

The men exchanged looks before the armed man turned back to Max. "And you're not squeamish, boy?"

Chapter Thirteen

Pollock clumsily knocked his shin against the stone rabbit sitting on Quentin's front porch and it fell askew. As he pushed it back into its original placement, he noted how uncomfortable the creature appeared to be. It was hunched over with its back leg forward, apparently scratching its ear. It was so contorted and bent, it made Pollock's neck hurt. "Poor fuck!" he said, popping a pool of drool from his lower lip. He began to feel sick to his stomach and swayed with his hands on his knees.

The front door swung open and Quentin stepped out in a grey silk robe, brandishing a shiny steak knife. "Pollock?" he asked, unable to fully make out his lowered face. Pollock heaved deeply several times without producing anything more than a tablespoon of bile. "Jesus Christ..." said Quentin, now fully recognizing his apprentice. He hoisted Pollock's arm over his shoulder, helped him inside, and lowered him into his recline-o-lounger. It had a valley worn into its middle from decades of bearing the same torso and thighs. Pollock fit inside of it nicely. Quentin poured a glass of water into a commemorative 1988 Ohio State Synchronized Swimming stein and sat it on the foldout snack tray beside the lounger. "You've really buggered yourself." Quentin said, lowering himself onto the couch adjacent to Pollock. "So what's the deal, huh? Is everything alright?" he asked, holding his face forward, trying to get Pollock to focus on him.

"Rat bastard!" Pollock spewed out belligerently, along with additional slobber. Quentin smiled and frowned simultaneously. Pollock had a trail of moist yellow bile leading from the edge of his mouth down his face and across his neck, ending in a smudge along his collar. Quentin wanted to pretend to be very upset by the intrusion. But, the truth was he had been wide awake, unable to sleep, and watching an edited hour and a half highlight reel of Jerry Rice's professional career as a wide receiver. The intrusion was welcome. Quentin was often up until three or four in the morning. And he was always in to work on time. Although, his niche position was such that no one would really care or even know if he came in at noon every day.

"I'm a rat bastard? You're welcome for the chair and the glass of water." Quentin said, amused but also with half-serious animus, pointing at his companion with accusation.

Pollock's eyes shifted to meet Quentin's. "No...not you. Silly bastard. You're...silly bastard, and friend...but not the rat bastard."

"Okay, so who *is* the rat bast—"

"That fucking Hans!" Pollock said, sitting forward with fury and smacking the leg rest shut, flinging the chair to its upright position.

"Oh God, Pollock, what did he do this time?" Quentin waved his palms as if shooing away pesky flies.

Pollock turned square and gave Quentin a death stare. "He has no character. He's like a gaping open anus, letting...nasty, hot anus air and...anus...leakage all over everyone!" Pollock said, thrusting his hands about like some totalitarian dictator instilling propaganda with such vigor it suggested he might even be trying to convince himself. The lounger squeaked forward and back, like the sad whinnies of an old arthritic workhorse.

He continued on as Quentin stretched his feet out in surrender, accepting that this would be one of those extended drunken tirades that occur semifrequently between those who have breached the artificial surface of common niceties and are late-night solemn, lubricated, and chatty. It was more an exchange of primordial forces than a conversation among fellow human beings. "His ratio of confidence to achievement, to…even potential, to talent…that's it, talent. His ratio of confidence to talent is preposterous. It makes me violent. I don't know why, but he just makes me want to hurt him. I really do want to hurt the…rat…bastard!" More frothy spittle abounded. "Why does he do that? Why does it bug me so goddamned much?" And with that, he leaned over, swiped the stein of water, and gulped his way eagerly to the bottom.

"Well, in order," Quentin said, "one: some people just don't get along. And that's fine. As far as Hans, which I suppose would be two, I would have to say that he has high aims and appears to be making the right friends for such an upward trajectory. And I know," Quentin sped up his words in anticipation of an interrupting rebuttal, "it's irksome to purists like you and me. But, be practical about this. You can't get drunk and prattle away your annoyance to me every time he trespasses against you. Trespasses will occur. You have to make a decision. Honestly, you've got to grow up a little bit. He's not the only, not the last person you're going to cross paths with like him in this line of work. And our line of work is really, at bottom, about categorizing and manipulating these kinds of interactions. Oye, that's what property is!"

The traditional carved Black Forest–style cuckoo clock on the brown family room wall paraded out singing birds and dancing nineteenth-century German school children with books hanging by their sides in leather slings. It chimed to indicate it was four o'clock. The clock reminded Pollock of his brief and unpleasant interaction with Mr. Ebersold. The thought put a foul taste on his tongue, which, for the briefest of moments, he believed to indicate a second round of stomach upheaval. It didn't. The animosity toward Ebersold intertwined with the animosity for Hans Flowers and created an infernal epicenter of aimless, nameless hatred and anger. Pollock really wanted to hurt someone. Quentin began to see the severity of Pollock's anger and began to take the conversation more seriously.

Pollock had taken everything Quentin had said sincerely, and the words had made their mark, demonstrating to Pollock his own childishness and indecision. Though, being drunk as he was and not quite aware that he really just wanted to run his mouth in vengeance, the realization of childishness and indecision melted right into that rage, keeping Pollock awake and chatty and thus keeping Quentin awake and chatty. Though, Quentin now was beginning to experience the foremost fringe of tiredness coming on, and it scraped up scraps of memories of a nine year old Quentin dutifully following his father's footsteps, the squeaky footsteps of black-rubber hiking-boot heels sliding and crunching on coastal Maine feldspar, granite, tourmaline, and chalky, compliant shale.

Salt spray from the crashing surf spritzed up against the jagged maroon cliffs and clacked against Quentin's brown rain jacket. *Click-clack-clack.* Iridescent fractals of sunlight mixed with layered dark grey clouds and eerie mist, creating for those who based their mood upon the weather, a deep anxious confusion. Days like these provided comfort to those experiencing great personal suffering by animating a backdrop wretched and expansive in comparison to their relatively small human turmoil.

It was the Park Loop Road in Acadia National Park where the two, Lovejoy senior and junior, volunteered on weekends between May and October. The volunteer work mostly consisted of securing, arranging, and maintaining large, smoothed, triangular boulders which lined the edges of the park's blacktopped scenic loop drive. The road wrapped around the low eastern ledges of the mountains along the center of Mt. Desert Island.

The work also required that they hike two trails, Gorham Mountain Trail and Precipice Trail, to make sure that no trace from previous hikers remained, and to realign all cairns and make sure that their positioning was sufficient to guide future travelers from the trailheads to the summits.

On these early morning weekend hikes, Quentin trod along behind his father Ian's steady strides, barely paying attention to the outside world and, instead, directing all of his focus to the inner theater of his mind. He had to keep himself removed from the stiff and cold boredoms, which were inevitable from hiking the same nature tails for the better part of a decade under the command of his father. Quentin's father had no other appropriate place to let Quentin be. And Quentin's mother, Janus, would be sleeping until their return in the early afternoon. Their rough and slamming entrance into the house would shatter and splinter her dreams.

Ian Lovejoy was a man who often lost his lobster-trapping wages due to poor hands of poker at The Crooked Shellfish, where he spent the majority of his time inebriated from, of all things, blueberry wine. His brother, Norman, was the sales representative for a local blueberry wine cellar, and through the laxness of his supervisor, provided Ian with cases of bottles free of charge. A long-standing debt reaching back to Norman's early twenties, when he borrowed six thousand dollars from Ian to buy a schooner, which, through fantastical circumstances, ended up as tourist fodder along the sharp banks of Otter Point, was being paid off in fermented Trenton blueberries.

The loan had come, unbeknownst to Janus, out of the fund which had, due to fruitful investments, grown out of their marriage gift bag. Janus had initially, and for almost three years, complained that it was odd how secretive Ian was about their funds and pleaded vehemently for him to discuss it with her, include her in the decision-making process of their investments.

He had obstinately declared that he would, despite their holy union, maintain his separate account, into which all of their inherited and household sums would flow. Her protests became more hollow, a stale formality from habit, as she realized that she had already conceded the point at the beginning by allowing the separate accounts. And besides, one of the foremost reasons she had ever, in the very beginning, shown favor to Ian, was because of his resourcefulness with money. She trusted that his designs were prudent. And so she often reassured herself that her share of the whole deal was being taken care of.

Several men had, at different times, made sideways comments to Ian about the perceived femininity of blueberry wine. Each of these incidents had ended in broken particleboard walls, blood, and a newfound understanding for the artifice of fermenting local blueberries. The Crooked Shellfish owner, Doran Wreathe was a close drinking buddy of Ian's and, coincidentally or not, weekly purchased his lobster catch. Doran was a cheerful fat man of Danish descent with the gift for commerce. He oversaw the operation of five separate tourist-focused operations between Trenton and Ellsworth. These included kayaking, hiking, horse-drawn carriage rides, and, yes, blueberry wine tastings at Bar Harbor Winery.

Thus it was that Ian was always sympathetically, if scornfully received after his defensive physical bouts. Doran would grab Ian's shirt through a beer-soaked bar rag, and from between reddened puffy cheeks, loudly say in a playful manner, "So, shall we charge you for the bathroom wall and surrounding damage, or can we count on half off your delivery this weekend?" It reminded Ian of someone talking to a baby. And, despite Ian's consistent pugilistic victories, the regulars at the Shellfish would always laugh mockingly at Doran's final word on these occasions, as if they made apparent that Ian had lost some larger and less tangible battle.

Ian was tall with a Hollywood-like musculature that, if anything, didn't do justice to his physical ability. His arms, chest, and legs, in their enviable, Greekgodlike formation, always delivered. It frightened Ian how well they accomplished the object of his desire. Oftentimes before he truly realized it was what he had wanted, it was already accomplished. The great, successful push-pull beasthood of his existence was frightening to him, as if a well-manufactured German bulldozer had gained the power of consciousness. He had wondered what to do once he realized he had been designed as a weapon.

His ability demonstrated to him, at an early age, that human interactions were all, at their core, a matter of force. Greater force ruled and decided. Lesser force lost and constructed a self-reinforcing tale for why the greater force was "wrong." He wasn't unfamiliar with these sour inclinations; they were all relative. Within him were the weaker attributes, the fantasies and oblique desires that never materialized into conditioned skills and habits, the secret longings that always took a back seat and popped out again when, he, in low spirits, contemplated a new line of work, a break with himself. These sour aspects, the lesser, the lower, the weaker, seemed to him more precious. More darling. And so he grew to dislike those features of himself that predominated. However, this turn of mind only had the unfortunate result of fueling such predominant responses.

In his sick, self-loathing reflections, he saw himself bifurcated. There he was, the affronted, slighted jester who could only dream of becoming, and there he also was, the enviable, muscular oppressor who gained the object of his desire with every impulse and breath. Ian was a man who was at odds with himself. Even in commanding young Quentin to get dressed early on a Saturday morning, follow him into the National Park–issued Ford truck, and eventually through his slated trails, he was confused. It was likely the common confusion of staring the creation of your own loins in the eye and thinking carefully about how you wanted to raise this creature. That, against the backdrop of guilt and history, his own father's history and its result, confused Ian. Then there was the fact that Ian's depressed wife would be sleeping until he returned and Quentin was an early riser who would be alone, for all intents and purposes, in a house without supervision or instruction. All of these confusions were normal. What concerned Ian was that he wondered about the kid's pains. More specifically, how much and in what ways he enjoyed his son's pains resulting from his weekend of work.

To Ian's mind came joy at knowing a young, impressionable creature was his to lead, to shape, and, hopefully, set on a track from which eventual success would sprout. He was also dreadfully afraid that any wrongdoing, any ignorance or missteps or innocent mistakes from inexperience he was stomping out in his son might actually be inward violence. He remembered once catching ear of some saying about how the things we criticize and molest most harshly are those things that double as images of ourselves. This saying, only half-drunkenly remembered in paraphrased form, haunted Ian.

And this haunting, as spilled through Ian's bifurcated belief system of strong and weak forces, confused him to no end. The result was a very distant, emotionally reserved approach in his interactions with Quentin. Ian, in his mountain-climber persona, felt if he and Quentin could come to terms using words and ideas, then they would have had a meeting of minds. Ian's lowly, envious, suspicious, but oddly pure and sympathetic custodian persona knew the kid thought of him not as a father but as a janitor cleaning up after his mother. Ian knew she said things about the size of his penis and his brain, behind his back. He was sure Quentin had seen the sadness in his eyes. Ian knew the boy was bright, like her. He knew Quentin was like her, not him.

Ian would shoo his lousy thoughts away and reorient his thinking until the progressions made sense. He always sided with the mountain climber and never with the custodian voice. But he always believed the custodian voice more, much more, which made him feel all the more cowardly for continually building up the mountain climber. He knew that the mountain climber was the fantasy. Ian was a suspicious custodian with the body of a gifted mountain climber. Those that were arm's-length acquaintances viewed Ian as a mountain climber. Those that actually knew Ian, treated him like the custodian he was. This was another manifestation of the confusing bifurcation that haunted Ian's life. And which usually, especially after many gratis blueberry wines, made him quick to engage his absurd gifts of concentrated protein complexes. At those times, the mountain climber would take comfort from having at least made intelligent investments with his monies, but then the custodian would remind him of his gambling.

It was on these morning hikes, following behind a confused and, more often than not, hungover father, that Quentin learned to create a taxonomy of different kinds of tiredness. One wasn't simply tired or not. There were flavors, phases, depths, regions, continents, even galaxies of tiredness with their attendant elements, chemicals, formations, experiences, and cures, aides, Band-Aids, etc. This was how Quentin dealt with the fact that both parents were essentially neglecting him. His mother, through her inattentiveness and his father, through his oversight. Together, they made it clear to him that he was something that needed "to be taken care of." As in, Janus was going with her sister to Portland, and Ian needed to drive to Rowe to buy tools, so what were they going to do with Quentin?

Neither parent ever truly tried to have a meaningful relationship with Quentin, except in those frantic introspective moments when they needed, desperately, someone to either second their hectic vocal spasms concerning their own private worth, or just silently sit and function as some mystic signpost for a verdict on their spiritual conundrums. Ian and Janus drank a lot of alcohol. They fought quietly, dejectedly in tones that slithered into Quentin's bedroom beginning at a very young age and reinforced in him the assurance that humans were generally all very sad and sure of their own uniqueness. Quentin became accustomed to his parents equally divergent nonparenting methods and learned to do things himself, in his own manner, at a very young age.

He began doing his own laundry at four and drinking coffee at six, a fact that a friend in college, Terry Gilman, once pointed out might have contributed to his small stature despite his father being "a freak, a behemoth" and his mother being "extremely tall for a woman, from tall people." The friend had never met Quentin's family but was spot on from descriptions to which Quentin hadn't realized Terry had paid attention. Quentin fished and gardened on his own to supplement food supplies for the meals he cooked himself, despite the fact that his father was a fisherman and his mother a gardener. Quentin would struggle at periods in his life to understand the concept of market competition because, at such a seriously early age, he was self-sufficient, without need to compete with anyone. Without need of anyone, really. His hobbies were all solitary. He could live from his two teak and oak self-made fishing poles and his natural green thumb. He worked at Luc's Diner, Don's Tobacco, and, of course, for his father, the "park ranger." This was all by the age of twelve.

So, Quentin basically declared to himself that he had never been young, that he was an adult since, "Say…nine," he said out loud to himself, his arms folded behind his head on his bare and sagging twin-sized mattress in his bedroom. And the young Quentin had no dreams. He was content occupying himself. The physical and mental labor of making meals, doing laundry, working a total of fifteen hours a week between his two legitimate jobs, fishing, gardening, hunting illegally, and drinking some while listening to music with varying combinations of his schoolmates kept him satisfied and fulfilled.

He didn't envision becoming a politician, or a movie star, or an astronaut's technical assistant, as his young friend Dabs foolishly wished, saying, "You know, the one who really does all of the math?" Quentin never filled up with all of that ambition to escape the small hometown, that unfair initial wound of place, which necessitated any outward route. What he really wanted was to live out of a tent as a bum, with nothing holding him down, so that he could live freely from hunting and fishing and use rivers and streams for washing and water. He wanted silence and free time with no obligations other than supplying his own sustenance and keeping himself healthy and safe and clean, as well as clean spirited. Occasional visitors would be welcome, of course. And he had grown fond of fine pipe tobaccos, coffee, and wines. Not blueberry wines, though. So he'd have to trade his earnings a bit, which would mean interaction in commerce. But as little as was possible.

The vision he had for his own future was partly responsible for why he took such a private, isolated disgust to following his father in those salty weekend duties. But, like his economic autonomy, he also maintained a fairly consistent mental autonomy. His mind and his imagination were his own. Words, conversations, these were tools for achieving things. They weren't to be enjoyed or engaged in for themselves. It never occurred to Quentin that this outlook had been instilled in him via his father.

Regardless, Quentin dealt with the task, one of those bare-minimum familial interactions he had to put up with. He was fully conscious of the fact that all of his friends and acquaintances had much more gruesome and taxing familial interactions. Quentin just thought of that as families being wrong, and he vowed at an early age to never have children of his own. This was a decision that, while seemingly flippant at his age and reversible, was permanent and came to be a great regret of Quentin's in later years, especially during his time spent mentoring Pollock.

His taxonomy of tiredness would depend upon how much booze he had snuck from the cabinet or other locations the previous night. Ian and Janus were each sneaking and replacing, in varying manners secret from one another, bottles of wine and gin and beers, and then drinking until passing out on the couch or in bed. Small, quiet whispers of argumentation, conscious of "the child," would occur: "Where is the booze, I need it now," or "You took the bottle, the last god-damned bottle. Are you really that worthless? Do you hate me *that much*?" Secret stashes were created outside of the cabinet and fridge. Ian hid his booze in his dirty clothes hamper under lobster-gut-stinking piles of white undershirts. Janus hid hers in her magazine drawer in the bedside table, which reeked of free samples of Curves and Voltaire, from the mall. Quentin, all the while, syphoned off enough for himself from both.

The syphoning process usually consisted of him, hunched on his hands and knees, gently unscrewing the caps of bottles—gin in particular; he loved gin because it tasted like Christmas—then smoothly pouring about two to three ounces into his empty old sixty-four-ounce metal coffee thermos and returned the bottles to their original position. He imagined himself a ninja on some critical mission to liberate stolen farm yields from an evil and undisciplined town mayor. He blended it all together, into a nasty and unforgiving mega liquor. Any given evening of theft could yield ten to twelve ounces from each parent. Every once in a blue moon, he would feel a bit ashamed for taking the booze because he knew the increased rate of perceived alcohol consumption only added to certain negative self-image issues that his parents clearly battled with. This acknowledgment also sometimes made him laugh, manically and ironically, after sipping from his thermos, shirtless and sweaty on his sticky mattress.

His bedroom was undecorated and very messy. His prized possession was a set of magazines that featured naked girls displaying themselves candidly atop motorcycles, dirt bikes, and four wheelers. His favorite edition had a voluptuous blonde holding up her plump bosoms with her elbows, and spreading her legs to reveal a completely clean and shaved vagina. The shave job, or wax job, had been expertly done. There was no trace of red irritation, no uneven stubble or growth. It appeared as though she had never been troubled with pubic hair in the first place. It was as smooth and sheen as when she was ten. It even seemed as though there was the slightest hint of moisture around the edges of her entrance. She was lying backward with her shoulders on the dark leather driver's seat of some modified dune buggy, muddy and dirt crusted from a day of heavy off-roading. Imagining the dune buggy tracking through untested earthen ruts was meant to be an allegory and suggestive. It was effective.

Quentin noticed girls, women. He appreciated their biologically produced attributes with severe focus and regard. He lusted after the Harford twin sisters as all males between the ages of nine and, well, between Ellsworth and Stonington did. He saw the glory in making their naked bodies work to bring him to completion. Perhaps he could even pleasure them some, in the event. Quentin charted the sexual maneuvers, the expected topographies to be encountered, the resulting assault of tongue and fingers, and the eventual tumescent finish.

He had had enough awkward basement meetings with looser female fellows throughout his grade school and middle school years to build up a repertoire of carnal tactics worthy of middling confidence in approaching the Harford sisters. And the younger twin, Helen, had once told him, "You are the cutest boy no one has noticed. No, really I mean that." As she spoke those words to Quentin at a pool party at the rich Ferris property, her eyes were nailed to the twilight silhouette of Brady Hoffman. He was talking to Sellas Chorn, the Alaskan transfer who was developed beyond her years and unafraid to reveal her tattoos located on her upper inner thigh to younger high school gentleman who could prove instrumental in her acquiring a local alcohol and marijuana source.

That look of Helen's bothered and ate away at Quentin for some weeks. At first, he believed it was because she had only talked to him to make Brady jealous. This was true, and it did annoy Quentin, but that wasn't what bothered him so much about it. There was something deeper, closer to the truth. It began to occur to him how much energy he would have to exude in order to force her gaze his way. He would have to tell her something impressive, show her something impressive, something rare. It would have to be rare enough to counterbalance the natural good looks and physical attractiveness of Brady. Quentin recognized the reproductive imperative, the drive to win the perfect oval sacs of fat fit best for raising young children.

It seemed absurd to him that a feeling of lust should weigh so heavily on his decisions. He couldn't see why he should bend his schedule to accommodate some ancient and obscene form of gene selection? He'd done his science homework. He didn't want children. And yet this archaic drive, the culmination of which resulted in copulation for the purpose of furthering the human race, still plagued him and terrorized his dreams, dreams which, in the hot summer Maine mornings, often ended in furthering the stickiness of his mattress. There crept up in Quentin some vague notion that all of the work one did in life would only manifest itself as the norm, the baseline, years, decades, centuries, thousands of years later. He currently was basking in the luxuries of his ancestors and saw that his descendants will reap all his hard work.

This idea, in and of itself, made Quentin feel quite exhausted. And it made him avoid all of the phony chitchat flirtation required to get close enough to smell the microscopic residue of body odor clinging to the pores underneath Helen Harford's neatly shaved and antiperspirant-glazed pits. So he just spit into his palm and masturbated to the pictures of sad older naked ladies on motorcycles until he came all over his knuckles. He'd wipe the semen off onto the bed or into a tissue and toss it into the trash can. After pulling his shorts up and repositioning himself on his bare mattress, he would feel fine, great, even, having made no efforts and experienced no drama. He felt he was making improvements that humans would appreciate hundreds or thousand of years from then if enough people came to the same conclusions he had and acted accordingly. Though he knew some will always have kids, some of those kids would think like him.

"Fuck! Not a living, or dead, or yet to be born, person, creature, thing will ever know fully! Never!" he shouted drunkenly, squatting and extending his clenched fists atop Beehive Mountain by himself at dawn in too little clothing. He had a recorded version of music that played one night on local public radio, *Morning Mood* by Norwegian composer Edvard Grieg. It played from a portable record player his funds had gained him. As he stood, thighs flexed, on giant protruding slabs of rose quartz and feldspar granite, the distant orange glow of the rising sun over the glistening green eastern Atlantic, he played the song on repeat and imagined he was time traveling. These were the places where Quentin Lovejoy lived: atop a mountaintop, confronting the rising sun with the fury of a wild creature. These were the types of situations in which he allowed his full expression to flourish without oversight. "Ahhhhhh," he exhaled in pure delight at the natural spectacle of it all.

But even this great expression of himself, the great solo adventure where he discovered his own truths alone, in the woods, at school, in his home, and developed a language and purpose wholly his own, grew tired. It grew as tired as following Ian on weekend trail jobs, staring at the mountain fork moss and the three-lobed bazzania.

After high school, when all of his peers were facing questions regarding "the future," Quentin began to think that maybe his tiredness would be quelled by going somewhere else. He began to wonder if all that hoopla about "escaping" the small Maine hometown, which had been transmitted back to Trenton, wasn't nonsense after all. Maybe some of it was transmitted directly from the Quentins formerly of the area that were relaying the positive gain back to their geographical brethren. For Quentin was under no allusion that he was special. He was just good at spotting where folks get tired. Maybe there was something to be gained in heading westward. Over a cup of coffee he had to admit was one of the worst he had made since he was four or five, he wondered if maybe the pioneers, the homesteaders, and the gold-miners had gotten it right. He spewed the coffee out into the stainless steel sink and lingered about a bit, watching house sparrows, terns, and seagulls sag in the thick, grey sea air. He figured he couldn't really know something like that until he went and found out first hand.

The tiredness of following Ian when Quentin was younger was that which came from having no control of the situation. He was more or less coerced into participation and complied only because many previous experiments had taught Quentin the futility in resisting his father's command. He always ended up treading that ground, that pine-needle-laden rocky path. He had looked down on it so often, in so many different areas, through so many different moods and seasons, that the Acadia Park hiking trails all blended into one aggregate of their component natural phenomena. It lay across the backdrop of Quentin's mind like a permanent computer desktop picture.

Certain things could be controlled, however. And, being a very stubborn person, Quentin drew his attention to those areas and enjoyed whatever freedoms they could provide. For example, he could walk in any way he wished. This was a small freedom whose amusement wore out quickly. He could think about anything. He could imagine the characters and setting of books he was reading in English class. He could take scenes from films that he loved and replace characters with himself and his buddies. He could fantasize about sex, about fistfights, about exploring ancient caves. His imagination was endless and, once properly acknowledged and courted on those long, dutiful Saturday-morning hikes, required greater and greater amounts of personal time to nourish it.

Quentin came to understand that the tiredness with his duty was the frustration of being bothered by those outside things that interfered with his devotion to his pure and seductive inner life. That was from where his truest, most authentic and potent freedom emanated. It was the place he trusted the most, loved the most, and which gave him the conviction that a man could live his life in this world alone. Which is precisely what had occurred throughout his life.

Quentin found things inside himself being rearranged because of Pollock, and this he found very frightening. It was as if, when their paths intersected, it was the time in his life when it would become clear whether or not the actualization of certain beliefs of his had proven wise. As he surveyed these beliefs and critiqued their application with the corresponding results, it wasn't that he was declaring those beliefs invalid as much as there was *something* in him declaring such. Thus, as Quentin indulged Pollock in his drunken outrage, he began inwardly cataloging a new kind of tiredness, the first new addition in some time.

"It's like everything most true about myself I have to apologize for!" Pollock said, flipping his fingers excitedly over his sweaty bedhead. His shoulders were slowly sliding down the back of the lounger, inching himself toward eventual horizontalness. Quentin consciously reengaged with the room in front of him.

"What?" he said, scowling at the sight of his sloshed mentee.

Pollock gave him a sideways glance of hatred as he tried to gather his thoughts, and when he failed, stared with greater anger.

"What truth?" Quentin said. "No one wants that—he used air quotes—'the truth.' What is the truth, anyway?" He gave an ornery smile and Pollock knew that meant he was going to teach another lesson.

"The truth is…the truth…is…" Pollock's eyes scanned the room madly searching for the right landing, mirroring his mental search for the right words, the right answer. Quentin's ornery smile gained real estate over his face as Pollock struggled. He now had wrinkles under his bottom eye lashes and his bulbous, pale, white-hair-littered ear lobes were retreating toward the back of his bald head with the growing of his grin. Pollock couldn't let the confident old fox defeat him. That would be such a disaster on top the night's earlier defeat. "The truth is that everyone just wants to tear down what you believe…to make certain that you know they got you. That others know they got you. Everyone is trying to get you. To get everyone else. And to do it in front of an audience." Pollock wondered if that was what he had been saying.

Quentin let out his healthy bottom-of-the-belly laugh. He whispered more than spoke. "Well said, well said." He admired the simple perceptive accuracy of Pollock's idea while, ironically, enjoying its clunky and poorly worded delivery.

"There's just no way to be around people…even when its good," Pollock said. "There's always some dark undertow where its clear that you are both competing, and when really put against it…well one of you would turn on the other without question…without question, and everyone has to be the man, you know? It's exhausting, living like this, monitoring every body gesture, every casual remark to detect their…their…latent violence. I'm infected with vengeance, aimless vengeance. And I'm exhausted, Quentin. I cant live like this, why would anyone want to? And then when you get to this point there's really only suicide or…or…" He glanced sideways back at Quentin, this time with less hatred and more compassion. Despite the stein of water, dehydration was setting in, and Pollock's speech rang with clicks and smacks from viscous saliva and sticking lips.

It wasn't appealing to watch Pollock air such heavy grievances. Quentin couldn't disagree with his observations but didn't approve of the way he was reacting to them with such indulgent and flamboyant lament. Quentin thought Pollock, at his age, really shouldn't be so effected by this general awareness of competition in life, shouldn't be prostrating himself like a beaten fool. He filed this distaste with all of his negative views on current education and parenting in the country. To Quentin, the pitiful political correctness of society—the coddling, the everyone-is-a-winner mentality where parents were friends with their children, the grad students living at home who paid no rent or board and expected professors to help them with tough essay questions on final exams—was a weakness that created weak citizens. The whole millennial generation seemed to feel entitled. They thought it their right to have a higher-earning job, the newest cell phone, a new car, a brick-interior apartment in an upscale neighborhood, three to five "mixologist-made" cocktails, and trendy, expensive burritos every night, all without any resistance or harsh language.

Pollock hadn't ever really fit into that general category of millennials, not in Quentin's estimation. Pollock had never really been irresponsible or expecting or inept in that general millennial way, the way that indicated one's parents and teachers and sports coaches and music instructors had told them too often of their special abilities and too rarely reprimanded them for all of their true shortcomings. The millennial descriptor applied to those who had been raised and prepared for a future economy that required little of the workforce and, in return, granted a hyperentertaining lifestyle. The baby boomers were complicit and, perhaps, even more responsible for the millennial shortcomings, as they were there at the ground floor constructing this failing methodology. They were the true authors and also perhaps, the best at spotting its wrongheadedness.

But now, tonight, with Pollock unable to hold his liquor and spewing out his feelings about what competitive and adversarial animals that life turns former friends and comrades into, Quentin couldn't help thinking that his protégé had no idea. This surprised Quentin's more analytical self as it combined with his new tiredness to create a robust throbbing in his chest that demanded release and satisfaction. Quentin experienced some vague intent to save something doomed, to repair something, to get "the plumbing humming" again, as he'd often sang while performing all levels of home repairs.

"You're, at its most basic, in the property business." Quentin spoke calmly with deliberate diction that gave the impression of rehearsal and purpose. He pulled his fat, sweat-panted legs up, tucking them sideways comfortably under his butt, nuzzling his toes into the pouch between the couch back and seat cushion. Pollock listened from his floundered, drunken surrender, just shy of horizontal, his moist cheek resting on the arm flap of the recliner. The shadows from the lamp fell on his mentor's face in a way that made him seem only nose and baldness, with dark teardrop question marks for eyes. He reminded Pollock of a Disney villain.

"Property is delineated by recognized rights under law. Federal law, state law, city and local municipalities. And, also, there was common law, which was passed down from England and through court decisions in all of the states here in the US. These property rights determine what actions the holder of these rights can lawfully take. These actions are actions either against others, other people, or against their competing property interests, which are really extensions of that other person anyway. So the property rights that exist are really, at bottom, a set of rules about which behaviors an individual may exhibit against another individual in relation to some object. Yes?" Quentin asked Pollock to make sure his words weren't being wasted on his glassy-eyed companion.

"Yesss..." Pollock answered, boyishly but submissively, indicating his commitment to the lesson despite his frustration with how rudimentary it had been thus far.

The cuckoo clock sang more briefly this time, indicating it was now half past the hour. The room was frigid from the central air unit that had been smoothly vibrating, thrusting cool, dry air through Quentin's metal vents. But it had been decades since any cleaning of these ducts had been performed, and chunky layers of dust fluttered about all along the fringes of the living room's lower dark wood paneling. This paneling lined the room in common 1970s fashion. It made the room seem ancient and reminded Quentin of his childhood. Quentin's tea spices filled the area with the odor of citrus and something similar to catching a whiff of grilling steak from several yards away.

"Easements, for example, grant the holder a right to cross or otherwise use someone else's land for a specified purpose. The dominant estate has the right and the subservient estate suffers the easement, of course in exchange for value, that is, money. Usually these are written into the land deed or in the developer's plats laid out for the neighborhood subdivision before it even goes up. Usually you can see what you're agreeing to. Then there are the implicit easements that aren't spelled out in detail in some instrument. The best example we've encountered would be municipal or utility easements in which the utility companies have a right-of-way on your property. This includes phone lines, gas lines, water and cable, and also electric power line maintenance. It is in the best interest of the community that these utilities be serviced, over and above your property interest. The maintenance must merely be done in a reasonable manner, so as not to unnecessarily burden or destroy your land."

Pollock listened intently, trudging through his memory from the first few weeks working at Trams and being given weekly Building & Zoning Services Department exams toward city certification. He had been keenly fascinated by the spatial categories of possible interests, the manifold reasons and designations for divisions of spatiality, and the different powers and players who manipulated such a difficult system. It was intriguing and engaging. But lately, and now as Quentin lectured, all of these property devices were taking on additional shadowy meanings, becoming allegorical for deeper, more human and archaic mechanisms dating back to the genesis of the great apes and perhaps before. The divisions of spatiality, as memorialized in various possible property rights and interests, began to resemble crystalized scars from ancient shit fights, primordial sorting of genetic futures, prehistoric and epic shuffling of the cosmic whole to land upon the fundamental rules of spatiality, movement, time, and interaction. All the entire way back to that damned almighty question mark that, at one point or another, plagues all minds, however adept or daffy, to wonder at the beginning, the original separation of things.

Of course this was all grandiose and drunken thinking, exaggerating the shadow of property rights over the whole dominion of possible natural phenomena. But that didn't seem to be incorrect to Pollock, already predicting the conclusion to which Quentin's thought was headed. Humans lusted for what there was, so battles ensued. The result was the formation of property. Thus, property and its laws, at their inception, pointed toward precursors such as crimes, torts, gene selection, mating, social ritual, history, custom, sports, religion. Pollock, listening to Quentin's lecture, put the meaning into his own form for more intuitive storage and recall.

Quentin continued, "Another kind of implied easement is the prescriptive easement. This easement forms from repeated and habitual behavior of the dominant estate. It is an easement that is earned by regular use. It is not something that is purchased, negotiated, or granted. Prescriptive easements often arise on rural land when landowners fail to realize part of their land is being used, perhaps by an adjoining neighbor. Fences built in incorrect locations often result in the creation of prescriptive easements. If a person uses another's land for more than the statute of limitations period prescribed by state laws on adverse possession, that person may be able to derive an easement by prescription. Under adverse possession laws, the use of the land must be open, notorious, hostile, and continuous for a specified number of years as required by law in each state." He spoke with rigid and rhythmic delivery, as if his explanations had been memorized from a textbook.

"So you see, the right to property, to *your* property, can accumulate legally even just solely from how you repeatedly interact with someone else." Quentin stopped abruptly. Pollock was slightly disappointed in thinking he had reached his point so soon, and it was a point that paled greatly in comparison to his allegory of all creation. But as the silence lengthened, the import of the point and its accuracy and bold fright blossomed in Pollock's imagination. He began to realize that his work project, which he had already been severely stressed about, actually stretched out much further and much closer to home than antecedent appraisal. But he knew this before the actual structure and granular particulars of the idea fully appeared in his mind, and so he tugged in suspense on the edges of the thought, as if lifting something submersed in dark waters in order to confirm preconceived ideas about what would surface.

Detecting Pollock's internal lifting, Quentin decided against pure patience and aided his pupil in the idea's upward course. "These are basic property interests which Zoning Development surveys, monitors, and amends experimentally for all sorts of reasons throughout Trams and sometimes the surrounding municipalities. Solon, for example, with their south side gondola. Our department partnered in writing the code which established easements for privately owned and operated inspecting agencies to regularly board the gondolas, shutting them down from time to time, to ensure their structural health and proper mechanical functioning according to state and federal transportation regulations. I know this was all before your time, but I remember you being somewhat thrilled when you relayed to me your discovering the project plans in the basement archives. Ecstatic, even. You kept mentioning "possibilities in zoning," and ranting about how zoning could help pave the way for alternative energy, smarter mass transit, better community housing and gardening projects. I could see your passion; the whole department saw your passion." Quentin paused for a moment and looked at Pollock, dearly remembering the kid's excitement for zoning and city planning. Pollock was still tugging upward on that submersed quasi-unknown.

"So I find no reason that you shouldn't be able to muster the same passion and excitement for your nemesis project, this trouble you're having with Hans in particular, but it also sounds like with people in general. You check all of your observations about Hans against the categories of property rights we recognize here and utilize for all of our city's organizing, for all of our code we've developed since Trams was chartered as a city. It almost sounds like he's working his way toward acquiring something of a prescriptive easement. Start there and work outward...."

The idea had been pulled into the light. Salty seawater ran down its edges and spilled back into it previous home. Pollock thought it wasn't so much as Quentin was framing it, though it was that too, but it was that all of the categories of zoning issues could be reformulated. They could be stripped of their geometric "land" qualities and placed solely in the context of two people interacting, face-to-face. "Yes, that's it," Pollock said. "That's what...I need...to finish the project. It's...a problem people. I mean it's a problem of people, not...the city's layout. The city layout will follow! I need to solve a problem about people...*People! See, it is* just people..." Pollock was near the point of passing out, his head bobbing up and down like that of a teenager in homeroom who had, between school, sports, and a girlfriend as committed as he was to exploring their burgeoning sexual curiosity, burned the candle at both ends.

Not completely following Pollock's revelation, his words created a confused look on Quentin's face. They had been having a somewhat different conversation. And, as soon as Pollock had said it aloud, he questioned both its accuracy and its profundity himself. The cuckoo clock indicated that it was 4:52 a.m. A curiosity spiked in Quentin. "Wait, you never explained—what happened with Hans?" he asked, a bit startled at how easily he had veered away from that important fact, which had provided the catalyst for the entire discussion thus far.

Pollock shakily ran his fingers through his short crop and rested his temple on his clenched fist. His elbow sank into the recliner's armrest. "He tried to emasculate me in front of Retta," he admitted in a confessing, surrendering tone. "It made me so furious. Rat bastard..." He said it softly, almost dementedly.

"What did he do exactly?"

"He sat down between us and introduced himself to her. He made some sideways comment about how he was taking over my position at the department. He…when it—" Pollock burped and spittle shot out the side of his mouth. He made no corrective action. "He told her not to worry, that he would take care of me and that his qualities would rub off on me, that he was already fashioning me his protégé…or…something to that effect."

Quentin thought this sounded like typical civil male combat and saw no foul, reaffirming his earlier disgust with his mentee's behavior. "And what happened after that?"

Pollock's long eyelashes were heavy with sleepy necessity, rolling upward and down, upward and down unbearably slowly. His response took a while to materialize. "Umm, we went home and had sex," Pollock said, struggling to enunciate against the click-clack of his dehydrated mouth and tongue.

"You and Hans had sex? Whoa…"

"Yea, we did. We did…" His eyes were now closed and his head sagging. He managed to fall asleep drooling onto the worn armrest.

Quentin thought the whole thing a farce. Pollock was distraught over the way people competed, yet he had won. After his confrontation, he had taken his girl home and copulated. Because he acted so wounded, Quentin thought Pollock a sensitive little lothario who should know most people were wretches, especially enterprising people. "Oye, he'll adapt."

And with that, Quentin concluded that Pollock was merely being silly and needed to come a bit out of himself. He pulled an old afghan throw over him and pushed the handle to recline the lounger into its most bed-like position. Pollock's limp body complied with the changes in contour. The cuckoo clock rang out. It was five o'clock in the morning on a workday. Quentin briefly surmised the doom that both of them were facing in such a situation.

Quentin had often occupied such a position of doom. Being a night owl and accountable to no one made for a potent form of allowance when it came to late night shenanigans, whether it be marathon reruns of *Cheers*, or a frenzied and apoplectic fit of writing memos to the department and the city and state senators addressing systemic slights against clear-headed zoning solutions which only presented themselves as problems on nights that Quentin drank. If he was drinking, he was drinking Willamette Valley Pinot Noir. Not blueberry wine. After those nights, Quentin would often slog into the office around eleven with circular, Lennon-like sunglasses and a fresh-baked baguette under arm. He'd go through emails and phone messages while listening to The Band, Frank Zappa, Warren Zevon, The Beatles, and of course Neil Young through his enormous, ear-covering headphones until about 12:30.

At that point he'd wander up the second floor stairs, casually yet sneakily making his way to the roof. There, he would edge out the end of the hangover with some nicotine. He'd sit in his self-made porch on the roof, "The Weight's" melody still swirling around in his head, his pipe hanging from his bottom lip. And he'd laugh at the absurdity and madness of what he had written the previous night. His spirits would rise from their lumbered morning drag and he would look forward to afternoon, where, with unadvisable amounts of coffee, he would accomplish work equivalent to what most of his coworkers would accomplish in two to three days. He'd return home in the evening, without any trace of headache or upset stomach, which were his two most pronounced symptoms upon first waking that morning. And so, feeling fine and proud and sure of the work that he had done that afternoon, he would be inclined to indulge in the Pinot Noir in like manner once again.

Now, the tiredness of aging had made itself annoyingly apparent, and repeat alcoholic offenses seldom occurred simply because the old-man tiredness would mount a sneak attack on Quentin, and he would be passed out on his couch by 9:00 p.m., his cats nuzzled against his body, purring.

Quentin had worked for Trams Building & Zoning Services' Department of Zoning Code Development for twenty-two years. It had been nine years since anyone had mentioned his work schedule. In the early going, he had made his name by espousing private-public partnership projects to renovate old railway lines. He envisioned a return to rail travel and rail shipping. It could be quicker, cheaper, and better for the environment, and there was already a preexisting infrastructure. Cheap travel throughout Trams, and later the entire region. His proposal to accomplish this consisted of pitching large corporations, whose headquarters and research testing facilities were already rushing into Trams and adjoining cities. He would have Trams suggest to these corporations that they use part of the tax rebates they were getting for bringing their businesses there in the first place to reinvest in what was slowly becoming a new concern of consumers: the green movement and the return of mass transit.

The big players of Trams laughed off Quentin's interest in reviving rail transportation, but they loved Quentin's ideas about how to fund city projects, his aim to partner private companies with the public infrastructure. Such a model would allow the income-driven structure of privately held companies to gain profits from publicly bundled taxes. And so Quentin instantly, inadvertently, became the darling of any important people involved in Trams city politics. The current mayor, the current director of Building & Zoning Services, and several council members who had been wooing company involvement in their constituents' districts.

Thus, Quentin's tenure as a city official began with a sense of welcome and much unanticipated glad-handing, which he felt were unearned but could be put to use in the future for something that warranted Quentin's full efforts. Over decades of experience, failed campaigns, and exhausted tirades, he came to see that his full efforts were of no consequence. The political city zoning and transportation machine was run by money. And Quentin had an uncanny skill for alienating anyone of wealth.

Chapter Fourteen

It was remarkable how well Hans slept. Having brushed his teeth, flossed patiently and methodically, gargled two cheekfuls of Cepacol mouthwash, and slipped into his pajama shorts and white night shirt, he would seemingly blink and the 5:30 a.m. alarm on his iPhone would be humming. Most mornings his eyes would open and consciousness would seep into him a mere three seconds before the iPhone's morning song. He would roll onto his slender shoulder and cheerfully silence one of Rob Durci's latest recordings. He would return to his flat-backed position, spreading his knees to arch and pop the base of his spine, his eyes peering upward through the skylight to gauge the condition of the climate, noting agreements and discordances with the Weather Channel's prognostication.

Hans slept on his back all night, every night. The caliber of his sleep was vital to him because he believed the success of each day began with the previous night's sleep. So he had invested in a high-end Tempur-Pedic mattress with firmness and temperature adjustments in five delineated regions along the body. The mattress was topped by two high-end Tempur-Pedic pillows, chosen especially to accommodate his posture. As he lowered his body onto, or perhaps more accurately into, the bed, it molded itself to Hans's lanky form. Then Hans would breathe in deeply, hold it until his lungs burned, and release the hot air with acceptance. And then he would be asleep, sleeping the sleep that winners sleep and losers only dream of.

A handful of years had passed since Hans last remembered dreaming. He was unsure whether this was because he didn't dream or rather that he forgot them all after he awoke. He didn't think about this long. It was of lesser concern when juxtaposed with the fact that he felt wonderful nearly every time he awoke and throughout the entirety of nearly every day. He had a distant and incomplete notion that a lot of dreams were the results of worries, fears, and distress that come with a dirty conscience. Hans's conscience was in mint condition.

After coming to a conclusion about the obstacles and joys in his life and the preparations needed for the weather, he would prepare for his morning run. He ran nine miles on Mondays, gradually working up to eighteen by Friday. He had built up and maintained this rigorous schedule since he began cross-country at his middle school. The activity had kept him skinny and strong.

Despite older influences in high school, Hans had never experimented with alcohol, cigarettes, or drugs. He hadn't even formed a caffeine habit, completely avoiding what he considered a base and unhealthy activity. Hans maintained his health and treated his body like a sacred organism. Instead of coffee, eggs, bacon, and toast or pancakes, Hans would opt for fresh kale, walnuts, dried apricots, and a little bit of smoked salmon. He drank water religiously; always pausing to take note of its taste, temperature, and the life-supporting hydration it was providing him. If someone spotted Hans, he was likely holding his high-end twenty-two ounce Nike thermal water bottle. He latched it onto his belt with a blue carabiner. The body of the bottle was shinning white and silver swirls that reflected the glare from the overhead fluorescent lighting throughout Trams facilities. The reflection got into people's eyes as Hans approached, creating an angelic or otherworldly effect.

Hans had worn the carabiner and Nike water bottle on his hip since his sophomore year of high school. He was second position on the varsity cross-country team, the Willerly Braves. Only senior captain and regional record holder Rob Durci was ahead of him in time. This was a great improvement over Hans's freshman year. At his final meet the previous fall, he eked into fifth position. But over the spring and summer, he shaved forty-two seconds off of his 5k time and, also, two senior varsity members graduated. The coaching staff and team were only mildly surprised when Hans finished first during the initial practice time trial in early August. Rob Durci finished third behind Hans and junior Trenton Moser, who was also the shortest member of the team and ran with a clunky, inelegant thumping that made him appear to be moving more slowly than he ever actually did. Rob conceded to his two betters that day with dignity and grace, blinking in acceptance with his hands on his sweaty knees, though he inwardly raged with frustration. He would not sit second to anyone, especially any sophomore. Rob began to approach his runs and stretches with the focus and discipline of a high-wire walker. Three weeks later, by the third time trial, which took place in heavy rain and slippery mud, Rob decimated his competitors. He bested Hans, who came in second, by twenty-five seconds. And he maintained his supremacy from that point forward.

The Braves practiced Monday through Thursday as a team but were encouraged to run on their own over the weekends to work on their individual areas in need of improvement. Head coach Tahir pointed these out with sadistic enjoyment as the boys sat along the aluminum locker room benches after practice. Assistant coach Reed stood quietly in the background, his pink arms folded over a clipboard, knowing himself as the true author of most of the critiques. "Hans, your stride is too long and your body rests too far back in your paces," Tahir screeched in his birdlike voice. "You're the anti-Prefontaine! If you ever want to beat Durci again, you'll have to shore that up." His smug smile inspired Hans. It was meant to. Tahir was the true author of *that* aspect of the team's training.

So, he would set out on Saturday and Sunday mornings that September and October, pushing his chest uncomfortably forward and stretching his forward trotting foot less distance than was natural. His time suffered initially as a result of his unsure approach to the new technique. It was hard to gain his previous momentum with so much attention paid to every movement. He shared his concerns with assistant coach Reed. Reed was an indistinct man without emotion but he delivered prophesies that always came to be and indictments that, after quiet consideration, were inescapably on point. Tahir was the motivational genius and passionate leader. Reed was the architect and tactician. The two played off each other very well.

Reed told Hans that a runner does not employ a new technique but, instead, becomes a new runner. And so, this new runner was starting from scratch and therefore needed time to pass through all of the tiers of success already behind the previous, discarded runner. The point was that the new runner would have more tiers ahead of him than the previous runner ever would. He was a better runner, perhaps eventually a great runner. Thus, the true test was in the commitment and patience of the new runner. It was a mental game. Hans understood this completely.

There was a tradition among the Braves to each have their own special water bottle which they took to each meet and had with them at most times: throughout the school day, to the movies, even on dates. It became sort of a superstition with mythical qualities, as if the bottle took on a personality and powers that could interact with its owner either favorably or negatively depending upon the degree of care given to it. Many of the great varsity runners at Willerly had gone as far as to name their bottles. The most recent state champion had been Jim Carbalter, six years before Hans entered high school. Everyone currently on the team knew well that his water bottle had been named Lucifer. Apparently, he claimed to have sold his soul for speed and endurance. Jim went on to a lackluster collegiate career. But in the locker room and on the light runs, his legend thrived as lore passed down through the upperclassmen. The slower and younger members huddled behind them to listen to tales of the Willerly cross-country pantheon.

Having decided wholeheartedly to become that new and great runner, to discard the old confident but limited Hans Flowers, he stopped in to Sole, the running specialty store in the Trams Mall, midway through his next weekend run, to obtain his talisman. High upon a shelf, above ankle braces and an array of three-pair packets of athletic socks in neon colors, sat his bottle. It was next to five others, all made by Nike. It was the furthest to the left. It was tall and slender, much like he was, and covered in silver and white. It looked like clouds and metal. It was kingly looking, as if fashioned by ruling nobility. It reminded him of freshness, cleanliness, and water. As others later told it, it chose him instantly with its long silver shine, like rays from Heaven.

The water bottle cost Hans $32. It had numerous impressive features. For instance, there was a layer of insulation, comprised of proprietary materials, which kept the water inside cool even in the oppressive ninety-five degree August afternoons of Trams. It also had an extendable nipple that would open its suction and stream water forcefully into the mouth when squeezed with one's teeth. The body of the bottle contained a middle section wrapped with memory foam that conformed to clasping fingers.

The bottle's name was unknown and of great interest to the team. If it was ever given a name, Hans never shared it with anyone. When asked by Durci, with some consternation and incredulity, Hans answered "Mmmm…" and tilted his head as if he wasn't sure whether or not it did in fact have a name. He repeated this maneuver whenever asked. And so, after about a week, Derek Mills began referring to it as "The Unnamed." The title caught on, and the bottle was thereafter called "Hans's Unnamed," and entered thusly into Willerly cross-country legend.

Robert Durci's bottle was blue with a black falcon outline in the center. It was named "Styx." Trenton Moser's was solid black, and it was named "The Wind." Alex Beddel had a tiny, cheap old thing that might have once been green but was sun bleached and appeared yellowish-brown. It was an advertising gimmick for a diner that no longer existed. He named it "Mommy-Daddy." Jeff Johansen had a mostly purple, tie-dyed sixteen-ounce bottle with an illustration of Jimi Hendrix emphatically riffing on his classic cream Stratocaster. He named it "Voodoo." Jon Riser had a silver and gold striped jug called "The Quickness." And lastly, the anchor of the varsity team that year was Don Shelby. He did not subscribe to the tradition of mythical worship of water bottles. He laughed sardonically at the whole practice, amused by the allegory it made of human irrationalities on a large scale. Don was fighting such irrationalities.

Assistant Coach Reed had himself been a state finalist during his high school tenure, fifteen years prior to Hans's time. He had placed fourth in his junior year and was a favorite to win it the following year, with Willerly favored to take the team title. But a college student working a summer job in Trams two weeks before fall training began maimed him during an instant of carelessness. The student, Stewart Rothbert, was mowing the short, steep slope that formed Mary and Calvin Lanscomb's front lawn on the west side of Merryweather Avenue. The Walkman latched onto Stewart's belt was blasting "Blue Monday" by New Order at a decibel level any attentive otolaryngologist would firmly advise against. Stewart had recorded the song onto a blank cassette tape several times so that the song would play on a continuous loop without requiring any rewinding. The Lanscombs' yard was one of eleven that he was mowing for drinking money that summer. On that Saturday afternoon, he had already mowed two other lawns

and was hurrying to finish the Lamscombs' in time to make it home for the Steel-
ers football game.

Stewart, filled with the rhythmic joy of the hit eighties song and the general
exuberance that accompanied his college summer days generally, shuffled and
pirouetted his fat cargo shorts–covered legs as he made crooked mow lines across
the crest of the slope. It was an act that Stewart had commonly engaged in during
his summer beer money mowing. And, he had already mowed the Lanscomb's
yard twelve times that summer, accustoming himself to its steepness and uneven
contours. The topography had intimidated him initially and given rise to the
higher rate that he quoted Mr. Lanscomb, who, with spunky-old-man chagrin, accepted. He accepted because he had severe arthritis and a wife who pointed to his
poor mowing performance as yet another example of his masculine inadequacies.

Young Peter Reed came chugging along the well-maintained concrete
squares of Merryweather's sidewalk, passed the long and thick row of mangled
and unkempt pine shrubs that lined the northern half of the Lanscombs', and then,
as he broke through the end of the great pine shadow and reached the steep grass
slope, he met with the sideways momentum of a bouncing John Deere
lawnmower freed from the grasp of its carefree attendant. The luck of the situation for Peter Reed was that the lawnmower was electric, connected to a 120v outlet located on the baseboard of the Lanscombs' garage. Upon Stewart's clumsy
release, the mower's cord, which was usually plugged into the outlet located at
the rear of the four season's room when mowing the back slope, reached its fullest
stretch and popped free of the outlet a mere eight inches before meeting Reed's
shins.

So, it wasn't spinning blades that did the damage to Peter Reed's legs, but
rather the blunt impact of its metal housing. The collision shattered Peter's left
tibia in three locations, ruptured his left anterior cruciate ligament, cracked meta-

tarsals one, two, and five on his left foot and four and five on his right foot, dislocated both of his ankles, and ripped the skin from his flesh in various undesirable locations as the impact made him into a clockwise-spinning projectile, which ground to a halt after five feet of blacktop.

Stewart watched this all happen from his elevated view atop the grass mountain as if in a terraced opera seat overlooking an unfolding Italian tragedy. It was an eleven-second opera. He experienced a sinking feeling that reminded him of a few times when pot had made him really paranoid around a group of strangers with harshly contradictory interpretations of the conversation. As the panic of the moment cleared and Stewart realized what had happened, a green woodchuck station wagon gently coasted to a stop adjacent to the boy and mower in a shambles in Merryweather.

Reed only caught a single still-frame of the green and yellow lawn mower from his hazy periphery before he felt the severe stinging blow to his left shin. Then he experienced what he later recalled as similar to having one's lower legs slid into a concrete grinder. Then a wave of curving street wrapped high over the sky and blocked out the sun. And he went out. He awoke to a blurry and bright hospital room surrounded by mother, father, his older sister Levina, his aunt and uncle on his mother's side, and his friend Tommy Tooley leaning against the doorway with his arms folded across his chest. The painkillers had eliminated the visceral impact of the event and made it hard to remember the incident.

The awful extent of Reed's injuries was delivered through the well wishes of his relatives and friends who all, save the perceptive few, explained to him how lucky he had been that the mower was electric and the cord had been stretched beyond its capacity. If the blades had been swinging, he would likely be missing parts and perhaps even confined permanently to a wheelchair instead of only needing nuts and bolts and a lengthy physical therapy and rehabilitation term. The horrible subtext was always his running career, the thing he loved most in this world and was best at, was gone forever. "But hey, at least your luck wasn't worse." The nerve involved in such proclamations made Reed just angry enough to wish he wasn't on so many pain medications. That way he would be able to get angry enough to hurt them. "At least it wasn't worse!" he mocked, sourly, bitterly from a bed for a few weeks, then from a wheelchair, then a walker, then crutches, then walking casts, and eventually only as the ably, if noticeably unevenly, walking shell of his former self. He knew this was how villains were born.

Reed never did run cross-country competitively after the lawnmower brought him low. But he did manage to run again, and even more surprising to himself, he moved on from his inward bitterness and decrees of unfairness. He forgave the indifferent universe that had allowed such a ridiculous set of circumstances to rob him of ever possibly being the best at something. Gradually, he thought about retribution on Stewart and Trams's street-lawn hedge rules less and less, and redirected his energies to other interests, some of which were as great as cross-country but which hadn't been afforded the opportunity to flourish because of the singular focus Reed had devoted to running.

One of these alternative passions was chemistry, which he decided to go to college for. He took the first teaching job after grad school he was offered, which happened to be in his home town of Trams. There he met a young and enthusiastic history teacher named Tahir, who had previously been kicked off an Olympic track team for drug use and was currently running a vocal campaign against the high school cross-country coach because he had allegedly made a sexual advance against Tahir's girlfriend and knew nothing about the sport.

"He's a cunt, a pussy, with just enough to make like he isn't always on the verge of running or crying, Wonky kink fuck! I'm going to run him out and get this program back on track. No pun intended," Tahir said, looking down at Reed with his signature self-satisfied look that made you believe him. "It's my winning charm. The power of belief and so on. That stuff is real. You know, Reed, what is real to the mind…" Tahir had the habit of trailing his sentences off in a way that allowed you to fill in the conclusion and later give him credit for its manifestation, forgetting that you were its true founder. Or were you?

But, to whatever extent, Tahir was correct of his assessment in then Coach Guernsey. After numerous and unrelenting attacks during meetings between school staff and boosters where Tahir finessed his oratory gifts to leverage community interest in winning to garner support for change in light of the poor recent record of the cross-county team, and school board meetings where several members openly spoke of Tahir's ability to turn the program around, Guernsey stepped down without a fight. He turned in his resignation to Principal Deeg and retired.

Tahir was named the new cross country head coach at Willerly and, only two days later, asked Reed to be his assistant. "You know, my man on the ground and so on…" Thus it was that the two of them, still relatively young men, began their tenure in charge of Willerly Braves running. It was a tenure that would eventually create more state champion teams than any other school in state history. And so, Peter Reed found a way to run again, with the young legs under his tutelage.

The trauma for Reed of having his dream, a dream fully realizable at that time, wrenched from him in his youth by an absurd iteration of inadvertent violence, authored primarily by a careless postadolescent, was communicated to his student runners. Each class of new students learned the story of his past from the older students in their healthy practice of passing along the cc lore. And beyond the story of his past, which grew some in exaggeration with each telling, Reed communicated the emotional and mental lessons from the incident in his coaching. It was communicated subtly, but it was communicated. It was communicated in the way he repeatedly emphasized the importance of his runners being aware of their surroundings when they trained on the weekends, driving around with a pedometer to ensure upon close examination that the weekly practice routes were free from oblique dangers. It was communicated in the way he got a faraway look when describing the type of runner his interlocutor could become, as if he were picturing something dear and painful within himself. At least that's what he did with Hans.

And because Hans could see this in Reed, there resulted an inspired reverence on his part for the coach. Reed became his master and commander, his science advisor and his personal confidant. Head Coach Tahir did little more than rouse his passions with well-crafted and delivered illocutions. These speeches had their own effect, mostly as enthusiasm for that which was preached by Reed. As was often spoken, "The two work well together."

And so it was that, after airing Hans's initial concerns with the new program, he submitted and put his full faith and efforts toward becoming a "new, possibly great runner." Once he did, his initial grievances proved to be ill-conceived and his subsequent efforts and faith in Reed's program paid dividends. His times began to drop as he grew more comfortable in his new stride. His knees and ankles stopped aching and his sacrum became less apparent to him as he walked throughout the nonrunning portion of his days.

The musculature near to Hans's bones readjusted to a more proficient alignment and consistency, one that allowed more give and also contracted with greater force. The whole locomotive enterprise of his lower half began to surprise him with welcome and encouraging gifts of prowess. He regained his position as second varsity runner two time trials after adjusting his stride. Minutes after having done so, Hans's eyes met those of Rob Durci from the other side of the ragged circle the team had formed on the main field in Echoes Park, all of them heaving from exhaustion and trembling from the aftershocks of exertion. It was a moment of unparalleled importance for the two boys, as was communicated by their nervous and circulatory systems and the look that flashed between them. The entire team and both coaches noticed. It was a moment that would later serve as the introduction to one of the great Willerly cc legends.

Hans began forcing himself to stretch three times a day and drink more water than he was naturally inclined to do. He bought a new pair of training sneakers, at a time when the old runner would have continued running on them until the next spring. The sound of his shoes against the blacktop matched the beating of his steady aorta. It became his mantra and eclipsed all other auditory data. He began to feel completely at home in the new steps. He did squats on Sundays and stretched for hours while watching *Nova* space documentaries. In the school cafeteria, he flexed his calves and pictured himself turning his head around in a race to catch a glimpse of Rob Durci falling behind him.

Rob Durci was the golden boy of Willerly, of Trams, really. There were none at any of the conference's high schools who gave him a run for his money. Only Hans, or the runner that Hans was becoming, could do this. And this idea tickled him like he had never been tickled before. He would work himself into ecstasy just thinking about it. He would tune out all of his surroundings and worship the fantasy, his true fantasy of being the first, of being the best. But it was even more than that, it was the idea of running his own kind of race, a race that none had run before and which none could replicate thereafter. It would be his brand. This is what Pre had done for the sport; he had made it more than a sport. Steve Prefontaine wrangled a simple running activity into a wrestling match with destiny, a forum to craft a statement of existence. He made running a religion, of sorts, with prophets and pharisees, the chosen and the forsaken.

And Hans decided that he was chosen. He had been chosen by the pantheon of running to be great. The only problem was that Robert Durci was tenacious. And much like his bottle's namesake, Styx, he was, for Hans, the great boundary separating him from entering the otherworld, the world of running legend. So on a

Thursday afternoon, riding in his father's Land Rover after a humdrum cc practice, he glared far and deep into himself and concluded that he had to do it all of
the way. "With everything or not even at all!" he whispered to himself, stone-
faced. "With every goddamned piece and all of the way!"

The next morning, he awoke from his uncharacteristically rocky sleep at
4:13 and decided to begin. He dressed himself in his favorite running outfit, black
shorts and white T-shirt. He laced up his new training shoes and took a long gulp
out of the Unnamed. He calmly made his way to the office next to the kitchen,
opened the drawer and pulled out a carpenter's knife. With its blade extended, he
sliced a two-inch divot into his left cheek. Dark red blood drooled out and ran
down his chin, over his neck, and down his hairless chest. He went to the bathroom and looked at himself with the viscous red mess over his face. What he saw
in the mirror was someone he did not recognize, it was someone he was about to
be. This thrilled him so much that he got an erection. He left the house at 5:30
a.m., headed for Rob's morning route.

Durci had instituted weekly morning runs into his training scheme. This was
something that everyone was advised against doing by Reed, Tahir, and basically
anyone who had experience running. Everyone except Durci. "He is a worker,"
Reed said to Tahir at the beginning of a conversation that would conclude with
Reed deciding to encourage Durci to begin morning runs twice a week. That was
two years earlier. Rob was now running twice a day, six days a week. And for
some unknown reason, it benefited him immensely. His quadriceps became shredded, and his speed increased consistently, every month, for the last twenty-six
months. He had never plateaued. His true potential was still murky, but many predicted college and even the Olympics. But Hans had other plans. He was going to
put him in his place, which was right behind.

Everyone knew Rob's morning route. He had explained it many times. Also,
the finish mark was the high school's side parking lot, and he usually finished

right at the time the morning crowd of tired teenagers was reaching its zenith. He often received cheers, sarcastic quips and snickers, and keen looks from all varieties of young females who, hard as they tried, couldn't deny their chemistry-based yearnings. The route itself was a three-mile loop folded over itself three times. Nine miles in total, with the final fold extended some to reach the parking lot finish sprint.

Hans caught Rob at mile five in a part near the end of the loop that crossed through a wooded area on the edge of a newer subdivision of large stucco houses. It was called Forest's End Estates. The layer of pine needles along the forest floor muffled Hans's approach. He tapped Rob on the shoulder. Rob jumped sideways to face the startling new presence but kept running.

"Jesus fucking Christ, Flowers. You almost made me drop a deuce! What are you doing?" Hans matched Rob's lowered pace, the occasional spruce interrupting his line of sight, and merely looked at him sternly through the eyes of the stranger he had earlier seen in his first-floor bathroom mirror.

Rob took note of the bloody path running down his face, the liquid renewed with the addition of fresh sweat. He crumpled his brow in some combination of fear and befuddlement. "One last loop for us both, Durci," Hans said without any change in pace or facial expression. The statement sent a rush of energy down Durci's spine. Hans repeated his statement. "One last loop." The second utterance had the gravity and monotonous delivery of a sentencing. It was as if some religious authority had the grave task of pronouncing the inevitable doom of his premonition. "One last loop." Spine shivers abounded.

The two took off in their respective idiosyncratic stride. As the Willerly Braves often poetically put it, it was on. The boys swept out of the forest side by side and rounded Forest's End Estates to find their way back to the beginning of the final large three-mile rectangle. They remained even until the final half mile, when Hans checked in. This was what the runners had been taught to do. When the race was whittling down, you "checked in" with your opponent to measure his reserves and try to find out if he had more, was barely holding on, or was playing you. It happened in every race. It was a thirty-second-long poker game enmeshed within the cross-country event.

Hans was known for his excellent poker face. He toyed with opponents, sporting a sour or hurting expression or panting slightly louder than necessary. Then he would pounce, tighten his gallop, and speed to victory. But this Friday morning, he did not do that. He turned his head, and screamed into Rob's face. It was a high, screeching shriek. It was something like an eagle or other great winged predator might emit before diving to seize the bounty afforded by its evolutionarily earned gifts, taking what was its own. It's stake, its claim. Breakfast. And that was just how Rob took it. Startled by the freakishness of the whole ordeal, he betrayed that he was teetering on the edge of his ability.

Hans pushed his stride into a gear previously unavailable, and the distance grew between the two. It began to seem as if the blacktop below him was moving and he was merely staying in place, observing the motion. Then he wasn't even in his body, but rather hovering over himself watching it happen. Hans's head emptied out completely and he disappeared. He was a floating emptiness, a great hollow void of galactic nothingness. A conduit of purpose without ego or consciousness. The tight, muscular pumps of flesh were locomotive beauty. The perfect meeting of design and execution. The distance increased until there were several hundred feet between the runners. Hans sprinted along the sidewalk that edged the crowded school parking lot, and he smacked his hand loudly against the aged brick school building.

He returned to his body just in time to realize that it was over and that he had won. Not only had he won, he had absolutely demolished Durci, who, some twenty seconds later reached the sidewalk. It was at that time the onlookers, those that were at all paying attention, awoke to what was taking place. Flowers had beaten Durci on his own route. A shaggy-haired Michael Penske called out from his squatting perch atop the hood of his rusty Dodge, "Shit guys, Durci just got smoked good! Smoked fine! Shrink wrap that and place it in aisle nine with a price tag!" Rob ran, grimacing, to the finish, where he quickly collapsed clumsily onto his side, scraping his legs against the harsh concrete. Because he wanted honest and fair competition and understood that he had snuck up on Rob, putting him at disadvantage, Hans extended an open hand to help Durci back to his feet and said, "We'll decide at practice." It wasn't a victory yet, only a pronouncement.

Hans beat Rob by an even greater margin that evening. Rob had pleaded with Tahir to allow the impromptu trial to take place despite the coach's disapproval. Afterward, sitting on his butt in defeat, arms around his knees, Rob surveyed his teammates' faces, searching for some grounding. All he found were avoidant eyes and a few sympathetic nods. Hans had since rinsed his face and neck of blood. But the cut remained, deep, the edges of its valley roughly apart and glistening. He stood over Rob smiling, pleased with himself, and basked in recognition from the others that he was now their leader, the best. This knowledge made him again grow slightly hard.

The emotional wake of Hans's emergence as first runner, in tandem with his intimate acquaintance of this new great runner born out of sliced flesh, thrust into him an unrelenting momentum toward dominance, toward feelings of having and executing his innate power. He increased his hold over first position the next few weeks. He won four more time trials handily, and finished first runner at both Hockeye Challenge and the Trams invitational, the last two meets of the regular season before sectionals began weeding out the weaker teams.

Rob's repeated defeats were enough to dishearten the promising senior. But, Hans, thriving off his new momentum, didn't stop at merely securing his position as head of the team. No, that wasn't enough for this new great runner. So, he continued to meet Rob on his morning runs and humiliate him, continually beating him by several hundred yards in front of their classmates. After a week, Rob wised up and conceded his morning route to the new runner, relocating to a farther-away ten miler he mapped using Google's pedometer the previous night. And for a few days, Rob felt relief from the embarrassment and defeat. He organized himself mentally to begin a comeback, a schedule of heightened intensity to propel him back to his preordained spot. And those next four days he ran like he had never run before, with a new severity to his concentration and a harder push at the end of his finishing sprint. He wanted, and his tenacity rewarded his want.

But during those four days, Hans was also running like he had never run before, or more accurately, he continued running like someone else to an extent unbelievable. He crossed into the fifteen minute territory, a must for glory, but something none truly believe possible of themselves until it happens. And he was experiencing no notice of an approaching halt or hiccup in his progress. His cheek was healing into a mild scar, which would one day be a mere faint line. His father had urged him to go to the doctor and get stitches, but he refused with certain that it wasn't so big a concern. As Hans put it, he was, "running the run that all runners dream of. The run that only dreamers can run."

After the fourth day, Hans made his way over to Fulton Street where he caught sight of Rob on his new route and began frequenting that route as well. Rob, with a stern face, advised Hans to leave him on his own during his morning training. Hans ignored him and continued to decimate Rob on his new route until Rob capitulated and stopped running in the mornings altogether. This lowered him in Hans's estimation. He knew that if his older teammate continued to chase Hans's tracks, the whole team would improve to greater heights. They had a strong chance at winning district and even regionals, if not at least placing top third, which would put them in welcome territory entering the state tournament.

Rob's capitulation expanded beyond his trademark morning runs, which had now been claimed by Hans. It seeped into Rob's running aspirations generally. Throughout October and into November, he began hanging out more and more with his musician friends, who made a habit of spending weekends playing nine-hour games of *Halo*, with intermittent trips to the bathroom to rip zero-gravity bong hits the size of their adolescent frustrations, in the house of whoever's parents were out of town that weekend. This pattern was usually conjoined with excessive consumption of cheap Natural Light or Coors Light, purchased by someone's older sister or via $120 fake and scannable IDs made by some boy-genius eighth grader. Then, at the end of these long video-game-party nights, everyone would stretch their gut beyond comfortable bounds to make room for piping hot pizza, submarine sandwiches, and gyros.

Rob didn't run on the weekends anymore. He was too hungover. His place dropped from second to fourth. Trenton and Alex, thriving off of Hans's competitive injection, were improving to Reed's quiet celebration. Tahir, who had taken a special interest in Rob from the start, began to raise the invective fury of his post-practice oratory. He would shoot a disgusted scowl his way and yell out, "Rob, you sad, sad boy. You're sinking. You are sinking. It's disgusting. Flowers is turning you into a cheerleader. A cheerleader." Rob studied his untied shoelaces amid the muffled chuckles of his teammates, who did not understand how seriously Rob took these casual jabs. Rob himself had chuckled at previous such jabs from the coach when he was safely in first position, and the harsh words were directed elsewhere.

On the second Monday of November, Rob didn't show up for practice. Rumors swirled as he remained out of practice the whole week. Meanwhile, Tahir was cornering Rob at every chance to get him to reconsider quitting the team. He was nice to him, for once, which only served to frighten Rob. Tahir and Reed visited with Mr. and Mrs. Durci to try and ply them. But they had strangely taken to

Rob's decision. The whole meeting was soaked in mysterious subtext, an aching awareness that there were other truer things at work in Rob's decision, things that couldn't be spoken of and likely dealt with mental health. Tahir maintained a sheen of composure as he shook Mr. Durci's hands on their front porch and pronounced with finality, "I'm very sorry to lose your son. We all are. Rob was our best runner. He was the leader and heart of the team." This brightened Mr. Durci's eyes, but lead to no revelations.

Rob Durci began studying less and gained fifteen pounds. His girlfriend of two years, Leslie Shemky, rather meanly broke it off with him after he failed for the tenth or eleventh consecutive time to produce a viable hard on. "You're not fun anymore, and all you do is sit in your room, depressed," she said. "You don't even take care of yourself. I don't understand; I thought you *wanted* to stop running. No, you don't know what you want. Limp dick Durci." Rob said nothing but concentrated on the burning churn of sensations flourishing throughout his upper chest and throat. After she slammed his bedroom door on him, he cried.

The world went on, as it does. Hans won a state championship as an individual that year, and rallied the team to their first ever team win the following year. Mostly everyone lost touch with Rob. He spent his days in his bedroom recording music on his laptop with a midi keyboard and condenser microphone. Over the next several years, he created four lengthy and creative solo albums. He posted them on Bandcamp where he had zero followers and made no effort to gain any. For years he had no website, no Facebook page. He never played out. He lived in his childhood bedroom as he passed on college and worked part time as a disc cleaner at an independent video rental store that barely hung on financially in the wake of Redbox, Amazon, and Netflix. Occasionally he would do yard work or cleaning for his mother, who loved having him around. In Mr. Durci's head was a kaleidoscope of analysis concerning his twenty-three-year-old, high school–educated, stay-at-home son. Rob's father remembered being about thirty before he himself "began getting his shit together."

"And the economy. It's a lot different for these millennials than it was for us," he'd say, repeating it like a mantra learned from an accumulation of *New York Times* articles and *Real Time with Bill Maher* panels.

Mr. Durci had reached out to Mr. Flowers a week before Rob quit the team. They met at Mr. Flowers's accounting offices. Alarmed at the awkwardness of the phone conversation a few hours earlier, Flowers was nervous. "Look, my wife doesn't know that I'm here," Mr. Durci said, his thigh bouncing rapidly up and down on Flowers's office chair, "neither does Robbie. Your boy is going to do very well this post season. And I hear he's a very good student as well." Opaque hesitation mirrored opaque hesitation.

"Thank you for saying so," Flowers said. "And your Robbie is the captain of the team. Hans said he is a really gifted leader. I think he really looks up to him."

The two men sat uncomfortably in their respective seats trading niceties until Mr. Durci finally revealed his purpose. He had wanted Mr. Flowers to maybe speak with Hans about letting up on the competitive wounding and maybe let Rob alone on his morning runs. "The boy has already won. And Robbie, he has a condition. His mother had a…well, you see he's going through a particularly rough patch right now. What, with college decisions, his girlfriend isn't exactly…supportive, not a good influence…and now with the thing between him and Hans. I just think it may be too much for him, and I wonder if you might just ask Hans if he would pull it back just a bit. Maybe just leave him his mornings…"

Mr. Flowers, who had been completely unaware that Hans had even become first position varsity, let alone that he was leaving in the mornings to taunt a teammate, felt very uninvolved with his family. He felt like an absent father, especially in comparison to Mr. Durci, who was clearly very involved and aware of even the emotional lives of both his wife and son. It scared him a little, and he had to fold through layers of unwanted feelings to align them correctly and tuck them away before talking with Hans. He knocked on Hans's ajar bedroom door, quickly strode in, and sat on the edge of the bed. Hans swiveled his computer chair to face his father.

"Tell me about cross-country," Flowers said.

"What would you like to know?"

"Well, for starters, I heard that you beat out Robbie Durci for first position."

"Yes, I did."

"Well, congrats. I know how hard you have been working," Flowers said with a pinched smile. He did not know how hard Hans was working, he was estimating.

"Thanks, Dad, but you shouldn't congratulate me until after state finals."

Flowers grunted with pleasure. He saw that his son was committed. But he soured a bit reflecting on his earlier conversation. "Well, look, I had a conversation with Robbie's father earlier today. He seemed…concerned about—"

"I know, Durci isn't handling it well. He's behind Trent and Alex now. I am trying to push him forward but he's become resentful. It's kind of disgusting. Who folds like that?"

Flowers considered his son's position. It made sense to him. He weighed that against the sadness in Mr. Durci's voice. "Well, maybe you could find another route for the mornings and let Robbie alone until practices?"

Hans looked pained. "No dad, that won't do anyone any good. Cross-country is a competition of individuals. Everyone wants the top spot, the fastest time. It's not my job to give it to someone else. They have to take it for themselves. It's a mental game, and I've just begun to understand my strategy. And it's working."

Flowers, who had never participated in organized sports beyond the neighborhood baseball pick-up, catalogued his son's statements as true and spoken by someone with experience greater than his own. He also saw that if he pushed further, it would require much more involvement of him than the casual presence at meets and nods of pride after reviewing grade cards. This seemed distasteful to him, and so he concluded that his son had a point, but at least he had broached the subject with Hans as Mr. Durci had asked.

Hans grew quiet when he heard his peers whispering "limp-dicked Durci" in the hallways or out on the weekends. He turned down sexual advances from numerous attractive and intelligent high school girls. And for much of his senior year he hung around Mr. Dallas, who was a retired architect and regional city planner of thirty years. He taught two elective classes, one on electronic rendering and structural programming and the other on the history of cities in the United States. Hans was unequivocally fascinated, and his interest in real estate and zoning quickly overshadowed his previous zeal for theoretical physics. His library record switched from *Nova* and Asimov rentals to law books on private property rights and documentaries on light rail systems and the development of mixed-use plats in US suburban fringes.

Chapter Fifteen

It grew dark. Max had been pushed forcefully through the small village in the woods, which consisted primarily of little tilting wooden shacks. They appeared to Max to be not much more than double-sized outhouses. There were a few dozen army tents and a handful of large fires blazing, with rings of dirty and quiet men warming their hands or shaking to and fro. Several men were uttering angry but indistinct words under their breath. His new armed friend shoved down on his shoulder, and his butt hit a short log seat beside a particularly large fire pit. His arrival garnered little reaction among the group of hand warmers. One of them merely looked up and noticed that there was a new member. Max's guard pointed a long finger in his face and said, "Sit here. We will be back. Don't you move."

The wind picked up and hurried a frantic whirl of snowflakes through the woods. It dusted over the men huddled by the fire. Pine logs blazed and cracked harshly. The men had an eerie uniformity, as if their bodies had once experienced freedom but were now sagged and hunched into a permanent cower, a cower that was inescapable, fated. The cheeks and lips of most were cut and splattered with dirt and yellow and white substances of unknown composition. None spoke. All that could be heard was the hiss and crackle of the flaming pile in the center of their circle. All shivered and swayed about for warmth. They rubbed their abdomen and shoulders with their gloved and shirt-wrapped hands.

The scene was wretchedly familiar to Max. He had been finished with the war for years. And he had fooled himself, time and time again, that there was something in which his revived hope would find reward. But time and time again, in his nomadic existence since his last battle, his last musket plug, he found that the war had never ended. Very oppositely, it hung around, heavy in the air. It had touched everything. The landscapes of the southern countryside he had traced in his search for Ethyl were all marred with cannon blasts, leftover confederate encampments, field graves, and dead bodies. The faces of those who survived betrayed their continued involvement in what was now "history." Max recognized that these fire-lit faces belonged to men who had fought. They were soldiers. He saw their military-issue jackets and boots. And at this realization, Max became extraordinarily sympathetic and also extraordinarily disappointed. Although he understood the scars these men bore, they showed him that with which he longed to be finished.

The thumps of war drums churned up within him. Memories flickered. He recalled the oppressively sticky June morning when he caught a Confederate pissing ten feet from his own urine drizzle, unaware that he had wandered too far and the double-take he made when he saw his bullet had slammed into a tree a confounding three feet above the soldier's head. He remembered the anguish at seeing the man level his own gun while he thought through the time it would take to reload and his swift trot forward, pulling his knife from his belt and holding the piss stained trousers up with the other. He could still smell the sulfur of the gunpowder the medic lit aflame to burn shut the bullet hole in his shoulder after retrieving the metal ball from within. The knowledge that he had triumphed, he had felled another man with his knife and had survived. Then had come the putrid revelation that this was what the war actually was, a theft. He was required to steal their lives from men. And in the process would likely lose his own. They were all death's pawns in a game that had a giant looming zero at the end. And all the while the drums, pumping, banging, seeping into Max's bones.

Max began to hunch like the others. And the frustration in not escaping those drums, not mustering enough distance to be finished with the thing, prompted him to reflect on his agreement with Mr. Rombathe, and the modified version he later made with himself to keep hope alive long enough to find Ethyl and then consider the other option. The thought of Ethyl stirred a calm into him and he reconnected with his composure, straightened out his slouch, and began clearly considering the situation in which he found himself.

"He Daddy forgot he Henry!" the man next to him said.

"What?" Max said.

"Er, Daddy, he forgot all about Henry. I done what I could. I know it ain't much. But it Henry. He Henry. And my daddy forgot all about Henry. Sister say don't do no good worry about Henry. I say…pudding!" His rot breath forced Max to turn his head away.

"Who's Henry?" Max asked with sideways eyes.

The man furrowed his brow, reached out his arm, and made a sturdy fist in the air. "Henry," he said, and pointed toward himself.

"*You're* Henry," Max said, with quasi-comprehension. Henry smiled to reveal brown teeth, and bobbed his head excitedly. Max noted the others had turned their attention to his and Henry's conversation. "Your father forgot about you?"

"No, Daddy forgot about Henry, is just saying. Sister say this saying, Mable say this saying. Get me, catch me saying this saying like I believe it. But it's all pretty lace. Truth is Henry never had no daddy. Daddy is all pretty lace. Old lace. Fine fine lace." The remainder of the group started moving uneasily, their bodies and eyes shifting.

"You were an orphan?" Max asked, at pains to retrieve coherence and beginning to pick up on the unease growing among the others. The conversation

seemed to be some kind of interruption, and though Max hadn't intended to provoke it, it seemed the more intelligent path might have been to ignore Henry.

"All sorts of orphanage. You in the orphanage now. Forget about Daddy.
Forget about that fireplace. Ain't Daddy after the lantern loses its light. We all
playing at daddy. We in the orphanage now. Playing at daddy, playing at daddy.
Fine fine lace…"

Max began planning an escape route. The others started whispering among
themselves, and throwing menacing glances at the two talkers. The drums were
building back up within Max, and he was preparing for combat. It would have to
be with his bare hands; the two sentries had disarmed him. A member of the circle
adjacent to Henry stood abruptly and formed his right hand into a salute. At this,
the remainder of men all jumped to their feet, saluting to someone who Max could
see approaching through his peripheral vision. He stood and turned, noticing that
Henry remained seated and continued, somewhat more softly, talking about how
his daddy had forgotten him, and he was now in an orphanage.

"At ease!" the portly man said, returning their salutes. He was clothed in a
Union Army captain's uniform. It was dirty and worn, with a blood-stained hole
in the lower left belly, just beneath the high-waisted leather belt. Turning his attention to Max, he said, "Captain Horace Deitland. And who stands before me
now?" Max, opened his mouth but no words came out. "Name and rank, son!"

Max's rote mechanisms took over, and he yelled as he had thousands of
times, "Lieutenant Maximilian Bellgrave, sir!"

Deitland smiled and nodded his head. He circled his hand around, as if
bringing the other men into his confidence. "You hear that boys, we've finally got
a lieutenant in our cavalry company. God has seen fit to answer our needs. Ah, its
a good time to be a soldier."

The men nodded compliantly and mostly returned to the slouched, passive
demeanor they had maintained since Max's arrival. All except Henry, who was

still muttering, "Daddy forget. How the hell Daddy forget? That mean sumbitch has the worst memory I seen. Can't complete a sentence without forgetting what words already come out that mean sumbitch's mouth."

"Men, return to your leisure time. Lieutenant Bellgrave and I have some serious considerations to make concerning our diminished artillery core." He looked upon Max and extended his arm in invitation to join him down the way. Max followed his direction, wearily. He was tired of meeting people, tired of changing scenery. His head felt like a steam engine puttering on with too little steam.

The battle within Max was between the need to identify or concoct a reason to keep trudging forth, again and again—confronted with perilous individuals and a seemingly permanent physical exhaustion—and a seething pessimism. Pessimism in the state of every fractured soul he came upon during his search, regret for what had been taken from him, and sadness for all the once-intelligent men who had forfeited their troubles in exchange for reflection, vagueness, and insanity. The whole damn country was confused to the point of self-destructive irrationality. Max's inner war provided just enough animus to keep driving him, to keep his eyes focused on the future, though he wondered what future he could have now. The masses of leftover men were all inwardly drawn to those violent reflections that the drummer summoned within him too, that bad and sticky bit of voodoo that haunted them, clinging with strong fingers to their animate parts and clouding their vision. They were all replaying the dark wretchedness, each man with his distinctive personal bent. Max thought about the thousands and thousands of pasts being relived with no future.

Deitland was very intense and conducted himself as many middle-aged captains did with which Max had crossed paths. Formal, tight jerks of the shoulders and wrists, subtle variations of contempt and dignity in the twitches around the eyes. Max was pretty sure that Deitland was absolutely insane. He purported to be reconstructing the artillery and two infantry battalions that were decimated in an unforeseen and devastating outflanking during a recent battle just north. He had no idea of, or otherwise had, perhaps out of necessity, chosen to ignore the year. For the war had been over for several years. But this was only another artifact that fit into Max's general understanding of the country since the war—just another man living in the past and putting forth nothing to craft a future.

Maybe Max was doing the same. Maybe his business with Ethyl was very backward looking. But *this* had been inflicted upon him. He owed her. He needed her. And beside, he wasn't averse to creating a future, but it had to be afterward. He had to find Ethyl and see her and know her. Only once this had happened could he begin thinking about something like hope, about uttering the word "to-morrow."

Unease sprang up from odd, unsure angles when he tried to distinguish him-self from the quicksand consuming those around him, like Captain Deitland. That was the hope side of the inner war he saw as being divided by a tugging line. And as soon as he approached it, he'd turn and join the fight on the other side of the tugging to maintain the line, where he revived his displeasure with having these unfortunate steps ahead of him. He'd fret at no longer having a thriving printing business to come home to. He'd think about Ethyl. Everything beautiful about him had been ransacked, turned over, mutilated, and hidden. And by this point, Max would be grinding his teeth, and his chest would tighten. The inner war raged on.

The potentially mad Captain Horace Deitland explained that any lieutenant worth a lick was more than welcome to recuperate at his camp, "so long as he pulls his weight and helps me repair my troop losses once oriented and rested." He showed Max to one of the "outhouses" and demonstrated in weirdly juvenile fashion, placing two complimentary hands against his cheek, that Max was to sleep there. Max took this as further evidence that Deitland probably had no busi-ness being in charge of these men. He pushed the door open and eyed the bare dirt floor. There was a heap of grey army jackets in the corner. It wasn't the shabbiest place he'd slept in lately. In fact, aside from his brief respite at the Rombathe estate, which now seemed like a fanciful daydream, this was among the higher tiers of accommodations in recent memory. He slept deeply and awoke gently in the early morning.

He stayed curled on his side with the three rebel army coats piled over his abdomen and head. It created a warm envelope of exhaled breath and stale cigar smoke. It smelled terribly bad, like day old fish guts and crotch sweat. And in an instant the floral scent of Ethyl's curly tufts washed over his recollection so strongly that he could actually smell it. The tenderness evinced by such recollection brought to mind his verbal agreement with Mr. Rombathe. He sat up. He was here to do an errand for Mr. Rombathe. And then he would be able to see Ethyl and resolve which side of the tugging line would win. The vacillations were growing harder to bare. He did not have long before he needed to decide, or have decided for him, what kind of future, if any, was possible.

With this steeled focus, he made his way out of the shack, and headed toward the closest smoking fire pit. It was thankfully unoccupied, and he took it upon himself to have a peaceful smoke to charge his cognitive faculties. Now in the early dawn, he could see the camp more fully. It was dominated by closely knit oaks along a gradual slope leading down to an unmaintained crop field. Max counted twenty-two similar sheds, and estimated a good forty-five or fifty tents. There must have been hundreds of people living in the camp. He wasn't even close to being the first to wake. There was activity along the slope among little groups. Mumbled breakfast conversations were occurring around other fire pits, and men cleaned guns, sitting hunched atop ammunition chests, their legs dangling. At the far end of the encampment, there appeared to be a beaten-up old farmhouse, but it was hard to make out with any detail because of the smoke, the thickness of the old tree trunks, and the mingling of persons.

From behind his seat, Max caught ear of grunting and high pitched cussing. "Shit, Denny!" He turned and made out two soldiers carrying a rectangular tabletop, six foot in length, with a large burlap blanket over it covering something round. Their cargo was heavy, and they were struggling to angle their way through the small gaps between the tree trunks.

"Gotta go sideways…uh…oh…there, we got it!" the other man said, as they tilted the top forty-five degrees and slid between Max's sleeping house and the tent behind it.

The sight captured Max's curiosity. Beyond that, it reminded him of his conversation with Mr. Rombathe, and his true reason for being there, in this encampment. Concluding that none around had the slightest notion as to his whereabouts or purposes, he cautiously followed the two men and their concealed cargo. He maintained a good fifty feet of distance and darted from tree to tent, peering around their sides to track the men's progress.

They passed a group of female nurses walking to a tent up the slope carrying boxes filled with folded cloths and metallic instruments. The women's faces were clean, with a look of duty that Max recognized well, having spent time recovering from a gunshot wound in a medical tent.

He recalled, specifically, one nurse named Rachel, who, unflinching, skillfully sliced away the gangrenous flesh from a soldier's leg while he writhed and howled from too little morphine. For twenty minutes, other nurses took turns holding the man down, but Rachel's intent stare never changed. She knifed away the foul yellow flesh to the bone, small rectangle by small rectangle, from around the soldier's knee. She had already sacrificed the lower leg to amputation a week previous. How odd it had seemed to Max to think that a woman had been tasked with such a vile bit of butchery. But it became apparent to Max that this nurse was something unusual, special.

She tossed the chunks of excised leg into a porcelain bowl, filling it with a mound of bloody, infected flesh. Rachel, staring directly into the mess of deformed joint and muscles, angled her head to see where the knife was still needed. The screaming filled the tent, causing Private Dugget to cry out, "Oh God, Jesus Lord! I have to watch this? O Jesus Mom! Jesus Lord. Mary have mercy, I am going to lose my supper!" The screams and blood and stench—none of this effected Rachel's resolve in the least. Max watched it all and fell a little in love with Nurse Rachel during the ordeal.

As for the soldier with the gangrenous knee, he died early the following morning. He watched the doctor, O'Henry, walk down the tent like a sulking child to deliver the news to Nurse Rachel. He couldn't hear their conversation from his dilapidated cot, but he saw O'Henry's arms extending apologetically like a man without an explanation in the face of terrible and pervasive doom. Rachel just nodded. But what she did next wrenched at Max's heart, and brought burning tears to his eyes. She softened her mouth in a gesture of mature acceptance of the unwanted, reached her hand out and cupped the doctor's cheek. O'Henry looked haunted, as if something paranormal had just taken place. Max rolled over in his cot and sniffled and worked at choking off the onset of teary hysteria. He didn't want to contribute to what he had heard within the medical tent on previous evenings.

Once the nurses had safely passed on and he had no fear of being spotted, he sprinted out in the direction the men had previously been traveling to find nothing in any direction. He was on the edge of the woods, where the dead grass and soybean fields stretched out flatly to the horizon in strange matted patterns, compressed from the recent heavy blankets of snow and ice. After scanning left to right, he lowered his head, listening, and heard a rustling and stomping noise and saw the burlap-covered tabletop far to the right, still underneath the trees' evil-looking branches.

The men zigzagged and stumbled along, leading Max farther along the edge of the woods. The brush grew thicker and more and more comprised of briar and immature saplings. It proved difficult for Max to manage his stealthy approach. He was forced to fall farther and farther behind and move with more deliberate steps, pushing aside the bowing branches and ducking to evade their punishing springing back into place.

Because the day had turned foggy and because of the growing distance between Max and his quarry, he began using his ears more than sight to follow their trail. He heard the crunching of boot heels and the clunking of the tabletop against tree trunks. "Dumb fuck! Way to use your head!" one said.

"Mother whoring Christ." the other said.

The crunching of the boots began to slur and faded into squishes as they moved toward the base of the long sloping hill to field's edge. The field itself was always hovering in the grayish-white mist somewhere just forward and to the left, as they made a line along the intersection of the two land features.

Finally the footsteps ceased and Max froze. "One, two, three…" A loud smack followed, what Max assumed to be the tabletop landing against the muddy forest floor. Max heard nothing for some time as he squatted, his hip against a tree stump. It had been gnawed off two feet above the ground, clearly the keen work of an experienced beaver.

An hour or so passed without another sound except the distant cries of predatory birds and the aching bends and cricks of dying trees. They hunched to the command of sharp gusts sweeping over the plateau and over Max in his tight coat. The wind cut openings into the mist, through which Max could make out the fuzzy, granular blobs of the two men moving around below his position. He traded off leaning against his other hip and then lower to his knees for a bit until they grew stiff and cold from the icy mud.

Max thought about his stomach as it gurgled with formidable discontent. He thought about the first time he had gone sledding; he thought about what life from another planet would be like and what it would make of this one and its peoples; and he wished that he could have a smoke and assuage the steady violence of his loud hunger. His lips stung and burned. He hated being still these days. It only highlighted the cold and the hunger and the memories, the good memories, which in their warm and distant glow made the present seem as if Max had left the atmosphere of earth and was floating in outer space. The stars and planets were fragments from his earlier existence, out of reach and impossibly quiet through the void of space, yet pulling at his attention.

"Uhhhhhh, just this one? That's it? Are there any others?" a high, nasal voice called out. It sounded like molasses on a whistle. Max perked to attention and peered through the widening gaps in the mist to find a wagon in front of his quarry. It had a large red cross on its side.

"Ambulance," Max whispered through savagely chapped lips.

"There is another wave coming from Ossiping tomorrow night. We'll have more for you then. Maybe ten or twelve. This is all for now."

A small man stepped down from the ambulance. He wore a distinguished-looking wool waistcoat and glasses. He approached their haul, swiveling his head back and forth between the men. He kneeled down, flung aside the burlap, and revealed a human body, which he prodded and tapped with a small shiny tool.

The two other men looked at each other with tired resignation. One of them exhaled impatiently and swung his head back and forth to an invisible tune, as a child might while waiting in a public space for their parent. The other man stood still and alert. It seemed fitting he wore a Union Army sergeant's uniform.

"And the circumstances…they are, the same as before?" the little distinguished man said, tilting his head. He lifted his bristly red mustache in a reflex of olfactory irritation, outwardly displeased at having to deal with the unpleasantness of his inquiry.

"Yes, just the same as before," the impatient one said. "The same as always, no one is gonna be looking for this fella. You have the same guarantee as you had with the rest." Their six eyes played pinball for a tick.

The mustache recoiled once again, out of habit. "Well, okay, then I suppose we are in business."

"Okay. Thirteen dollars and we will be on our way."

The well-dressed man paid the impatient man from a leather billfold he pulled from his striped vest. The first two men hoisted the tabletop back up and rounded the rear of the ambulance. After pausing there for a moment with strenuous grunts from both carriers, the impatient man let out a loud and extended, "Ahem."

The fancy man said, "Oh, right! Very right!" He darted over and lifted the latch and opened the rear doors. The two men slid the tabletop part way into the wagon, tipped it up, and jerked it back out, roughly sliding the burlap-covered corpse onto the ambulance floor. Having completed this task, they turned and headed back up the muddy forest slope. Their boot steps were less pronounced due to the diminished weight of the tabletop, now relieved of one fat dead man.

The purchaser called out in a wavering voice, "Pleasure…as always…," holding his hand with the indistinct instrument high. The impatient man shook his head. Max watched as the fancy purchaser reentered the front compartment of the ambulance and the driver whipped the two quarter horses. They struggled momentarily to gain adequate traction in the deep brown mush of mud and grass and dead leaves. But they eventually caught momentum, and the ambulance disappeared into the mist.

Max was relieved to be in motion once again. He almost sprinted up the hillside, neglecting to take the care with which he had evaded the thrashing springs of briar and sapling branches on his descent. His stomach was twisting dreadfully in hunger, the bile seeping upward. He could taste the acid with the back of his tongue. He was going to go back to the camp, take advantage of Deitland's deranged state, and use his former lieutenant rank to garner something substantial to eat. After quelling his hunger, he would have something to report back to Mr. Rombathe.

* * *

When Jasper was in elementary school, he used to get stomachaches that forced him to lie on the ground hugging his knees. They came on quickly and without regard to activity. It had happened often during backyard pickup football games with the neighborhood kids and at recess during disorganized kickball contests. It even happened during math exams, when he would slide onto his side and squeeze his thumbs into his ribcage and quietly writhe, perplexing and amusing the other distracted test takers. The school nurse called it "active stomach." An HMO physician later diagnosed it as irritated bowels. "Doesn't help that the boy eats like an alley cat," the slick and sweating doctor said to Jasper's young mother.

The stomach affliction followed Jasper throughout his adolescence, making him the victim of many insults flung from other kids. Add to that Jasper's slight build, and it wasn't surprising that he had few friends by middle school. Though when he was occasionally asked out or to join in on the activities, he would always employ his token refrain: "I would love to but I'm really tired." He eventually learned to master his abdominal pain without falling to the floor, but he was

not able to evade or delimit his gaseous outputs. And so, not wanting to be sub-
jected to further familiar hostility and harassment from peers, he spent most of his
time alone.

His stomach problems resulted in unpredictable and strange appetites. He
loved applesauce with ketchup, hotdogs with pumpkin flavored jam, which was
always in steady supply by twelve-ounce bottle in the back of the fridge. And often times, mostly because he was so frequently alone and because he was, secretly, a very emotional child, Jasper would create meals to ease his anxieties. He
ate his feelings. If he got stressed thinking about his first sexual encounter, then
he would fry beef gristle and eggs in lard. If he was depressed about getting
tagged out first in capture the flag, he would make a bologna sandwich and eat it
with a big glass of fruit punch.

And he would make his meals larger than were necessary. He wasn't merely
satisfying a need for physical replenishment; he was seeking nourishment of
spirit. So his meals would be large enough to feed three or four people. He would
eat fast and clumsily, with long and painful gulps aided afterward by emergency
swigs of whatever liquid was ready at hand. And he would cough from intake
down wrong passages, and he would often be farting and laughing while doing so.

Having completed his meals, and hopefully approximating anxiety-free satisfaction, he would lie down for a nap. The nap was important because, if he
stayed awake long after his gluttonous sittings, he would experience bouts of gut
discomfort far worse than those average pangs that he had mastered. These were
so bad in fact that, the few times he did remain conscious during them, they
brought him to generous tears on the bathroom floor, praying to some vague deity
to allow him to vomit it up and be done with it all and crumpling the yellow-and-
orange-flowered bathroom mat into knots with his clinging fists. This whole kind
of episode made him feel dumb. Sleeping allowed him to bypass the pain without

having to forfeit that which was gained by the gluttony. And in this manner Jasper became obese by the age of fourteen.

But the public outbursts and the embarrassing horizontal submissions subsided as he aged, though his gaseous output and tepidness toward social engagement remained intact, always garnished with his robotic refrain, "I'd love to, but I'm really tired." It wasn't until he had crossed off the first name on his list, over a decade later, that his physical mastery proved unequal, and he fell to the ground, plagued with dry heaves for some twenty minutes. As name after name was crossed off of the list, the heaving and the weak legs let up, but still always threatened.

And so, in the second-floor hallway of Wicker Home, as Brass Knee's pupils slowly dilated in recognition and fear, Jasper felt the old familiar tickle running up his gullet. Mocha and papaya chunks launched from between his quivering lips, smacking against Brass Knee's prominent brow ridge before splashing outward into a radial spray that stretched out peripherally, reaching both hallway walls. It projected forward around Brass Knee's neck and shoulders, spilling onto the waxed wood flooring behind, and misted Martin's hands and forearms. The flow of flying chunks grew in girth for several seconds, reaching a full cylindrical six inches at its zenith, testing the capacity for torture of the skin along Jasper's mouth's edges. Eventually it petered out into slow moving sludge sliding down his chin onto his concave chest. A stench immediately invaded the corridor as if it were a pressure-filled, airtight container. The odor was a toxic blend of bourbon, smoked salami and milk.

Martin had closed his eyes just in time to evade the digestive explosion's wrath. Brass Knee was not as fortunate, suffering the worst of the blow in the form of slimy nodules of grease, meat fat, and astringent stomach acids. The mess was slithering its way into his eyes, but he wiped them to restore his vision.

Larger pieces slid down his forearms, which he had raised in an instinctive defensive posture.

Ms. Corin's face turned with disgust as she covered her mouth, trying to keep the smell out. Corin Junior, who had always had a weak stomach himself, without a moment's notice, returned Jasper's favor in kind all over the shoulders of his mother, who, though he had backed up abruptly after running in to her, was still right before him. Undigested corn and beets spilled down over her breasts and onto the floor, forming a yellow and lavender river that merged into Jasper's pool just behind Brass Knee's boots. The whole messy moment seemed to happen in slow motion, lasting for minutes, when, in reality, the last of the propulsive vomit had settled within fifteen seconds. Jemmy, who could not see what had happened, only heard the splat against the floor like a 5 gallon bucket being emptied. Then she received the foul, stomach-curdling smell creeping under the bedroom door.

The surprise and subsequent smelly offense boggled Brass Knee's usually indomitable reasoning skills and required him instead to employ animal impulses. Recovering from his defensive huddle, he launched his massive body through the air at Jasper, who, with his gun still raised, pulled the trigger. The bullet cut through the left edge of Brass Knee's rib cage, splitting off dancing fragments of bone and plasma. The bullet continued its trajectory out Brass Knee's back and made its way into the molding at the end of the hallway.

Brass Knee's momentum carried him into Jasper, who did not have time for a second shot. The two spun in circles of struggle until Brass Knee's two hundred plus pounds dominated Jasper's light frame, smashing him backward and right onto Martin. The tangled pile of bodies slid through Jasper's waste and over the top of the stairs. The knotted trio bobbled and bounced, clunking their way down, two steps at a time, until they finally reached the kitchen, broke their connection, and each slid out beside one another. Their bodies formed a Roman numeral three atop a welcome matt under Martin's aching legs.

Ms. Corin stood rigidly, her knees locked, staring with wide eyes at the disaster of filth spread out in front of her. She watched intently as the lavender of the beet river comingled with the mocha-colored salami and bourbon river. It was forming mesmerizing, inwardly tightening swirls. She thought it was strange that something so beautiful could come from something so vile. "Praise be His name!" she whispered, hysterically. "Praise be His name!" It was a good minute before she realized her son was pulling her forcefully backward.

"Mother, back into the room! The room, goddamn it!" She succumbed to his pull, and they flung around backward into her bedroom. Junior slammed the door behind them. Ms. Corin made her way wearily to the bed, where she lowered herself slowly onto her flowered comforter, which she had made by hand years earlier.

"There is a revolver in my desk drawer," she said. "Please be careful with it dear; it is loaded and cocked into firing position. You must handle it with great care," she said flatly. It scared Junior, whose mind was speedily passing through all of the horrific scenarios his mother had anticipated and which he had previously considered alarmist and overwrought, the paranoid machinations of a lonely old lady with too many responsibilities. The fact that he hadn't paid detailed attention to any of her prophesies of doom made the fear greater in its lack of definition, it grew power in its indefiniteness. Gulping and wiping the smeared digestive overflow from his cheek, he walked over to the desk and slid open the warped wooden drawer from its slot.

The steel was cold against his soft palm. He applied barely any pressure as he closed his grip around its handle at a near-sloth-like pace. Then he stopped, standing foolishly staring down at the weapon in his hand. "Give it here," Ms. Corin said, approaching her son. He met her eyes and searched them for recognizable features, as if meeting a strange species and determining to which known category of animal they belong. He had always assumed the more severe pronouncements of her religious convictions to be mere flamboyant flourishes, passionate decorations of a personality that required faith and dogma. But he was now seeing that maybe there was something else behind it entirely, maybe even something bordering on justification. He gently placed the gun in her hand and dropped his eyes in bewildered submission. She took it, kissed him on the forehead, then opened the door and crept out into the hallway. Junior stared at the layers of shadows stretching out from the doorway on the bedroom floor and listened to his mother splatting her way through the vomit-covered hallway with a loaded revolver in hand.

Having the wind knocked out of him, Martin did not move, other than to arch his back reflexively, and sucked air, trying to catch his breath. Jasper had regained himself faster than the other two and was dragging himself toward the dining room, his limp, lean legs trailing behind him. Brass Knee's back was to the others, and he was doing his damnedest to keep his eyesight straight, suffering blurriness in whole quadrants of his field of vision. He had instinctively wrapped his bottom arm upward and cupped his right hand around the leaking, sinew-laden wreckage of his ribcage.

Fully underneath the kitchen table, with his back up against the stained-cypress table stem, Jasper realized he'd lost his gun. He quickly pulled his legs beneath himself and began crawling around the linoleum tiles on his hands and knees. He scurried about, keeping Brass Knee's presence in his peripheral field. He was fully aware that the gun was the only advantage he had over the large man, who, to Jasper's growing terror, would likely recover from what had been only a grazing, definitely no organ damage or internal bleeding. It was a gunshot wound that Jasper himself could recover from quickly with enough adrenaline, the proper tilted posture, and shallow breaths. Martin appeared to be having troubles of his own, flopping around like a suffering bird nailed out of the sky. Jasper saw

Martin was more frail of a build and about eight inches shorter than he was, so he didn't consider him an immediate threat. This calmed him somewhat. He scanned all but the other side of Brass Knee's body for the gun, without success.

This job had been botched so badly that Jasper considered just running out of the door and regrouping. Once he was sober and had some better sleep behind him, he could run the situation through his mind and find the proper recalculations. He experienced a deep, mournful tug of regret. Regret at having had bourbon, more bourbon than he had promised to allow himself. Regret at knowing, perhaps all along, that he was destined for some such cataclysmic failure. Regret at the thought of his father. It was all so much, in an instant, and it was choking him up and threatening to further the disaster. Jasper was paralyzed in jaundiced self-absorption. All around him he could see his incompetence. This was the mess called Jasper. "I've made such a mess," he said under his breath, eyeing the expanse of drying vomit, blood, and wood chips around his fellow recovering tumblers.

This mess could perhaps be salvaged, but only after retreat. And retreat meant admitting that there was a problem, that he had the problem, that he *was* the problem. Which he had understood really the whole long, lonely way here. That was what kept him so constantly piqued and petulant, so dissatisfied and vexed. He was lowered in his own eyes. And yet something unclear, and seemingly undeserved yet pressing, urged him not to even consider retreat. That would be a blatant and truly irredeemable dishonor to the Narduccian purpose, to his father, to himself, to the very thing that gave him, made him himself, which all at once seemed more of a question about how to clean the mess than the mess itself. There was still more work to be done in the definitions. So, despite the clear rational appeal of leaving, while he still had clear passage, and regrouping, Jasper instead became resolute in his decision to push through and salvage this name on the list. It made his skin crawl and his blood boil. "Alright you old fool, you fix this. Clean the goddamned mess! Clean it up!"

Jasper remained still for a bit, trying to pick up on any audio or visual cue, any indication whatsoever as to Brass Knee's condition and intent. Having divined nothing but speculative possibilities, he began working on employing his recent swell of determination and courage toward completely crossing the kitchen floor and searching the remaining corner for the weapon. He thought himself an old fool, but he knew he had to clean the mess. He stood and took a shaking step toward the large curled body, keeping Martin in his peripheral vision now. Martin had regained his respiratory rhythm but was still frozen on his back, carefully watching an upside-down Jasper take a long step just two feet from his head.

As Jasper's foot noiselessly planted beside Brass Knee's back, Martin raised his eyes from between Jasper's feet looked through his legs toward the motion that he had detected on the staircase. There, upside down, Martin saw Ms. Corin holding a rifle and a handgun and peering down with a horrifically sadistic smile on her face. It was the innate grin of a great predatory beast who had just cornered the worthy prey after a tremendous pursuit. Jasper, now bending carefully over the large man, was unaware of her presence. Martin kept very still and very quiet, tension making his back sore.

A hole erupted in the linoleum beside Jasper, and he sprang to attention. He looked directly at Ms. Corin, and then, with great agility, barreled back across the room, flipping the kitchen table loudly onto its side and kneeling behind. Martin remained on his back, frozen in fear and watching the events transpire upside down. He had a panoramic view of everyone's position.

Ms. Corin kept her smile, cocked the revolver with a steel *ting* and aimed it at the overturned table. An explosion blew a hole the size of a baseball in the tabletop, throwing bits of oak through the kitchen air. The bullet went into the cabinet door directly next to Jasper's head, leaving a clean and narrow entry hole. Jasper kneeled down, tighter into himself. He had caught sight of her for only the briefest of moments before his adrenaline and fear propelled him to his makeshift fort, but it was long enough for him to see that she had two guns. If there were only one, then he would time her cocking procedure and wait until the exact second she had fired a bullet and then rush her, with the hope that he would arrive before she could fire again.

This tactic had worked for him when he fell through a run-down nightclub's office floor in Chicago while lying in wait for the floor manager to arrive in the early afternoon. The floor was imitation granite laminate. It was sticky and smelled like popcorn butter. There had been no drinking prior. It was only the second name on the list, and he was still overpreparing for these affairs. He was still fresh and keen. He was also much lighter in the midsection. A soft spot in the floor near a closet opened up and took his left leg up to his waist. The edge of the hole raked his testicles so badly that he tasted foulness on his tongue.

His swallowed leg had rocked through a feeble two-by-four, ripped out a mass of antiquated electrical wiring, thrust through the plaster ceiling and pushed through a foam panel of the dropped ceiling above the main bar downstairs. The spritz of foam particles drizzled down onto the bartender and the head of security, who were arguing over some irrelevant detail about the word they had pieced together for the morning crossword puzzle. The word was "ornery." They stared in wonder at the leg protruding from the ceiling above them.

Jasper wrestled with the knots of wiring, pulling desperately to free his limb from the hole. Just as he succeeded, the door swung wide open, letting in a long arm of light leading right up to Jasper, still on the floor. Jasper looked up like a fawn in headlights. And much like one, he made no movement, but clutched his six-inch buck knife.

The security man pulled his thirty-eight caliber and fired. The bullet went into the floor just beside where Jasper's head had been before he jumped up and sprinted toward the shooter. He arrived before the man could pull the trigger again, and he pushed his buck knife into the security man's stomach a good ten to twelve times in rapid succession before the security man lost his footing and fell. Then Jasper, consumed to the state of zombification by the adrenaline, began thrusting the blade into the security man's eyes. He managed a good twenty or thirty stabs. Thick blood spray coated his face, and he began laughing and farting from the stress.

This was how the bartender came upon Jasper, with the white hallway light upon him as if revealing some terrible demonic tableau, a demented laughing face of red launching, again and again, with all of the great might in both arms a dripping dagger into the eye sockets of his coworker and friend. The edge of the knife squeaked and squealed against the eye sockets' bony orbits. When Jasper had finished, the bartender dropped his eyes and let Jasper walk calmly past him and out of the nightclub.

The failure, one Jasper later made up for, educated him to the necessity of a firearm. But here he had brought a gun along, and now it belonged to his mark. It was testament to the damage that the bourbon had wrought in him. He was no longer fresh and had not been for some time. But all intoxication had evacuated his system by this point of crisis, and he was no longer under the bourbon's influence. This thought brought him confidence. But the problem remained; she had two guns and could fire at will. If he were going to charge her, take that route, then he would likely need to be prepared to mend a bullet wound later that evening.

Another explosion erupted in the tabletop, another clean entry hole in the cabinet behind Jasper. He slid quietly but promptly to his right, near the far end of the table, sensing the pattern in the shots. Ms. Corin was working her way across the length of the table, ensuring a hit at some point down the line. Martin flicked his eyes back and forth between the shooter and the target. Ms. Corin did not speak but, now growing comfortable, dropped the wry smile and began taking a step down the landing with each shot. By the third shot, which whizzed through the middle of the table and into its thick pedestal base, she had only one step left before she was at ground level.

Jasper's internal machinations hummed and kicked like a panicked engine, running through any coherent solution, any escape. He rejected the door as too far. He thought if he charged her, he might die right there from a fatal gunshot. The table was far too heavy to slide at her, and the floor too solid to break. He closed his eyes sensing that the options were petering out, that it was either a bullet wound or death. He turned his back to the table and surveyed what was behind him: cabinets, no windows, and a wall he could never break through. With a deep, long breath, he decided that he would not die in that kitchen. As he reopened his eyes, he saw the cabinets, again, and drawers. And with that, he reached over and yanked out the nearest drawer, its many years of paint coats sticking and dragging against the inside of the framing on its way out. He applied more force than was necessary, falling back on his butt, the drawer landing in his lap. Within it was a disheveled array of cooking utensils, a cheese grater, a potato peeler, a meat-tenderizing hammer, three or four good pairs of shears, a long cleaver, a turkey baster, and a good dozen or so butter knives, forks, and spoons, their upper-class silver dull from lack of polishing. A rush of relief overcame Jasper. He nabbed the cheese grater and lobbed it sideways, with one arm, over the table. The grater's path pronounced a half-parabolic arc, twisting with backspin just below the broken ceiling fan. Due to its great downward velocity, Ms. Corin was unable to evade its impact, suffering the brunt of its nipping bite on her nostrils and lips. She merely whipped her head to the side and spit in pain.

Having launched his initial weapon, Jasper swiftly switched to the second phase of his kitchen attack. He stood, half hunched, in a position directly out of the military special-ops training manual's guide to evasive action, swung his leg over the tabletop and emerged on the other side. He launched the meat tenderizer from his left hand, and reloaded with a handful of forks from his pocket. The hammer whizzed past Ms. Corin's head and danced around percussively on the steps behind her.

The nature of Jasper's plan now apparent to Ms. Corin. She dropped the rifle and raised the hand gun's barrel, steadied with both hands. She clicked its hammer hard with her quivering thumb. For years beyond years she had been anticipating this moment, fearing it, dreading it, wanting it. And now that it had come to pass, it seemed trivial, nonsensical. The last in a chain of oft-breeding Narduccians was directly in front of her, sprinting with all of his speed, tossing sharp silverware at her face. And there she stood, well-armed and with the responsibility to make the fatal blow to her adversary. This was the meaning of her entire existence, the moment of definition. And yet it seemed so very simple and rudimentary. She pulled the trigger twice. Smoke from the tiny controlled explosions within the gun barrel slowly flowed outward and dispersed into hazy tendrils around Ms. Corin. Jasper continued on through them in his desperate charge, one bullet in his shoulder and one in his cheekbone.

* * *

Pollock awoke on Quentin's couch, covered in a brown throw. Sitting atop the throw was Stanton, staring at Pollock's face with his green pupils. Once he realized Pollock had awoken, the cat hopped to the floor and disappeared into the dark hallway. Pollock felt embarrassed, and his head stung. He quietly folded the throw, and let himself out of the house. He had a text.

When your dreams are this grandiloquent, whichever reality sits in front of you becomes an insufferable wasteland.

Pollock read and reread the text several times, trying to approach its meaning from different angles. It seemed so defeatist to him. It seemed to be telling him that, in order to enjoy one's life, one must temper their aspirations, their mental beauty and musings, or it meant that one's personal, private mental life was the most special aspect of living, which sounded very lonely to him. Besides, the text was unlike Cabe. He was never philosophical like this. It must have been a quote borrowed from someone else. And that was something that was beginning to really anger Pollock, that sucking up. Cabe was really catering to him, clawing into his good graces, tailoring and tilting the communications to areas where Pollock felt comfortable. And this made him very uncomfortable because that wasn't something Cabe did.

Of the two, Pollock was surely the more compliant. That wasn't to say that he was in any way less headstrong or less vital to their combined projects and operations. Quite the opposite. But he was always keenly aware of how others preferred to function, to speak, and to give meaning to themselves. And he would always adapt to that. His adapting was testament to the ability that Pollock possessed to hold many multiples of systems, schemata, and personalities in his head at once. Pollock could understand someone who thought spiders were vile creatures and hated their very notion, while also fully understanding another who worshipped them as a biological marvel. This was why Pollock often felt hindered in the possibility of creating for himself a concrete personality. At least, a consciously constructed personality. There were too many truths for one to turn his back on any certain set of them without sharp and obvious hypocrisy. But on the other hand, a life without killing off some certain quantity of truths, is a life without determinate coordinates. It was the life of a lost soul.

And thoughts like these turned Pollock into a quagmire of turgid and animated self-reproach. He had read too many treatises on postmodernism in city planning. It all revolved around intersections. Not street intersections, but intersections of ideas, of systems, of traditions, of disciplines. The whole area of thought always brought him back to some notion that he believed to be a correct interpretation of Derrida, which was that real honesty in intellectual analysis always kept the analysis going further and further. There was never any resting place. The truthful mind exhausted itself in an infinite, all-encompassing approach. But always approaching and always expanding. This was the anxiety, the trickster of mental faculties that kept Pollock from ever landing on something sturdy with which to use as his lens, his personality, his identity, but instead continually shifting all about from intersections and new angles, wrapping himself in layers and bundles and knots until it was unclear what part of him was doing the thinking.

And it seemed to Pollock that this was why it was so hard for him to have any community. Because community necessitated some acceptance of shared truths, or at least an understanding of which architectures were safe and which were taboo. Pollock could spend hours, days, weeks, analyzing the meaning and social consequences of three minutes of light banter with an acquaintance. Cabe was likely the last true friend that he had had. And their days together at university were the last that he could identify as taking place within a community. It was the last time he was inside the beating organism, part of something functioning for a bigger whole, instead of being alone wandering, wondering through intersections, traps, being honest. He didn't want to be honest. He was tired of being so honest with himself. He wanted to be with people.

Community. Belonging. Social purpose. Social cohesion. Interaction without paralysis and paranoia. Family. These were the grandiloquent dreams within Pollock. And they indeed did make his reality an insufferable wasteland. His was a wasteland of competition and privation, where each individual functioned covertly with ulterior motives to outdo one another for scarce resources. Each interaction with a living entity was potentially the most heinous of terrors. It was potentially an unacknowledged, or only obliquely acknowledged war. Being alive had become a death struggle. And the cerebral processes for working one's way out of such a position only amounted to cognitive quicksand. Having lived with these realizations for the past few years, Pollock had begun to believe that he, himself, was the problem. He brought these bleak views to everything, carried them like an infection that polluted his surroundings. And people noticed and responded with apprehension or evasion, silent divorces that Pollock believed he could perceive. He had quietly become persona non grata in most circles and social arenas. Pollock often came to the conclusion that the only two real solutions were murder and suicide. Both were untenable and unacceptable to him. So he decided, essentially, that he would keep himself out of the equation of the world and suffer quietly alone, without expectation of solution.

Of course, deep and integral portions of Pollock didn't believe these things at all. He made an online dating profile, which led him to Retta. He worked diligently to make the city zoning code more rational and beneficial to the greatest number of Trams citizens. He listened to Quentin's silly yet profound wisdoms, internalized them, and employed them as he understood to be prudent. He reminded himself of these things but only occasionally and to no great relief. Cabe was arriving the next evening and it was dredging up his most powerful concerns with a renewed vitality.

Cabe angered Pollock to no end. The reason wasn't that he had merely betrayed him; it was that there was never any reckoning, which, in all fairness, followed logically from the nature of their friendship. The tear between them had been too large and unwelcome to even name. So the two of them danced around it, flirted with it, prodded at it, and left it in various different locations over the last few years. It was some curious, pathetic puppy dog routine. Neither had the balls to just pick it up and shove it in the other's face and yell, "Look at this fucking debacle! Can you believe it? And also what are we going to do about it now?"

For Pollock's part, he kind of figured that his balls weren't on trial as much as Cabe's, because it was Cabe who had been the transgressor. But Pollock did know that he was somewhat of a coward for letting the incident expand into such a large object. And this object had become like a symbolic shadow hanging over the whole problem of community and truth that Pollock struggled with daily. He wondered to himself whether the rift between he and Cabe had been the catalyst for all of his mental wandering. But then he would scan his memory and recognize the indicia of despair and realize that the rift was not the catalyst but maybe only a very powerful example, a high-resolution magnifying glass over the whole bundle of social issues.

Pollock believed Cabe must be close to the crux of it all. There was some secret, some key, some understanding to come that would only come from walking into the dark epicenter and not leaving until there was evidence of a solution, or otherwise, all reference to hope, however dim and sideways, would be quashed. So Pollock welcomed Cabe's arrival like a man on death row welcomes the injection. mostly tired of living in wait. Because that was one of the side effects of Pollock's outlook. He wasn't going forward. He was in a looping pattern. That realization brought him back to his disgust at overinvolvement with postmodern theory—the breakdown of the concept of progress.

Progress for Pollock required that there be some picture, however ill defined, of that toward which he strove. Without it, there was no direction. But, in order to arrive at that picture, he must extract values from his experiences, which, hopefully, more fully and consistently exhibited those values as time went on. Pollock was stuck in analysis of how to derive the proper values. Once again, his ability to hold many different views at once corrupted his ability to formulate a simple linearity. He couldn't say for certain if he wanted a girlfriend, a female companion. He understood his sex drive, but wasn't sure he wanted children. He wondered if a friendship could have sex added like ice cream to up the pleasure quotient and whether that was bad, to move toward something for physical pleasure. The question game made him sick to his stomach. His thoughts made him sick. He needed to escape himself, change himself, and be something other than what he was.

Retta had been informed, rather vaguely, that Pollock and Cabe were college roommates and buddies who parted on shaky terms, and that he was staying at Pollock's place for a few days, and that it was Pollock's intention to try with all efforts to patch things up between the two of them. Therefore, Pollock would likely not be able to spend time with her until after the weekend. The conversation was face to face and felt harsher to Pollock than it actually was. He felt somewhat slimy for essentially claiming space so soon after their first having become fully physically acquainted. It was too similar to the dominant male modus operandi of conquests and craven farewells. And he also felt somewhat disingenuous for conveniently leaving out the detail that his and Cabe's schism had involved a female companion of Pollock's.

The question of Retta, however, seemed to mandate such withholdings on Pollock's end. Because, if the "Retta question" was going to be answered in the affirmative, then these other long-lingering issues from his past needed to be sorted out properly first. And, being issues from his past, they needed to be sorted out without involving Retta. Later on, having come to some concrete understanding, having some picture of how to move forward, then and only then could he disclose these matters to her. He did find it odd how much time he was spending justifying his actions regarding her. Maybe she was already beginning to answer the Retta question for him.

Regardless, he had squared away his time to spend with Cabe. And Retta was very accommodating and understanding. He had also held, at his request, a short and terse meeting with Mr. Freedman, wherein he claimed that he had had a great breakthrough with the presentation and was working feverishly to get it completed for the following week. Of course this was all bullshit, almost. Pollock was betting that the Cabe resolution would clear his thinking for land usage. And also, his confrontation with Hans in the food court had sparked something within him. He felt confident now in his ability to substantially contribute to the conversation of future zoning projects for Trams. It was as if an idea had already been reached, he just didn't know yet what the idea was.

Mr. Freedman was inspired by Pollock's initiative to have the face-to-face, and it restored his waning confidence in Pollock indeed being the correct code developer for the task. The past few weeks leading up to this Wednesday face-to-face, Mr. Freedman had been increasingly considering allowing Hans Flowers to craft a presentation on his University Corridor idea, and then weigh it against whatever Pollock came up with. It was a contingency plan that Freedman later felt was mildly unnecessary, having witnessed the passion and conviction in Pollock's eyes as he excitedly spoke about a new approach to city land rights, something that would invigorate community involvement in planning and development. The language was specific enough to garner interest from Freedman, while being empty enough to apply to whatever it was that Pollock had already discovered and merely needed to put into a memo.

So, aside from an abbreviated Friday workday that week, Pollock's slate was clean for Cabe. That Thursday afternoon, he lounged around at home taking care of various chores. He still hadn't fully unpacked from the move. Having done the dishes and finally scraping out the dead leaves from the gutters with an unscrewed broomstick, he sat on the couch and stared at the ceiling. It then occurred to him to read some more of his great-aunt's journal. He had found it lying on its side, leaning against the wall molding. He picked it up slowly, unsure exactly of how it had ended up in that location. The last time he remembered handling it was on the front porch the night that he, Retta, and Quentin had discovered Martin's tent city. It alarmed him somewhat, the gap in his memory. He sat back down on the couch and opened it up.

The late afternoon carried a cool breeze, which was a welcome relief from the unbearable heat that had run through Trams the past couple of weeks. Pollock knew that it wouldn't last and so felt obliged not to become acquainted with it, the tease of it. The sunlight danced in orange arcs along the back windows above the couch, littering his reading with shadows.

1-24-77

Another visit from Richard today—these are becoming like routine. It was my silly ambition to make mother's pirogies recipe with poached eggs and jam. I thought that would be so nice. I followed the instructions to a tee and they looked just as I had remembered them. It must've been twenty years since I have seen mother's pirogies on a plate. The taste was off. Too sweet. I tried to temper them with salt but it still wasn't right. I wonder now if I hadn't made too much fuss of them. Maybe they always tasted so. Maybe my taste has changed.

Anyway, Richard knocked on the garage door just after the breakfast disappointment. He had brought over vodka and tomato juice for Bloody Marys. "Mary for my Mary?" he said. I didn't like that—how he used "my." But Richard is a harmless man. And I thought that I should reward myself for doing so well lately. Only three drinks a day the past week. He added chunky salsa to the top instead of celery. It was authentic Honduran salsa that he had bought at an ethnic market downtown. It wouldn't be my first choice but I warmed to it after the second.

Spent the afternoon completing the blanket I have crocheted for Saul. If I am honest, I would still say it is top-notch work. It makes me happy to be helpful to a young family that is just starting out. Must stay useful in old age, as they say. Kept looking over to the stack of estate papers in the dining room. Not excited to have to square those away. But it must be done. Still a few months before the court deadline. Executrix. Sounds sexual—dominatrix. Anyway, I am putting it off for another week or so. I wonder, should I name an executor/executrix? It is curious—will someone be reading these very words after I die?

It has been overcast most everyday this January. I remember being so taken by cloudy days when I was younger. It was intriguing and eerie. Mostly now the clouds seem to dampen my moods. Maybe I am getting softer lately. It is hard to find activities to fill the days. It was much easier with Bud around. He was always bringing life and mayhem on his tail. What a fun man. Anyway, must stay active in old age, as they say. Very aware and thankful of having my health. Many friends with hospitalizations. Walkers. I

am thankful I am still able to get around on my own. Dreading ter-
ribly the eventual "old home" conversation. And I wonder—with
whom will that conversation be?

Pollock made himself comfortable on the couch by extending his bare heels out onto the coffee table. He leaned back against the cushioned lumbar support of two pillows and shortly thereafter was asleep. His head was back and mouth open in the snoring position preferred by his father, and that of many other fathers. It was a sort of echo of simian surrender and abandon during times of peace, and thus was a sort of youthful display as if saying he had no real responsibilities right now. And since this often occurred in those with many and great responsibilities, it became ironically emblematic of a man who's tired body demanded escape from the grueling task of his life. Penetrative and awkwardly revealing dreams often flourished within these slumberous retreats. So it was with Pollock.

He was walking in a bright white kitchen. Blinding sunshine spewed in through large bay windows over the white marble counter tops. The kitchen appliances were stainless steel and white plastic. It all appeared very Ikea-esque—cheap, modern European trendy. Out through the windows, held open by a complex crank-handle system, Pollock could make out a laundry line within the bright glare. There were rows of wrinkled white linens curling in the gentle breeze. The fresh air poured through the window and warmly kissed his cheeks. Ambient music emanated from an invisible sound system, with layers of droning piano and strings overlapping extended major chords in dreamy and haunting harmonies. Pollock looked down to realize that he was wearing his red and blue striped onesie from his childhood. It had the feet sections carefully cut off and hemmed, for air circulation. He wriggled his toes over the pristine shale tiles.

He turned toward the eating area to his right and saw a completely naked Hans leaning his butt against the kitchen island, wearing a Spartan war helmet.

Hans was tossing his head back and grunting baritone yelps of ecstasy. Pollock lowered his eyes in alarm, and saw Hans's long, hard erection extending far outward. Its circumcised head was quivering with crimson turgidity. And there, just below the large specimen was Retta, crouched on her knees in what might be termed a "worship" position, also entirely nude. Horror clasped tightly around Pollock's chest and throat. Retta was licking circles onto Hans's inner thigh region, her hands palming his lower abdomen and convulsing twitches fluttering through her fingers. She moved her head quickly up to Hans's long erection and placed her hands along the penile stem, one above the other. She began working with her tongue along the underside of his crimson head, in long, wet licks, the end of each pronounced with a devilish stare upward at him with her narrowed eyes.

Pollock's heart sank into despair at the sight, but his pajama crotch tightened up a bit. After a minute or so of this tonguing action, Retta repositioned her hands onto Hans's abs. Then, after a prolonged upward glance, proceeded to slide her lips over and slowly down around the entire erection, all the way to its shaved base. The erection's bulging end announced itself in subterranean fashion through the side of Retta's throat. She then pulled back from her gagging gulp and began making steady work of the top two-thirds of the shaft in an up-and-down motion, incorporating her entire head into the rhythm. She began to emit high pitch hums enthusiastically, her hands once again writhing in pleasure as she gripped Hans's chiseled lats with her fingertips. The act lasted a harrowing three minutes with Pollock locked into place in the corner of the sleek, blindingly white kitchen. It ended with Hans erupting into Retta's cupped lips, some excess spilling over and leaking down onto her tight nipples.

With her hand, she removed some of Hans's seed from her mouth and, extending three outstretched finger tips, inserted it into herself. Hans, having relieved himself with such gusto and force, turned his gaze upon Pollock, with a knowing look of appreciation, as if thanking Pollock for being a swell pal and letting him borrow his gal for a minute to work out some stress.

In the next instant, Retta was hip to hip with Pollock's great-aunt Mary, both adorned with tattered and stained aprons, working studiously at washing a heap of leftover-crusted glass bake wear. The aprons were all they were wearing, their backs turned and their bare asses exposed beneath the neatly bow-tied apron strings. Mary's wrinkled ass, with webs of green veins running throughout, made Retta's smooth alabaster cheeks appear fantastically ideal and youthful by comparison. "Your play date is here, Polly!" Mary said, her head slightly turned, still focusing on the scrubbing in the soapy water–filled sink in front of her.

"Your play mate is here, Polly!" Retta repeated in a sarcastic and mocking manner, one which said "Hey, kiddo don't you worry about what you've seen here. You focus on playing with your friends. Now run along."

And with that, Pollock trotted past where Hans had had his pleasure, through the dining room, through giant sliding glass doors, and out into a sunny afternoon. There were bees and dandelions and monarch butterflies hovering in maddening loops near to his face. He toed through the luxurious grass. The sun gleamed down hard and hot. Pollock walked the length of the yard and came to a rectangular sandbox, contained by two-by-fours stacked three high. The sandbox was littered with *Star Wars* actions figurines, GI Joes, model vintage Ford trucks, and a scattered assortment of hand shovels and rakes. The sandbox was strikingly dissimilar to the one that had been in Pollock's back yard as a child, and yet, in that uncanny dream world manner, he was certain that it was one and the same. And with the realization, he was once again calmed, forgetting the shocking sexual scene from inside the house. Pollock sat himself in the corner of the sandbox, cross-legged and, with eyes closed, smiled deeply within himself, feeling safe and free from fear. In the yards surrounding his, the healthy green leaves on large trees swayed and danced in the warm breeze, shimmering under the sharp orange sun's rays. All around, life seemed accommodating and beautiful.

Eeeeaawwwk! Eeeeaawwwk! In the middle of the sandbox, within a low valley of dug out sand, lay a black Labrador. The dog exhibited clear and harsh evidence of unimaginable abuse. Its snout was missing pieces, whole large chunks, which had to have been either burnt off or sliced off with sharp tools. It was hard to tell from the complicated regrowth patterns of hair over the area. One of its eyes was missing, with porous and wide lateral scars extending over the entire socket. Chewed nubs remained of its ears, and various sorts and sizes of pocks, cuts, scars, burns, and open seeping wounds ran over the poor creature's entire body, all the way back to the hacked off tail. *Eeeeaawwwkk!* The Labrador pleaded to Pollock, fixing him with its lone, desperate eye. With an unsteady teeter, and great stress upon its front legs, the dog tried to stand and move toward Pollock. Its hind legs had been snapped or torn at the hips and knees so that they curled unnaturally and unevenly inward under its torso in severe bends. Thus, with struggle, it hobbled, predominantly with its chest and forelegs, up to Pollock's crossed legs, and gently laid itself against him and whined.

Hesitation briefly paralyzed Pollock, but he stretched out his hand and grazed the dog's short head fur with his knuckles. The dog squealed, but in a lower note, indicating the reception of comfort. Pollock thought about which human or humans could do something so catastrophic, so monstrous to this pup. It choked him up a bit. His knuckles extended their petting down onto the thicker fur along the Labrador's neck. "Fucking worthless pieces of shit!" he muttered, his sadness and shock turning to anger and vengeance, those familiar burning sensations manifesting yet again within his loins. His fingers ran into a collar, loose around the pup's neck. He twisted it clockwise to reveal a bronze, bone-shaped nametag. Engraved in its center was "Pollock." He panicked, let go of the tag, and realized, in that uncanny dream-world way, that he was this dog.

Pollock was thrust back into the reality of his living room. It was dark outside and in the house. He hadn't anticipated sleeping for any great length of time
and so the lights were all still off. A pounding resounded from the front door.
"Shit, Cabe…" he muttered, in a post-REM-sleep haze. He stood and felt a wet
stickiness in his boxer briefs.

Pollock swung the front door open, still strangely distanced from the phe-
nomenal world in his drowsiness. There stood Cabe, with his shaggy hair, a red
hiking pack dropped at his feet. He smirked and said, "Jesus, for a minute there I
was starting to wonder if there was anything alive in this house." Pollock didn't
respond but merely studied Cabe's appearance. He was wearing a loose fitting
black T-shirt with a picture of a grizzly bear standing upright. His skin was tanned
dark brown and even burned red at the edges nearest his matted hair and along the
ridge of his wide, curved nose.

His old friend was more muscular than Pollock had remembered him to be
back in the days at university, and his brow ridge was more prominent. Perhaps
this was from subsequent changes, or perhaps an error in Pollock's mental accounting. He couldn't land on which bothered him more, or if he was, in fact,
even bothered at all. The blue khaki cutoff shorts, which were more pasted onto
rather than worn on Cabe's chunky thighs, revealed, below their frayed edges,
badly pricked shins with apricot-colored ruptures in midhealing. They were the
shins of one who had walked through thornbush or briar, and they lead down to
his simple grey Tom's slip-ons, worn sockless. He seemed juvenile and reminiscent of a neighborhood child running between houses, who existed within Pollock's reservoir of malleable early memory. Summer camp came to mind. And the
whole motif was aided by the fact that Cabe, despite being approximately the
same height as Pollock, was standing on the concrete pathway, which sat a good
foot below the house's floor level.

The crickets on Nyqvist were deafening behind Cabe and seemed to Pollock to somehow add comment to his youthful character, as if the crickets and he had traveled alongside one another and arrived together, as if Cabe had some mystical power over the insects of the world. Perhaps they spoke some grand echo language intrinsic to all creatures of the universe. Pollock caught himself in this digression and returned to the present moment.

Cabe took note of Pollock's stoicism and said, "You haven't changed a bit old bud." He grabbed the top strap of his pack and lifted it with his dark, muscular arm. "May I enter?" he said in a mock British gentleman's accent. Pollock stepped to the side and switched on the foyer and porch lights. The whole exchange had flustered him. He was still reeling from the import of his recent dream, still with drying stickiness clinging to his pubic hair and lower belly. He slammed the door shut, snuffing out the loud roar of insects amid soupy summer.

Cabe had always preferred to drink scotch and so Pollock, in anticipation of their time together, had stopped off at Apollo and nabbed a pricey bottle of Ardbeg Islay single malt. But, in typical Cabe fashion, he struck first on the booze front and slid out an unlabeled 1.5L bottle of red wine from his pack with a lilt of his wide wrist and slapped its bottom onto the kitchen table. He discarded his pack haphazardly onto the living room floor. Pollock timidly followed Cabe into the kitchen, where the only other lit interior light hung over the kitchen table emitting a flickering dim orange glow. The whole scene made Pollock think of classic noir films. And that was the kind of mood he was in too, the mood for an interrogation.

The two old acquaintances sat silently while Cabe made a job of unscrewing the bottle top and smiling wildly, as an adult in charge of entertaining a group of five year old children might smile, forcing good cheer. The two exchanged anxious glances. "Glasses for the occasion?" Cabe asked, pointing up to the cabinets.

Pollock nodded, knowing he had the advantage in the situation, letting Cabe squirm and put forth effort.

Two mason jars were extracted from the glass-faced china cabinet with great care, and Cabe poured generous portions into both. "I'm pretty excited for you to try this. I had a hand in making it. I'm interested to hear what you think," he said, excitedly, bestowing subtexts of truce and gift giving. Cabe had always mitigated any unease by becoming a busy body, a ringmaster—orchestrating non-stop activity and conversation, constant commotion and process, so that the un-ease couldn't seep in and flourish. Pollock had always secretly found this a bit cowardly, like slaving oneself to avoid encounter with what was most pressing. But, he also always abetted amicably, if in solemn and slightly bemused fashion, so he was complicit in the cowardice. And what an unease there was here, this night.

"So, you're fermenting your own wine?" Pollock asked, cupping his glass and sliding it under his nose. He took an extended whiff. The wine was arid and made his jaw tickle at its back ends. He liked it.

"No…em…actually, I helped grow and pick the grapes. And then I also helped out a little with the fermentation too, yes. But, mostly with the grapes. Growing, grooming, and picking the grapes." Cabe smiled and took an enormous gulp of the wine.

"So you're growing grapes. Where do you do all of this?" asked Pollock, raising the mason jar to his lips.

"Australia," Cabe said.

"You've been in Australia?'" Pollock asked skeptically, accusingly. "How did this happen?"

Cabe smiled amicably. "I know we're not Facebook friends or anything, but I figured you at least knew that. I've been there, uh…just over two years. Don't you keep up with any of the old gang?"

Pollock took a swig. The wine was sweet and dry, and he sloshed it around his rear molars. The jaw-tickling recurred with greater effect. He swallowed loudly. "No, not really," he said.

"Yeah, I knew the answer to that question. You know, a lot of people wonder what happened to you." The sentence stung like a punch, and Cabe regretted the look it produced on Pollock's face. "You've only been here in Trams a few months, right?" he asked quickly.

"Going on five months now." The conversation was cursory and rigid, and it made Pollock feel like the two had grown quite old, older than the years they had lived. It seemed forever and more since they had been buds. "So why Australia?" Cabe had finished off his glass and poured another. Pollock followed suit, sliding the bottle over to refill his own.

"I needed something different," Cabe said. "I was stressed out and I...,"—he looked Pollock in the eyes and stretched his smile to one side in discomfort— "well a work friend had been talking about his cousin who was in a program called WOOF."

"Woof?" Pollock asked, the orange glow from the light tinting his pasty face.

"It's a program. They set you up with a farm or vineyard. I think some other kinds of businesses participate as well...I don't know. Its been a while since I've looked into any of this. But basically, you provide your labor, and they give you food, board, and a small stipend. Anyway, that's what brought me out—it was a three-month program. And it was just a good fit, so they offered to keep me on after the program ended, and I agreed." Cabe took a look around the kitchen. It was dark and sparse. Behind Pollock, in the pantry, there were stacks of canned tuna, sardines, and smoked oysters. Next to the pantry hung some binoculars above a

stack of bird books. The kitchen counter was clean and empty except for the machete that Pollock had found in the alley out back. Cabe scrunched his forehead in
curiosity. He pointed over to it in question.

"So then why are you back in the States now?" Pollock asked, purposefully
ignoring Cabe's curiosity. This was his conversation to administer and direct.

Cabe smirked, understanding the dynamic that was being established by his
old acquaintance and also deciding that he would play along, be subservient. "I'm
fickle, basically. Don't you ever get tired of routine, need a different rhythm?"
Cabe took another large swallow of his Australian bounty. Pollock thought about
the routines in his life and, for whatever reason, all he could picture were panes of
overhead florescent lighting, stretching out along an endless paneled ceiling.

"Yeah," Pollock said, capitulating. "It makes me sick to my stomach."

Cabe nodded, perfunctorily. "Not enjoying your work? You're working for
the city, right?" he asked, finishing off his second glass. Pollock was trailing far
behind now, with a good two-thirds of his glass remaining.

"Yea, zoning." The refrigerator hummed, its icemaker cracking and drib-
bling water droplets throughout its labyrinthine plastic mechanism. The two were
silent for a moment, each squirming to find the next linguistic cover, safe harbor
of neutral talk before the embarrassment of their discomfort made itself unavoidable. Conspiring in cowardice once again.

"So what else is news, Polly?" Pollock had always resented the nickname,
but never spoken against it. Until now.

"Don't call me that. My name is Pollock."

Cabe raised his hands defensively. He felt like he was dealing with something very slippery.

"What's news?" Pollock said. "Well I am seeing a girl. Her name is Retta."

Cabe lit up. Pollock had supplied him with substantial chatter fodder. "Good
results, baby! Is it serious? What's she like?"

"Well…yeah, no, I mean, I guess its getting serious. I'm not sure. She's in nursing school. She has a lot on her plate right now, though." Pollock took a swig. His cheeks and jaw had become accustomed to the wine and no longer quivered with each taste.

"Like what?" asked Cabe.

"Well, she has a younger brother who is very autistic and a father with well, uh, other mental issues. He's just not around much, not really there. So she has had to step up. She handles all of the bills and credit cards for the family, for example. Cooks a lot." Pollock raised and drained his glass, beginning to feel the alcohol work its way throughout his bloodstream, calming him with tingling endorphin. Cabe slid the bottle over and Pollock poured another. He was catching up.

Cabe asked, "You like her? You feel responsible, or is it heavy with the baggage?"

Pollock nodded, acknowledging to himself that the questions hovered somewhere near the crux of the Retta conundrum. "Eh, baggage? I don't know. Yeah, I guess so. Mostly I just feel guilty for taking up so much of her time. I mean, she has work, studying, babysitting, and then the chores, the errands. It's a lot different for me. I am pretty freed up. And yeah, I do like her. God, I really do." Pollock was picking up momentum, talking more to himself and more freely with the help of the wine. And yet he couldn't help sounding defensive at the same time. "She's fun to be around. Really witty, she has a good sense of humor. And she is kind. She's become a confidant." He hadn't noticed it but he was smiling.

"So you two are getting married soon, then?" Cabe jibed. Pollock looked at Cabe with dejection, as if caught in lameness. Cabe held his hands up and shrugged. "I'm just sayin', you're talking like a World War II postcard."

Pollock snorted. Despite his commitment to holding Cabe at arm's length until proper atonement had occurred, whatever that would be, he was beginning to remember the fun of being Cabe's friend.

Cabe picked up on this. It was part of his plan—to charm Pollock with humor and booze. With Pollock allowing him to crash there, he hoped the whole issue of their past might never arise again.

"But then there's the other side of that," Pollock said. Cabe was intrigued and remembered how much he loved it when Pollock got on a roll about something. He used to love listening to his late night manic rants. He finished his glass and poured another. Pollock did the same. The ancient groove was reemerging. "People don't stay together, you know," Pollock said. "It doesn't stay fresh. Eventually, if you take that path, that monogamous choice to be with someone, really be with them, eventually you always end up resenting them, or hurting them or—"

"Or getting hurt?" Cabe said. Pollock nodded to himself. "So you're saying the honeymoon era will come to an end, and then you'll be left with homework assignments?"

Pollock looked down at his palms. They were moist and pale, glistening orange. He rubbed his fingertips. "Maybe . . . And, yeah, the novelty will just wear out. And I'll look elsewhere. And then I'll be caught in my promises, promises I made when I was high on the novelty. Or she'll get restless first and something will break. But I can't know until I am there."

Cabe's smile widened. "Is that where *we* are?" They caught each other's large eyes and finished their current glasses. "Look, that's probably all true," Cabe said. "But where is the honor in not trying? Wouldn't that just be surrendering to your fears? That's no way to live, is it?"

After mulling over the question, Pollock stood and turned the other overhead kitchen light on with a loud snap of the switch. The harsh orange was replaced by the soft yellow-white light of the 75-watt bulbs housed in the clear plastic hanging orb. It swung limply in its rope frame. Cabe's features protruded more brutally now. Pollock sat again in the chair, feeling the drunken waywardness of his legs as he bent down.

Cabe took note of the unsteadiness with giddy appreciation. It seemed to him that perhaps his foot was already in the door. He had Pollock three glasses deep into his potent outback cabernet, and was fueling the beginning of what he foresaw to be a long and interesting conversation juggling numerous concepts and ethics. This was what he missed about the old roomie. Next they would only have to find some trouble to get into and it would by like old times indeed. He thought it was a good result.

"It's just unfortunate that I am so attracted to certain shapes," Pollock said, concentrating on certain alabaster and freckled feminine curves, which had remained blazoned in his mind from the nightmares earlier in the evening. Cabe let out a thunderous clap of laughter, forcing a wispy spray of vino outward, which misted lazily over the glazed table surface. He leaned forward and said, "Yep! The male human libido. Sexual desire. Lust. Attraction to them fit mammary glands, divining that they are well suited for baby rearing. Proper maintenance and furtherance of our seed. Keeps the species healthy, as well as baby car seat manufacturers, but definitely destructive of the whole monogamy program." Pollock smiled.

"But look," Cabe said, "things get strange pretty fast when you're sleeping around, when its open. That's how things were down in Perth for a bit. I . . . spent two months there before I jumped back over to the US. Shacked up in a fairly cheap hostel, $120 a week for a bed, locker, and restroom. No bedbugs. Great wrap around porch. I was dragged into the whole debacle by Margee, a girl at Desert Cat's. That's the vineyard. Marjorie Swills-Buckle. Went by Margee. Relentless cunt. Sharp as Vermont cheddar. She pretty much owned my soul. Maybe still does." Cabe's eyes sort of glazed over, like the glare of lamplight washing out the image on a television screen, while he conjured up his near past. "She convinced me we should have a go at an open relationship . . . shortly after convincing me to follow her to Perth."

"Margee, huh?" Pollock said in a suspicious tone. He was determined not to warm completely to his old friend until the inevitable accounting.

"I had saved up a bunch of money from my wages," Cabe said. "There isn't really much to do in rural Queensland. Besides, I was beat after working all day. A beer and some downtime was enough to get me to sleep at night. Beautiful sunsets there though, man. I started reading again but . . . that's a different matter. So anyway, I was pretty well funded. Margee showed up my last two weeks looking for work. Mac is a pretty fair guy, so he set her up with the square deal. Square deal. Money for stay. She was Icelandic, backpacking with a group of friends. They had slightly different itineraries, so she decided she wanted to see what it was like on a vineyard and meet back up with them in Perth two weeks later."

The crickets outside were becoming apparent again. "Iceland, that's interesting," Pollock said, regretting the banality immediately.

"Yeah, that's what I had thought. But boy, she didn't want to say anything about where she was from. I mentioned her family, school and the chat just suffocated. Reminded me of you in that way. She was evasive."

The comment both complimented and offended Pollock, who, now lacking confidence in his contributions, quickly said, "Two weeks. So you guys must have hit it off pretty quickly then?"

Cabe chuckled. "Oh my, God yes. I noticed her right away. I mean, you know, noticed her. Straight long black hair. She had a crooked smile that made it seem like she enjoyed watching small animals suffer. *Schadenfreude*, the Germans call it." Cabe squinted then raised an eyebrow. "Well, maybe I noticed that later on. Anyway, to keep it brief, we were sleeping together before too long. And she convinced me I had to see Perth. So we got a private hostel room together, and her friends showed up two nights later. And you know, for a while things were pretty great. Just restaurants and parties and beaches and sightseeing . . . er, you know, like a good-times montage in a film?" Pollock smirked and nodded.

"We really were. Almost like music was playing, like we had our own soundtrack. A few of the friends picked up hubbies, international hostellers—eh, I can't even remember their names. Its not consequential, but we all of us just kind of roved around in a gang, from moment to moment, sight to sight, completely on a whim, boozing and rolling and it was great. Wasn't too bad on the funds, either. For a minute I was like, 'Wait. Wait. I could keep doing this for like a year, maybe two.' And, you know, we were having sex regular. Margee. Fantastic sex. Freaky stuff. And she used to beg me to read to her aloud in bed. Sir Arthur Conan Doyle."

Cabe had begun speaking more rapidly, with detectable mania. His elbows were now up on the table's lip, his hands dancing, flamboyant gestures that mirrored the rhythms and punctuations of the narrative. Pollock noted that he himself was already strongly buzzed. The bottle was still half full, and Cabe was showing no signs of slowing down his rate of imbibing. Pollock could feel the heat in his cheeks and scalp from being wine drunk. And it occurred to him that, if this was the first hour of their reunion, the weekend was going to turn into one hell of a bender. "One hell of a bender," he muttered under his breath with a crazed look. He was genuinely excited for the raucous mayhem that lay ahead. It had been too long since he had cut loose, and the looming liberty tickled him from all odd angles.

"What?" Cabe asked with a confused look on his face.

"Sounds like one hell of a bender." Pollock said, course-correcting.

"You said it, baby. It really was. No hangovers. Hair of the dog, and so forth. For a while. Then Brooks showed up and things got weird." And with that, he chugged the remainder of his glass with a high elbow and slammed it down

upon the tabletop. He refilled it with alarming speed and agility, as if he had practiced the very same maneuver thousands of times, as an Olympic gymnast might
practice an idiosyncratic pummel horse dismount. He then stood, knocking the
chair far back along the tiling and into the corner of the refrigerator. "Now where
might your pisser be located?" Pollock made a sloppy twisting motion with his
raised ring finger, which, in his mind, communicated that the bathroom was up
the stairs and to the right. Miraculously, this was exactly what Cabe took it to
mean.

While Cabe was tending to nature's call, Pollock took inventory of his current status. He was still upset with Cabe, and he still intended to address the subject. But they were both already well on their way to being absurdly intoxicated.
That was no time to handle such pertinent matters. "Half-assed," he said, in his
best recollection of his father's voice. He didn't want to broach the reckoning
half-assedly. So he decided to bracket the entire matter for now. He had the whole
weekend.

And yet, Pollock had to admit that he was enjoying himself. The wine was
actually quite exquisite, doing strange geometric throbs of flavor. Cabe was more
familiar than he had anticipated, and Pollock was earnestly interested in hearing
the rest of his story about Margee. Perhaps there was more to gain, more to learn,
than his prior angry self had believed. Maybe they could just be friends again.
Maybe there didn't need to be any dark, obtuse sore hanging over the relationship,
and they could just pick up and start fresh, without the remediation. "Maybe,
maybe, maybe," he sputtered, in his best impression of his mother's impatience.
He carelessly snagged the jug of wine with his middle finger and poured more
into his already three quarters full glass. It overflowed a little before he compre-
hended his misstep. He ceased the pour and bent over, slurping up the spill
through pursed lips. The job just came to completion as Cabe emerged from the
dinning room.

"Pretty sparse upstairs too," Cabe said. "Pollock, how long have you lived here?" He slid clumsily into his displaced chair and then scooted back up to the table.

"Like I said, about five months now." Pollock was still reeling from nearly being caught in his sipping procedure.

"That's right. Forgive me, it was a long flight, and I'm just…uh…I'm not in place, full form." He pulled a faded blue bandana out of his pocket. It was already neatly folded into a two-inch-wide band with knots at either end. He merely placed it out on the table and ran his index fingers along its length from the center outward. He then pulled it to his forehead and tied it in back. Pollock figured that accounted for the napped hairline which he had noticed at the front door. "That's better," Cabe said, and sighed.

"So what happened when Brooks showed up, who is he?" Pollock asked. To Cabe, it was a classic Pollock moment. Cabe could recount hundreds of times when, as a conversation was getting interesting, when its participants where beginning to fire on all cylinders, interjecting right-brain-generated associations, and the entire enterprise was being pushed along by lateral connections and far-reaching relationships. often because everyone involved was stoned or drunk, Pollock had a habit of reminding everyone of some earlier signpost in the conversation, which marked the beginning of the long and interesting aside. He would track the divergence, the sideways hop, and sort of gently steered everyone back to the original direction so that they might conclude that train of thought before taking up another. It was an interesting bit of social management, and one that sometimes frustrated its subjects. Cabe always thought it was impressive and also admirable that Pollock demanded these conclusions before moving on. Cabe found it impressive that someone stoned could consistently recall the previous details of their scattered thinking, let alone of a conversation.

"Brooks, right," Cabe said, holding a finger up as he took another long swig of cabernet. Again he demonstrated the physical mastery of his high elbow–table slam signature maneuver. "Uuuuuh-huuuuh," he howled, in a strangely southern-gospel-like manner. "Hate to toot my own horn, but these are some damn good little grapes."

Pollock held his glass up and said, "Cheers!" Cabe nodded absently and slouched against his chair's wooden back.

"Right, so Brooks. Brooks that fuck." Cabe shook his head fervently in the negative, repositioning the bandana, which had slid a bit from the motion. "Margee and Brooks had had something casual going on in Amsterdam. That was like, a month before she showed up at Desert Cat. Brooks was an art critic." Cabe used air quotes as he sarcastically pronounced "art critic." It was quite clear that he did not believe Brooks was an art critic, or if he was an art critic, then Pollock decided Cabe must think "art critic" was a term not too dissimilar from "pretentious waster," or "soiled doucher," or "voodoo butter."

"He wrote monthly five-hundred-word articles about street art for some independent student-run magazine in Toronto. He is a trust fund baby. He'd been traveling through Europe for like a year. Part of the motivation for me to come home. Maybe that's giving him too much credit. Not sure, bud. Not entirely sure! The three of us went to the Art Gallery of Western Australia at his suggestion. This was before he really started to bother me. I listened to that fuck talk about the paintings for the better part of an afternoon. 'You can see the vagueness of the shapes suggested within the image. This is a common technique of abstract expressionism.' Ugh." Cabe frowned.

"We got to the modern art section, man, its all fucking careless scribbles. I could paint these things drunk with my dick. He was praising them, using ten-dollar words and Margee was eating it up, just eating it up. Lapping it up like a grateful kitten. Sure I was a bit envious, but even objectively, it would have been frustrating to watch it happen. For such a smart gal, she sure was being obtuse. But, the guy *is* like six foot three and has a face like Anderson Cooper. It's no mystery. I tried to reclaim some attention for myself by suggesting that perhaps the real art involved was the spiel that the art dealers and the critics spun for the pieces to get them bought and sold." He pushed forward, his elbows on the table's lip again, rocking it slightly with his weight. "Takes real art to sell a turd, right? I mean, right? Anyway, nothing. She was *enrapt* by him…"enrapt," is that correct?" Cabe squinted and tilted his head in true confusion.

"Um. Being taken up with someone? Ra-pt-ennnn-rapt. I think. Yeah, that seems right!" Pollock said in careful, measured syllables.

Cabe nodded appreciatively and continued. "Okay. So not long after the museum visit, Brooks had a room of his own at the hostel, and Margee was slyly trying to convince me of the virtues of an open relationship. In hindsight, it was all very clear, and I kind of feel like a real sucker. Ah, Pollock its good to see you again, bud. I needed this." This was followed by another Olympic maneuver.

"Jealousy does kind of shock the system. For better or worse, it really wakes you up. I mean, I don't really want to get into all of the detailed carnage. I'm sure you can imagine. When I finally acquiesced to Margee's request, I basically told her that it would only work if we were honest with one another and disclosed all of our…encounters with others. You know, whenever there's a relationship, usually one of the two is more jealous than the other. Maybe it changes, I don't know. But I am pretty sure that I was the more jealous one, at least at first. Brooks aside, which was hard to put aside.

"But aside from him, the whole reason I took a while to come around on the idea was that all I could picture was Margee in bed with other men. Sure Brooks, but others too. Like nondescript, faceless men. Just *men*. And incidentally, always with very tan and muscular backs. I imagined nicknames like "Daddy" or "Ice

Pick." I wasn't thinking about any of the adventures that *I* could have had. And probably it had to do a bit with confidence. I mean definitely it did. Margee, an attractive girl, wicked hot, she could likely manage to pull together whatever fantasies she wanted to. Men would comply. Me, on the other hand, I'd inevitably have less success, and it would require much more effort at any rate."

Cabe was coming to terms with the words spoken as he was speaking them. He hadn't yet talked about these recent matters to anyone, and he was surprised by how affected he actually was. Initially, he had opened up this topic so matter-of-factly and with no more forethought than for a clichéd idiom dropped nonchalantly into unsophisticated chatter. He readjusted his shoulders nervously, hoping the depth of his discomfort over this failure was not apparent. In fact, to Pollock, Cabe seemed to be presenting his story in a comical, farcical tone, betraying no concern. Cabe had always been this dryly self-deprecating around him. There was no contrary evidence now to suspect the existence of any more acute psychic pain in this particular instance.

Cabe continued, "Needless to say, Brooks was her first extrarelationship fling. They fooled around pretty much immediately. She didn't tell me. Nope. So much for our agreed transparency. I got wind of it from her friend Ashley, who asked me basically how on earth I was okay with her spending the night with him, sleeping in his room and everything too. Apparently, Margee had told all them back in the Netherlands that she was in love with Brooks. Like head over heels, actually beginning to finally think about marriage and children in love with him. World war two postcard, heh-heh." He nodded at Pollock. "They had some pact to part ways and then, in two months meet, and if they still felt the same way then, that was it. But when—"

"Wait a second. So she had this pact when she met you?

Cabe pursed his lips, then said, "Yeah. I was taken for a fool. I played the fool. Honestly, I think she saw all over my face how easy I was. You know, compliant. That's Margee. Like I said, cold bitch. But smart. She played me like a homemade family heirloom didgeridoo. I probably knew her game all along. Maybe not. Eh…whatever. I ended up banging Ashley several dozen times. I mean banging. Like a fucking monster. So there's that." He sliced the air with his hand. Finishing the contents of his glass, he lifted the jug to his mouth and chugged five loud gulps. Wine leaked down his neck and underneath his grizzly bear t-shirt. Pollock snorted in approval at the spectacle and finished his glass. "Music!" Cabe said. "That's what's missing, brother; we need music."

As Cabe was rifling through his pack in the other room for his iPhone, Pollock ruminated a bit on Cabe's open relationship. He asked loudly, "That's what got so weird about the open relationship? Hooking up with her friend?"

Cabe hopped back over to the table on one foot, his other flailing to get free of one of the backpack's straps. He sat, breathing heavily and scrolling intently on his phone. "No…no, not you either…no…yes!" He sat the phone in the middle of the table as the tremolo-laden intro riff to a psychedelic surf rock song rang out. Pollock noted that both of their drinking glasses were full again, mysteriously. He had no recollection of either of them doing the refilling. And, alas, the 1.5 liter bottle was sitting empty on the table, reflecting the white-blue glare from the electronic album artwork displayed on Cabe's phone screen.

"I was saying that that doesn't really seem all that weird to me." Pollock said, angrily. He meant the statement to somehow call out Cabe, a subtle attempt to try to use everything Cabe had just disclosed for competitive advantage. The memory that Cabe sought to pass over would not so easily be forgotten.

"Right, right," Cabe said, breathing in deeply. The animosity was received. "Well that wasn't the end of the experiment, bud. Like I said, Ashley and I were sleeping together for a bit. This was week two of Perth. First off though, you have to understand um…you mentioned that it was a bender? Well it really was. I mean we had coke and pot, and I did molly a bunch of times, and drinking all the while. Days kind of…blurred. Anyway, I don't remember all of the steps that lead to shacking up with Ashley, nor do I fully remember, or even really fathom, the steps that lead to our foursome." The word foursome dropped out of Cabe's mouth like a lead anvil onto a concrete shipping dock ,and it sent shivers down Pollock's neck.

"A foursome…wait, with who?" Pollock asked, with interest catching and spreading over his previously tight face.

Cabe smiled madly, seeing now that he had truly hooked Pollock. "Ah, Pollock, you little pervert," he said, with a hearty chuckle. Pollock blushed, aware of his eagerness and waved it away with a thrusting waft of his hand. Cabe continued on, merrily. "Ashley and I had a foursome with Margee and Brooks." Cabe's smile grew and grew, pushing his fleshy earlobes backward as he saw the confusion and shock set over Pollock.

"What the *fuck?*"

"Yes," Cabe said. He was beginning to sound haggard to Pollock, and maybe desperate. His inner reticence was pushing through the forced exterior. "Yes," he hissed, "so it was Brooks's idea, apparently. I am told, I have been told this. Doesn't matter. I told Margee about Ashley per our agreement, which she hadn't kept, and she told Brooks. Brooks recommended the soiree. Something about it making the most sense in these scenarios. Ashley was in immediately. Margee had laid out, in detail, the many virtues of Brooks as a lover to Ashley. So she was curious. In the end, it came completely down to me to make the decision." Another, less graceful, and leakier drink from the bottle ensued.

"And you went through with it! Dude, why?"

"I wasn't going to do it. Ashley's whole proposal put a bad taste in my mouth. Right, this fuck, Brooks, took my gal off of my hands and was now going to get me naked and make me watch as he, as he, well, played with two girls that were both clearly lusting for him. Fuck that! Un-uh!" Cabe again pursed his lips, sunk his shoulders, and looked down. Pollock had a sudden desire for him to end this story and regain the youthful vigor with which he had conducted himself before. "Yeah, but then I started thinking about what would happen if I declined, right? I mean, if Ashley and Margee were already willing, then without me, they'd just have a ménage à trois. At least if I were there, I could have some control over the situation. I mean, it started to seem scaredy-cat not to go through with it. And I guess once I started thinking like that, it seemed fated, fatal-ed. So I said yes."

Pollock wanted all of the raunchy details of Cabe's foursome. Cabe's emotional discomfort became apparent and made Pollock feel like a gossip enamored by tawdry exploits. Yet it was painfully true. "So what happened? How was it?" he asked with regret, resigned to hear the meaty conclusions, the ones he deserved, before endeavoring to spring Cabe, and perhaps himself, back into high spirits. He was experiencing a weird paradoxical pull to both torture Cabe by prodding the story onward, and restoring lightness and gaiety to the evening.

"It was confusing. I mean, it was awkward and then…well…" Cabe flipped through his mental Rolodex of foursome memories. The memories themselves were like pictorial freeze frames. He glimpsed an outstretched Margee indicating to Ashley with a sly index finger that she could come hither. Then he rotated the Rolodex, and next up would be Brooks's meaty thigh backs strenuously thrusting against Margee's buns. Another turn and he saw himself in Ashley while she tended to Brooks. "Things converge on the horizon," he said quietly. "It was like entering a porno. And afterward I remember being smelly and feeling guilty. I couldn't look any of them in the eyes. I mean…it went well enough. Everyone got off, no one received special attention. And in all honesty, I don't recall anything particularly special about Brooks's sexual prowess. Dude wasn't even as well hung as myself. Which, now that I think about it, that's kind of a victory. But its just hard to be intimate with someone after you have those images in your head, you know, of her basically just getting rammed by a guy you despise. And her loving it…just fucking loving it and begging for more. And then her best friend is flopping around on top of you, tits flinging and bopping all over hell and back. Yeah, Ashley was stacked like…well let me put it this way, if she were on the Titanic…"

Pollock felt his pants tightening a little. It bothered him that he was turned on by sex involving Cabe. Such a matter implied questions of predetermined sexual identity boundaries. Things Pollock didn't want to have to think about. "How long was the foursome?" he asked matter-of-factly, readjusting his butt on the chair.

"Oh man, I think it was like two or three hours. Like I said, things got smelly. Especially because Ashley was really adamant about anal. That's how I finished the last time. Same with Brooks. I got off like four or five times I think. That bed had sweat and saliva, vagina, ass, semen, hair, skin…ugh!" Cabe shivered in disgust.

"That sounds heinous. Where did you guys do this?" Pollock asked, his erection diminishing as he contemplated the postcoital odor involved in Cabe's pornographic affair.

"Oh on Ashley's. She had a king size. Thank God. If it had happened in my bed, I would've had to check in to another room to sleep. It wasn't just the bed, either. You know, even though the bed was large enough, the events sort of took place all over the room."

The two had finished the wine and Pollock uncorked the expensive scotch he had picked up for the occasion. "We are going to have a mammoth of a hangover tomorrow, but this is all I have unless you like sherry." Cabe shook his head in the negative, and Pollock poured generous portions into two new glasses. The scotch's usually bruising edge wasn't so harsh to Pollock, having already downed so much wine. He received the spirits with admiration. He looked at Cabe, and around the room, and realized that he was drunk and that he was happy to be drunk. The alcohol had confiscated his cynicism, his planned pettiness toward Cabe, and he was thankful for it. The night, the whole weekend, had potential for shenanigans on par with the days of old, and Pollock made a conscious decision, then and there, that he would surrender to its possibility.

Cabe wrapped up his tale with a tidy epilogue. "Yeah, so I paid my bill the next day and decided it was time to head back stateside. That's when I texted you." Pollock did some arithmetic. He was now leaning hard onto his elbows, halfway across the table, next to the empty bottle. Cabe's phone was now emitting some jazzy sounding big-band music from the 1930s. It reminded Pollock of black and white scenes of New Year's Eve, women with extended cigarette-holders and flowered veils. "Wait, so what have you been doing in the meantime?" he asked.

Cabe's head was swaying and he was flicking his fingers against the lip of the table, poorly mimicking the jazz beats. "Mostly ignoring texts," he said.

"From the others?"

"Yep. Like I said, things got too weird for me. I'm done with all of that garbage. I am a serial monogamist, my friend. And I am just fine with that. We're doin' just fine. Just fine. And that is the end." He held his glass out, and the two clinked their diminishing scotches together for the third or fourth time at this point, eager in drunken camaraderie, neither entirely 100 percent sure about what they were celebrating.

"So what's this job that brought you to Trams?" Pollock asked, feeling the extreme heat coming off of his cheeks.

"I have no idea!" Cabe said, loudly with a smirk.

"In your text, you said you were here for a new job, right?" Pollock asked, sensing some vague double cross on the horizon, his cynicism yawning back awake.

"I am here for a new job. I just don't know what that job is yet. Any suggestions in that regard?" Cabe answered, his grin now devilish and severe, admiring his own deceptive yet technically accurate communication.

Pollock rolled his eyes. "I don't know, Trams isn't known for its wine but there are some vineyards. They're pretty far out, though. Not really in Trams. Not Trams proper."

Cabe pulled out a white cigarette package from his pocket. "Spanky's Orange Flavored Suck Sticks" was written in bold black cursive on the package just above a girl in 1950s attire. She was sitting on the hood of a vintage Ford with fins typical of the era. Her name tag read Lo-Li-Ta. She was smoking, or more precisely, sucking on a Spanky's, which was approximately the size of a small baguette. Cabe smiled at Pollock, who was unconsciously flickering disapproval across his face, and howled out, "Good results, baby!," He flung his noggin back and balanced the chair on the hind legs before slamming back down onto the tile with a soda can–cracking pop.

They marched out onto Pollock's rear stoop and spent the next two hours pulling drags from the loosely packed orange flavored baguettes, and then back into the kitchen to sip the expensive Islay scotch. There reached a point, roughly corresponding with the edge of plausible sobriety, at which the lively naïve spirit of the two young men triumphed over the reservation and pessimism and self-loathing. This was especially true of Pollock, who required greater chemical influence to give up the ghost. Things were flowing. Serotonin production patterns were being disturbed.

Pollock and Cabe took turns regaling each other with moderately corroborating accounts of their college days. Details of drunken escapades and crammed study sessions unfolded, louder and faster, with each competing to finish the story. It was as if some strong natural phenomenon was creating one, hyperfluid, multifaceted creature out of the two conversing humans, comprised of the music and their clumsy desire for brotherhood. It was exhilarating and dangerous. Pollock ripped his blue T-shirt on the rough brass ring that ran around the backdoor catch and lock. He laughed and pushed his finger through the hole in a pecking motion against Cabe's upper thigh. At this, Cabe playfully shoved Pollock away with two much force, pushing himself back into the pantry, knocking several cans of sardines across the kitchen. "Saaaardiiiines!" Pollock called out in his deep raspy cartoon impression.

At Cabe's suggestion, they made a decision to, "go out among the people of Trams!" And from there, the evening became a sloppy hop from bar to bar, with increasing slurs and gaiety. At one point, in Tuft's, Pollock considered himself fortunate that they hadn't run into anyone he knew, because he didn't believe he had the resolve to formulate coherent sentences. He grinned madly to himself and finished off the rum and coke he had been sipping just as Cabe's arm landed heavily upon his neck.

* * *

Bastien Ebersold's pubic hair was longer than his penis. When he stood naked in front of the mirror, the top third of its shaft reached approximately the crest of the brunet bush. It hinted at the presence of a tan peanut below, like a bald baby gerbil tucked into a nest of rotten alfalfa sprouts. When Bastien urinated, the spray emitted from beneath the hair and often caught the edges of many individual hairs, forcing the stream to refract and to spritz wildly in various directions. This phenomenon kept his pubic region wet and rather smelly, especially because Bastien drank very little fluid other than coffee and liquor and so was dehydrated, with concentrated and odorous urine. There was a constant yellow-orange stained region on the front of his tight white underwear.

Often during meetings, or merely while absent-minded, Bastien would twiddle and twist the brass strands of his protrusive pubic bush. His slender fingers would gently run along the sharp edges and then tear down onto a mass, strongly mangling them clockwise into a knot until it hurt form the pull at their roots. The motion lifted his crotch skin upward into little red and white teepees. The pain that this produced was satisfying. Bastien enjoyed hurting himself because it allowed him to feel the pain that he was inflicting. And, this was an improvement over hurting other people, or animals, because then he would have to imagine the pain he was inflicting. There was a distinctive difference. Both were divine.

He had been inflicting pain since before he could remember. The earliest incidents he could remember occurred around age five. He would hold the heads of the family cats under water and take note of their struggle to break loose from his grip as their capacity to hold their breath reached its expiration. He always let them up before any permanent damage resulted. The cats were always very aware of where Bastien was and became more violent in their defenses, which only strengthened Bastien's resolve to continue. As he held their heads in the fountain's water, what he felt was so powerful and appeared so right that it made him cry and laugh and heave uncontrollably. It was his secret ecstasy.

This was before Bastien made the move from Switzerland to the United States. He grew up on a rather large estate in the mountainous countryside. He was home-schooled by a private tutor named Ida. Most of his afternoons were unstructured, allowing him ample free time to roam around the estate's expansive gardens and back park. His parents were rarely present, even less so were other children, and so the cats became a main source of socialization. His secret dunking did make him remorseful. But he then enjoyed feeling the remorse, which

pushed him again to continue. After some time, he decided to expand his repertoire and began setting the animals' fur on fire with matches he stole from the service kitchen cabinet.

The burning was delightful to young Bastien because he could look the creature in the eyes while producing the pain. This added a whole new aspect to the
experience, like one who enjoys roasted chicken discovering salt and garlic for
the first time. The smell was first unpleasant, but soon became associated with the
delight of inflicting pain, and so Bastien came to treasure that as well. He would
conduct these sessions in the large cellar below the east wing, where the estate
staff only ventured while exchanging the stored seasonal decor four or five times
a year. Next to an incinerator, there was a large chemistry table that Bastien's father had used as a child to study polishes, acids, polymers, creams, rubs and other
potential Ebersold Family Clocks proprietary compounds for varnishing and treat-
ing rare and sensitive woods. The table was perfect for his sessions.

Once he realized that pain was an enterprise with which he had an affinity,
and one which he was going to pursue further and throughout his life, he started
incorporating additional props. First, he took two travel cages and sat them along
the table. Next, he liberated a blowtorch from the service garage. Thus, he could
place one of the eight estate felines in the cage, and then angle the torch toward it.
The flame was long enough that, regardless of how the animal contorted and
flopped about, Bastien could reach it. This process prevented the scratching and
biting, which for a short while he had enjoyed, but the marks eventually became
so obvious on his arms and neck that questions from Ida and other staff members
began to mount. Bastien was perceptive enough to understand that his enterprise
needed to remain private.

What really got young Bastien's rocks off was an audience. Two cats in two
cages. One being attended to, and the other witnessing with horror and dreadful

anticipation of what awaited it. This Bastien loved, the anticipation. He would often get more pleasure from watching the other cat anticipate its fate while he burned its sorry compatriot. He would toyingly bring the torch over toward the second cage but then hold it next to the metal wiring without igniting the flame. Sometimes he would deliver what the viewing cat had anticipated, and other times he would merely go back to the first cat. Every once and a while he would let both of them go, with the realization that this might be the outcome the creatures would expect on the following occasion. And the next time, he would begin to unlatch the door, eyeing the look of relief on the feline. Then, just as the cat felt that it had evaded the worst, Bastien would unleash the blue-white torch. Delivered pain after first stoking and then quashing the little thing's hope was as good as it got for young Bastien.

He felt terrible for days and even weeks at a time, and thus the sessions would subside for the duration. Much of this time would be spent in his grandmother's rocking chair in the west living room, which sat beside the wooden cabinet with all of the board games and his mother's extensive collection of classic music. With an afghan on his lap, he would rock back and forth listening to Handel, Beethoven, Verdi, Bach, Brahms, and Wagner and ponder the purpose of living. It was from this vantage that young Bastien began to see that the truth of all things in life was agony, pain. He would smile sadly, his imagination alive with dreams of hurting people.

Other times he would eavesdrop on the kitchen staff, responsible for cooking for the entire estate's help and the few actual Ebersolds, mainly Bastien, who held extended residence on the premises, as well as Ida. The younger ones would rap about their weekend dalliances at pubs and city parks, and the older ones would affectionately relate the most recent milestones of their children. Bastien would sit on the cold granite floor of the long service hallway and wish to have friends with which to play. But then a real coldness would come over him at seeing how no friend would ever accept him for what he did, for his experiments with pain. This world would ever only be *his*. And that pain felt spectacular and true.

Bastien's work eventually did draw the attention of the staff. Especially, the young Michael Billet, who was responsible for, among other tasks, feeding and cleaning all of the estate's cats. He started taking note of the scarring and hairless sections cropping up on the animals. He hypothesized, to the drunken amusement of fellow Ebersold staff members, that the cats must be encountering ibex, wildcats, foxes, or bears that had made their way into the interior of the Ebersold property. "Perhaps a battle for territory?" he said. "The cats do string together, much like a pride." Michael brought his thinking to the attention of the head-of-house, Balton, who, in passing, mentioned it to Ida, with instructions to find out whether Bastien had noticed anything and to make sure to tell him to find his way inside before dark.

Although he saw that he could go on inflicting pain on the cats without suspicion pointed directly at him, Bastien did feel uneasy about Michael's waxing interest and therefore made a decision to find other subjects. An option quickly entered his mind. The estate was nightly thriving with opossums. A week wouldn't pass without a sighting. Once he had the idea, he was in motion. The switch from species to species was almost instantaneous. He acquired two raccoon traps that hadn't been employed for years from the hunting cabin out back and loaded them with bread and jellies. He set the traps behind the pond, underneath the thick purple plum trees, which the opossums seemed to favor. Within three days time, the boy had made a full transition and was back in business with three fully grown possums in cages on the chemistry table.

Half of Bastien's mother's records were stealthily transported from the west living room game corner down into the basement, and he would play Richard

Wagner's *Das Rheingold* while engaging in his activities. This was an even further addition, which he prided himself on discovering because the musical element enhanced his pleasure at inflicting pain so exponentially. It frightened him. And he liked that, feeling a bit beyond himself, a bit out of control. It was new. The opossums were fed and given water bowls and blankets upon which to lie and burrow. Aside from the few hours every week in which they were tortured, they lived the life of a pampered hamster or, rather, guinea pig. Bastien maintained a consistent rotation of opossums, keeping two as audience together in one cage, and then pulling one of the audience out to next serve as recipient. The previous recipient would then get two sessions as audience.

There were long stretches when Bastien would feel no impetus to inflict pain. During these periods, sometimes lasting up to a month or two, he would regularly check on the opossums and chat with them as if they were his closest buds. The point of these monologues was to review all of the best parts of the opossums' lives that they were missing by being his playthings, stuffed away in the dark basement. He would imagine himself in a comparable situation, trapped in a cage with some giant beast burning and cutting and poking him all of the time. These thoughts in and of themselves felt pretty dreadful, and so he could almost receive the desired pain without having to use any tools at all. This made him feel powerful and came in handy in later years when he didn't have the liberty of an abandoned wing of a mansion and oodles of free time.

The three opossums, which were never named, were all female. Bastien kept them in rotation for just under a year until the spring that Affie appeared. Then everything changed. Affie was the son of Bastien's father's business attorney, Dale Reiser, who disappeared during a weekend camping trip, and whose mother was subsequently forcibly checked into a mental ward. Following the discontinuation of search parties for Dale, Bastien's father took in young Affie out of his sense of loyalty and obligation stemming from his successful twenty-seven-year relationship with Dale, which centered on intellectual property, contracts, and real estate advice from Reiser, Holder & Associates. Don Holder, Dale's partner, had been on the camping trip and suffered the same fate.

Affie's arrival and introduction to Bastien and the estate's staff was awkward enough initially, regardless of the child's circumstances, because the presence of Mr. Ebersold was such a rare occasion in the first place. He was always traveling on business or vacationing with his mistress, who was known and adored by Mrs. Ebersold. She had open, extramarital proclivities of her own. Bastien, who was so starved of interaction with children his own age, was almost aghast at the sight of Affie. His presence, standing with his arms behind his back in the main estate foyer, was foreign and full of dangerous and wondrous potential to Bastien.

The boy was ten years old when he came to dwell at the Ebersold estate, two years Bastien's senior. He was shy and quiet. The first couple of days, he remained primarily in the game room, pacing around, fiddling with all of the Swiss globes and knickknacks that Grandma Ebersold had collected. They were spread across the mahogany mantel above the majestic marble fireplace beside the entertainment center, and also below on the hearth. The room was lit entirely by outdated oil-lamp chandeliers. The flickering of their flames tossed shadows about on the walls, which tended to play tricks with one's eyes.

Affie had a habit of scratching the skin below his lower eyelashes with the backs of his thumbs. The friction made the skin smooth and reddened, like a Jonathan apple. He would do this three or four times a minute as he walked in loops around the room, blankly observing the little porcelain village displays, but mostly just exuding a clear discomfort and uneasiness. Bastien watched the kid from the rear courtyard. He reminded Bastien of the cats as they adjusted to their newfound captivity in the cages in the basement. It was a terrible association to make, and in an instant opened Bastien's mind to the possibilities of having a human subject. He felt terrible for days.

Mr. Ebersold had made a very formal and cold announcement upon Affie's arrival. "Bastien, my son, this is Affie and he will be staying with us for a while. His father has been a dear friend to our family, and it is my wish that you show him the benefits and rules that attend accommodation in our summer home." And with a gentleman's wave of the hand, he had left the two boys alone, staring dumbly at one another in the foyer. It struck Bastien that his father had referred to the estate as their summer home. Bastien's residence there was year round, and thus the expression only further illustrated the distance between the Ebersolds. His father had a migratory pattern that was undisclosed and entirely separate from Bastien.

"Hi," Bastien said, displaying his customary intense facial expression.

"Hi," Affie said in an effeminate voice, shrugging his shoulders.

As he left the foyer, Bastien beckoned Affie to follow along. He strolled all throughout the premises, describing each sight that was worthy of note or otherwise not self-evident. "Service kitchen. Good for midnight snacks…Linen closet. Towels, undershirts, socks…Rose garden…Record collection…All of the cars in the garage have their keys just below the driver's seats." The tour lasted a good thirty-five minutes and ended with Bastien saying, "This one will be yours," and swinging the door open to a nondescript guest bedroom. It was one of eight on the east wing's first floor.

Then Bastien left Affie to himself, but never went far. He tagged along out of sight observing his new housemate, watching him trying to navigate the halls and examining family memorabilia and all of the traditional Swiss decorations. Affie walked oddly, and it delighted Bastien to think about it. The elbows were tucked close to the body with the wrists far outward. The steps were harsh and absorbed by deep bends of the knees, like overdone suspension. The whole production appeared clumsy and ill-suited for movement. Bastien guessed the boy lacked agility. This gave Bastien confidence in his ability to physically overpower Affie. They were approximately the same height, and with nothing particular to distinguish their builds, it was the muscular ineptitude displayed by Affie's hobbled waddle that convinced Bastien he could obtain the upper hand, especially through surprise. And so the possibility of a human subject opened up into a probability. The anticipation was titillating and salacious, like microbial little ringing bells spinning and echoing throughout Bastien's skull and gonads simultaneously.

But the plan was aborted when Bastien realized there was just no way to get away with it. The kid would scream, and he'd talk. Bastien couldn't keep him locked up, because the staff checked on him, made him meals, changed his bedding. And since Mr. Ebersold had come home with Affie, he had remained at the estate and worked days in his offices on the third floor of the west wing. Though it was only once or twice daily, Ebersold senior had made a habit of checking in on Affie. No matter how well Bastien coached or forced Affie to keep his mouth shut, Mr. Ebersold would surely be able to tell if something was wrong.

Besides their part in foiling Bastien's plans, Mr. Ebersold's daily check-ins with Affie deeply offended Bastien. It made him envious and angry. His father had never displayed any equal emotional investment in him. "His father passed on." Mr. Ebersold whispered into Bastien's ear, expounding Affie's tragic present circumstance. Bastien hadn't experienced any great tragedy, but still thought the mere fact of fatherhood should supply enough motivation for affections. He knew that he wasn't really after the answer because he had long ago concluded that he and his father would never have some kind of close and casual relationship. His father was the progenitor and paterfamilias, he was the only son and heir apparent to the Ebersold Family Clocks business. The relationship was transactional, which in some way, he told himself, indicated nobility and sacred ritual to his father.

Now, here his father was, patting Affie's back and smiling and asking him about whether he enjoyed sports or skiing. This unexpected solicitousness should've been Bastien's. But it was someone else's. And not even another sibling, but a complete outsider, a foreigner in the house. But then Bastien realized *he* was the foreigner. It became apparent quickly. The staff preferred Affie as he opened up and began talking and conducting himself more freely and comfortably, growing acclimated to his new surroundings.

Michael Billet especially warmed to young Affie after having realized that he would laugh at almost any story or joke he told. The boy would sit and listen intently to Billet's ramblings for hours. Stuck on a wooden stool in the service kitchen, the room smoky from cheap rolled cigarettes in the late evenings, Affie would just eat up each morsel of monologue as it rolled off Billet's tongue. It was a stark contrast to the derisive sneers and mockery that Billet received from the rest of the staff. Because Affie listened and laughed, he became sacrosanct and familial to Michael. And because Affie spared them from having to also listen, the cooks and valets warmed to him as well. His presence became expected in their late night card games and drinking congregations after their shifts were complete.

Bastien would stand outside in the long service hallway, with the cold somehow emanating from the tiling, and he would listen to their laughs and jokes and sharing it all with the ten-year-old houseguest. The houseguest had taken over Bastien's house. He was the odd person out in his own home. Nothing had made him feel lonelier.

Bastien blamed himself a little. He knew that he was a quiet person. Aloof, as he had overheard his mother describing him to giggling party friends one evening, covertly from the main stairwell. "Oh yes, well he is still very young now, isn't he? He'll come around," one of the partiers responded. And he was always curt and standoffish with all of the staff. He never meant any offense; he just happened to have a stern face and never found chitchat all that purposeful. But it did register that people tightened up when he came around, like he brought a gust of cold wind with him or even something more paranormal and suspicious. He was unwanted.

Ida had many times tried, slyly and with great tact, to broach the subject of Bastien's lacking interpersonal skills to him. She had been prompted to do so by Mrs. Ebersold, who had grown embarrassed of her estranged child's behavior at her frequent social events entertaining wealthy socialites, businessmen, and politicians, into whose circles the Ebersold Family Clocks wealth had thrust her and Mr. Ebersold. These occasions were also the only real time she spent at the estate, and so by influencing Ida to help young Bastien improve his ways of relating to others, it was a nearly intimate gesture on her part because they would otherwise practically never cross paths.

And though Bastien recognized Ida's efforts plainly, he put none of his energies toward appearing better adjusted. It seemed to him that some terrible trespass had already been committed by his family asking him to be different than he was. Besides all that, it didn't appear to him that there were any fundamentally desirable rewards in behaving as his mother and her frequent party guests behaved. They all lied through their teeth and talked about each other with hatred and disdain. Bastien, being an eavesdropper at a master-class level, used a stethoscope, which his father had shipped to him for his seventh Christmas from England, to listen to bathroom conversation during these parties. The comments all faded into a monotonous stream of backstabbing pettiness and jealousy. Everyone present was sure they were better than the rest, and everyone was also sure that everyone else was stupid, sometimes for the same reasons that other people thought themselves better.

It all seemed a nasty and infectious circle of wasted energy, this being nice and this school thing. Bastien hated social. He loved being alone and feeling awful. He figured at age six that he was going to die alone and all of his thoughts would be only for him, and so there really was no legitimate advantage in trying to share things with others. And yet, when that discombobulated little houseguest Affie came and illustrated to Bastien what things would be like for him if he indeed did begin sharing and valuing the good report of others, it drove him nearly to tears.

Ida had begun a project with Bastien. He was prompted to imagine a future in which he was happy. Where would that be? What would he be doing? Who would be there? Ida specified, after numerous questions from Bastien, that it could be an alternate world where the rules of nature were different or even in the past or in the future. The point was to capture some understanding of what he wanted out of his life and who he thought he was. It was an exercise in identity. "It is called introspection. It means looking into yourself. This is where there is truth," she said in her strong Swiss accent. Bastien ruminated on this statement with growing admiration until he was exuberant, with genuine wonder, about the fact that he could construct his own truth, his own world,

Bastien pictured himself with the ability to absorb pain from others. If someone slipped and nicked their shin on the curb, then the resultant stinging would be transferred to Bastien's leg. If someone had a headache, it would be in Bastien's skull. And maybe he could invent an apparatus that did the transferring of the pain. This way, he could use the apparatus on others. For how bad would it feel to have another experience the pain of the world. Bastien imagined a husband and wife. The wife would be attached to the apparatus. He could then slowly dissect and torture the husband, all the while sending the feeling of it to the wife. The husband would see himself being mutilated and hear the cries of agony from his wife.

Bastien thought it would be quite an experiment. The apparatus, when pictured in his racing imagination, was organic and cocoon-like. It was a thick fleshy sac hanging down from a dome-shaped steel frame. A tangle of electrical wiring spilled out from the sac and connected to a television screen display fitted with a complex of knobs and dials, as Bastien had seen in old films depicting mad scientists. At the front of the cocoon was a small viewing window made of material similar to saran wrap, in a little four-by-six-inch rectangle. Thus, the subject receiving the pain could look out upon the room.

The apparatus, as it appeared to Bastien in more detail, tickled him to death, and he found himself flexing his abdomen and letting out low-pitched howls and yelps somewhere between cries and laughter. Vowel-like sounds began to accumulate from out of the guttural cacophony. The vowels condensed and turned into a word. "Sarrrgusss," Bastien said. And again, "Sarrrgusss," with an extended hiss on the ending "s."

After a few days of uttering "Sargus," Bastien, subconsciously and then consciously, acknowledged that would be the name of the apparatus. "The Sargus! The Sargus!" he would call out. The idea of this contraption, which concentrated all of the pain in the world, the universe, into one enwombed subject, made his experiments so pale and dull in comparison. He felt underachieving and somewhat defeated, as if he saw how he could never really equal the grandeur of his aspirations. He took to estimating how long it would take a subject in the Sargus to die. He really had no scientific basis, but he came to the conclusion that a human subject would last approximately one month before their heart gave out. "The month of the Sargus!" he mused, melancholic. "The month of the Sargus for Affie."

Having been marginalized in his own home, Bastien began spending more time talking to his opossums. He had taken great care to maintain their secrecy and began to view them sacredly, as the only semblance of true kinship. The conversations he had with them were tantamount to upholding his self-esteem. "Affie's eyes look like mermaid boobies. Isn't that strange? Don't you think so, girls? I want to cook them. Eh, maybe I don't want that. But I don't want him to have them. They shouldn't be in his head. You know, I could probably let you guys go during the month of the Sargus. Wouldn't need you anymore."

He would lay on his back atop the workbench adjacent to the chemistry table, his arms tucked behind his head. The antiquated heating pipes rumbled and vibrated his body against the surface of the bench, eventually leaving his thoracic vertebrae sore. Through the narrow windows near the top of the brick basement wall, Bastien could see the tops of hedges in the row out back flittering about in the wind.

He lay in that position tens of dozens of times over the next few weeks, wallowing a bit in his isolation, a new sensation for him. He was also despairing of his technological shortcomings, which disallowed the invention and employment of the Sargus. But a new and exciting notion did brighten his outlook. He came to realize that even if he were caught for molesting Affie, say burning a spot on his lower back, his father would never take it further than chastising him verbally. Perhaps he would sequester Bastien in his room or otherwise extend punishment to some variety of privation of his passions. He would likely be unable to tend to his possums. But there would be no corporeal consequence, no legal matter. Once Bastien realized this, his fear and reservation faded.

It wasn't entirely clear to Bastien that Affie, in fact, would squeal. Bastien thought he might be able to hurt him bad enough that he would be too afraid to speak out. Maybe Bastien could trade him less pain for silence. But even if he did squeal, and Bastien was caught and punished and, therefore, couldn't repeat the experiment, he hoped it would be enough to alter Affie's behavior. Bastien's desire was for Affie to lose his zeal and, consequently, cease his healthy engagement with the staff, Michael in particular, and of course with Mr. Ebersold. The risk of the entire scope of anticipated punishments that Bastien could conceive of seemed to merit going forward. And so Bastien decided, although he hadn't the pain contraption of his imagination, he was going to commence the Month of the Sargus to the best of his means and accept any departure from his dream.

A warming calm resulted from Bastien's decision to work on Affie. It relaxed him, and he made no haste in beginning preparations. Instead, he spent the next two days continuing his supine conversations with his "girls," staring out through the high basement windows and watching the winds have their way with the hedgerow. It was a cold autumn, with snows regularly occurring that early October. He watched the individual flakes of snow twirling and dusting the evergreen tips. The thermometer behind the service kitchen window had read minus two degrees Celsius earlier that morning. It made Bastien wonder out loud to his opossums, "The cold can be pretty painful...until it isn't, right girls? Because it always stings and nips, especially in the fingers and toes and...well the limbs, I guess, but then the cold overtakes you and you go numb. I bet freezing to death isn't that painful after all. You probably just get numb and then real sleepy. For the pain, you would have to freeze and thaw, freeze and thaw. Now that would hurt good. Wow, yeah!"

Bastien thought of all the times he had come in from sledding or wandering about with stiff hands that turned into little knives of warming pain. His ears, nose, toes, and lips would follow suit. The feeling was penetrating and massive, like it combined into one continuous throb throughout the parts of the body furthest away from the heart. It felt like flames, like he was burning at the edges. If one were to have to enter and reenter this thawing/burning period again and again, the toll would be great. "I wonder if you could speed it up...the freezing and thawing? Do you think you could, girls? Do you think? Oh, a hot bath tub. Yeah, a hot bath tub, and then back out into the snow and ice. Then back into the hot tub, with fresh hot water running. Um, but where to do this? Well, you know what, girls? I bet we could do it down here with the tub sink."

With that he sat up and glanced across the basement at the deep, oversized plastic industrial sink. It was yellowish-white with spatters of yellow and orange from repeated splashes of acidic and base chemicals. Bastien's father had spent many evenings in his youth mixing various polymeric compounds, searching for patent pay dirt in this basement. Bastien hopped to his feet and walked over to the tub sink. He wiped its smooth inside slope with his fingers. A slight grey silt appeared on his hand. A flash of the inside of the Sargus's womb rocketed into Bastien's imagination. It was gooey with a substance roughly resembling puss in its viscosity and composition. The inside walls of the cocoon were warm and tight around the subject, almost suctioned stickily against the subject's skin like a mucous coated throat in midswallow. Bastien shivered in reverie.

He twisted the left metal lever above the tub and held his hand out underneath the sputtering flow of water as it slowly increased in temperature. Within thirty seconds or so the stream was too hot, and he had to jerk back his hand. He shook it outward and wiped it against his pant leg, visualizing a plan coming together. "A month in the Sargus for Affie."

That night, just after 2:00 a.m., Bastien carefully transferred all three of his girls into the smaller of the two cages. He had long been using leather pruning gloves to handle his subjects, but on this night, it struck him how calm and accepting the possums were. Their eyes gleamed up at him; their smoky fur was tattered from burns and tears and healing round wounds from drill bits. Bastien twisted his pubic hair, contemplating how he would miss his girls.

The woods were a wall of black just beyond the reach of the latticework and sculpted shrubbery at the farthest eastern edge of the yard. And as the girls ran off, hesitating now and again as possums tend to do in approach and flight, their little charcoal bodies slipped out of sight as if swallowed by the night. Bastien sniffed his fingertips. They reeked of pubic sweat and urine, and the smell was almost akin to sulfur and garlic. For a small moment the emotion of releasing his closest friends overtook him, and he deeply regretted having done so.

The next morning, Bastien woke up late and angry. It was Affie's fault that his girls were now out on their own, out of sight. He thought Affie a dim-witted little socialite who didn't, and couldn't possibly, understand the span and fury of Bastien's influence at the Ebersold Estate, but soon would. This was the day or, rather, that night. As soon as Bastien mentally committed to the timing, the anger completely disappeared, and a steady concentration orbited him serenely.

The consideration Bastien was directing toward Affie was all distant and reserved. He hadn't, in the three months between Affie's arrival and the release of the girls, spoken more than a handful of sentences to the boy. This was not lost on Bastien. It was apparent to him that Affie most probably had contributed nothing to Bastien's own social isolation and feelings of exile in his own home. But whenever he meddled with this tangle of thoughts, he ultimately justified going forward by attributing the decision to his need to expand upon his experimentation.

Bastien considered himself a scientist. And he was working in fringe territory where other less fortitudinous scientists merely acknowledged that the field existed and, with great trepidation, tiptoed back into conventionally accepted areas. But in their beds before fading out, these scientists reflected upon the domain and submitted to its power and their own fear. It was the dynamics of pain. Bastion recognized that, if he were able to let go of what he thought was right and wrong, he would learn all sorts of things. One only really needed right and wrong in a group. Everyone, to Bastien, secretly threw right and wrong out of the window when there was no audience.

So Bastien kept no audience and could be honest and throw out right and wrong. And Bastien came to believe that anything you hurt enough will end up loving you. In fact, that thing will love you so much, it will crave your punishment. And once it has fallen in love with your infliction of pain, when you stop, it will do anything to get you to resume. Bastien also learned that, in hurting his subjects, he was really hurting himself. For that was why he did it—to feel truly terrible, that rush of grave horribleness, so brash and complete and stark and unrelenting that it must be the most potent of truths. And so, he came to see that every experiment was really a plea for the same to be done to himself.

Beyond this point, Bastien's learning ceased. He could not figure why it was that he craved abuse so ravenously, but it was truth. And he wasn't exactly confident about what that meant. It was obvious that people reached out in communication to others because of their sheer terror of loneliness. The communications were also abbreviated approximations seeped in conventions and conceits. But they seemed to make the people feel better. It made Michael Billet feel better. It made his mother feel better. And, apparently it made Affie feel better. But it didn't make Bastien feel better. It made him feel fraudulent and weak. He felt he was being strong and true by turning to the terror inside that drove others to communion, and dealing with it directly. That, to him, was at the heart of the dynamics of pain.

But there was still a looming blind spot for him. Because, for all of his experimentation and desire to feel the true terror at the heart of himself, he still had to live a life. His life couldn't be just one experiment after another, continuously, until he passed on. Bastien did have his interests. He loved walks and music and cooking. And he loved animals above all else. He had loved his girls more than anything else, more than his family, more than Ida. And so it seemed to Bastien that maybe he had his own conceits. Because, if his experiments were indeed confirming his hypothesis, than he either needed to quash his loves and interests and just die or revise his hypothesis. He wondered if maybe part of the truth consisted of good things,

These were the questions pressing at the edge of his fringe science, and a large impetus for why he did not hesitate to go forward with a human subject. He needed to push the science forward. He needed to know. Bastien knew the saying "curiosity killed the cat" and decided that's what science was—curiosity. He believed science required scientists to kill cats. Bastien repeated this phrasing to himself as he mentally walked through the plan for Affie, again and again. The saying had initially been an amusing and silly play on words, but through its repetition had become akin to a motto or creed.

That evening, Bastien sat cross-legged on the rug in Affie's guest bedroom. He had a red and yellow woven climbing rope in his right hand and a folded, chloroform-saturated square of terry-cloth bathing towel in his left hand. Affie was snoring gently on his side, facing away from Bastien. On the nightstand sat a nightlight, a rotating cylinder of plastic into which was cut bird-shaped holes. The light shown through the holes and projected the birds over the blue walls. Bastien felt the birds moving across his face. The turning motor at the base of the night light made a low, hollow clacking sound.

His body wrapped by the thick down comforter, Affie's breathing was steady and slow. Every exhale produced a quiet whoosh, and each inhale sounded like the teeth of a bread knife dragging over a hard loaf of pumpernickel. The organic rhythm seemed to coincide with the clacking of the night light motor. Bastion couldn't hear any other sound throughout the house.

Bastien stood and leaned over Affie. Affie's face was completely relaxed in sleep and it made him look like someone else entirely. His cheek sagged down toward his jawline and Bastien could make out the beginning of jowls. The eyebrows, in their relaxed state, slanted upward toward the middle of his forehead. It made him appear sad and pleading.

Bastien found it eerie how well his plan had been executed. He merely dropped the chloroform cloth on Affie's lips and he was out. When he awoke, he was in his undershirt and boxer shorts lying just out back in a drift of snow, his wrists and ankles bound with thick horse rope whose ends led in through the small basement window. His mouth was covered in several layers of duct tape. Bastion yanked him in and plopped him into the industrial sink, steaming with hot water.

Affie's muffled cries and writhing illustrated the discomfort that Bastien had anticipated. He lifted him out, dried him with a towel, and replaced his shirt and shorts with dry ones he had taken from the linen closet the previous day. Then he lifted Affie and shoved him back through the high basement window, his feet on the tool bench's wobbling surface. He used two broomsticks to push Affie's body back into the snowdrift. Affie tried to get to his feet, but Bastien, through various angled tugs on the ankle or wrist rope, stamped out each effort with little bother.

After the third trip back into the tub, Affie had become quiet and tears ran down his cheeks. Instead of any of the previous writhing and yelling, he had become resigned to his fate. Bastien did detect a modest noise coming from Affie. It sounded much like a whistling teakettle heard from rooms away. Bastien lowered his ear to Affie's head, protruding from the bath, and heard a continuous high-pitched humming. He turned and looked into Affie's eyes. They were unfocused, aimed at nothing in particular.

The ringing hum was something that he had experienced with none of his previous animal subjects. It was terrible and delightful, and he couldn't help but smile from ear to ear. The newness and uncanny pure agony within the hum exceeded Bastien's expectations of discovery. He mimicked the hum, adjusting to match the Affie's tone precisely. He hummed until losing breath and then reloaded his lungs and resumed his own high-pitched humming. With each hum, he was louder, and at a certain decimal level, the sonic vibrations at the rear of the roof of his mouth where it met with the upper throat began to tickle and itch. He

scratched it by coughing abruptly with gusto, caught his breath and then continued in the humming frenzy.

Affie's limp, resigned body lay in the giant sink, only his head and shoulders above the water as it cooled. Bastion, in his state of unparalleled elation, was
dancing around with his arms in the air and continuing with his mimicking hums.
He traipsed in circles, his arms modeling the wings of airplanes, humming and
coughing throughout the basement as the sink water became room temperature
and then chilly.

Being fully satisfied, Bastien cleaned up after himself. He chloroformed Affie again and put him back into bed with a dry set of clothing. Anticipating the
fallout from his experiment, Bastien returned all of the supplies that he had
amassed for experimentation over the past year and a half to their previous and
rightful locations. Each tool or supply's theft had caused minor trouble for many
of the staff members who were responsible for their care and use. Bastion was
cognizant of this fact, and wondered sometimes whether they knew it was he who
was guilty of taking the tools, the cages, the clothing, the wiring, the knives, the
fuel, all of the necessaries. He thought that if they did know it was him, that might
be the reason that they disliked him, not because of anything he was. But the idea
made no sense to him because Bastien knew very well that none of the staff
would reserve their judgment and open admonishment of his thefts had they discovered him to be their author. In fact, Bastien had overheard his father instruct-
ing the staff, as they stood aligned in the living room, to treat Bastien as their own
child and spank him at will for misbehaving or not following their instructions.
Just such spankings had happened from time to time throughout Bastien's childhood.

Regardless, it brought Bastien some vague appreciation to know that he was
returning the items back into the possession and purview of the Ebersold Estate
staff. Having done so, he lay in his own bed listening to Mozart's *Requiem in D*

Minor. He was asleep before the "Dies irae." When he awoke early the next morning, his body ached and his forehead was on fire. In an instant, it was apparent that the experiment had made him sick. And he was appreciative. After an event so groundbreaking and emotional, it seemed almost proper and necessary to him that he should spend a few days on bed rest. Besides, it was a practical advantage to be ill when the wrath of his father would come down on him after Affie found his way to tattling. The illness, to Bastien, was merely his body being prudent. And with that, Bastien returned to his deep slumber.

He awoke late the following afternoon to his father sitting quite upright in the great bedside chair that Bastien's grandfather on his mother's side had crafted himself. Very intricately carved eagles and snakes topped the ears on the back of the chair. Mr. Ebersold was reading a thick stack of what looked like legal papers held together by a black clasp. Bastien's pulse sped, fearing that this was the moment of his reckoning. Despite accepting the inevitability of its coming, its actual approach was far more worrisome to him now. He covertly pulled the comforter's edge up from his neck to his cheek and, then, upward still.

The move was unsuccessful. Mr. Ebersold saw the motion from the corner of his eye. "Ah, Sebastien, you're awake. I was wondering if you were going to make an appearance today or whether I should come back tomorrow," Mr. Ebersold said in his raspy low whisper, as he tossed the stack of paper down hard on the bedside table, discombobulating the doily and rattling the lamp. He crossed his leg over the opposite knee and held an expression of expectancy. "Ida has told me you are fevered and all. I told her you are a sneak and cherish sick days away from lessons. But she has assured me that she took your temperature herself," he said, after receiving no response.

Bastien's eyes grew wide, and he did not move. He was waiting for the true topic of discussion to emerge. "Are you feeling any better at all? Any better than yesterday?" Bastien continued in his unresponsive hunkering down behind the thick downy comforter. "Sebastien, I am speaking to you. Can you hear me?" Mr. Ebersold said with growing concern. He reached over and pulled the comforter down to Bastien's chest and placed the back of his other hand against Bastien's wet forehead. "Mmm. Sweaty but cool. I think it has broken," he said, and returned to his casual cross-legged position, leaning back into the creaking eagles and snakes.

"Have you talked to Affie?" Bastion said in a haggard voice, wishing to end the suspense.

Mr. Ebersold frowned and said, "Why, yes. We were just at hearts earlier in the parlor. He is a sweet boy but really has no gift for cards."

Bastien's heart sank in confusion, wondering if his father was toying with him. "How is he doing?" Bastion asked, his voice becoming more normal with use.

Mr. Ebersold again furrowed his brow and smiled curiously, as he often did during the rare occasions when he was being playful with Bastien or Mrs. Ebersold. He maintained his mirth for a moment before his expression grew quite severe. He cleared his throat, uncrossed his legs, and leaned a bit toward Bastien. He put his hand on the comforter over Bastien's thigh. The position was intimate, fatherly, and it alarmed Bastien. "Well. It is a very hard thing, this thing that he is going through. It is hard enough when you lose a parent. I remember when I lost both of mine. Tough. But with Affie, he doesn't... You see, when my mother and father passed I knew why. Heart attack and pneumonia. There was a reason. Here, no one really knows exactly what happened to Affie's father. The investigation ended without answers. And his mother... well that is a shameful and unfortunate thing. All of this... all of this, and Affie is interested in learning how to play hearts. I think he will be okay."

Mr. Ebersold made a pained face and looked away from Bastien. He said, "You have to imagine this situation that the boy is in because you have never experienced any loss so great. But it's real for him. His parents have been plucked away from his life. And now, he is in a new home with mostly strangers. He is searching for something sturdy you see? Something dependable and familiar. And that is why it is important that you are good with him, that you treat him more as a brother than a houseguest, eh?" Mr. Ebersold nodded his head, redirecting his eyes to Bastien's. In all of the anger and exhilaration, Bastien hadn't really considered Affie's loss. It didn't quite register. Perhaps this was partly because of his own distance with his parents or his jealousy with Billet. And it was strange now, the closeness and solicitude his father was exhibiting. It made him squirm somewhat under the covers. "Yes?" his father said.

The question mandated a response. "Yes, sir," Bastien answered, perfunctorily.

"Okay. Well get some rest. I'll be in my office. If you require attention, Ida will be checking in on you." Mr. Ebersold cleared his throat and got to his feet. Collecting the stack of legal papers, he turned and exited the room. And that was it. Bastien's mind wasn't entirely up to task, its content sort of swimming in fevered dream waves, but he did wrestle to the conclusion that Affie had kept the molestation to himself. This puzzled Bastien, and he wondered why Affie would keep quiet. Further, the new discovery of the intensity of Affie's loss and displacement made the experiment seem more severe.

As strange as it seemed to him, he was afraid to see Affie again. Bastien knew he had the upper hand, having hurt Affie bad enough to shut him up. He assumed Affie was afraid but Bastien didn't know why the boy's face now scared him so much. He wrestled with this reticence to see Affie again, holed up in his room for far longer than his illness necessitated. He indulged in a total four days of sleeping long hours, living mostly in half-remembered fragments of dreams.

He finally emerged from his room on the fifth day. It was late morning on a Saturday, and the house was mostly quiet. His slippers' soles clicked down the hall stairs. He could hear the clanking and clattering of Billet and company performing routine maintenance on autos in the garage. A distant motorized landscaping tool droned in a faint hum. Upon turning the corner into the kitchen, he stopped immediately. There sat Affie, alone at the long bench seat, yellow in the early autumn sunlight. He was still in his undershirt, as he was when Bastien had left him in his bed.

Affie had been scraping hardening wads of oatmeal from the sides of his bowl until he caught Bastien's panicked face out of the corner of his eye and ceased his eating. He rested the spoon against the lip of the bowl and returned his gaze to the table, stiffening his entire torso. Dread and sickly feelings previously unknown to Affie cascaded through him.

Bastien's adrenaline and norepinephrine spiked. He went numb in his hands. The horror of the confrontation caused him to look peaked and he felt flush. The moment of the two's silent recognition of one another seemed to last longer than time itself. Bastion saw the morning sunshine through the translucent little windows spreading across the floor as it did at sunset, and he longed not to have to move his body or use his hands. He wondered if he would be able to overcome the crushing inertia that the stark reality of the moment birthed.

And then, as if pushed from behind, he just traipsed right into the kitchen, loudly poured himself tea from the warm kettle, and sat down next to Affie. Affie didn't move as Bastien scooted into a comfortable position, nearly shoulder to shoulder with him. "I'm feeling much better now," Bastien said with an air of excitement in his voice. "It seems like I slept for nearly a month." He sighed and took a generous slurp of tea from the porcelain mug. Affie continued in his rigid posture but lowered the spoon down to the base of the bowl and rested it there.

"Mmm," Bastien said in satisfaction. "It's good to be up and about again. This is my favorite time of year. I absolutely love watching the leaves change. Interesting that they're dying when that happens. And excellent when we have these early snows. Do you share my affection for autumn?" he asked Affie, raising the mug back to his lips. Affie inhaled deeply at the question and blinked his eyes sporadically in a series of rapid-fire flutters. "I...prefer spring."

The fight-or-flight mechanism was inflamed throughout Affie, most acutely felt in his flexed thighs. He was preparing himself to hop up quickly and leave the room. In his head, he counted down from five, but at two, Bastien thrust himself upright, causing Affie to flinch. Bastien, already warm with the satisfaction of having confronted and conquered that which he feared so much, reached out and patted Affie's head three times as if to say both "There, there now" and "You are mine." Then he almost strutted out of the kitchen.

Affie spent the remainder of the morning and the larger part of the afternoon contemplating running away form the Ebersold Estate. He was given great autonomy and privacy, which he had never had in his previous household. He used these to walk the gardens and forest paths by himself, and it made him lonely and bored, not being accustomed to such long stretches of silence employing nothing but his imagination. His imagination had a habit of turning against him. It showed him horrible vignettes of his father being savagely maimed and eaten by a bear or falling into a hidden cave and starving to death in the dark. He saw his mother locked away in a grimy basement cell, unable to find any sense.

It was because of these inflictions from his imagination that he clung so heartily to Billet and the kitchen staff and sought out Mr. Ebersold whenever he was free of his office. Affie thought little about his ordeal with Bastien. Perhaps it was so horrific and jarring that he wished to keep it free from his tyrannical imagination. Perhaps he felt that he deserved what was given to him. But one of his few concrete thoughts on the matter was that he would welcome its repetition rather than have to run off or be alone again. There was enough at Ebersold Estate for him to cope. But the unknown, out there in the woods somewhere with his imagination, that was beyond what he could accept and make do with.

So he decided that Ebersold Estate was his home. And he hoped that Bastien had discovered or proven that which he sought and would no longer harm him. And he really hoped that Mr. Ebersold would stay and work from the estate for much longer.

The flush of new experience and dense information riding the wake of Bastien's human experimentation with Affie left Bastien confused. He was proud that he had seen the whole process through to completion but needed time to come to articulate conclusions about the import of his actions. So Bastien kept his distance from Affie for a while thereafter. This was possible largely because the two boys, due to their school level differential, had different lesson times with Ida. Affie, being the older and more advanced student in his maths and histories, went first in the morning. Bastien then had afternoon sessions. The lessons took place in the corner study at the far end of the west wing.

There was a thirty-minute gap between their sessions, so they never had to cross paths unless they desired to. Affie began winning Mr. Ebersold's attentions with greater frequency and for longer periods of time. He really took an interest in the boy once he realized one day how dexterous and mechanical minded he was.

Long hours, the majority of Mr. Ebersold's time in his office, were spent tinkering with cuckoo clock guts. He would repeatedly disassemble and reassemble the machinery, looking for ways to improve upon the design, usually to no avail. Scattered on his desk were all sorts and shapes of pins and cogs, braces, framing, tin wires, rubber stops, wood shunts, nimble little screwdrivers, and specialized, elegant, curved metal implements that resembled those found in a dentist's toolkit. The clock's innards would be laid out deliberately in neat rows atop the felt-covered worktable and studied and ruminated over resentfully until, eventually, the clock was reassembled with no improvement. Following this, Mr. Ebersold would either work on repairing a dysfunctional clock or focus on novel woodcarving for a new model.

Most of the Ebersold fortune had been earned back in the 1600s, 1700s, and 1800s, through cuckoo clock sales and contracts throughout Switzerland, Italy, and Germany. The acquired fortune had since grown steadily through an investment portfolio containing a plethora of stocks, mutual funds, real estate, intellectual property licensing, and subsidiary clock repair and design shops that carried on their business under the Ebersold Family Clocks banner and trademark. Predominantly, all of the clock-related activity still carried out by the surviving Ebersolds revolved around participation in regional and basically ceremonial tournaments, conventions, and pageants.

These international competitions hosted many fine clockmakers and craftsmen. Despite the rogues, the mavericks, and the up and comers, late night enthusiasts by the hundreds who had enough skill and savings or paid time off to make the travel itinerary of the circuit, all in all there were really only a dozen ancient families who dominated the scene. The Ebersolds were one of the dozen, and thus superb performance at these meetings had become a matter of longstanding pride and tradition for the family, a sort of community survival. Mr. Ebersold had been feeling his family's grasp on inclusion in the upper echelon slipping. It had been several years since anyone from the company had taken a first prize for design, craft, or vision. And if he was honest with himself, his own interest in the family business was waning greatly with age. He had never truly been that interested in clocks. But it was the family business, and he did what was expected of him by his father and his father's father.

Mr. Ebersold had been sucked into the business via chemistry and a little sleight of hand. As a child, he was fascinated with the subject, partially in response to his own father having purchased him a fairly extensive set of beakers and boilers. Along with the set came the opportunity to shadow their head wood craftsman, Mr. Egerrick, with the impossibly long neck and hairless arms, who was in charge of polishes and varnishes. He was nicknamed the Egret. Mr. Ebersold followed instructions handwritten in barely legible cursive by the Egret, sitting at a desk mere feet behind him, while he worked on family woods and metals in the basement lab, beside the constant hiss of a Bunsen burner.

The gift and the apprenticeship were seen by the child as a magnificent indication of fatherly love, but they were actually a sly way of reeling young Mr. Ebersold into the fold of the Ebersold clock concern. Within only several short years, Mr. Ebersold had patented some seven proprietary concoctions. Many of these were antirusting agents for brass and copper cog edges. Several were for heavy-shine wood finish.

Mr. Ebersold's office emitted the pungent patchouli odor of burning incense sticks with the uneven syncopated hand drums of traditional north Indian music. Either alone would have been exotic and unusual to Affie, but together they proved to have an attraction supremely potent, hypnotic even. He found himself standing lock-kneed and peering through the opening of the ajar door time and again.

"All Anger Left Inside is Prayer for Death" was painted in script on the wall above the large purple-felt worktable. Now Mr. Ebersold was staring at the words, sitting, his back hunched, atop the pine stool, resting his chin on his fist and his elbow on his knee. The man was shrouded in white incense smoke. Affie's shoulder leaned against the doorjamb as he shifted his weight from left to right, and the humid maple jamb creaked as it took Affie's weight. Mr. Ebersold—at wit's end over the furtherance of pioneering cuckoo clock technology—turned and smiled upon recognizing the spy. He was happy to have been interrupted and eager to dispense with his consternation. "Come in, young man," he said in high spirits.

It was then, through a series of questions from Mr. Ebersold that inadvertently functioned as a job interview, that Affie displayed his propensity for clockwork innovation. He had nimble fingers, and he could reassemble and understand the entire working of any given clock having only watched Mr. Ebersold quickly tear it down once. For Mr. Ebersold, the rest of that day swept by as if directed by the mad Indian music, with he and Affie intuitively trading ideas about mechanics and choosing component piece combinations to fit together to form unique new clock designs and housing facades. Both art and engineering were present in the results. It was great fun and a surprise to both. The smoke from the incense even seemed merry as it billowed, spun, and twirled through the bright room that fall day.

Eventually, Affie was collaborating with the directors of all of the creative departments in the Ebersold company. He introduced new lines of facades, made innovative refinements in clock construction, and even took part in the marketing of the products. By the following autumn, the Ebersold staff, championed foremost by Michael Billet, openly referred to Affie as "Ebersold Heir." It was a fanciful title but the scorn it created in Bastien was real enough. He watched Affie's climb in importance from a calculated distance, protecting his secret reservoir of shame and envy.

It had always seemed to Mr. Ebersold that Bastien held no interest in ever joining in on the family activities. He held this belief throughout Bastien's adolescence. Part of the belief was spawned from his own regret at having not been more vocal and forceful about his own independent pursuits as a young man. He actually identified with Bastien and wished to garner for him a different opportunity, one he hadn't quite had the wherewithal and foresight to snag those forty-odd years ago.

And so Mr. Ebersold molded Affie into his replacement as the future director of Ebersold Family Clocks. If Bastien ever exhibited passion of his own then the door would still be open for him as his birthright. But even without any involvement, Bastien would still be entitled to his inheritance and eventual control over the vast wealth and its attendant properties and investments. Such a future necessarily put him on a much more privileged and powerful trajectory than Affie could ever hope for.

Yet Affie had something that was far more rare and inspiring than the capital and monies coming to Bastien. He had social cachet and the devotion and respect of practically every person he met. This proved extremely useful in the mansions, convention centers, and large labor halls rented out for the conferences and competitions across Europe. Mr. Ebersold began taking a back seat by the time Affie was fifteen, and allowed him to do all of the talking and presentations.

Bastien would remain at the estate during their business ventures. He began to develop a knack for piano composition and the fine arts. He knew well that he would be able to live the life of a leisured man and thus felt it reasonable enough to put all of his focus and energies into mastering painting and piano. The Ebersold Estate was equipped with an exquisite grand piano in the drawing room, which joined the two wings of the house. Bastion would sit at the stool and let his fingers wander for hours and hours.

He loved interacting with the keys, playing the notes. They were inanimate and yet so real to him. It was much easier to communicate through them than with language and among human beings. Music seemed somehow more truthful to him. And still the pain at the center of his philosophy found its way into the notes and the chords. He gravitated toward sour minor keys and dissonant, clashing chords with distressing and sinking progressions. His songs would drone on and dissolve into unpatterned, scattered melodies.

Ida would routinely inquire about his newest pieces, she herself being proficient in music. Bastien would occasionally demonstrate, as he found the words used to describe the songs borderline useless. Ida found the music to be very powerful but of a sort that had no business being listened to. It was more of a soundtrack to something. She said as much in a very tactful manner. "Bastien, you would be great at writing scores for plays." Bastion took this as high praise because it seemed to him to say he had honed in on making audible that which people felt. He was bringing out the subtext that actually drove people.

Michael Billet referred to Bastien's musical endeavors as "clanking drivel." "Car exhaust sounds better," he said. "I drive a car; I suppose that *I* am a musician!" Remarks like these always garnered laughter, as much for imagining Michael a musician as for agreement with his judgment of Bastion's music. Bastien overheard similar statements, as he never abandoned his penchant for eavesdropping. It was the way he preferred to be social, from around the corner. Ida was an inconvenience, which he had suffered because she gave him so much. In fact, it was she who recommended he begin piano in the first place and went on to train him in measures and chords. It didn't last long. Within two months of starting, Bastien had taken to teaching himself from the sheet music and scales books that had amassed jointly from Ida's personal collection and casualties from the numerous professional pianists hired to play for evenings when Mrs. Ebersold was entertaining guests.

Drawing and painting were always part of the curriculum at the estate. They had been even back when Mr. Ebersold was a student. Aside from Bastien's grandmother, nobody in the house had ever shown any noteworthy talent for either medium. Bastion had always been mediocre as well, until he was thirteen or fourteen and began focusing on representational drawing. He realized that if he looked at something hard enough and truly saw what it looked like, he could reproduce it exactly on paper with charcoal and lead. The activity also suited his need for isolation because it took him three to four days of nothing but sitting, looking, and drawing in order to render a complete picture.

His first drawings depicted the gardens behind the estate. Then he moved on to the forest beyond the yards and specific trees. He focused on an eddy in the river beside the roadway for a week in late May. It was fascinating to attempt to capture motion in a two-dimensional picture. But he did, with great success. And in doing so, it dawned on him how peaceful of a person he had become. While his music seemed to tease out the internal dramas and frustrations, the drawing seemed to wipe his insides clean. It was simple; focus on what there is and repro-duce it exactly.

He thought about how nice it would be to spend the rest of his life doing drawings and never feel anything again. Such thoughts seemed to contradict his earlier hypothesis about the terrible truth of all things, but he decided that truth might be just a concoction, a feeling. Bastien didn't think feelings were the truth. In fact, he believed the truth was empty of feelings, that it was just three dimen-sions plus motion. There were just space and shapes. He considered everything else to be nonsense. He began to think about turning himself blank, emptying himself out of everything other than contemplation of the visual data in front of his eyes.

Having spent some awkward years on this seesaw of conflict between his musical motifs and his drawing motifs, he began introducing colors into his art. His first undertaking was to make a portrait of Ida using oil paints. He first sketched the portrait with his preferred fine-point lead pencils. Then, he went over the sketch with the oils. Ida's face was very pale and almost green in the middle of her cheeks. She was a plump and supple specimen, with coarse blonde hair that curled and split at the ends. Her eyes were yellow and brown, and they were deeply sunken above low and wide cheekbones, which were littered with brown and sienna freckles. Bastion did a fine job, and the colors were accurate. Ida appreciated and modestly celebrated the accomplishment by framing the portrait and hanging it above the chalkboard in the study room.

But color was baffling to Bastien. There was no way to talk about it. He couldn't describe maroon or beige to someone. Its only description was in its name. This titillated him fiercely. Color was, to him, a weird intersection of what he admired about music and what he respected about drawing. It was truth outside of language, asocial and incorruptible.

The skill and style of Ida's portrait drew the attention of the staff. Billet and Mack, a part-time valet, admired the painting over a bottle of gin on a long weekend in August when the estate was nearly vacant of staff from vacations. After Billet was drunk to the point of losing some motor control, he barreled up to Bastien's room, woke him with his loud voice and stinking breath, and demanded a portrait. Mack followed along with gleeful gaiety, pleased at the hilarity and absurdity of the task. "You paint my face…and shoulders!" he slurred.

Bastien was awestruck by the demand. Billet had always been such a detractor that, if he would possibly win over his favor through his painting, then he was equal to the challenge. The three of them found their way back to the study room, and Bastien began mixing his paints and sharpening his pencils. "Come on, come on, get to it!" Billet clamored, falling back into a chair.

Mack laughed and said, "You are an ass!" And with that Billet laughed and grabbed the bottle of gin back.

Billet had passed out in his chair by the time Bastien was ready to begin his preliminary sketch. He looked over at Mack, unsure of how to proceed. Mack merely waved his hands, dismissing himself from the ordeal. He then stood, buttoned his tweed jacket, and with a tip of the hat left the study room. Bastion sat staring at Billet, seated upright with his head forward, his face still showing the tension in his neck. Bastion shrugged his shoulders and went about what he did best.

The portrait took a little over seven hours and he was finished by the time the smell of burning grease and brewing coffee began wandering through the halls of the estate. Billet awoke some hours later to the sight of himself on a three-foot-by-four-foot canvas, the easel turned toward him. What he saw was a shameful image of a man who had failed to hold his liquor properly and appeared devoid of his honor. He looked like a pub crawler. "Bog trotter…," he whispered aloud, recognizing in himself something akin to a story from his youth that his older sister, Rochel, told about how folks trotted out of the bog to get stinking drunk. She used it to explain the men passed out in an alleyway.

Therefore, despite the exactitude of the portrait and the clear skill demonstrated by it, the painting made Billet despise Bastien from an even more rich and internal place. Bastien was now walking around and breathing within Billet's violent subconscious. Billet believed Bastien to have found some higher ground against him that night, to have somehow made the portrait as a message to him, as a token of Bastien's superiority. It tore Billet up a bit and he was defensive and revisionist when he interrupted Mack's telling of the story to the kitchen staff at a poker game two nights following.

As for the portrait, Billet rolled it up and kept it underneath his bed. He never looked at it again, and it gained more power over him. Though the image seemed to communicate to him that he was becoming the type of man that had frightened him as a child, a type of man vile enough to prompt his upstanding Rochel to dissemble in order to protect him from it, the recognition ironically thrust Billet into a more advanced state of alcoholism.

And in Billet's alcoholism, he became an angry drunk. On weekends in Foist, he would get his head in drink and challenge much larger men, men more experienced in fighting, to box him. Outings like these would always meet the approval of a dozen or so other men in the pub who were primarily drinking away the monotony of their mediocre and routine lives. They saw the fight, which was clearly stacked in one direction, as a welcome diversion. A circle would form out back on cobblestones or the concrete of the train station, and bets would be made.

These nights would end with Michael's cheek firmly against the brick or rock of the roadway or station lot, blood leaking from multiple cuts and swollen bruises. Charity always sprang from an onlooker, cued by the twist and jab of sympathetic sentiments. Billet would wake in a stranger's apartment, sore beyond belief and sweating and with a migraine too painful to bear but too routine to take much notice of. He would thank his patron and repay the kindness with breakfast or a drink the following evening or a week or two later.

But after a while, his reputation grew, and the kindness of onlookers shrank. Eventually, the onlookers disappeared, and later still, no one would fight him. So he would get deeper into his drink until he was slurring completely beyond deciphering. Someone would sigh in agitation and meet the solemn eyes of the other pub regulars, knowing that they had the unfortunate task of ejecting the town drunk yet again from their establishment. Then Billet was getting punched by the ground as he landed, tossed from the arms of those men who sought to protect the decorum of their watering hole. "Bog trotter," he would hear as he crawled to some wretched corner of a building or porch to pass out for the evening. And eventually, he never woke up. But Billet's descent into the creature so despised and lamented by Rochel took many years, and by that time he was no longer working at the Ebersold Estate, nor considered by Bastien.

Bastien's pain experiment on Affie was not a solitary event. To the contrary, Bastien, after a settling period following the first experiment, routinely enlisted Affie in furthering his knowledge of the economy of pain. Affie never really resisted or struggled against Bastien's efforts but, instead, solemnly accepted the tortures as a necessary and unavoidable side effect of being wrapped into the Ebersold bosom. And he never said a single word to anyone.

This all initially shocked and exhilarated Bastien; it was a gift to have a compliant human participant who was nearby on most occasions and who would never reveal what would likely be perceived as depravity by outsiders. But as the occasion became more commonplace and the consequences more predictable and assured, Bastien eventually fell into taking this privilege for granted. When he was eleven, he lacerated and burned Affie's ankles and heels with a smoldering soldering iron. The tight pink skin curled and oozed under the heat. Affie cried quietly and wore thick high socks over salve the following week. There were always months-long hiatuses afterward, with little to no interaction between the two.

And though it became clear that Bastien could continue his investigations with impunity, he still maintained his surprise approach to beginning each session. Thus, the horror of the event would always unfold with Affie coming to from his slumber in the latest apparatus of pain infliction Bastien had conjured and assembled. The smell of chloroform and the aches of his limp body were also constants. Affie would come to terms with what was happening and shift his mental focus into his imagination and memory. He often times pictured moments as a youngster with his mother before she lost her mind. Even then she was peculiar with her white mittens in summertime, petting Affie's head and whistling.

He began a ritual, rushing through visceral vignettes from childhood memories, engulfing himself in their details, thus saving himself from the problem of being present during his suffering. And so he learned to check out and weave an ever-growing landscape of interment. It was apparent on Affie's face. He looked like an apoplectic monk or an epileptic in a fit. And Bastien took careful and curious note. It seemed something very human, something he had not noticed in his animal subjects. He only recognized it because of his ability to divine emotion from the facial expressions of a human subject.

Bastion often wished for better instrumentation, for a proper laboratory and assistants. He would eventually have all of these things and be able to perform pain experiments so haunting and magisterial that anyone encountering them for the first time would find such proceedings to be far more terrifying and preposterous than the contents of any horror tale. Frankenstein himself would have blushed. One day, Bastien would have the means and the ability to install his desired apparatus. One day he would truly begin the Month of the Sargus.

Affie allowed this to evolve and progress, never taking the opportunity to avail himself of justice. There were only a few such opportunities before he had already internalized the notion that his situation was inescapable, deserved, or out of his control. By the third or fourth experiment, the entire procedure, however novel each instance was, had become bearable as an accepted, if not understood, part of his existence.

His discomfort was balanced out enough by the long periods between Bastien's experiments and the generosity and affection given by Mr. Ebersold. Affie was being groomed as the future mind of Ebersold Clocks. And he was reminded of this by the chorus of his fans throughout the estate, Billet serving as the vanguard's spearhead. But Bastien was the blooded heir apparent and would be the one who would truly receive power. And so, the tiniest kernel of prudence within young Affie knew that it would be to his advantage to remain in the favor of the son who would one day pull the strings of the purse and be the eldest of the Ebersold name.

Chapter Sixteen

"Good results, baby!" Cabe howled, with fat cheeks of jubilee. Pollock spotted him on the other side of the dark and teeming crowd at Smooth Henry's Pub. Cabe had been dancing with a middle-aged woman named Nancy. They were underneath the black lights that swung in their aluminum casings above the brick walkway running from the bar to the bathroom corner in the back. Pollock was beginning to find appeal in letting his eyes go unfocused. He wasn't tired, really, but just tired of putting forth the effort to see straight.

Cabe and Pollock had bounced from pub to bar to pub, using, at the behest and initiative of Cabe, Uber drivers for transportation. Each round of drinks deprived the pair of more refined motor graces and increased the obtuseness within their frontal cortexes. At one point in the evening, a barback's friend, who had lent a cigarette to Cabe, recommended that they come see a cockfight. The conversation took place beside a dumpster and a fragile stack of egg carton racks, which Pollock shook with wry irony at the mention of cocks. No one responded to the action with more than an annoyed sideways flicker of the eyes.

It didn't bother Pollock. He was glazed over and isolated, enjoying everything as somewhat soft calamity. Everything seemed washed out, as if projected with too bright a light. And all around was the kaleidoscopic and cacophonous mingling of sensory data: the tacky year-round plastic Christmas lights at Jabsonen's, the black biker vests crowding the pool table in Stormdyke, the peppered hairy upper lips and quacking lubricated saps spittling out bamboozling madness from all around.

"Good results, baby!" Pollock said roughly like the furious exhaust of an idling Harley hog, aping his friend's catch phrase. He held his hands over his belly to mitigate the heaving of guttural laughs. His knees bent far forward and his head slung upward like a common drunk in the thralls of the hilarity of it all. But by this time, Cabe was shushing him and nodding to indicate a giant mustached man in a beige trench coat staring down his nose at the two of them. Pollock was immediately sprung back into the present where he, Cabe, the barback, and his buddy were all carefully navigating the social intricacies of admittance to an underground cockfight. Pollock's face instantly became sober and serious, his posture following suit.

The hefty man looked over the foursome with his chin raised. Then, without a word, he smiled in a wide display of yellowed teeth. The group then walked past the man and entered the crummy basement. Ten minutes later Pollock would still be rummaging through his memory to discern exactly what about the man's actions qualified as consenting to their passing his guarded threshold. "Good looking chaps, we are," Pollock mumbled, unable to picture the barback or his friend's face.

The basement was vast and in an advanced state of dilapidation. The walls were variously crumbling, sagging, or marred with deep and concerning cracks in the cinderblocks. Despite his potent intoxication, the condition of the basement did worry Pollock. On the approach, he had noted that they were entering what used to be a mill at one time. There were three industrial stories above, pressing down on the wavering foundation. And here, below it all, they now roamed.

Large black halogen lanterns lined the perimeter of the space, providing barely enough light, harshly outlining the people walking about. The sweeping blackness of shadows obscured the walls. The clicks and claps of boot heels sputtered about at confusing distances. In the center of it all was a large circle of backs, most in suits or jean jackets, underneath a bright hanging fluorescent bulb with a wide funnel of a shade. Cabe and the others nosed up close on the circle's outer perimeter, keeping enough distance between them and the necks in front of them.

And through the six or seven layers of weight-shifting spectators, Pollock made out a caged area at the center. It was a ten-foot rectangle of wired fencing with some hay was strewn about in patches. Feathers were floating amid the crowd, occasionally flirting with someone's shoulder before latching onto a fresh stream of air and whipping toward their next momentary place of rest. Pollock also detected the taste of iron on his lips. Subtly, Pollock took in those around him. There were swaths of five o'clock shadows on husky men in expensive grey suits, young Hispanic men in jeans with colorful tattoos coming out from under their collars and sleeves, and a few older men, two of which were wearing sweatpants and had the general appearance that Pollock associated with sexual predators.

"The Dalsom Falcon lusts for blood!" a soprano voice rang out from the center to unanimous applause and cheering. One of the spectators heckled, "That's no falcon you heinous cunt!" A few others laughed; the man in front of Pollock scoffed and folded his arms. The crowd settled back. "But sirs, let us not forget that the Loud Cloud will spill!"

The crowd exploded even louder at that. Various fellows echoed the sentiment. "Loud Cloud!, Loud Cloud!" Pollock pushed up onto his toes to see and made out the two cocks.

At the left end was an enormous black specimen with white speckles along the sides of his face and neck. A small man with a gigantic bun of grey hair was holding the creature with orange handling gloves stretching up to his elbows. He smiled and bellowed out, "Falconer!" Falconer strutted and paced, pecking at an imaginary foe with enough force that the man struggled to contain him in his padded grasp. The cock's beak was long and thin, reaching up to eyes that had clear scarring. It was magnificent and provoked confidence within Pollock.

In the other end of the caged area sat a pathetic looking cock. It was only half the size of Falconer and remained completely motionless. Short white feathers sporadically covered the thing's body. Around one of its eyes was a yellow oval of featherless skin. A child no older than ten was gently resting one hand atop the little animal's back. "We can't sleep on this one!" Cabe yelled, as his hand came down hard onto Pollock's neck. He turned and saw that Cabe was pointing at Loud Cloud.

"You've got to be kidding, look at Falconer...that thing is a beast!" Pollock slurred with an air of incredulity.

"Barney has seen him win three weeks in a row," Cabe said. "He's a strategist, fells much bigger opponents. And he says the odds are thirteen to two. We gotta get in on this, brother!"

"Who the hell is Barney?" asked Pollock, a little too loudly for the comfort of the man at his front. He turned his head to display annoyed side glances.

Cabe turned and pointed to quite a short man in overalls. His face was pale as computer paper. "Barney," he said. Cabe turned back to Pollock and reiterated the information. "Barney."

Pollock joined in for good measure. "Barney," he said, which was met with another annoyed side glance. "I don't know...I think I am going to keep my money where it is," Pollock said. He didn't want to let on how intimidated he was by their surroundings. He'd never thought that he would be much bothered by a cockfight, but now that he was there, it was clear to him how dangerous the situation actually was. The activity was illegal, there were all variety of shady individuals, and two horrific birds were about to try and tear one another apart.

"You're crazy. I'm listening to Barney, dude," Cabe said, and waited with an expectant look on his face. Pollock stood still while the whole circle scattered and shuffled about to put in their bets and talk about the respective birds. As scuttlebutt was being exchanged, each creature was outfitted with two razor blades on each of their legs. They protruded outward like cute little built-in swords. Pollock's horror swelled.

Cabe and Barney returned with confident nods, the chatter expired and the mysterious announcer voice returned. "Ah…Batella!" he screamed and the crowd howled with vigor. Pollock joined in, if only to expel some of his insecurity and attempt to make himself somewhat belong. In doing so, he noticed that a few little bits of saliva had shot forward and hit the short black hair of the annoyed side glancer. Terror surged, followed by sheer relief at realizing that side glancer was none the wiser. But there it was, a blast of Pollock's mucous coating the neat little black tufts, shimmering in the oblique light from the far-off halogen lanterns.

As soon as the man howled for the fight to begin, Falconer was released and charged toward Loud Cloud, who, though he was free to move about, chose to remain completely still. The two opponents were nearly face to face by the time Loud Cloud exhibited his brilliance. As Falconer bore down on him, Loud Cloud deftly sprang straight up four feet in the air where he seemed to hang in slow motion directly above Falconer who was still barreling forward. Then, the little white bird stretched out his legs and shot down onto Falconer, razor blades leading the way. Red mist spurted out in a wide radial spray, hitting the midsections of all of the first-row gamblers. Falconer fell on his side, legs twitching, the frightening sounds of gurgling and retching resounding through the silent basement. Loud Cloud slowly trotted away from the dying carcass and plopped himself down, ass against the fencing, and waited for his owner to retrieve him. The boy removed him from the cage and quickly disappeared behind the circle.

Commotion erupted as the gurgling and retching ceased. "The Loud Cloud has spilled rains of blood!" the voice yelled out, joining vibrant howls of invective and joy.

"Oh my god!" "I've been cheated." "Heinous cunt!" Disarray close to mayhem began, with several fistfights starting, only to be broken up by other men. Pollock was knocked to the ground by a rough sideways shuffle of the side glancer. He popped back to his feet and backed away, regaining composure at the edge of the gathering, near one of the longer stretches of darkness between the lanterns.

As he was stepping back, he bumped into something soft and lost footing for a moment. He jumped back, pulled out his phone and shown its flashlight down. There was a man in tattered clothing lying sideways on a heap of folded cardboard boxes. "Jesus, I'm so sorry!" Pollock nearly screamed.

"No bother. Common occurrence. Comes with the territory. Expected downside. Accepted setback. Not your fault. Design flaw," the sleeper responded in a listless monotone that suggested rehearsal. Pollock had nothing to say to that. His thoughts were discombobulated and he instantly desired to go home and go to bed. The sleeper never opened his eyes, but merely rolled over on to his opposite side, facing away from Pollock, and quickly resumed his slumber.

Pollock raised his flashlight and discovered another sleeper a few feet beyond atop a roll of towels. He raised the flashlight still farther to discover that there was a trail of sleeping people stretching backward down a dark, wide corridor the length of which wasn't visible but seemed a great distance. There must have been dozens of people in total, all in some level of unconsciousness, all on low makeshift beds of cardboard or clothing or dirty blankets. The sight seared into Pollock's mind. It was made eerier by the cold blue hue of his phone's light. He killed the flashlight and rejoined the group of gamblers, which had settled back into a quasi-neat circle around the cage.

"Good results, baby," Cabe said from behind happy eyes as he found Pollock. "I've just made enough cash to subsidize our drinking habits for the next month! Dude. Dude. You should have listened to Barney," he said with a forced sternness.

"Yeah." Pollock said, his mind replaying what he had just seen beyond the darkness. For a few seconds he debated sharing his discovery with Cabe, but decided that he would keep it to himself. He felt weirdly guilty about having seen it, and he wasn't sure that he could trust Cabe's reaction. Having come to each of these conclusions, Pollock was pleased with himself for having such control of mind to think this clearly despite the amount of booze he had consumed by that point.

"Did you see that ridiculous dive Loud Cloud did? He-he…That's the funniest thing I've ever seen. Ever. Absolutely ridiculous," Cabe said gaily.

"He has tactics," Barney said, joining the two friends.

"Ha-ha. He has tactics. Did you hear that? Barney said he has tactics!" Cabe howled out with great enthusiasm.

"Barney said he has tactics," Pollock repeated dully.

"Oh what a night. What a night! The most ridiculous thing I've ever seen," Cabe said in celebration. Barney bobbed his low head in agreement. Pollock geared up to introduce the idea of retiring for the evening.

The three looked on from the backmost row of gamblers and witnessed, with strained necks and shuffling feet, two more matches. Both lasted much longer than Loud Cloud's blood rainfall, which proved to be the highlight of the evening. Pollock continued his fall from intoxication to sleepiness and, after several poorly received suggestions to head in for the night, finally convinced Cabe that they could return another time if he felt that his betting quota and thirst for animal brutality was unfulfilled.

Cabe had lost both his bets on the second and third fights and was barely still in the black. Barney's insider knowledge of the cocks proved to be limited to Loud Cloud. "Yeah, its probably best we dodge out about now," Cabe riffed as if the idea had just occurred to him. Pollock nodded with frustrated agreement and the two said their good-byes to Barney, the incredibly pale and phenomenally short businessman.

"On down the pike…" Barney said, without so much as a gesture or turn of the head. He was absorbed in the spectacle.

As they carefully sauntered their way back to the staircase exit, unsure once again of the protocol of it all, Pollock caught sight of a familiar face. At the edge of the circle, standing back a little to puff on a curled pipe, stood Bastien Ebersold. He was shaking his hand to extinguish the burning match that he had just used. Pollock skidded to a stop and did a double take. As if keyed in on the same wavelength, Bastien looked up, and for a powerful moment, the two locked eyes. As the length of this moment increased, so did Pollock's inability to employ use of his legs. And finally, just before he reconnected with his lower limbs and sketchily, hastily scuttled off, he made out a slowly forming, knowing sneer on Ebersold's face. It was haunting.

The journey home went unremembered by both Pollock and Cabe. This was congruent with the sheer volume of alcohol the two had ingested. It also led to Pollock not making it in to the office for his half day on Friday. He didn't wake until noon, at which point breakfast odors of sizzling bacon and burning pancake batter caught his nose immediately. He went downstairs to find that Cabe had taken over the kitchen and apparently must have gone grocery shopping because Pollock had no supplies for any of the numerous breakfast delicacies Cabe was hectically jumping between. "Hope you like crepes, and breakfast burritos, and toast, and Bloody Marys," Cabe said loudly, seemingly unaffected by what Pollock considered to have been a borderline train wreck of a night.

"That's just because you haven't gone over all of the events, measured the blowback yet," Cabe said, after spotting the seriousness on Pollock's face. Pollock gave him a questioning look as he sat down at the table, offering no help with the vast morning smorgasbord. Cabe said, "You can go so far away from your own life, return and find that there really is no evidence of any detour. There are like…cracks running sideways, like, uh, parentheticals. And you can just kind of pick up where you left off and no one is the wiser. But to you, the difference, the excursion, its a mammoth. It's a mammoth inside of parentheses. So long as you remember the parentheses are there, you're safe."

Pollock thought this over and dryly replied, "I didn't make it to work today. That's not parenthetical."

Cabe switched from stirring hardening scrambled eggs to blending a mixture of salsa, tomato juice, and vodka, then over to the tortillas smoking on the back burner. "Call in and let them know that your house was broken into," he said.

"I can't lie like that. Plus I've already taken a half day. It'll seem too convenient."

Cabe turned and pointed toward the front of the house. "It doesn't look too convenient to me,"

"What?" Pollock said.

Cabe kept pointing. "Yeah, front porch. Go check it out."

With that Pollock's heart sank. But he complied with Cabe's request and quietly strode out to the front door, which he found ajar. He had failed to notice it when he came downstairs. He pulled the door inward, and with it came the white light of afternoon. There, on the floor of his porch stoop was his great-aunt's journal. It was open and the hatchet, which he had found in the alleyway out back, had been stabbed into the pages so that its handle stuck sturdily upward. The edge of the brittle pages waggled a little from the dry winds scraping across the porch.

Pollock's mind went berserk. It ran to Bastien's face in the darkness of the basement. It went back to the face of Martin who ran an enormous homeless town that somehow no one in Trams seemed have any clue existed. His mind went to Cabe. He wondered if his friend was pulling a harsh prank on him.

It felt as if he were smack in the middle of some giant mystery, some layered and complex conspiracy. He pictured Hans setting himself down on the picnic table. His paranoia spiraled through dozens of amalgamations, possible ways that he was being screwed with. He surveyed the street, beginning to feel that perhaps he was being watched. Everything was quiet; no one was outside. He knelt down to inspect the tableau, and as he was nearing it with his outstretched hands, he noticed small dirty shoe prints, the size of a child's. They went up to the door, looped around in circles and led back down the step and outward to the street. Another set with different tread and a shorter stride made similar designs. "Little fuckers," Pollock said, as it dawned on him that it was the Ne'er-do-well gang.

Sherry had been looking forward to spending the majority of her Friday morning watering the numerous potted plants in her cubicle while listening to voice-led meditation through her ear buds. She was frustrated and disheartened to find a thick pile of papers waiting atop her desk with a pink Post-it note from Mr. Freedman stuck on top. The note read:

> Sherry, interesting developments with curious plot of Trams. Need
> much info. regarding who owns the property (city land bank?) and
> how Zoning should proceed, if at all. Many thanks, SF.

Sherry glumly pulled the note off the top page to find a *Trams Gazette* article about an old bulldozer and tractor manufacturing plant that had been unused

for several decades but was now inhabited by a large swath of homeless and destitute individuals who had organized into what they referred to as a "family union,"
headed by an elected leader named Martin Danburry.

The article went on to indicate that a local business owner, Bastien Ebersold, whose commercial interests include business and property investment companies, has filed a complaint in local probate court seeking a declaration of ownership of the plot of land.

> On the Trams City Land Bank website, Mr. Freedman, director
> of building and zoning, published an article last May that included
> the specified stretch of land as part of a tract for consideration as the
> future site of a publicly owned city market and park. Mr. Ebersold
> has plans to put in two hundred units of high-end condominiums tar-
> geted for the working professionals of Trams, whose growth as of
> late, due to growth in Trams in general, has outpaced suitable living
> space. Neither the mayor's office nor the zoning department has
> commented on the issue.

After reading the article and letting its implications sink in, Sherry, who was
still wearing her backpack and hunching over the desk, at once recognized the
time and hassle involved if this research was to be done competently. Therefore,
she decided to procrastinate a little and, dropping her pack in between a poinsettia
and aloe plant, she strolled lackadaisically toward the coffee cubicle, her feet
dragging a little like a disappointed and distracted schoolgirl.

The coffee cubicle was a well-known and unspoken about refuge, a haven
from computations, drawings, and any other real work. It was only twelve by
fourteen feet and without seating. At the end opposite the narrow entrance sat
three ancient wooden desks, side by side, serving as a counter of sorts. Atop the

counter were two Mr. Coffees and an extensive, if eclectic, assortment, including sweeteners, sugar, cream, a milk carton which remained unrefrigerated all day, creamer packets, tea, raspberry and vanilla syrups, cups, and straws and other odd stirring devices spiraling up from a deep ash tray, which always presented the coffee drinker with the problem of deciding if they had previously been used or not. The desks had shelves below where pupils had placed their books, on which sat an equally eclectic collection of mugs.

Aside from a large brown trashcan, whose shape and size suggested it should be found curbside or garaged, the cubicle was empty square footage, available for Trams zoning workers to uncomfortably stand and mingle. On this morning, it was empty, which meant Sherry would return to her cubicle not having had the twenty-minute bare minimum of conversation and procrastination that she had been seeking. She sauntered back to her desk, amassing fortitude within herself to confront the task that her boss had assigned her.

Because the issue involved a question of ownership, and because the city was going to be a party to the upcoming court decision, Sherry knew that she would have to go down to the basement where the physical copies of plots and deeds were held and, also, that she would have to involve a city attorney. This second conclusion meant travel between the Trams Facilities building and city hall, which further meant that, for however long this assignment was her priority, she would have to begin driving to work instead of walking, which was her preference.

For a few moments of uncomfortable sitting atop her tucked in legs, she fiddled about with the idea of passing the work on to someone else. Pollock was first among her considerations. The notion sparked joy within her, which was quickly dampened by the thought of Mr. Freedman's expectation of her involvement. Indeed, the note was handwritten by him and left specifically for her. She let that marinate a little until it became clear that Freedman had chosen her because of her proficiency and intelligence.

Mr. Freedman had, much more often than not, sided with Quentin whenever there was internal disagreement about zoning matters. He had sided with Quentin against Sherry in their infamous electric car charger argument. And Quentin received a much larger number of personal requests for consultation with Freedman and city attorneys and even council members. This didn't mean Mr. Freedman liked Quentin personally, but just that Quentin was higher up in the food chain, despite holding a parallel position to Sherry within the department.

So this was perhaps an opportunity for her to gain back some ground, shore up her gravity and importance. The possibility did an enticing lap dance for her pride, eventually securing its seduction and moving her to stand and head down into the Trams Facilities basement. On the way, she stopped and refilled her coffee mug in preparation for what would inevitably be a lengthy and hair-pulling experience.

The Trams Facilities basement was a glorious catastrophe of inept organization. The long western and eastern walls were lined with large filing cabinets six feet wide, with short, full-width drawers, that were stacked on top of one another, reaching up nearly to the twenty-four-foot-high rafters. The poor structural integrity of this arrangement was manifest in the crumpling and splitting edges of the middle and lower units, unable to take the weight of the higher units. And so the individual columns of cabinets were leaning one way or another. This resulted in some of the drawers resisting opening, their sliding frame mechanism bent beyond functioning.

The problem had existed and been dealt with for decades. A stack of wooden roofing ladders leaned against the far end of the east wall, to aid in the unfortunate situation where one was required to acquire maps, surveys, plots, parcels, or deeds beyond one's tiptoed reach. Next to the ladders sat a plastic bucket holding a number of hammers, pliers, chisels, and pry bars, any of which might be necessary when face to face with an uncooperative drawer.

Each drawer had some approximately coherent label, mostly a date in permanent marker on a strip of masking tape. *Nov. 1971*, for example. But the direction and sequencing of the dates was scattershot at best because numerous cabinets in the stacks had been replaced in different years and not all with the same sort or size of cabinet. Thus, the dating organization had succumbed to the greater importance of the size of the various cabinets and the physical condition of each column. Often times, navigating the stacks was like following the intersections of a dozen different minds with disagreeing notions about the definition of common sense.

Not to mention that many labels had faded beyond legibility. Others were incorrect, didn't appear to be in English, or were missing altogether. Further, not everyone who used the stacks cared enough to return the inspected document back to its proper location within the structure. So a drawer labeled "Nov. 1971" may contain, for whatever reason, zoning codes from 1998, twenty public sidewalk charges from 1960, and a survey by metes and bounds of property surrounding a presently condemned mansion dated May 12, 1899.

Every two to three years, the interns, who were placed by O'Cott Community College, would be tasked with the process of reorganization. But, being a summer position that was unpaid, and because of the sheer volume of documents within the facility basement, the three or four interns would only get so far before returning to autumn semester, their efforts akin to another mind to understand when locating one's query.

If all of this weren't enough, many who were responsible for placing the originals in the records room basement, had abandoned the stacks in favor of piles which sat atop of foldout dining hall tables with pale white plastic tops. And there were at present 117 of these tables, each with, at minimum, ten piles and most with, at minimum, another ten sitting on the floor beneath them. Because these piles were unlabeled, their order conformed to an oldest-to-newest layout. This could be divined by the hue of the papers, the oldest being tea-colored with dark orange and yellow around their perimeters. The newest were closer to the bluish-white Adex 2250 papers on which all official property documents in Trams were currently printed. The older piles were in the southeast corner, the newest in the northwest, where two tables had been set in place despite holding no documents, a level of foresight ironic for such a room.

But this pattern wasn't always reliable either, because, as with the stacks, many of its users were irresponsible and careless with refiling. Though the topmost documents of each stack maintained coherence with the progressing date ranges, documents underneath usually jumped all around. The tables were accompanied by rolling stools and uneven metal folding chairs. Some tables had magnifying glasses or splintered rulers left over from likely abandoned searches. The room was always hotter and more humid than seemed prudent for the storage of paper products, and it was lit by a grid of hanging fluorescent lights whose flickering made reading a painstaking task.

It was here, in this insane breach of order, that Trams stored the authoritative reservoir, the final say of property ownership records. And its infamous disarray had become accepted so widely that often judges, lawyers, and businessmen went forward with their disputes or development plans in whatever way allowed them to circumvent any interaction with the true record of land in the city.

And yet Sherry, intent on tracing the line of ownership of the property that once housed a bulldozer factory and currently housed a tent city of the poor, creaked open the sagging door and stood upon the metal terrace overlooking the mess of information. Her willingness to do so was testament to the bitterness she felt at having a long-overlooked, even neglected voice within Trams Building & Zoning Services. And maybe it was something much larger within her, something connected to things that were long years passed. Whatever it was working against her, she felt today the tide would turn. Passing the fire extinguisher whose carriage box had scraped into it "All Ye Who Enter Here, Abandon Hope," she took a deep breath and descended the stairs, grasping the rickety handrail with one hand and balancing her coffee mug in the other.

* * *

Max sat with folded legs in front of the curious painting DeBeers had recently produced and leaned against the hearth. The canvas was wide, stretching nearly ten feet. It dwarfed Max. The vast expanse of the image was predominantly black, with little dots and spackles of white and grey with sharp pointing tails of light beams emitting outward. It was a night sky. Except for a little bit at the lower right corner, where upon close examination, one could make out a naked woman staring upward.

The picture suggested to Max that the universe was unimaginably vast and the whole world, let alone one person, so cosmically tiny. It also reminded him of Ethyl. She was gone. Who knew where. He had convinced himself that he would find the body. The letter he received while away, the letter from the Randalls written by the eldest, Roy, had stoked his horror.

Titius had explained a little about the encampment before Max ventured off. Years earlier there had been the Waukegan farm, which stood at the base of the long sloping valley. It had been a small operation, used primarily for housing supplies and slaughtering cows which grazed the adjacent field. The oldest Waukegan boy began growing marijuana plants in the same area where the slaughtering occurred. The plants grew out of the same earth where flesh and blood and brain bits rested and absorbed down into the soil. Young Waukegan was skilled enough in the endeavor, and the plants produced significant and potent buds.

But when he and his brothers began smoking its yield, they turned strange. They began speaking incoherently, striking out violently at others, including Waukegan family members. They eventually retreated into living permanently within the slaughterhouse, aloof in their madness, the three brothers, doing God knew what all day and night. And when Mr. Waukegan came to roust them and tried, with a full measure of understanding and force, to snap his children back into productivity for the coming autumn harvest of their cash crops, they attacked and killed him. Or so Titius intimated, with his two hands gesturing in the manner of driving a pitchfork into someone's skull.

During this time, all sorts of veterans and hobos were wandering the war-torn country, looking to function as factotums or farm hands, seeking shelter and food, slinking about in the night, sleeping under shade trees in the day. The specific circumstances unknown, dozens of such wanderers ended up at the slaughterhouse, sampling the maddening pot and succumbing to a similar aloofness and propensity for violence. Before too long, there was a whole little village of strange folk, always huddled about the slaughterhouse, behaving furtively like guilty apes.

Eventually, as the group grew, the slaughterhouse became too small, and they erected cabins to house their number. Nurses, thieves, ex-prisoners, estranged university students, and all other manner of people flowed into the encampment. It was like a signaling beacon for all of those who had trouble with society, all of the fringe individuals, troublemakers, losers, vagabonds, lost souls, crazies, mentally deficient, abused, forsaken, and otherwise unfortunate.

But in the midst of all of the anarchic personalities and madness abounding, there was a loose orchestration to it all. The rumors had made a high to-do about a nun turned voodoo lady at the heart of it all. This "wicked mama," it was believed, had a tight knit group of soldiers to whom she had proven her proclivity for magic and sorcery. And it was this group of high-ranking ex-union soldiers who carried out her orders and kept the village running. They would venture for supplies, farm the fields, tend to the maddest members, and employ the nurses.

Of course all of this knowledge was hazy at best because, for a long time, no one had reason to investigate and confirm the gossip. And the gossip ran rampant throughout all of the surrounding towns. Every month or so another newcomer to the slaughterhouse encampment would be ejected, or repelled therefrom and head out on a new path. Over pints or at their next room and board, they would boast gushingly of the humor and oddness living within those woods or whisper about evil doings of the wicked mama. The audience would always play along but secretly question the validity and accuracy of such reports until another stranger would arrive with frighteningly similar stories.

The tale of the slaughterhouse encampment in the woods run by a mad old lady became common lore, equal to "Little Red Riding Hood" or the tale of Hansel and Gretel. The lore mounted and spread throughout the region for years. Mothers would speak of it to their children while tucking them into their feather quilts for the night as a warning to refrain from wandering aimlessly into the forest, or straying from the farmhouses with friends. "Wicked Mama will get you! She eats little children!" The stories were effective for a certain cross section of naive or otherwise compliant youths.

However, very recently, a rash of grave robbing had sprouted up all over the Righteous Buhle Woodlands and surrounding areas. Over two dozen graves had been robbed, including the grave of Amelia Rombathe, Titius's daughter. But there was something even more concerning than the robberies. Upon examination of one of the targeted graves, belonging to one David Hempstead, DeBeers found a whole pile of legs and arms underneath the jostled casket, each limb neatly sawed off clean at its end. This was two days and one night prior to Max's capture.

Titius, as Max had correctly perceived, was a very forthright person. He believed in personal responsibility and civic duty. He was industrious and headstrong. He started his farm on two acres and turned a profit. The farm currently stretched some four hundred acres and employed over sixty workers. Both his wife and child had died of tuberculosis. His friend Dana DeBeers had thereafter moved in and began helping to run the day-to-day operations. Occasionally the estate would employ someone who had recently stayed at the encampment. Titus had always believed that the rumors were exaggerated, and besides, he preferred to focus on running his vast and time-consuming farm.

Even as a younger man, and especially since the war, Titius was averse to free time or any undisciplined contemplation. He had done too many bad things, things that grew in the quiet hours. And this angered him, so he would shove it back down and use the anger in a physically arduous task—repaneling the indoor staircase or chewing out an employee who had a recent misconduct on their weekly docket.

But when it was communicated to him that his only child's remains had been disturbed in such a heinous way, it was too much. Then he found Max and his "friends." Titius's men pummeled Max's friends until they disclosed that they had first seen the fruits of stealing from the dead while they were shacked up in the "loon lagoon." That was how they referred to the encampment. They admitted to three previous robberies, no more. And they had received enough pain that DeBeers and Titius felt confident in believing them at that point.

Titius was a religious man, though he did little to advertise such. But the combination of their confirming his previous suspicions that the robberies were related to the encampment of lore, in tandem with his mysterious and nearly in-

stant trust in Max, registered as a sign from above. Thus, he could use his leverage over Max, that wayward son, to scout the situation within the encampment,
gain intelligence, and assess the level of involvement required of Titius and the
tactics necessary for such. Max was his little spy.

What Max reported was far worse than Titius wanted to know, but approximate to what he feared. Ex-soldiers were being lured into the camp and drugged
to death, their corpses sold on the black market to doctors for science. Beyond
that, Max had learnt that the operation was being funded in large part by several
former lieutenants cashing in the soldiers' pensions shortly before they were made
caput. The entire enterprise was run off the war monies owed to the dead.

This news soaked into Titius's psyche like a longstanding annoyance. One
summer, several years past, the nob atop the newel-post of the staircase leading to
his third-floor study began squeaking and teetering with each grip. He knew from
the very first that it needed attention, but he was a busy man and was always juggling scores of annoyances, all more pressing. This meant that this specific annoyance had to be ignored until its due time. And so he went about trying to tune it
out, yet each time it rattled its little thumping tune, it came across to him as a petulant complaint, as if it were a child demanding attention from a father, the child
unaware of the manifold adult duties and resulting stresses.

The knob squeaked with his every touch, each time bringing Titius closer to
his pressure point, sounding more and more like a child begging for attention. It
was finally all too much, and Titius knelt quickly, arched his head back, taking a
long fortifying breath as if from heaven above, and launched his forehead into the
four-by-four column of wood, ripping it out of its step entirely and sending it
crashing to the landing below. "Not...now," he pronounced slowly, his skull
throbbing with pain and relief, having finally addressed the nuisance. Three
weeks later he replaced the column and ended up sanding most of the attached
railing as well.

Amelia's disheveled grave was Titius's pressure point for the whole strange-folk squeak. It was finally real, beyond rumor. It was finally a problem. It was *his* problem. It pissed him off. They'd touched something sacred of his. This was more than a rattling newel-post. This was more akin to rabid vermin in his house. Which, had happened. A dog belonging to the Bielers, neighbors whose soy crop had failed and were going bankrupt, had broken through the flimsy screen in Titius's kitchen door. There it stood, rigid and snarling at Titius as he ate breakfast. He knew the only way to deal with an animal in that state was with a bullet to the brain. It could not come back, there was no correction, no rehabilitation. And so, after slyly fishing his revolver from his jean vest, he cocked the hammer and fired, and the room filled with the smell of sulfur. Titius abandoned his bacon and begrudgingly summoned up the energy to bury the beast and notify his downtrodden fellow farmer, Mr. Bieler, of this further misfortune.

So, because Titius knew just how fully he would have to commit to dealing with this problem that had so deeply and mortally offended him, he had Max retell his findings several times. During the three days he had spent with the strange folk, Max concluded that there were approximately two hundred and fifty people permanently residing within the village. "Most there are confused, and many think they are still fighting, they're still at war. Day and night they congregate around fires and wait for orders. And they don't know why, for what. That is, they don't know what they're fighting for." Max was affected by his time in the woods. It had been the capstone to his understanding of just how lingering the violence of the war and disillusionment of humanity was. The conflict had surely infected its survivors and torn asunder all recognizable order. The marijuana only added to the destabilization.

"So they are really insane people there, mad people?" Titius asked in a measured tone.

"Well, yes, most of them," Max said.

"And the marijuana?" Titus inquired.

"They all smoke it. Unimaginable amounts. It still grows in the slaughter-house where—"

"You saw this?" Titus said.

"I wasn't allowed into the slaughterhouse. Nor the barn. No one was. No one there is allowed in except Wicked Mama, not even her helpers."

Titus stood in front of his regal family tree and rubbed his throat stubble. "So," he said with a despairing baritone, "all of that gobbledygook about Wicked Mama is actually true. A crazy voodoo lady running a looney bin in the woods with the help of some crooked ex-officers who sell dead soldiers after embezzling their war pensions. And otherwise respectable doctors actually subsidize this lunacy, do…business there…" His voice trailed off as he scraped his palm over the salt-and-pepper shadow on his cheekbones and rubbed his greasy temples.

Titius and DeBeers spent the next week gathering what could only be called a posse. Max had explained just how well guarded he had found the perimeter of the encampment. Numbers with guns would be required, whichever way the confrontation went down. So DeBeers began visiting local watering holes at second toast, when most gentlemen were in higher spirits than usual but still in command of their better reasoning.

Many of these gentlemen had at one point, in some manner, been employed by the Rombathe Estate, or otherwise had agricultural dealings there. Most were receptive and even enthusiastic about joining the expedition. Occasionally, DeBeers would come across a drinker who had known someone whose family member's grave had recently been disturbed. They would add to the momentum and general sense of duty about the whole scheme, relieved at having an identified source of the baseness. "Sick business, that is! As low as it gets! Rotten heathens!" The opinions spread and grew louder with more drinks. A mob was germinating throughout Righteous Buhle Woods.

As per his deal with Titius, Max unearthed the grave that he had been working on the night of his capture. Underneath was a corpse badly decomposed but wearing Ethyl's clothing. He recognized her floral dress, sweater, and her hair immediately. The decay that had already taken place left her soft features unrecognizable, her skin stretched tight over the underlying skeletal structure. It was gruesome in a way nothing during the war had been. This was new and closer to the heart of the matter. The being of his greatest aspirations and desires lay supine, defaced within the dirt below another's tomb. S.G.'s tomb, as per the hint in the letter from the Randalls. Max had lost. He now had the unavoidable evidence. The Randalls had taken everything. And seeing Ethyl there now, in that state, was somehow worse for having been warmed and softened after a few days' stay in the Rombathe Estate.

He did his absolute best to keep strict composure and solemnly and carefully laid her remains in a proper grave. The switch took less than a full day's work of digging and piecing together a sturdy casket of pine planks from DeBeers's workroom. DeBeers quietly and almost gracefully inserted himself when necessary in the construction, while otherwise providing Max space and solitude. Anger helped push the production along quickly for Max. Anger at the Randalls, anger at his failings, anger at the general quality of human life. The cold winds gusted over his nose and down his collar as he stood over the fresh hole in the southwest region of Titius's cemetery. Max knelt down at the perimeter of the grave and once again brought her face into his mind, her youthful, living and healthy face, flush with warmth and happiness. Rouge around freckles.

"Ethyl...I..." Max floundered for the words. "I am so sorry. I can't believe it happened...this way. If anyone deserved a good life, it was you. You deserved something so much better. And I was supposed to give that to you. I should have never left you alone. All I wish for is to go back. Oh God, I just want to go back and do things differently. I'm sorry. I...I..." He thought about how much he was saying "I," and it became utterly apparent to him that he was speaking to himself. There was no Ethyl, not anymore. He was alone, talking to a wooden box in the earth. The image of DeBeers's painting returned to Max and he realized that his knees were numb from the cold dead grass.

Max had procrastinated over making any examination of his own life, instead making his sole focus locating Ethyl. Now that she had been properly interred and put to rest and Max had vocalized some approximation of closure with his failure, he was left with the problem of what would come next. He had no illusions about settling down or trying for a family with someone else. That life no longer existed for him. The war and the Randalls had left too much rubble; they'd obliterated any indulgence in notions of a restful or proud existence. Simply, Max was ruined. But he was still breathing.

The Rombathe Estate had come to life in the wake of DeBeers's pub recruitment. It was teeming with all sorts of men, young and old. They were drinking from shiny tin flasks and sharpening knives along oiled sandstone at the long main dining table and cleaning their rifles and shot guns on the numerous rockers along the porch which wrapped around the home. Most of them had seen battle and were experiencing anxiety from the return to civilian postwar life. There were finger tremors and chilled sweats. They were preparing to raid the enclave of insanity within the woods as if it were the enemy's fort. Burlap bags, wool blankets, and foldout army cots were put about on the floors in the upstairs bedrooms. The beds were untouched, or otherwise displayed a neatly organized design of weaponry.

Max blankly strode about, honing in and out of conversations. He felt pointless, as if he were a ghost haunting himself. His lungs were heavy with sickness, as they had sometimes become from too much gin. "Are you okay, son?" Titius's fatherly voice questioned from down the hallway. He stood, shoulders square with Max's and pondered him. And in his pondering, he recognized himself in Max. More than himself, he recognized in Max the same absence within most everyone around, and the wounded look around the eyes. The recognition brought out tenderness in Titius and a swelling in the throat. Max didn't answer the question. He just stood, plain-faced, basking in Titius's recognition.

"Of course, you can help us here. There are only a few men that know the land. It would be beneficial to have you on hand when we embark," Titius said, acknowledging to himself that the offer had fallen short of its aim. But, the question Max was entertaining was a question that Titius himself hadn't answered, aside from throwing himself into rapid action, and successive tasks all of the time. He was in constant motion. In fact, most days Titius could be encountered in two states: intensive and laborious activity or asleep. So, in a way, in his offering to Max, Titius was reinforcing, once again, the same offering to himself of distraction through work.

It was enough. Max nodded in acquiescence and began to surrender to the general mood of the Rombathian mob. At dusk the following night, the men gathered into a crowd in the front yard. Their horses neighed steamily into the dark cold and stomped, pulling at the reins tied to the long porch rail. It rattled under the strain. Eyes of farm hands, pub employees, mechanics, and of all sorts and varieties of men wandered around looking for a signal or direction.

The gathering didn't last long. Mr. Bieler stepped forward and gave a rousing speech about civic duty. "And my family, we are working our hands to the nubs just to make ends meet. We have nothing leftover. And now the bank, a group of leisured city men, men of means, tell me they have to take my house and maybe even my farm to make dividend on the mortgage. Many of you men are in similar situations. Wives, kids, debts...bad memories. Memories so bad they work as a yolk on our shoulders." His voice was raspy, his lips curled and badly chapped. The group wrapped closer around him as he paced about in a semicircle, speaking to the earth as if calling upon some natural force to wake and aid them in their quest.

The specific aim of this quest, other than confrontation regarding the up-ended graves, hadn't quite been made apparent to all. Titius had taken note of this fact and intended to address all of the volunteers and work out unanimity in the results they desired and the means by which to achieve them. He had planned on making a speech of his own and taking a tally of the men. But, before he could, old Mr. Bieler, bent in stature and with wiry strings of white hair madly fluttering about from his temples, continued his tirade.

"But we have not given in. We're not holing up in a rut like some woodland deer, or frothing at the mouth and attacking those who try to help us like a rabid dog! Such beast needs to be put down!" He made eye contact with Titius, listening intently from the innermost ring of the surrounding men. He nodded in silent accord. "That's no way to live. It is no way to live. And now they steal from us, and they desecrate the dead? Well, gentleman I am not content with this at all. Not at all. Are you? Well, *are* you?"

The crowd shuffled a bit and several men scratched their heads, musing over the potential distinction between rhetoric and true questioning. Bieler repeated, "Are you?" Max, who had been left further back in the body of people, thought of the Randalls and what they had done to Ethyl but also what they had done to him. A surge of violence, of unadulterated bloodlust spit up into his gullet and he damn near howled like a maddened wolf. "No!" Max yelped out deep from his gut and stomped his foot involuntarily to dispel the excess of energy within his system. Men turned their heads to look at the one who spoke. Max thrust his way between shoulders and into the center, where he stood with Bieler.

"I am not content at all." Max breathed it more than spoke. Bieler smiled and held out his arm in communion, and he and Max clasped forearms.

Bieler continued, now addressing Max directly rather than the ground. "No! Not in Righteous Buhle. Gentleman, the war is over. We've brought enough of it into our homes, into our beds. And that's for us to carry and, if we are lucky, share the weight with our kin who were there. But we can't let the battle carry us from our homes like crazed dead men, to live like Indians in the woods. We have, have, *have* to begin rebuilding. We've got to come back from all of this or at least give our children a chance. I don't want this for my younger boys. I don't want for them to hear stories of what we've done and feel terrified from the stories. I want them to be happy and peaceful at heart." The men in the crowd searched within themselves, thinking tenderly of romances and family members, waxing optimistic about future business enterprises, and seeing quaint visions of sturdy homesteads. Eyes met eyes with admiration and quiet camaraderie.

Bieler's voice was now raised to a high yell as he bit in to the conclusion of his harangue. "As long as these cowards are having their little party of despair, so long as they are thieving otherwise good working men and supplies and waking the dead, as long as they are out there, they are keeping the terrors alive and stirring all about. They are infecting our countryside. Let us be the scalpel to slice the putrid flesh from the body so that the man may live. Let us deal with our demons face to face!" He left off speaking and the crowd of men, forty-two in total, were now riled and flexing fists. Many were pacing about with anticipation.

The speech worked brilliantly. Every man among the mob was very motivated to destroy the mysterious enclave of degenerates. Bieler had just told them that by doing so, they were fighting the internal pain that each man harbored, each man suffered, from bearing witness to the brutal violence of war. But that violence was forever within them now. And Bieler knew this, so he gave the violence a worthy and sentimental target: itself.

And so, on a dark winter night, the Rombathian mob rode out from the estate on horseback, wildly energized and with the confidence of those on a holy mission. It was the first time that they had felt so purposeful in their actions, so unified in ambition. The turning and tuning of righteous anger was so abrupt and so magnificent within each man, that no one asked prudent questions like where was the enclave getting supplies? And what exactly were they going to do once they reached the encampment? Were they just going to open fire and slaughter everyone there? Were they going to relocate the residents?

Mostly, everyone assumed that someone else had a plan of action. What was most important was that they all felt good about themselves and what they were doing. And many of the men did assume that, if the folks out there were as crazy and unhinged as the stories they had heard, then perhaps killing them wouldn't be such a burden. Perhaps, killing these unfortunate lunatics would be a graceful move, perhaps even merciful.

Max rode along on one of Titius's quarter horses. He convinced himself that he was going along with the posse for the sake of Ethyl's memory. It didn't compute for him that the Randalls were not the same as the people he had recently spent several days with in the woods. For him, they represented the same madness that possessed the Randalls and drove them to do what they did. It was all a part of the same unreasonable violence. And now, Max was carrying out the final chapter of this violence, seeing it through to the end even if it resulted in his own end. This thought did cross his mind. He felt the pendulum had come to rest, and he knew on which side of the line he fell.

* * *

Retta had to be by herself. Fox and Remy were together downstairs, and she decided to skip class and stay in listening to records. The needle scraped over the vinyl ridges and settled into a groove, enunciating the twang and frolic of dueling bluegrass banjos. Her back sank into the mattress and it was both somewhat painful and a tremendous relief. Once relaxed, she squeezed her eyes tightly shut and took a long breath. "My feet are stuck in drying glue," she said aloud.

Retta was receiving glimpses of an older version of her self, some two decades further along the way. And what she saw was a very confused and lost person, middle-aged and suffering quietly, covering up her anxieties with distractions. This was a person bogged down in a job that was mildly fulfilling and time consuming. But it was mostly a daily grind of slogging through tasks without enthusiasm. When she thought more about it, there seemed a chance she didn't even want to be a nurse anymore. She was tired of cleaning up after and taking care of. She wondered if she was becoming what she hated. She let out a self-deprecating grunt, shaking the rickety bed frame.

This older person would get home from work, turn on the television, and sit in an empty apartment. After eating something that cooked quickly, some variant of a microwave-steamed meal, she would sit on the couch and binge watch TV sitcoms and network dramas until she fell asleep on the couch. This seemed like a reality most of her acquaintances were headed for. Water cooler talk about which character on a popular series one identified with most would become the keystone of conversation throughout the day. Perhaps stop off at a gym several days a week to keep the belly in line, keen as it would become to expand from such a starch, carbohydrate, and sodium-laden diet, not to mention high blood pressure issues. Her greatest accomplishment would be the degree to which her walking between the kitchen and living room wore a path into the carpet.

In this future scenario, her older self was almost hollow. There was nothing sturdy and certain in her life; she hadn't really figured anything out. There was no code, no creed, no worthy agenda. She didn't have much savings, because of her school debt. She didn't travel, because of her obligations to her family and to work and, probably, out of laziness. There would no longer be any pressing explorations into science or religion and philosophy. After her daily shift, her active mind would dissipate into near-automaton mode. She didn't use her hands for making art anymore.

It was all a very dull outlook. There was no joy, no curiosity. There were only bleak duties and responsibilities interspersed with intermittent entertainment, to most of which she was indifferent anyway. She wondered what it said about you if a highlight of your life was sprucing up the house with new drapes and re-upholstered couches or finally getting those records framed, so they can hang with pretty dark wood borders on the wall in the foyer. She didn't know for sure, but it did seem like a fearfully plausible version of the future for her.

She thought that having someone in her life might help. She knew that's what people did and figured they did it because of how bad things get alone. Then it occurred to her that perhaps that was why she was spending time with Pollock. She thought it a spineless state of affairs if true. It bewildered her to think that an otherwise dastardly failure of a life could become something acceptable, even aspired to, just because there was another person in the picture. "Connection. No matter how bad it gets, things are gonna be alright, baby. So long as we're together, baby," she mocked aloud, as if some dashing Romeo were reassuring her in a cocksure manner.

Retta recalled a saying that had wandered in and out of her consciousness over the past decade or so. The saying went, "Wherever you go, there you are." It had mostly seemed to be a cop out to her, if an obvious truism. It made her wonder how anyone would try to get away from themselves. She thought new scenery would at least help with the endeavor. The idea was lately gaining traction with Retta, even seeming reasonable in proportion to the amount of time she fantasized about getting away to Australia. This, of course, was fitting. The idea of Australia was almost more appealing the more vague and less definite it was. As she filled in the fantasy with the details of how such a move would unfold, it became more obvious that Australia was a flimsy salve. Her anxieties, her worries, her disappointments would all still be there. She would spoil Australia by arriving fleeing her own life. She'd come to this conclusion many times over, but her mind loved to dredge up anything painful and bandy it about ad nauseam until Retta wanted to give up on thinking all together.

Her problems were much more than, and independent of, her physical surroundings or the climate. They were permanent and personal challenges. It felt like anything she did to address these challenges only seemed to push her further into the rut. This evening, she had skipped class to basically wallow in her room alone. How this was a solution was beyond her. And so it only made her feel worse. She made fists and slammed them down onto the bedding, shaking the entire mattress. She imagined she looked like a toddler throwing a hissy fit. The inclination to leave the house and go on a bike ride entered into her hazy mental machinations, quickly performed a swift disappearing act, and ultimately left only the faint whiff of its rejected possibility. Bike riding and music were the two main activities that helped Retta maintain her sanity and continued engagement with her life, and both were currently failing her.

She entertained the notion of calling a friend for a drink or at least a comforting chat. But the truth of the matter was that she couldn't think of anyone who would bring comfort. Any conversation would be veiled in counterfeit levity. It would be an awkward and shameful project: calling someone and feigning casualness while actually desperately seeking human interaction to stave off the crushing belief that she was doomed and alone. It put a bad taste in her mouth. "Maybe another time, darlin', maybe another time," she said aloud sarcastically to the hypothetical phone mate whose specific identity she never settled on. Fists on mattress once again.

Retta's social life was almost entirely dried up. All that remained were the infrequent messages and shared posts via Facebook and Twitter, like guerrilla communications. There were also the online dating sites, which she had not indulged since she and Pollock had begun hanging regularly these past few weeks.

The record skipped to a stop. The entire nine songs of music had gone by and Retta hadn't paid attention to it beyond several seconds of the first song's intro. She let out an exasperated breath and sprang to her collection of vinyl. They lay disorganized in messy heaps and leaning against the foot of the bed and the footlocker upon which the record player sat.

Retta pulled the record off the turntable and threw it onto the outdated brown shag carpet, which she had begged her mother for. Retta fingered through the selections. She often believed that the music one picked said a lot about one's emotional state. After sifting through a decent number of albums, she caught sight of a single, "Sure of Love," by the Chantels. It was one of her mother's favorites. She put it on quickly and sat on the floor, her back hunched over and legs spread out wide.

The needle scraped and fell in. Then the piano and the choral refrain, "So sure, so sure, so sure, of love…" Then the lead came in with the percussion, "I need no stars to guide me. I need no sun to shine. Long as you're here beside me, no greater love could be mine." The lyrics cracked against Retta like a wildebeest on cocaine. Her shoulders sagged, pulling her back into an intense arc. She recalled what her mother referred to as Rainy Day Celebration.

In elementary school and perhaps before—she found it hard to know exactly because all of the instances blended together, and Remy's prompted recollections were only so useful—Retta's mother would insist that the two of them play hooky on certain rainy days. She'd nab Retta from bed and they'd get dressed in their rain boots and jackets. The back yard dipped in the middle and there was a narrow strip that flooded with every rain for several hours. They'd get a sled or, once or twice, set up the Slip 'n Slide and lunge, sliding out of control into the impromptu pool.

The two would also do more traditional rainy day activities, such as folding origami ships and letting them sail along the flow from the rain gutter downspouts. When the outside activities were done and they were thoroughly wet and chilled, they would head inside, strip their outer layers off, and put on hot cocoa. Retta's mom would serve her as she snuggled under plaid blankets and pillows on the living room couch. Her mother would then hunker down at the large wooden hutch, which housed the record player and vast record collection that she and Retta's father had amassed throughout the late sixties, seventies, and eighties.

From time to time, she would surprise Retta with her pick, but if Retta had to bet, she would always put her money on "Mr. Blue Sky" by Electric Light Orchestra. It amused Retta the way the singer, Jeff Lynne, who was legend in her household growing up and whose decisions and mastery in sound engineering and song structure was lectured on by both parents almost weekly, addressed the weather. She'd rustle and spin about madly, twisting the cotton throws and rough show pillows into knots and strange tunnels through which she would stretch out and roll, sucking her cocoon closer and tighter around her little cocoa-heated body. The whole room was brown and orange and yellow, remnants from a color scheme that predominated in the late 1970s and which her parents had never really aesthetically evolved beyond.

This type of outdated interior decoration represented safety and healthy curiosity to her. It was the visual backdrop to the magical rainy day celebrations. Between her awe of these celebrations and the more alluring Wiccan rituals, Retta damn near worshipped her mother. Things always seemed like they were really going to be okay going forward. At the very least, Retta learned at a young age that, despite what travails and ill-fated catastrophes transpired, there was nothing that a little ELO and hot cocoa couldn't solve, especially on rainy days.

Those rainy days would always end with Retta's mother fixing supper for Remy and they would have family dinners. Remy would swing in through the garage at 5:45, his hands and face washed but still stained with the resilient hues of oil and grease. He'd grab Retta's mother around the waist and make some deep-throated moan, sexual in classification. And the three would sit while Remy told anecdotes about various customers and their car troubles, always in comic fashion and always elaborating on his internal dialogue in a self-deprecating manner. "And I'm thinking, when did they begin installing volcanoes into the air intake on Camaros? Anyway Jack's face and my hands were covered in molten lava…And I'm screaming, 'I don't speak Samoan!'" Retta and her mom would laugh and wriggle in the their seats. Remy would kick his seat out and begin doing characterizations and miming his business interactions.

But the day would always end. Earlier than usual, because Retta would be exhausted from the activity and enjoyment. And often on these nights, before falling behind that black wall of pressing sleep, she would hear her parents having sex. There were never any furniture sounds or bangs on the wall. She would later take this to mean that they were trying to be quiet and respectful of the fact that Retta would likely hear such disturbances.

Instead, what she heard was the guttural grunting and moans of pleasure. Her bedroom was at the far opposite end of the upstairs hallway, and she always kept her bedroom door slightly ajar so that a ray of light could shine onto the floor and provide some illumination, however minimal. And that strip of light stretched far up onto the bed and could be made to cross her face like a tremendous scar if she angled her head just so to the far right side. She understood what sex was and was not bothered or disgusted by hearing the act, merely rather curious.

The sounds were so violent and painful sounding, she thought it could have been a pig being slowly skewered alive. And yet these were the sounds one makes when experiencing the highest levels of physical pleasure. It was interesting to her and stoked inquisitiveness about the anatomy of the opposite sex at a very early age.

However, there was always also sadness present at the end of these rainy day celebrations. Retta realized that the following day would inevitably be unbearably plain and humdrum compared to what had just ensued. She was sentenced to boredom. And boredoms did loom large in its approach. Then again, she knew it was necessary, for the rainy day celebrations wouldn't stand out if not surrounded by a plethora of ordinary and uneventful days.

The memory churned up both appreciation and disappointment in Retta, like an interrupted catharsis being stopped at its midpoint. She straightened out and lifted the needle's twitching arm from off the record. She thoughtlessly replaced it with Peabody's "Revenge." She had purchased their debut album on sale the previous week when she went with Pollock to see them play at the open mic night during the food truck fest.

After the post rock–funk fun began, she jumped up back onto the bed and resumed her supine position. A memory popped up from in class, sometime in the past week. She had overheard a conversation. The context involved someone's friend who wasn't coming out for drinks anymore because he was depressed. "Depression?" one of the listeners responded. "What, you mean sadness? Just some whiny bitch-ass shit. We all depressed. You've gotta man up and get over that shit." The sentiment seemed preposterous to Retta, who knew well and good that depression was a clinical disease with chemical and neurological symptoms, but she said nothing. Nor did anyone in the conversation. The comment seemed even odder when she considered that everyone in the class was studying to become a nurse and, in some capacity, fancied themselves members of the medical profession. She imagined the commenter as a future nurse with some patient wallowing in great pain from some ailment, and he leans in and mutters, "Man up and get over that shit."

And yet, for all the hilarity and stupidity of the comment, Retta couldn't help but admit that she agreed. Down there within herself, she secretly believed that she could overcome her travails, her anxieties about her current situation. Retta believed in solutions, she was a problem solver. Indulging in feelings of doubt and defeat was how Remy had dealt with his own bad hand. She couldn't follow that route. Though she loved him dearly and never really held his actions against him, she also knew that she had to do better.

She thought she had been doing better, but still there was no relief. She had finished undergrad, stayed in town, and earned a scholarship to nursing school. She managed the house finances, cooked and cleaned, cared for her brother and even her father. She never got into trouble and never took selfish risks. She had been walking a straight line. Every wild and fantastical impulse to lead a more adventurous or more fun lifestyle had been constrained, choked, or otherwise given the cold shoulder upon its arrival in Retta's head.

All of this responsible, task-oriented behavior was supposed to lead to some advantage, some reward. But it was apparent now, leaning into her midtwenties, that all it had created were habits which made it easier to keep on keeping on in this same way. Now the pressure was beginning to mount. Perhaps there were too many repressed desires, too little youth, too few flights of fancy. But she felt, dearly and viscerally, that she was most certainly not living the life she wanted. Instead, it was the life that circumstances and her more prudent side demanded. She felt sorry for herself. And as soon as she did, she heard again the phrase "Man up and get over that shit."

Her thoughts were circular, and she wasn't getting anywhere. She'd feel guilty for feeling bad and then realize that the only way too feel less guilty was to continue in all those same behaviors that made her feel bad in the first place. She flopped onto her feet, snapped the off button on the turntable, and ran downstairs and out the front door without checking on Fox or Remy. She swung her leg over the frame of her bike and took off toward town.

She turned onto Boundary Road, which she rarely did because it was a wavy 55 mph country two-lane that was poorly lit, with slim shoulders and a history of accidents. Boundary ran around the other end of the older housing developments, past Nyqvist where Pollock lived. She put her troubles into the pedals and did not relent on either ascent or descent of the maddening crescents of the hills. She knew that if she tired herself well enough, there would be no trouble left in her thoughts. Under such circumstances, she could continue on living as she had without these distracting regrets and ambitions for another week maybe, at which point she could return to the road or experience better success with music.

The inclines gained ferociously in their resistance as Retta's quadriceps and hamstrings turned closer and closer to shaky gelatin from her abuse. Her legs shook, testing her grip on the rubber-covered handlebars. She continued on in this fashion for twelve miles, well past Nyqvist, even past the scattered country homes that started beyond the municipal limits. Eventually she came to the bottom of a large decline and skidded to a stop. Besides the sporadic gusts pushing the high forest canopy branches against one another, all she could hear was her own heavy breathing.

Orange dusk leaked through the leaves and left faded prints across the crumbling blacktop. It was beautiful and strange. Retta had accomplished that which she set out to do. She was empty and alone. After gathering her reserves, she could jaunt home and would fall asleep without much worry or effort. She could get a fresh start tomorrow. She lifted her bike frame and hobbled out a half circle, turning to face her return voyage.

On her right, there was a rustling and a moaning. Retta froze and squinted her eyes. The moaning continued and turned into grunting. It was a deep male voice. Some thirty feet in, she made him out. A man in blue sweats was leaning against a large tree trunk, rubbing the bark with his hands in circular patterns. He spoke loudly. "Help me, goddamn it. I am an evolved human being in the twenty-first century, and I cannot live like this. Save me goddamn it! Take it all, just take all of it, I don't want it! I can't have it anymore!" Then, he resumed grunting.

Retta used her toe to lift up the pedal into attack position so that she could take off. The motion made a loud click of the chain against the gear ring, and the man turned abruptly and faced her. His face was swollen, with a few days worth of stubble. He looked embarrassed. Retta did not move. The two remained still, staring one another down, unsure. The man held out a hand, taking a step forward and said, "I'm sorry, look I—"

"Don't come any closer to me, stay where you are!" At that, the grunter obeyed and froze, nodding emphatically.

"Of course, of course," he said. "Fuck this is embarrassing, I didn't expect anyone to be out here. Maybe the occasional car, yeah. But no one in person."

Retta let out a large breath, her body trembling in the wake of her exertion. She kept her toes on the pedal and her fingers tight around the handlebar grips and asked, "What are you doing? Like, are you okay?"

The grunter let out a snort and smiled abashedly, his cheeks reddening with the simmering embarrassment he felt. "Yeah, I'll be fine. I'm just in the middle of a little ritual of mine. You can go along, I'll be okay. Thanks!" He waved her away and turned back toward the tree trunk. Retta began to push on the pedal but stopped short of a full rotation and slid her opposite shoe to a stop.

"What ritual?" she called out. The man turned back to her and raised his eyebrows. After a pause, he chuckled and nervously said, "Well, it's to help me forget about some things that are giving me trouble." After seeing that this limited explanation fell short of quenching her curiosity, he continued. "I'm obsessed with parts!" he yelled, slapping his left pectoral.

"Parts?" Retta yelled back. "Like, what do you mean, parts?"

"Women's parts!" the grunter yelled back, throwing his hands up. Retta thought on this a moment, trying to make a connection but it wasn't happening.

"What?" she said, emphasizing the depth of her confusion in the degree of upward pitch at the end of the word.

The grunter chuckled again, looking downward and nodding in avid agreement, almost endorsing her confusion. "Okay, okay. It's boob—breasts. Women's breasts. And asses. Butts. And hair. I can't...well..." He began chuckling again and rubbed his forehead in obvious discomfort. "Look, I am thinking about proposing to my girl. I *am* proposing to her. Only problem is that I can't stop thinking about Regina and her breasts. I wasn't supposed to see them, but I did. And there is the internet. It's...well. I can't concentrate anymore. I have too many lady parts in mind."

"Okay." Retta said. She was becoming alarmed, fearing that she was in the presence of some sexual deviant or insane person. She prepared to flee quickly when the grunter continued on in his explanation.

"Anyway, my brother told me about tree therapy. I guess it helped him out when he came back from the Middle East. I figured I'd give it a try, you know? I mean, I am a thirty-five-year-old man, and all I think about are tits, naked girls. What the hell? You know, just shapes and colors of women's parts." Retta could hear the desperation in the man's voice. It had become too uncomfortable. She shoved her weight against the pedal and lunged forward.

She was nearly home before she let up and settled into a comfortable coast. Her empty Zen-like state, which she had achieved in her outward journey, had been completely crushed by the tree therapy man. She felt more stressed and unresolved than when she had darted out of the house an hour and a half earlier. It dawned on her that she would need to make some changes.

The familiar smoke plumes rose out behind the kitchen window. Retta jaunted through the living room, slammed open the sliding glass door, and strode across the creaking back deck. Remy acknowledged his daughter's presence, casually, with a sidelong glance. He took a nervous toke. "Dad, you have to come inside right now," Retta said gravely, holding her hands out to the sliding door. Remy merely quivered his eyelids as if the smoke was getting into his eyes and stayed quiet. "Dad, I'm drowning. You have to come back. You have to come inside *right now!*" The old deck rocked under Retta as she shook her arms, wringing her fists, and shifted her weight from one leg to the other. Remy lowered his head and tightly pursed his lips.

"I can't do this anymore," she said. "I have to figure things out for myself. There is too much. It's just too much to. And I know you're...well...I know that...you've had your time, and now I need you to come inside. Right now! I need my time." Retta held her hands back out toward the sliding door, as a butler might escort someone along. Having said, however awkwardly and inarticulately, what she wanted, she felt relieved. But she also felt as if she had crossed some important line. She could see the pain that her having crossed this line inflicted on her father's face. Remy was grimacing and shaking his head in denial. The two, father and daughter, had a longstanding agreement to remain silent. That they would never directly vocalize their obvious misery. The contract was implied and had formed out of their habitual obedience to its decree, itself birthed out of silence. But the contract no longer suited Retta. And it likely was not suiting Remy. She needed to break it. Still, her need felt like violation.

This precise moment, this instant of fracture, though foreign in the particulars of its manifestation, may have been something that Remy was waiting for, abstractly. It rang out like a bodily alarm clock, waking him from his prolonged estranged posture, his castaway rumination sessions behind his rotting house and in his cluttered garage. Something tender and slippery moved in him, ecstatically dredging up life-affirming forces. It made real everything he had been taking pains to avoid. The bodily alarm rang out, calling him to return. "Okay," he said, his lips trembling and his head still down. His response scared him. It scared Retta.

"What?" she asked. She was startled by the quickness and simplicity of her father's answer.

"Okay," he repeated, "I'll come inside now." And with that, he bent over, dabbed out his burning cigarette on the lawn and stepped swiftly past a stunned Retta. The deck wobbled greatly.

Retta remained outside and was rather bewildered as she watched her father, renewed in focus, go into the kitchen and begin pulling food items from the cupboard and fridge. He gathered what appeared to be ingredients for dinner. Having brought a bowl of water to a boil and set a box of fettuccine noodles beside it on the counter, Remy laughed loudly and moved over to the sink. There, he ran cold water and put his face beneath the faucet, rubbing soapy bubbles over his forehead and neck. He rinsed and dried it off with a wad of paper towels he clumsily ripped from its roll.

Remy cooked the pasta and reduced shredded Parmesan into a tasty Alfredo sauce. He, Retta, and Fox sat down and enjoyed a pleasant and unusually vocal family supper. Remy, like a statue come to life, asked all sorts of questions of Retta. About how her classes were going, about the young man she was spending time with lately, about Fox. And Fox even noticed the difference, responding with laughter and a repeated refrain of, "Asta allo mena sane! Asta allo mena sane." It was a phrase of sounds, which Fox favored and uttered when happy or excited. He kept it up that whole evening, cementing the clear emotional shift that had occurred within the household. Remy, and especially Retta, received the phrase with uncontrollable laughter.

The entire scene of Remy suddenly switching back on made Retta muse on whether she had slipped into an alternate universe where Remy never retreated into himself at all. It was bizarre in how it was exactly what she had wanted for so long. And yet it happened so automatically, so easily, once she addressed it. She wondered if all she had needed to do this whole time was tell him that he wasn't allowed to be absent. The thought gave her sour guts, thinking about the time she might have lost abiding by their silent accord for so many years.

And it was curious how Remy's old self needed no practice in its return. It was as if that previous personality, the happy-go-lucky, goofy asshole version of Remy had been existing all along and was merely overshadowed and prevented from appearing by the shell of austerity and despair. There was no gradient, no phasing in. It was a switch. He was brooding and aloof, unreachable. Then— *fffft*—he was there again and telling jokes and interrogating his children in that familiarly warm and spirited way.

Retta spent no more than a day or two thinking over the wild hurry of this transition. Once Remy was back, he was back. And the ball was rolling. He took back dominion and control over the finances, haggled with the credit card representatives, started leaving work to drive Fox to and from his daycare and instruction, and even began work on replacing the back deck with a friend from work. Once this all had settled in as the normal flow of things, Retta noted to herself that Australia didn't seem so seductive as it once had. She renewed her concentration on nursing classes, with a zeal to finish and begin practice. Because, if she was no longer looking after, caring for, her brother and father, then nursing was not an extension of her domestic responsibilities but rather a free choice. And it was one that she made cheerfully, even with glee now. Her passion for the healthcare profession had been repaired. She had remembered, or rather rediscovered, the reasons she'd wanted to become a nurse in the first place.

In the wake of such an upturn in fortune, and because Retta had been focusing on how fractured and isolated her friends had become, she decided to put a party together. Seeing her father smiling and chatty reminded her how much she missed being part of a community. And it had been such a long time since she had had people over. But with the deck soon to be rebuilt, and semester finals coming up, she decided that she could make a Facebook invitation scheduled for a month or so down the road and hopefully rope in a few dozen old friends and acquaintances for a backyard fire. It was settled.

It took little time to arrange the Facebook page and she sent it out to all of her friends without distinction, even ones she knew lived in other states. It felt right, like she was turning a corner and signifying the beginning of a new phase in her life, a lighter and more fervent chapter, one where she was more open and welcoming to possibility. Retta knew she was "getting over that shit, man." She wrote down the event in bubbled lettering in her planner while working on the Facebook invitation. In the invitation's header, Retta had pasted an image of a dream catcher that she had nabbed from Google images. Initially, it had been nothing more than an appealing object to stamp her personality upon the digital visual facade. But after thinking about it for a bit, Retta understood that the party would be a dream catcher–building party.

Retta had owned dream catchers when she was younger, and in high school, she adorned her car mirror with one that she had purchased from the Trams farmer's market. It had been lost or misplaced somewhere down the line. Though the device itself was not associated with Wicca, both of her parents had expressed to Retta their fond sentiments toward the ideas behind the catchers many times. Her mother had said, "It's a protective charm. You keep it near to your bed. It works like a sifter to keep out the bad dreams, and only let the good ones in—the happy dreams. Mothers used to weave them for their children. I think it was the Lakota, maybe other Native Americans. It was a tradition."

Retta decided to build a giant dream catcher for the neighborhood at the party as a fun arts and crafts project and keep it in the backyard. She wanted to make it out of wood and rope and twine, materials that weather.

The thought excited Retta and she typed it in to the description segment of the Facebook invitation. It was set and she got almost teary eyed, looking forward to receiving RSVPs. She was thrilled about her life, which, really, hadn't been the case for quite some time. Things were coming together, and she was thinking a little bit less about her mother and a little bit more about the future.

Chapter Seventeen

Jasper opened his truck's door as wide as he could. The seat felt cold and sticky as he reached for the far side of the cushion and pulled himself up onto his side. He rested there for a few moments, trying to catch up with his breathing, which was growing more and more shallow and elusive. Blood dripped from under his coat and pooled on the frozen carpet on the driver's side floor. He had been shot three times.

Because of the difficulty involved in breathing, the loss of blood, and the exertion from hiking back to his truck, Jasper was light-headed, and his vision was blurry. The edges of his sight were closing inward with swells of throbbing distortion. He let out a chuckle that ended in tears. He found it fairly hilarious how fucked he was. Every bit of his body stung from the cold, from the tumble down the stairs, from the gun wounds. But the stinging was beginning to fade as he grew more numb.

Reaching his left arm out, he slapped the overhead sun visor downward and a rectangle of folded, aged paper fell down. It landed in the pooling blood, which had warmed the carpet and was now soaking into the fabric like an aerial time-lapse video of an evaporating lake. Jasper wheezed in agitation, then lowered his hand clumsily and began the task of unfolding the bloodied paper against the floor. Once the paper lay approximately flat, Jasper examined its contents.

Six names were enumerated, with a space in between each. The names were full, with a first, middle, and surname spelled out in cursive. Each of the first five names had been crossed out and only the last was left. It read "Hannah Lynn Corin." Jasper smiled to himself when he saw the last name. It was the most important, the most personal on the list. He had left it for last, and now he could cross it off. Unable to even contemplate where his pencil was located, Jasper instead stretched out his bloodied index finger and pressed its tip against the name. He lifted up and was pleased to see a smudged fingerprint of blood over "Corin."

It was quiet outside. The winds had subsided and all Jasper could hear were the clicks and claps of the truck's underside interacting with the temperature. He was sure that he was going to die, but warmed to the idea of prolonging it just a little bit and began patting his pockets with his free hand, searching for the keys.

He managed to get the truck started, with a painful twist of his arm against the ignition's resistance, and aim the lone front heating vent downward at his midsection. He thought about his father, Perini, who had sent him down this path. He had told young Jasper, "This world is mostly a brutal and thuggish place where violent and obtuse men do well. There is no consolation prize for being ethical or having depth of thought. All that matters is the register of guts, of goddamned guts that you put forward in getting what you want, making what you want become yours. Everyone else loses. Maybe it doesn't appear so on the outside, but in their heart of hearts, almost everyone knows that they've crumpled when it counted. Everyone recognizes immediately when they've been done over. Some just paint it over better than others. Some make justifications."

Perini was a short man, with unending alcoholic depravity, and seemed always to be speaking with fellows who weren't present. He would pace, manic-eyed, iron stein at the end of a bowed arm, splashing bits of froth and beer over the edges at the turns. And he'd yell and mutter and rap vitriolic about the state of man and society. It was clear to Jasper at a very young age, three or four perhaps, that his father was very bitter and very embattled. It seemed to Jasper that Perini spoke against everything that Perini himself was, as if he was unaware that he was no different from what he was disparaging with passionate vigor.

"But you see Jasp, we're Narduccians! We have the ability to account. You see, all the horror, the aggression, well, it gets into you. Right in there. You cannot avoid it, Jasp. Sure, you've got those numb brains practicing meditation, and you've also got the ones who choose to evacuate in the emergency." He pointed two close fingers to his head and imitated the best gunshot sound he could conjure. "But neither of those kinds make it out clean. The only reason they seek an alternative option is because they have already seen the problem within themselves. Why else would they retreat or blow their brains out? Fucking cowards! So you see, the problem finds its way in no matter how you handle it. So why not handle it like a fucking man? Huh? Can you tell me that? Well, I say we are Narduccians, and that is exactly what we are going to do. We are going to push back. The problem has found us and we are going to push the problem on some one else. Who? Huh? Who do we Narduccians pass this problem onto? That is why we make an accounting. And the accounting doesn't cease. It passes on down the line. Time does not forget. Narduccians do not paint it over!"

Jasper pulled his knees up into his chest and wrapped his arms around them. It was now nice and hot in the compartment despite the driver's door remaining open. He had mulled over the idea of closing it, arched upward to confront the task, but the pain and the exhaustion put him back down against the seat. Now, in a tight ball, he smiled at Perini's words, reflecting in his final minutes.

His father ranted on in Jasper's head, aggrandized by the quasi-mythical status Jasper's imagination and admiration had granted him. All of this while the life was leaving Jasper's body. "We can't forget our fathers' work. We don't enter into the world from a vacuum. You see, so much has already happened. The stakes are already set. Otherwise I'd have been born a wealthy oil magnate with a revolving harem. But I wasn't. And I can't be. Because time does not forget. There is no maneuver to erase time's memory. Okay, so those Jesus freaks and bitches that need to feel protected and in control will tell you that you can, that there is a choice. But they are the same one's choking on themselves, huddled in a corner with an imaginary lover. Jesus was a cunt! That's right, he is a nice wet imaginary cunt for forlorn lovers coming up dry. The only choice there is, is whether to step up to the plate or take a nap in the dugout. Either way, the game goes on."

These late night pacing monologues occurred routinely, two even three times a week since before the beginning of Jasper's memory, and they continued up until his twenties when he was finally given the accounting, the first names for him to start on his father's work. And now he had completed his father's work. And he had made an accounting of his own, but he had no children to which he could bestow it. He was going to perish alone, without a legacy. No one but the names on the list would know about his life's work.

But maybe none of that mattered at all. Because Jasper could imagine that wherever Perini was, he was smiling at his son who had stepped up to the plate. He hadn't cowered and deluded himself into fucking that imaginary lover. He had done his father's work, finished his father's work. He had followed through on the accounting and balanced it all back in favor of the Narducci name. He was a true Narduccian. In measuring the worth and impact of a man, that was, to Jasper, the pinnacle of greatness. His life was a success, and so he could die at peace.

His vision was virtually blurred over and he could not feel his lower half. The rumble of the truck's engine shook Jasper in little circles. It soothed him like a baby in a rocking cradle. He wondered how long the gas would last and whether the heater would run until he was gone. Though it really didn't have to, just long enough so that he no longer felt the cold at all. Jasper closed his eyes and committed to the end.

The mental theater opened back up and Perini reappeared, now smiling and patting Jasper's head. He said, "Everyone knows when they've been put over on. It's only your job to prove something to yourself. It doesn't matter what it is, in the big picture, but everyone knows what they need to prove it to themselves. And that is the only way to rest easy, as they say. You have to answer your own question for yourself. And you can only ever do that by making an accounting and balancing the sheet out in your favor. And the accounting is always in place before you even begin. So, you see, you can rest easy, Jasp. Rest easy."

Perini's smile faded and he turned his head away from Jasper. "Oh, and the problem never ceases, son..." he said, staring down at Jasper's feet. The armrest cracked hard against the back of Jasper's head. He pulled his eyelids open and, through the blurry rings, barely made out fiendish beast eyes staring at him. Jasper focused all of his concentration, pushing his chin down to his neck to see more clearly.

Standing on the seat above Jasper's now more prone body was a coyote. It was straddling him on lean grey legs and bent down, licking the blood from the open wound in Jasper's left side. He could not feel any of it. The coyote then spread its jaws and bit into Jasper's shirt and flesh with its canines, pulling skin and fat and cotton up until it tore off. Still Jasper felt nothing. The animal had not noticed that Jasper was now conscious and continued on methodically in its eating. It took care to pull its lips back toward the rear of its mouth and fully chew the gristle with its mangling teeth, cocking its head to the side. It almost seemed to Jasper to be smiling.

Jasper briefly considered doing something about the situation. However fucked he had been before, he was surely far more fucked now. He laughed hysterically to himself without sound or movement. His feeling was at a minimum, now not even fully aware of his head. The rumble of the truck and the stream from the heating vent were now beyond his perception's reach. And so, he con-cluded that nothing about his ending had changed, except for the specific manner of its execution.

He was being eaten alive by a coyote, and the thought caused the slightest of smirks to emerge upon his face. The thought repeated and the smirk grew. It didn't even matter whether the coyote was real or he was hallucinating this entire episode. There was no bodily communication left to decipher. He repeated the thought to himself one last time for good measure, allowing the finality of the proposition to sink in. The idea brought him pure joy. He could think of no better compliment. And so he dropped his head back and relaxed all of his mental facul-ties as the animal continued pulling and gnawing on his exposed flesh.

"We left Miles. He's still there," Martin said, looking out the rear passenger window. "We left him." Dead treetops flashed by, their shape warping along the glass as the car sped on. Sarah glanced over at Brass Knee, who had not spoken since the beginning of the drive, and then back at Martin.

"Hey. Where are you driving to?" she asked Brass Knee.

He remained silent a moment before answering. "You said that you needed to go far away from here." Sarah nodded in anticipation of something more. "I can help you with that. A friend…"

Sarah was still unappeased. She asked plainly, "Why?" Brass Knee took his eyes from the road and set them upon her, without another word. But she could see the thoughts flickering quickly about within him.

Martin was heartbroken, slouched against the plush Corolla interior. Miles's needful eyes kept appearing to him. He wondered what would become of the poor kid, now. It alleviated his devastation only somewhat to know that Ms. Corin would no longer be the wicked overlord of Wicker Home, but he didn't know what would happen to all of the kids. It seemed to Martin that every transition in his life yielded worse results for him and those around him. The more things changed, the worse it got. He had thought that he had it bad before, in the picking circuit. "Stupid," he muttered.

Watching Corin's death had not brought Martin any respite in the way that he had occasionally fantasized it would. Her end only seemed to add to the mess, like an additional tally. However, he was out, and Sarah was out too. His sister and he had made it. She was his only family, and they were sticking together.

The terror of the past, with its prickly turns, was powerfully still potent and seductive. Plus, Martin had just seen a woman murdered and was caked in dried vomit. Still, with imagination, he mustered some hope for the future. After all, they were out and on their own. "The future...," he said under breath.

"What?" Sarah asked, catching his face through the side mirror.

"Nothing," he said, a bit startled. He looked at Jemmy, snoring in the seat beside him.

Brass Knee drove into the cargo yard through the back entrance and parked beside the far loading dock in Bay 4. He pulled the keys out and said, "Gabby will get here within the hour. I have to speak with my manager. You guys sit tight and maybe get some rest. I'll be back before she gets here." He looked over at Jemmy, her neck crooked against the plastic window trim, snoring loudly. "If she wakes up, fill her in." And with that, he hopped out of the car and, with an elegant jump, pulled himself up into the loading dock with his upper arms.

Sarah and Martin were left quiet, looking at one another in the mirror. Sarah turned onto her knees and faced Martin between the car seats. "Are you okay, kid?" she asked, her usually motherly face stern.

"Yeah, I am," Martin said, flatly. "Are *you*?"

She took a deep breath. "I'm not sure. I...will be. I will be," she said, in a way that convinced Martin she was primarily reassuring herself. She let out a high-pitched gust of air that squeezed through a range of tones before settling into a hearty laugh. Her cheeks flushed. Martin raised his eyebrows, a little alarmed, but he could not help laughing himself. The two continued laughing riotously for several minutes, staring at one another, working out their stress. And this is what Jemmy awoke to.

Gabby arrived in her eighteen-wheeler, hell-bent on a timely transition through the distribution center, so that she could make her long return south. It took some aggressive convincing from Brass Knee, but in the end he managed to persuade Gabby to accept two minor stowaways. Their business relation had been one of mutual respect and, more importantly, trust. They'd each taken turns calling in favors, and this time it was Brass Knee who needed one.

Sarah, Martin, and Jemmy watched the two talking in a shadowy corner next to the loading zone. A handshake punctuated the deal, and Gabby continued on smoking while the morning crew of Bay 4 slid the usual fare out from her trailer. Then Brass Knee drove the gang away from the warehouse and parked alongside the state route. There, they all managed awkward yet sincere farewells before Gabby's now-empty truck found its way to them and rolled to a stop behind the Corolla.

Behind the cockpit, there was a sleeping compartment with a couch and bed where Sarah and Martin spent most of the trip to Florida. Gabby had rarely suffered guests and it showed. She would shout back to the two searing warnings concerning their personal conduct and the limits of her own hospitality. "You shits break anything and the next exit will be your destination, you hear me?" And later, "Here, it's a snickers bar to tide you over. Don't let any of my cushions get sticky, you hear me?

They made it through the limited late-winter daylight and, by the following morning, were watching the sunrise behind palm trees. Sarah and Martin had slept as well as could be expected hunched side by side on a love seat whose spring supports had long ago lost the resolve to continue on, clutching an itchy wool packing blanket to cover themselves. Gabby maintained her aloof crankiness, weathered and resigned to her agreed task.

Once stopped along the gravel perimeter of a trailer park, there was some verbal commotion outside, which Martin and Sarah overhead from inside the truck. Then the side door flung open and the two were shuffled about and hurried along by two women speaking Spanish. The women placed their palms on the back of Martin's and Sarah's necks, ushering them forward along the gravel road-way between rows of double-wides, rundown Winnebagos, and the occasional vintage Airstream trailer. They took a sharp turn to a smaller gravel path, which led down to a palm-forested ravine surrounding a meandering brown river.

The path turned into a serpentine trail of worn dirt and trampled blades of marshy saw grass and bromeliads. They were sun-bleached and brittle and crunched underfoot. Just before reaching the low, mud-caked riverbank, one of the women pointed upward along the thick and twisting roots composing the trunk of a pale fig tree. Martin looked up. Above, within the knots and woven mess of roots and branches, was a dark wooden structure. It was approximately the size of a small woodshed or yard barn and sat just slightly uneven, likely made crooked from the unpredictable growth of the tree's wrapping and winding appendages. Martin looked to Sarah for clarification, who unfortunately was equally per-plexed.

"There," the lady said, pointing her finger and shoving a heap of clean clothes into Sarah's hands. "There you stay." Martin looked back from the lady to Sarah. Sarah shook her head, dropped the clothes, and held her hands out as one does when failing to comprehend the meaning of another. The lady looked to her partner who spoke rapidly in hushed Spanish. She then tried again. "There you stay. Two months. Two months. Okay, yes?" It was clearly enunciated in the uni-versal tone of a question, and yet there was no pause for a response. Instead, the lady pulled a matted bundle of single US dollar bills, pried Sarah's hand open and slapped them in place. "Two months. Okay, yes?" Again intoning a question but leaving no time for a reply, she turned and trotted back up the narrow path through the southern jungle. Her friend followed along, hiking her skirt to keep it from the sharp edges of wetland plants.

"What…the…fuck?" Sarah said. Martin had no answer. The two twirled about, looking for sources of guidance. Eventually, Sarah tickled her bangs with a puff from her bottom lip and began climbing up the pronounced fig roots.

The tree house's door was hinged, and inside were two aluminum cots on which sat a neatly tucked stack of orange sheets and thin pillows without cases. It was not so unlike the sleeping accouterments at Wicker Home, slightly down-graded, and of course without the mistress monster. Upon settling in to that no-tion, Sarah shook her head and placed her palms backward on her hips.

The edges of the US currency rubbed her skin, calling out to her attention. "We've got forty dollars." Martin watched from below while monitoring the slow moving river water and wondering about the presence of alligators. The surface was brown, and there were swirls of white bubbles churning about in spirals here and there between eddy and current like a settling foamy latte.

The warmth of the locale was a welcome change but it was sticky and the heat horrendous. Martin and Sarah spent that first evening lying in the cots, trying to make up for the rest they lost in Gabby's truck. But not long after hunkering down within the room, it had begun raining harder than any rain they had previously known. It was so hard that all of the leafy vegetation in the surrounding for-est bent down to the ground, which ran with water, spewing madly into the river so hard that, within the first hour, the bank had disappeared and the river's width widened threefold.

Swarms of innumerable mosquitos traveled like destitute refugees into the safety of the tree house and began waging an unrelenting campaign of blood lust. The smacking and swearing remained constant. Sarah believed she had outfoxed the heinous menaces by pulling the sheet completely over her body. Her sanctuary lasted a good minute before it became apparent that the mosquitos could penetrate the coarse threads of the cheap fabric. "This is hell," Martin said. "What are we going to do? I can't stand this any longer. I'm going to go crazy."

"Agreed. Let's bail," Sarah said, enlivened by the prospect of escape.

They swung the tree house hatch open to the crushing torrents of the downpour and tried to make heads or tails of the condition of the jungle floor. But it was too dark. Lightning crashed and the two ducked down against the tree house floor. The fig tree shook mightily, overturning Sarah's cot onto the now-wet floor. They peered out again. Again a flash of lightning. It wasn't long enough to get a picture. Martin thought of just jumping for it, taking a leap of faith. The room was only twelve or thirteen feet from the ground, and surely the rain had softened the soil and the plants. But the fear of the unknown was potent, and he had no idea if there were alligators, poisonous snakes, or thorny plant below.

The second clap of thunder shook their fig tree again. Again came a flash of light. This time it was much longer. Sarah had extended her neck far out, putting weight on her bent wrists and palms like a large cat lapping from a puddle, and she saw the water had risen right up to the tree house. There was, at most, two feet for it to climb before taking their room. "Oh, goddamn it!" she screamed, more annoyed than truly fearful. The problem felt like an extension of the biting, itching bugs, an extension of Corin's religious ceremonies, an extension of her bastard of a stepfather.

Sarah grabbed the door handle and rapped it closed, not unlike the slam of a pouty teenager miffed by her mother's pronouncement of grounding and confinement to her room, except she and Martin were literally confined to their room. "We have to wait this one out, kid," she said while putting her cot back in order. He followed her lead in lying down and covering himself over with the sheets as best as possible. And they spent the next few hours quietly slapping and scratching. The rain outside raged on and both imagined the horror of the impending moment when the water line would rise above their relative haven and necessitate their further action.

"At least we're kind of dry," Sarah said through the roaring and rumbling from her side of the dark tree house. The words seemed heroic to Martin. She had decided the situation would not beat her. Flashes of lightning illuminated the outlines of palm and pines, tortured by the winds and heavy rain, visible through the chinks in the walls' wooden planking.

"Yea, kind of…" Martin said, attempting to emulate her valor. But it came across to both of them as sarcasm. She began laughing instantly. It was contagious. And there, in a shanty tree house in the middle of what seemed the monsoon of all monsoons, they both laughed uncontrollably from deep in their guts, shaking about and gasping for air. It had become their habit.

When the sun came up, the rain had ceased and the water level had retreated well below the tree house. With the fortunate turn in weather, the bugs almost entirely ventured off, and life seemed a little more bearable. They were now covered in dried mud. It was smeared thickly and unevenly over their faces, their necks, their bellies and backs, and their arms and legs.

At some odd hour in the night, once the water had risen above the floor and inched toward the cots, a bunched knot of saw grass growing around a leg-sized chunk of driftwood knocked through the door and floated inside. It spun between the two cots, which were only being anchored by body weight. Martin, then sitting cross-legged, reached out to investigate the object. The saw grass's hair-like roots were intertwined with clods of dirt and pasty mud. Martin rubbed the substance between his fingers before applying it to his forearms.

Having watched several mosquitos land and unsuccessfully try to penetrate the mud, Martin rapidly spread its dominion. Sarah, who had been lying on her side and watching Martin with resignation, followed suit. Once the bites ceased on the muddied areas of exposed skin and became concentrated on the skin below their clothes, the clothes came off, and the two of them furiously rubbed the muddy mix all over. Eventually, Martin was in nothing but his plaid boxer shorts and Sarah, her sports bra and panties, all of which were also covered in thick, oozing, and drying mud. They were eyes and teeth.

The bites then dissipated altogether, and they were able to lie back down in peace. Once the rain lessened and the water level plateaued and then lowered, they were able to close their eyes and get some sleep. The sleep was deep and welcome. But it was short-lived, as all of the creatures of the jungle rejoiced at the storm's end with their respective songs and cries. And there was the intermittent crashing and creaking of branches, wooden planks from porches and docks, lawn chairs, and all other sorts of flotsam running into trees and each other as they washed downstream.

Now that the particular panic of the storm had abated, Sarah and Martin had to face the much more general problems attending their station, and they pondered how they could find a shower to get the pancaked earth off of themselves, where were they, exactly, how long would forty dollars last them, how would they get more when that was gone, and were they really going to continue living in this jungle tree house for more than a day or two? These questions rode in on the welcome sunrise's coattails and nestled into Sarah's and Martin's heads like a bad hangover.

The two wandered to the edge of the trailer park and skulked around like nighttime vermin. Fortunately, the park had public restrooms with showers near a community playground, and they were able to wash themselves. There were enough units in the trailer park to allow for strangers, and no one thought twice about their presence. Having air-dried and patted his face with the disposable paper towels, Martin returned to the tree house refreshed. Sarah sat cross-legged, her wet hair pulled into a ponytail.

Neither were in a trusting mood and the lack of care and sustenance, which they daily received at Wicker Home, was woefully felt. Sarah spent a great deal of time fretting and musing over whether their faces would end up on the television news, whether they could freely walk about in public places. She also became quite curious about the reasons for Brass Knee helping them flee instead of just calling the police and leaving them there. The resolution that she settled on was that he must have, in some way, identified with her and Martin. She couldn't think of any other reason.

The trailer park, named Flamingo Lagoon, was located on a four lane commercial drive surrounded by seedy pastel motels, more elegant high-rise hotel complexes with pools behind, seafood restaurants, and Putt-Putt courses around plastic volcanoes and pirate ships. Just north, Flamingo Lagoon ended and the river on its east side spilt into the Gulf of Mexico near sandy white beaches where tourists vacationed on neon beach towels and feigned reading lofty literature for several minute intervals in between naps and fruity cocktails.

There was no city proper, but the whole area was known as Sands Step and it was 90 percent vacationing middle-class families. Once learned, this fact loosened Sarah up a bit about walking around. At least no one would be able to see they were out of place. She and Martin found a little diner with a beachside porch and devoured pancake breakfasts. Sarah noted the "Help Wanted" sign posted in the diner window. She nodded to it and said, "Looks like some of these places are looking for workers. I wonder if they do background checks."

The wooden seat was hot against Martin's back. He was gazing out at the public beach area and caught sight of a father swinging his two daughters around under his large tan arms. A woman, presumably his wife, stood a few feet removed and hunched down over her large black camera. A little further out into the water, a family madly clung to a long yellow inflatable being dragged behind a Jet Ski. Each wave crest popped their butts from the seat and they landed back down harshly, crooked and with a compression of necks.

Dotted across the beach as far as the eye could see were American families enjoying leisure time together. It was another look into what Martin wanted most in life and would never have. The sun's reflection in the dark diner window glimmered white into his eyes and he returned his attention to his compatriot. The two sat, Martin bewildered with scrambled thoughts fighting against the inertia of digestion, Sarah figuring how to acquire more funds. The breakfasts had cost $9.50 with tip.

Employment practices in Sands Step were unscrupulous. The vast majority of the service industry's labor was Cuban. And the vast majority of Cubans were illegal immigrants. Thus, the immigrants were open to less than minimum wage, longer shifts, and under the table, untaxed payment. In exchange, it became in the best interests of the small business owners and chain managers to conduct as little prehire investigation as possible. Just enough to cover their own ass should questions ever arise, which usually never did.

Sarah was hired instantly upon inquiring about a "Cleaning Maids Needed" sign in the Sandpiper Inn next to Flamingo Lagoon. She was white and spoke perfect English. The manager, Kat Jamejam, in a gravelly smoker's rasp simply asked, "You have a social security number?"

Sarah, sure that she did but nowhere near capable of remembering what it was, simply said, "Yeah." Kat was sitting sideways on a barstool in the Sandpiper's front office-cum-coin laundromat-cum-bar, watching a tiny black and white TV playing *All in the Family*. She raised an eyebrow and looked Sarah up and down. Sarah, though scrawny and pale, always possessed an aura of competence.

"Sure, sure. You will start the second shift tomorrow. It begins at 1:00 p.m. You should arrive a little early, so we can get you a uniform and introduce you to coworkers. They don't speak much English. It can get lonely round here for a white girl." The raised eyebrow remained. Sarah nodded and, before turning to leave, took note of Kat's curled grey quasi-afro and how it reminded her of a similar haircut on one of her elementary school's lunch ladies. It was endearing, almost familial.

Martin, being years younger and still owning the face of a child, had a harder time acquiring employment. His first efforts, being attracted to the idyllic visions of vacationing beachgoers, were applied at the banana raft and Sea-Doo rental tent. He was dismissed, with the wave of hands, as an overly eager child drawn to the watercraft. These things spelled out liabilities.

So, for the first few days, while Sarah accustomed herself to what essentially amounted to motel room scatology, Martin was entrusted with the majority of the remaining cash funds to perform other chores. He dropped in and shyly purchased a few outfits for the two from Goodwill far down the strip. It brought their stash down to a total of twenty-six dollars. A quarter from the change he diverted to acquiring a blue gumball. He chewed it eagerly as he hiked through the grass highway shoulder drooling blue juice down his cheek in the rank humidity.

During the tail end of his return trip, he came upon a yard sale in front of one of the more gaudy doublewide trailers at Lagoon. There he handed the silent fat man two dollars for a mostly full bottle of Deet deep woods bug spray, an afghan blanket, and a battery-powered lantern. Then he sat alone, in the cramped and dank tree house. There was nothing for him to do and no one to talk to. The sounds of birds and the wide river overtook him. He felt forgotten by the world.

Over the next weeks, Martin spent most of his time strolling the beach and eavesdropping on vacationers. He had acquired a couple of beach towels, flip flops, sunglasses, a wallet, and a book bag left behind by multitasking fathers and errant late night bonfire partiers. While toddlers waddled into the surf for the first time, ecstatic camera-faced mothers in tow, Martin would nap atop the fruits of his scavenging and dream of his mother, his mother who had been taken from him.

While preteens, kids his age, were attempting to skim board he would wonder about where Miles would end up. He wasn't sure Wicker Home would still exist after what had happened. And he wanted to know why Jemmy's friend helped them get away, and why they were brought here. The questions kept coming as he basked in the sounds of a normal life he would never fit into. He wondered how many other isolated kids like him and Sarah had been shuffled to the side of life by woeful forces out of their control, without families, unattached outcasts and drifters.

It was during these sun drenched afternoon beach naps that Martin fully came to see how good it had been back on the orchards and the farms. Even though it was only he and his mother, there were so many familiar faces with so similar lives that it felt social, it felt like belonging. There were friends and routines and rules. There were surrogate aunts and uncles. The longing to return to those days stung strong.

But Martin recalled that even then, in what now seemed to be the good old days, he longed for what was outside. He had wanted to be enrolled in school and have a father who came home at 6:00 p.m. on weekdays and complained about politics. And so he now wondered if maybe everyone felt outcast, even those children on the beach surrounding him. They were the protagonists of his American idyll. Yet, maybe they too were inwardly sullen and lonely and wishing for something more. He wondered if that was how most everyone felt.

The origin of this want began to nag at him. He thought about his longing for that other, better, normal life and whether it had been programed into him through the few movies he saw. He searched his memory for hints that it came from his mother. Experiencing the way the field hands were treated on the migrant circuits might make anyone wish for a better life. Martin didn't settle on a final answer. The considerations involved scared him. He transitioned to ogling the abundant bikini cleavage. He wanted to have sex again. It had been so long, since before Wicker Home.

He had shoved his few possessions into his pack and was walking along the strip of surf shops and seafood restaurants when a voice called out to him. "Oye, you there!" Martin stopped and turned. It was a skinny boy in black jeans and buttoned-up jean shirt. His clothing seemed absurd to Martin, given the heat. He didn't respond. The boy was at the brick corner of the convenience store leading into an alleyway entrance to the public beach.

"Come here. It's okay, come on!" the boy called, waving Martin over and shooting his head around furtively. Martin thought of running, but his curiosity and boredom got the best of him, and he complied with the stranger's request. "Good, you're in. You can be look out," the boy said, pointing around to indicate where to be looking out. He spoke impressively fast and over enunciated. "You have to work your way up to doing the actual job. It's harder than it looks. I fucked it up my first go around. I'm Fitz, by the way. Them's Wombat." He pointed to another similarly dressed teenager, who was hunched over one of three pay phones in a bay, finagling and tapping angrily.

Martin squinted and said, "Are you—"

"There is a lot more money than you would expect. We got just over fifty bucks last time. Twenty-five split two ways, uh, um, little less, three ways now. We'll split it three ways, right? Good. Okay, crow sounds to warn us. Like, *ca-ca ca-ca*." And with that he ran over to assist Wombat.

There were people all around. The alley was right off of the main thoroughfare. So it seemed wildly impractical to Martin for them to expect not to get caught or at least spotted and have to scurry off. But the theft exhilarated him, and so he stood at the corner looking as casual as he possibly could. He crossed his legs and leaned into the brick, whistling nervously a little under his breath. The families strolled right past him on the sidewalks, never even noting his presence. They just walked on, absorbed in their own vacation bliss or frustrations.

One younger girl with a rapidly melting ice-cream cone in one hand and her other hand in her father's, looked up at Martin and then back upon Wombat and Fitz, who were grunting and arguing. Martin watched her little face shift from blank acceptance to frightened curiosity. She lowered the cone outward and it was torn from her grasp by the other corner of the alleyway as she was pulled along by her father's grasp. Her eyes stayed on the phone booth thieves until she was gone. "Oye!" Fitz hollered back at Martin while Wombat finished stuffing the dismantled payphone body under his loose shirt. "Great success. Come on."

He chased after Fitz and Wombat through the sand below the backside patios of all the restaurants along the main strip and then across an empty portion of the beach and down under the fishing pier. In the shade below the intersection of the boardwalk and the pier, Wombat fell harshly upon his knees in the cool sand and uncovered his bounty. Fitz and Martin kneeled across from him, the three of them catching their breath and scanning the area for others. Martin wondered how old his new fiends were and guessed about sixteen.

The footsteps on the boardwalk and pier above were loud and made the wooden beams underneath vibrate. Seagulls fluttered and cooed from nests tucked into the trusses and crannies. Thin slivers of sunlight shining through the planks made bright pinstripes through the darkness. "All right, man. You did good. And you kept up," Wombat said to Martin, still breathing hard. "I sure know how to picks, huh?" Fitz said, smiling as he patted Wombat's exposed pale belly.

"Alright, alright. So we're a trio now," Wombat said, pulling his shirt back down..

Once content with their solitude, Fitz stood up and looked down upon his conspirators. "Okay. You guys protect the goods, and I'll go get the pick." Wombat nodded dismissively, still struggling to catch air. Fitz took off into the darkness where light and wood disappeared into the black sand under the foot of the pier. Then for a moment it was only Martin and Wombat, who was finally slowing his gasps and breathing through his nostrils.

"That was the easy part, really," Wombat said. "Getting it open is much harder and takes a whole lot longer. And it's all change too. Which is annoying, but money is money, right?" Martin nodded, excited for what lay ahead. He was tickled by the fortunate turn that his day had taken. All of his thoughts about loneliness and his fevered feelings had subsided. Here, under the pier with Wombat and Fitz, he was a part of something. Something fun.

With this understanding, it became urgent within Martin to make sure that this excursion would not be a onetime affair. These were his new buds, and he was their lookout. It was so much better than scavenging and napping along the beach, trying to blend in. It had to happen again. And again. He was going to make sure of it.

Fitz came jogging back with a long pickaxe over his shoulder. Martin stepped back as Wombat and Fitz took turns throwing all their might into swinging the pick down hard against the steel box. The blows cracked loudly and Martin looked upward, convincing himself that the boardwalk was loud enough to drown out the swings. Each blow emitted bright sparks from the friction. They looked like little firecrackers in the middle of the night sky. After some two and a half hours of laboring, almost to the point of both swingers being clearly exhausted, their shoulders slouched under drenched buttoned-up denim, the reservoir of coins was exposed through a sliver of the pick's bite.

Wombat pulled a used grocery store bag from his back pocket, and he and Fitz poured the coins slowly into it. Martin once again kept lookout, as best he could through the narrow pinstripes. The two veterans then counted their bounty, one quarter at a time, moving them from the bag and back into the phone reservoir as they tallied. The total was $32.75. Martin agreed to settle for $10.00 even since it was his first venture, and he did not help out with any of the disassembling or the pickaxe swinging.

"Thanks for being so swell about that. You did well. Tomorrow. Two o'clock. Meet us under the Dundee Hot Dog Cabana. You know where that is? Can you get there?" Fitz asked, getting real close to Martin.

"Yeah, I'll be there. For sure. Right at two o'clock under the Dundee Cabana," Martin answered with the enthusiasm of a believer on Christmas morning. It brought a smile to Fitz. He wrapped his arm around Martin's neck and pulled his head tight into his wet pit. It was hot and foul but Martin did not resist.

Fitz looked down at Martin and spoke more slowly. "You are our lookout now. Reason we needed you was our last lookout grew a conscience. You're not going to grow a conscience are you? I mean, you did take some of that money already, didn't you?" Martin could understand that this was a test. Fitz was feeling him out. He closed his eyes and pictured Aurelia's smiling face. He couldn't tell if the image was a memory or a dream, but she seemed to be supporting him, encouraging him.

"Hell no. No conscience here," he said, reopening his eyes.

Fitz studied him sternly and then grinned ear to ear. "Well look at that, Wombat. He's a natural!" He turned toward Wombat, Martin's head still in his pit. "Isn't he?"

Wombat had dug a deep hole in the sand with the pick end of the axe and was presently pushing the evidence of their crime down within. Once fitted therein, he began pushing the excavated sand over the phone with cupped hands. He did not acknowledge Fitz.

"Wombat!" Fitz howled. Wombat turned his head only slightly and continued on in his task. "He did good today, didn't he?"

Wombat grunted. "Yes, you've already told him so several times. Haven't you? You two boyfriends now?"

Fitz chuckled, delighted with the jest. "What, ya afraid you're mom will be jealous?" This grabbed Wombat's attention, who was clearly not as amused by the heightened slight. Fitz said, "He needs to hear from you. So that it's unanimous. Remember?" Wombat stood up, having finished covering the hole. He shoved Fitz sideways and grabbed Martins shoulders. Wombat's irises were so dark they looked black.

"You were ok. Good enough. So we'll see you tomorrow then, right?"

The intensity of his look and the severity of his tone quieted Martin's enthusiasm. "Yes," he said.

"Okay, now run along!" Wombat said, slapping Martin's behind with his sandy palm. Martin exited the pier's underside looking over his shoulder. When he reached sunlight, he could no longer see his new friends but only hear laughter and undecipherable chitchat.

He had tossed his share of quarters into the bottom of his book bag's main compartment, and they hopped and crunched together rhythmically with each of his strides. The pack pushed his T-shirt up into a wad below his shoulders and rubbed against his sweaty lower back. Martin replayed the events of the afternoon over and over in his mind. The anticipation and excitement to show Sarah what he had accomplished was nearly unbearable. But she wouldn't be off of work at Sandpiper for many hours.

Sarah opened the tree house door at a quarter past ten. Martin practically tackled her at once. "Easy, easy. What's going on," Sarah said noting the presence of the lantern and the blankets.

"I'm a thief! A bandit. I stole a pay phone, and well, my share is ten dollars!" Martin shouted, his face aglow.

"What? Your share?" Sarah asked, pushing Martin down upon his butt on the cot.

"Well, yeah, Wombat and Fitzy, they took their shares too. They were a little bigger because they knew how to do everything. But I kept lookout, and I mean, it was so sweet." Martin slid the book bag out from under the cot and unzipped it to show her the money. She took the bag and sat down next to him.

"Okay, so you met some boys and stole a payphone." She was somewhat annoyed at the seeming stupidity involved in what she considered a hoodlum act. But she was also somewhat impressed, even relieved. It would be a week before her first check would come to her, and they could use more cash in the meantime. She also didn't have the spirit, especially after her long and disheartening first shift, to dampen Martin's. She was glad to see him happy. And besides, she wasn't his mother.

The two talked for a while that night before getting to bed. Sarah took possession of the quarters and planned out a budget. Martin told her all about the heist and his new friends. He explained that they were going to strike again the next day. It was clear to Sarah that he sought permission from her. She felt heavy with responsibility as the perceived adult. "Martin," she said, "just be really careful. You don't know these boys, and I'm not sure what will happen to us if we get into trouble. I won't be able to protect you if you get arrested. I won't be able to do anything."

Sarah's words sunk deeply into Martin and irked him. He desired so earnestly not to disappoint her. In fact, the thought broke his heart. He said, "I won't get caught. I promise." That was the last thing said before they turned off the lantern and lay down to sleep. Sarah, whose feet and back ached from the day's labor, fell into deep sleep after a minute or two of trying to memorize the names of her coworkers that had thrown scattered Spanish at her and mimed her orders. She hadn't smoked any cigarettes since getting off work.

Martin took a little longer to fall asleep. The insects outside were roaring, and though the bug spray mostly performed, occasionally a mosquito did break through and find blood. He detected the kerplunks and splashes of unknown creatures moving in and out of the river below. The wooden planks in the walls and floor creaked and moaned, stretching with the micromovements of the fig tree. It seemed that the forest was trying to intimidate him.

Some hours later, after he was asleep, he dreamt he was a professional cat burglar. He wore all-black tights and scaled the sides of modern skyscrapers, breaking into chic minimalist-decorated apartments belonging to wealthy businessmen. There, he'd crack safes and dismantle expensive paintings from their wall fixtures. He'd retreat into a hidden bungalow in some corner of the woods where Sarah would be waiting, chain smoking and looking through a giant telescope, which his money had purchased. They'd smile at one another, content that they needed no one else.

The dream brought a smile to Martin's unconscious face. He didn't wake up until nearly noon, his right cheek covered in layers of slobber and sticking to the pillow. The heat and attendant humidity was already oppressive and unwelcoming. Martin longed for the northern weather. He wished for air conditioning. Sarah had already left for her shift but a note was on her folded blanket. Martin grabbed it and read:

> Remember to be careful.
> I will see you tonight.
> P.S. Buy A Fan!!!!
> – Sarah

Sarah kept Mason's goofy smile present in her mind throughout the day as she obediently pushed the supplies cart from room to room along the exposed passageway. Once inside a room, Clarita would direct her like a musical maestro, with hand movements abounding. And she'd spit out Spanish like a threatened bulldog. Sarah kept her head down and tried her best to be fastidious and learn fast. However, Clarita's harsh tones were always received as grating invective.

The shift went by quickly enough; it was tiring work and they were always on the move. Besides, the exposed two stories provided clear line of sight to watch most of the guests coming and going. Sarah saw very quickly that the two main types of guests were middle-class businessmen and bargain-shopping families on vacation. The businessmen's rooms were tidy and sparse, usually several empty glasses of booze or beers at the desk with an array of papers and notes. The families' rooms were a cluttered wreck of suitcases, child bathing suits, and all varieties of half-eaten leftovers from local restaurants carelessly strewn on the chairs and dressers.

But there was something special going on in the last rooms at the far end of the first and second floors. These rooms abutted the alleyway, and every couple of hours, a man and younger woman in heels would enter and then exit not long after. Sarah was busy and it was tough to get a good take on the situation while under Clarita's iron fist, but the couples always seemed uncomfortable and moving faster than necessary. Sarah instantly guessed that the rooms were being rented out to prostitutes.

Clarita and Sarah never cleaned these two rooms. They were handled by Jamejam's second in command, Roselle. And she would always wait until Clarita and Sarah and the other two maids, Coco and Maria, were done with their rounds and inside doing the laundry and other duties. This portion of the shift was the most lonesome and boring, because Sarah was outnumbered. Clarita, who was unmistakably the queen bee among the maids, Coco, and Maria would all circle around and laugh and gossip while loading and emptying the washers and dryers. It seemed like gossiping to Sarah. She did pick out words here and there, the easy ones like, *gato* and *mujere blanca*. They'd all turn their heads to her and lose their smiles and then grow real quiet for a bit.

The laundry room was located beneath the front office. Four washers and four dryers. The room was air-conditioned, and it provided a nice respite from the heat. But the accumulated sweat from the afternoon rounds would cool and dry at the small of Sarah's back, under her knees, and in her pits. She'd get chills, and the heat would be welcomed back when the maids reemerged from below, clanking the glass doors open and pushing the plastic carts piled high with stacks of clean sheets, pillow cases, and towels.

The entire motel was concrete and stucco, painted beige. Along each and every interior and exterior wall surface were three stripes of yellow, orange, and red stretching out toward a pink orb at one end that emulated the setting sun. For any temporary visitor, especially one at the beginning of a much-needed tropical getaway, the color scheme and layout was inviting and refreshing. But for Sarah, it became oppressive.

The white sand beach and the turquoise water, the sound of the tides and the smell of salty surf had initially taken her in. It was a paradise to her, a place she'd only previously visited in film and books. But after several shifts at the Sandpiper, she began to loathe the beach paradise. She narrowed her mental vocabulary down to sunburn and fish smell. She had to reapply sun lotion a dozen times a day to keep from turning raw, and the oily substance oozed over her pores and combined with her sweat to form some kind of ubersweat. And everything, everything smelled like coconut.

It was as if all the signifiers of an ocean getaway—the seafood, the watercraft, the inescapable seashell motifs, the sound of Styrofoam noodles, the smell of chlorine, sunglass reflections—had all ganged up and began taunting Sarah.

Between this phenomenon and the disdainful Spanish Clarita hurled at her, she started to get down on herself.

And after all of this, she'd have to slink back to an un-air-conditioned tree house and put on a brave face for Martin. She began to wonder if they had gotten anyplace better than Wicker Home. She was grateful there was no Corin, but there, they didn't have to work. It was clean and they had comfortable beds. Full meals were cooked for them. She'd come around after thinking in this way for a little while. She knew she was just struggling with being responsible for herself for the first time in her life. If she could survive through the transition, make it past the initial shock and become accustomed to it, the freedom would be much better in the long run.

Things went along this way for some time. It was uneventful and Sarah began to get into a rhythm. The other maids even began warming up to her a bit once she had demonstrated that she was good at the work and didn't complain. Jamejam mostly stayed in the office, watching her little television and checking guests in and out with her charmingly offensive demeanor. And the couples kept going in and out of rooms 1 and 16. Sarah eventually noticed it was the same five or six girls, and this only reaffirmed her suspicion of a prostitution operation. She wondered how much Jamejam was making by renting the rooms out to hookers.

Martin continued stealing phones with Wombat and Fitzy. After three successful heists with them, Wombat walked Martin through the actual theft, and two heists later, Martin was responsible for detaching the reservoir box from the booth. They also began letting him take turns swinging the pick, though he was much less effective than the other two. It was mostly to allow Wombat and Fitz some rest. All in all, Martin had proven himself a quite useful addition to the gang. The three started hanging out when they weren't stealing phones.

Fitz explained that he and Wombat both went to the same high school. "But school is useless, anyway. You can learn all of that stuff at the library, if you really wanted to. So we skip most days. We have our whole lives to get jobs. But we're young now. Wombat has a funny idea that old people should work so that young ones can be retired until a certain age. I mean, we are the ones that can do things with our free time, you know? What use is retirement to some crotchety old geezer who spends all day complaining about dentures and solving crosswords for the billionth time? Uh, and old people sex, don't even get me going on that." Martin would laugh and Wombat would nod his head in agreement.

Neither of them asked for many details about Martin's life. For the most part, they were content to know that he lived with his older sister Sarah in Lagoon. They never wanted to come to his place and they never seemed curious that he wasn't in school. He was their boy, and so long as he kept performing their heists with them, nothing else really mattered.

They stole a surfboard and Wombat tried to show Fitz and Martin how to stand and turn once the swell comes. "You walk it, front first." But the knowledge was lost on both, neither of which made it past a brief stand before crashing down into the wake. They ended up watching Wombat, who had a demonstrated skill. His body was long and gangly atop the board, his black jeans clinging to his narrow legs beneath.

Sarah and Martin would share their days with one another when she returned from her shift at night. With their collective earnings, his thieving yield and her paychecks, they had made the tree house about as comfortable as they could. They had sheets now and a fan that spritzed water from a bottle when you squeezed a handle. They'd each bought and stolen numerous outfits, along with toothbrushes, soap, and conditioner for the public restrooms in Flamingo Lagoon. Sarah installed a lock on the tree house door and they each had a key. There was a

small shelf, which contained an assortment of dry goods. There was a bug-repel-
lent candle.

It was around the time that the tree house became almost a bearable habita-
tion that they started discussing renting a room, a proper apartment. Martin had
grown fond of their little abode in the woods. He fancied himself a renegade of
society, an outcast. It seemed fitting to him to live in a tree house in the woods
where there was no rent and no one to bother them. Martin felt like Robin Hood
living in the woods with his merry band of thieves.

Sarah harbored heavier considerations. First, she worried that the women
who showed them to the tree house in the first place might return to check in or
even bring others there. She didn't know what would happen then. Or if someone
else found them out there, like the police. Plus, though the river had not flooded
again nearly as badly as that first night, Sarah did not rest easy. It was only one
strong storm away from happening. And then all of their improvements on the
structure would be for naught.

But the alternative scared her too. She knew well enough that background
checks were lazy at best in the area, but two teenage-looking kids renting out an
apartment together might raise suspicion. Or worse, it would give the owner some
kind of power over them, some leverage. She briefly considered reaching out to
Jamejam. Based upon her presumption that she was renting out rooms to call
girls, it wasn't a stretch to believe she'd rent out a room to Sarah and Martin in-
definitely.

However, that would mean Sarah would be living at work and that seemed
unappealing. It also wasn't clear that Jamejam would be receptive. The inquiry
might dampen her standing at the Sandpiper. Sarah couldn't risk that because, as
much money as Martin was making with his friends, Sarah's pay from the motel
accounted for the vast majority of their income. She needed the job, and so she
decided to think on the matter longer before making a play.

Her shifts continued on, under the punishing sun that hovered above the state in late spring and into early summer. On a Tuesday, as Sarah was finishing pulling the clean stacks of towels into the maid closet, she caught a man staring at her from the parking lot just beyond the front office. It was a tan man in a linen leisure suit. He had shining chrome sunglasses and he was leaning far back against the hood of a black sedan.

Sarah stood up from the closet shelves and cast a shadow over her face with her palm. The man did not move. His face was deeply wrinkled around the glasses, which concealed any details behind them. He bit his lip a little. The moment of staring lasted longer than Sarah was comfortable with. Just as she contemplated retreat, the man turned quickly and trotted into the front office. His dress loafers clicked against the blacktop as he moved with long, measured strides. It was the way of a man without worry. Sarah's gaze followed him until he disappeared into the dark office, its double doors rattling closed behind him.

Though she was not unaware of the attention of men, Sarah had never been ogled so openly and so directly. It made her skin crawl, as if the stranger had somehow touched her without even reaching conversation distance. The interaction reran in her mind as she finished her shift, and she walked with a little more caution on her way back to the tree house that evening.

It may have been that the stare reiterated to Sarah just how fragile her and Martin's situations was. They had no one to protect them, and any recourse to someone that could would likely result in their return to Wicker Home or someplace worse, which Sarah's imagination always struggled to conjure but she knew inevitably existed. She withheld this rumination from Martin, who seemed to be contented in his new surroundings.

Wednesday, as Sarah was putting on her uniform and closing up her locker, Coco poked her head around the hallway entrance. "Jamejam want you, now!"

Sarah slinked into the office, hyper vigilant for any unusual attention, as her recent experiences had taught her to be.

Jamejam met her with a scowl. "Have a seat, doll," she said, pointing to one of the barstools against the office counter. A barely audible rerun episode of *The Brady Bunch* played on the little angled TV. Sarah situated herself and waited for Jamejam to turn her gaze away from the show.

"This motel does well enough. But part of that is the business we can depend on from a few of our benefactors. This constant business is vital in such a spotty tourist economy. It keeps income reliable, treads through the lulls. You follow?" She finally looked at Sarah directly. Sarah nodded though she had not the faintest notion of why Jamejam was telling her this. She'd learned long ago that in these situations it was best to feign understanding long enough to actually arrive at it.

"Mr. Knudsen is one of these benefactors. It sounds like you two have already been acquainted." Sarah did not follow. "Well, he…How do I say? He's taken an interest in you. Something about a Nordic goddess." Jamejam dismissed the phrase with a wave of her hand. "Men, you know how they get sentimental. If it's not something about their mother, then it's an adventure book they read as a kid. Tinto's sister, you know? Or do you know?" she asked. Sarah did not respond, still working on deciphering what Jamejam was attempting to communicate.

"He's taken an interest in you. And he asked me if it would be appropriate to approach you. Mr. Knudsen knows very well how much I value a good employee. You haven't been here long, but I can see you're going to be one of the good ones. So I told him that I would ask you. It's not a bad opportunity." Jamejam awaited a response. Sarah said, "I'm not sure that I understand…" Jamejam smiled, a bit amused at the innocence, the naivety, in front of her.

"Mr. Knudsen has pull around here, he has money. A lot of it. If you were inclined to spend some time getting to know him, he might be tempted to help you out." Jamejam could see Sarah still lagging behind and decided to speed it up. "He wouldn't expect anything right at first. Just dinner. And he'd likely enjoy hearing any stories that you have. Or, do you enjoy singing?"

The terror of the position was now sinking into Sarah. "Um, no not really," she said.

"Well, that's too bad. Knudsen enjoys a good voice." Then the two sat silent for a moment. *The Brady Bunch* now seemed much louder as two voices argued about something involving a broken lamp. "Look honey, you don't have to give me an answer right now. Think it over. But like I said, Mr. Knudsen is very important to the Sandpiper. He's very important to us keeping staff on, you understand? And, things being as they are, he's not an unpleasant man." Jamejam managed a conciliatory smile and then returned her attention to the little TV.

Sarah left the office in a daze of horror and confusion. Reflecting during her shift, she pieced together that, at a minimum, she was required to go on a date with Mr. Knudsen to keep working at Sandpiper. Coco, Maria, and Clarita's gossip and chitchat seemed more sinister than usual. It was unclear whether they knew anything about the proposition, but they seemed to be somehow linked to its general unfairness. Mostly, Sarah wanted to be mad at someone because she had already decided she would say yes.

Later that evening, when she informed Jamejam that Mr. Knudsen could approach her, Jamejam closed her eyes and pursed her lips. It was the look of someone deeply satisfied, proud even. Sarah didn't find Jamejam familial looking anymore. Instead she appeared like a haggard, wizened witch. Someone who had been shit all over so many times, she forgot there was anything else in this world.

Once again, Sarah kept all of this private from Martin. She was making a habit of parceling off information with which she felt she need not burden him. It made her feel like she was declaring herself the adult. It also made her lonesome and troubled. Conversation dwindled between the two over the next few days while she waited for her introduction to Knudsen. During those days, Martin had been spending so much time surfing and running through the thoroughfare with Wombat and Fitz that he often was already sleeping by the time Sarah made her way into the tree house.

The thought, which made Sarah feel the most confident in her decision, was that she could stop it all if she were uncomfortable. If Knudsen wanted something she wasn't willing to give over, she could flee. She held on to this thought. After all, Jamejam had assured her of it. She figured there was still a chance that Knudsen was a nice man, as she had been told. But in the back of Sarah's mind, she entertained a dark intuition that he wanted her to become some kind of sex toy for him to use at his discretion. She felt helpless.

It was that Friday when Mr. Knudsen finally approached her. Sarah and Clarita had swung the door open to begin on Room 9. Clarita looked up and there he sat on the edge of the bed. He was again wearing a tan leisure suit and sunglasses. Clarita froze in her tracks. "Afternoon ladies. Sorry to intrude," he said with a southern drawl. Sarah, who was pulling the cart backward into the doorway, stopped and turned at the sound of his voice. Mr. Knudsen stood and removed his sunglasses, tucking them into his chest pocket. Sarah noted that the skin beneath did not appear tan anymore but more pinkish and sallow, like a sunburned pig. However, his features weren't unpleasant.

"Miss Clarita, if you would be so kind as to excuse us for a few moments. I'd like to have just a brief conversation with young Miss Sarah here," he said, extending his hand out to Clarita's elbow and directing her past the cart and out of the room. He left the door open and spun back to Sarah. "Pleased to make your acquaintance. My name is Damon Knudsen. You should call me Damon." He gently grasped her hand, bent forward and kissed its back. His lips left a cold oval.

"Please, come have a seat with me. I am just dying to get to know you a little," he said, pulling the chair out from the desk for her to sit in. He smelled like pepper and garlic, almost like Chinese food. It was pungent and of curious origin. She sat in the chair, keeping silent. She noted that there were two Sandpiper Inn complementary pens in her apron, which could be used to stab if need be. She resolved to check on them regularly.

Muffled laughter came from the next room over. Sarah and Clarita had just passed by the room, and she remembered that, inside, a father was crawling around on the carpet with two young girls on his back. Another boy was jumping on the bed. The proximity of the others comforted her. The large air-conditioning register hummed from behind the bed on which Mr. Knudsen sat himself.

"Mrs. Jamejam doesn't seem to know much about you, Sarah. But she was adamant that you were a dearly valued employee of the Sandpiper Inn. She has a talent for, well…for finding talent." Mr. Knudsen raised his eyebrows and chuckled, rocking his head side to side. He calmed and gave Sarah a conspiratorial wink. She remained silent. "You don't speak much do you?" Sarah forced her eyes up to meet his but did not say anything. Mr. Knudsen smiled. "Look, I don't bite. In fact, I am what they call a pacifist. Means I don't fight. Old Luck—er, Mrs. Jamejam and I have been in various businesses together for a while. We have a habit of checking in on one another, and well, it's always in my interest to follow up with employees she praises."

Sarah nodded and said, "She's been good to me. It's been fine working here." She could tell he was pleased to hear her voice.

He straightened up his back and said, "Well, I'm tickled to hear that. Is there anything else that you need, any issues I could help clear up, Sarah?"

She estimated he desired a "yes" to his question. "No. Like I said, its been good working here. I'm grateful."

Mr. Knudsen smiled despite feeling miffed at losing the opportunity to intercede on her behalf. He wanted this girl, in every way. He loved her untamed hair and the feisty aspect of her demeanor. But he was unsure how much she knew of the kind of game they were playing. So, he decided he would consider her a beginner.

"Do you like Cajun food?" he asked.

"I've never had it. What is it exactly?"

Her interest enticed him. "Well, Sarah, its spicy. Do you like spicy food?" he asked, stretching his legs apart, his beige suit pants riding up his socked shins. Sarah could hear his ankles cracking as he lifted his heels off of the carpet.

"I love spicy food," she said, "just not seafood. It's not seafood is it?"

He shook his head and lowered his heels. "Doesn't have to be. It's mostly just Cajun because of the spices and the sauce. But there is a wide variety of meats and vegetables in the entrees." Sarah nodded, checking in on the pens.

Mr. Knudsen pulled forward the pant-leg fabric at his knees, tightening it around his crotch. Sarah glimpsed the outline of his penis within. An involuntary grimace crossed her face, and she worried about its detection. Mr. Knudsen had been concentrating on the peach fuzz over her earlobes. He could barely make them out through the sun-bleached strands spilling around the side of Sarah's neck and jawline. He cleared his throat and said, "Crawls, down on 19, has the best jambalaya I have ever ingested." He leaned forward and cupped one side of his mouth. "Don't let my mother find out I told you that." He straightened back up and winked. Sarah displayed an obligatory but effective smile in response.

"Well, it is divine cuisine and plenty of turf options for you, Sarah." She noted the outline was gaining size within the bunched triangle. Mr. Knudsen noticed her shifting eyes and his smile deepened. "And, well, I would be delighted if you joined me over dinner. Mrs. Jamejam explained you have Sundays off. I'll pick you up here at 6:00 o'clock?" he said, somewhere between question and command. The impending finality of the dinner soured Sarah's insides. But she felt compelled, if only to not muddy the water at Sandpiper.

"Okay," she said flatly, "I'll be here."

Mr. Knudsen's smile reached its pinnacle before he grew serious. He said, "And Sarah, let's see if we can't find something that helps with this, uh, quiet nature of yours. See if I can't get you livened up. I already have a few ideas about that." And with that he stood up. The triangle dissipated but the outline beneath it was as visible as ever and now at Sarah's eye level. She pushed the chair back and stood up.

The two were face to face. Mr. Knudsen pulled his sunglasses out and slid them onto his little nose. "Well Sarah, it was a pleasure making your acquaintance. I won't keep you any longer. Wouldn't want you to get behind and fall out of Mrs. Jamejam's good graces."

Sarah said, "Oh, right." He pulled her hand up from her apron pocket and kissed it again. He turned swiftly and, as he strolled through the door, called out, "Until Sunday." Then he was gone.

Sarah spent the rest of Friday performing her duties like a zombie. Inside, she was beating herself up for being so compliant with Mr. Knudsen. The image of the outline would not leave her mind. And it had become entirely clear that continuing forward with him would entail getting very intimate with that outline. And, though she had figured that he smelled like spices because he had been eating Cajun, she couldn't help but imagine the outline smelling like hot spices as well. It made her gag a little. Clarita raised an eyebrow, curious if her coworker was getting sick.

The situation stunk. She knew that she needed to play it cool. But she also wondered if the young prostitute girls at the end of the motel had once been asked out to Crawls for jambalaya. The girls didn't seem much older than Sarah. She wondered where they had come from, how they ended up selling themselves several times a day in a midrange motel on a vacation strip. And she wondered about Knudsen's ideas about how to liven her up. She guessed it was an allusion to alcohol.

These thoughts crowded and bumped against one another. Again the feeling of helplessness returned, as if she were not in control of the forces in her life. It made her angry as hell and she snapped at Martin a couple times that night when he pushed her for details about work. "Enough, dammit! I'm tired. I'm going to sleep." And she laid in her cot for hours, stewing with a growing hatred for Knudsen, for Jamejam who was complicit, for the dumb young girls that were foolish and weak enough to ruin their lives, for the whole beach community full of its vacationing families. It was only spring, and the crowds were bad. She didn't want to think about how out of control the tourists will be in late summer.

All of the night sounds coalesced again. The teeming of the forest and the bugs and the river—it made her skin crawl. It felt like one big pressure point stretching over her entire body. Her mind frantically tried to find ways to escape. She wondered if it was time to go find Mason. Again, she thought about the women that brought them to the tree house. She could picture them somehow in cahoots with Knudsen. She even thought it possible they knew Clarita or Coco or Maria.

Saturday's shift passed uneventfully. Sarah performed her tasks efficiently but perfunctorily, inwardly distressed and focused elsewhere. Clarita, who never really took any interest in Sarah, noticed the difference but paid it no mind. She had her own troubles brewing at home. And it wasn't her job to look after a young girl. Clarita had two girls of her own, and they were almost teenagers and beginning to pay attention to the neighborhood boys.

Around eight o'clock, Sarah heard a strange sound as she was unlocking the dumpster in the alleyway to drop off the last of the day's garbage bags. It was a shrill squeaking coming from behind an adjacent dumpster. Sarah dropped the garbage bags and reached into her apron pocket and pinched the head of a pen, as had become her custom over the previous days while ruminating on her hatred of all things. She approached the corner slowly.

"Hello? Is there someone over there?" she asked, tiptoeing closer. The sound stopped. Sarah reached out and placed her free hand on the edge of the green dumpster and slowly leaned in to get a look around its side. The whole alley was hazy with the orange afterglow of dusk. Sarah could see a young girl lying in the alley, her back up against the wall. It was one of the girls who frequented the rooms at the end. This was the first time Sarah had seen any of them in close proximity. She realized the girl was even younger than she had first thought, per-haps even younger than herself. The girl's shirt was askew and her skirt was hiked up on her midsection so that her undies were exposed. Sarah noted dark track marks on her forearm and thighs.

"Oh my god, are you alright?" Sarah asked. The girl cocked her head up-ward and smiled absently. The girl said, "Hey friend. I just need a minute. Have to catch my…" The girl continued moving her lips as if she was speaking but no sounds were coming out. It was obvious to Sarah that she was loaded. Judging by the marks on her limbs, it was from something in a needle. It was a pitiful sight, painful to look at, and it concentrated all of Sarah's anger. She saw her future.

In that moment, Sarah fantasized about murdering Knudsen. She fantasized about cutting off that outline and also murdering Jamejam and her stepfather who had made improper advances toward her, always rubbing the small of her back in circles. She condemned the whole world as a worthless piece of shit, full of hei-nous beasts that didn't take care of their children, one giant meat grinder. Sarah refused to become processed meat.

She let go of the pen and reached behind the girl's back, hoisting her up, an arm over Sarah's shoulder. She was thin and light. It was easy for Sarah to walk with her in this manner, even with her plastic heels dragging along the concrete. They made their way to the corner of the alley, next to the rooms at the end of Sandpiper. Sarah scoped out the facade and parking lot. No one was around, and it was now dark enough that they would have cover. She could see the flicker of the little television through the double doors of the front office. Sarah helped the girl out of the parking lot and across the main strip at the light and headed west, back toward Lagoon. She took a break to rip off her maid apron. She watched it fall and lie in the grass beside 19, pink and white curled over dark green. The image brought her great pleasure.

There were always drunks stumbling to and fro along the strip. College boys were often carrying their incapacitated buddies back to their hotel rooms while woo-hooing and laughing. They didn't look out of place at all, making their way along as they were. They received a whistle from a black pick up truck as they were nearing the entrance to Lagoon. "You're comfy...mmmmm," the girl said into Sarah's neck. It was hot and tickled.

Martin was not home when Sarah and the girl arrived. She had left a good hour before her shift was up. It struck terror in her as she realized that Clarita and, likely, Jamejam were probably already looking for her and wondering what had happened. Add that to the fact that she had become paranoid about who knew that she and Martin were living in the tree house, and she began to feel very anxious about waiting there for Martin to return. He was always there when she got off, so she knew he shouldn't be long.

Sarah unlocked the door and slung the girl into her cot. Her lips were still mouthing nonexistent words mixed with the occasional grunt or sigh of delight. Meanwhile, Sarah scurried about collecting clothing and supplies and shoving them into a plastic grocery bag. Martin's backpack was absent. She then pulled out the ziplock bag from between two floorboards, sat on Martin's cot, and began recounting all of the pay she had saved to make sure her previous accounting was correct.

There was a grand total of $211. But Martin had been keeping his earnings in the pack, a lot of it in coin wrappers. Sarah hovered over the girl and shook her. "Hey, what's your name?" she asked.

The girl smiled widely and replied, "Betsy. I'm either a briar patch or a ramekin..." The words droned out woozily and faded. Sarah tried to make sense of the meaning. Betsy curled into herself and returned to her low humming.

Outside, Martin was making his way up the ladder. He was whistling the melody to "Johnny Comes Marching Home" and synching his climb to the beat of it. His whistling ceased when he swung the door open upon Sarah and Betsy on the bed. "What the..." he said, gaping. He was amused more than perplexed, but confused nonetheless. Sarah stood and approached him with an alarming seriousness.

"We have to get out of here, out of town," she said. "Tonight. People will be looking for us now; they may know where to find us; I'm not sure about it, but...Oh God, I'm not sure about anything except that we need to leave." The rarity of the pitch in her voice scared Martin.

"Why?" he said. "Who is she? What happened?" His otherwise good day was turning sour. He passed by Sarah and looked down at Betsy. Her gratuitous eye makeup had been smeared and reached the far corners of her face. Her hair had been styled and doused with spray, but it was shaped now like someone's that had just awoken: asymmetrical and bulbous. "What a mess," he said.

Sarah, standing behind him, took a deep breath. "That's Betsy. She is a prostitute, or...well..." Martin turned to her, his fear growing in proportion to the confusion of the situation. She took his hands and sat him next to her on the free cot, avoiding eye contact. "Look, its Sandpiper. They're not good people. They're selling young girls to older men. And…and, well…" Sarah searched for her words.

Martin watched her and waited. The anticipation reached its crescendo. He yelped, "And *what*?"

She met his eyes. "And I'm pretty sure that's what they hired me for." Martin broke his gaze with her and looked at Betsy, who was still humming lowly and smiling like a lost fool. Martin now saw the track marks and how pale she was. He saw the high heels with chips knocked out of their backs and the scrapes on her legs. And when he pictured Sarah's face instead of Betsy's, his whole being sank.

"Look, kid. I know how much you like it here. You have friends. And that's why I never mentioned all this to you before. I liked it here too, for a while. I thought it was something I could manage on my own. But *this*, this is too much. If I stay here I'm going to die, *or worse*. I mean, look at her. She's younger than me." Martin imagined what must have happened along the way for this girl to end up like this. The bitterness about his good day turning sour disappeared and was replaced by a familiar anger.

"Kid, we've been together every step of the way. You're the only family I really have. So I want you to come with me. I need you to come with me. And I also think that you need to come with me. I was going to offer you half of the money and let you stay here. But, like I said, I don't know who all is in on this. Or how. I'm not even sure if Jemmy's boyfriend was doing us a favor or not. If you stayed, someone might come looking. And that might not work out so well for you."

Martin considered Sarah's words gravely. Even though he had so enjoyed running around with Wombat and Fitzy, as Sarah had just made clear, they were family, the only one he had. Having concluded this, a wellspring of camaraderie and admiration jolted forth within him. He turned back to her and said, "Ok.

Where are we going to go?"

Chapter Eighteen

The plot of land at issue in the action to quit title, presently held by the Trams Land Bank and known as Plot 547, was located at 3 Wikstrom Road, just off of Boundary Road. The land, and the entire surrounding region, was originally occupied by a network of Lakota communities, "originally" being approximate in its reach but sufficient in purpose. Oral and drawn Lakota histories demonstrate a sustained presence for what likely amounted to centuries. Such presence inevitably traces backward to the Bering Straight migrations during the last ice age, 10,000–13,000 years ago, the natives being not far removed from Asia. Previous to that, there is no perceptible record of peoples claiming any level of dominion over the land in question. It was uninhabited wilderness.

The first European people to make their way to the region flew the Dutch flag and claimed title of ownership by right of discovery. Not long after this "discovery," a large group of British, members of a rather large corporate trading outfit, arrived in the area led by Lieutenant General Candie. Their private exploratory mission had been subsidized by the crown, and its purpose was to find countryside unknown to all Christian people. In service to achieving this goal, they haughtily denied any claim by the Netherlanders. With dueling national prides at stake, the matter was settled by the sword, and the British came out standing.

Having quashed the competing European interest in the lands, the British turned their considerations to what claim the natives, who were dwelling upon the land, had. It was eventually established that the natives, being un-Christian and heathen in their wildness, could not assert any right to ownership. They were merely occupants, subject to the fluctuations of circumstance attending the greater glory of the Lord and Savior. There, the precedent was set that prior legitimate title flowed back to either the earliest discovery or conquest of the lands by any Christian peoples.

Relations between the British and the Lakota were varied and often bloody. It was a relationship that paralleled that between the crown and its colonies. With the Treaty of Paris in 1783, which concluded the Revolutionary War, Great Britain bitterly relinquished all title to property on the continent that it previously held. These titles passed to the newly formed United States of America government. Letters patent were created, and the entire region was converted into large, geometrically pleasing tracts.

The Lakota, over several decades, both pre and post US independence, became savvy in the procedures of transferring ownership of land as property according to deed. In consonance with measurements made by survey and metes and bounds, Plot 547 was in fact transferred by Lakota tribal leaders to a successful young frontiersman and entrepreneur named Will Dieterbund. He was seeking a location to build a headquarters for his trapping and mining operations as they stretched further west. The Lakota were happy to oblige, both because of the apparent inevitability of encroaching white men and the handsome amount of goldbacked US currency offered up as purchase price. It was an intelligent play because the Lakota inhabited so much land that the relatively tiny parcel they sold off was much more valuable as liquid funds.

The same parcel was subsequently granted by US letters patent to one Samuel Dance in consideration for his accrued agricultural talents. The two men found themselves involved in a sticky and confounding altercation when they both appeared on land supposedly solely owned by each respectively. Dance and Dieter-bund, both being relatively reasonable men, took the matter to court. The case worked its way into the hands of the Supreme Court justices.

The justices, referring back to the previously established principle that land titles were settled by priority of European discovery and that the native peoples held only the right to occupancy, decided that the Lakota had no rights to sell the parcel of land. Indian sovereignty over their lands was limited. Thus, the federal government would intercede in disposition of such lands. Therefore, the Lakota grant to Dieterbund was deemed invalid. Dance was declared the rightful and sole holder of title to the parcel.

Dieterbund, after federal pressure, evacuated the land and Dance began his farm. The farm, though quite small and inhabiting only a very limited portion of the parcel, flourished and was passed down through the Dance bloodline for several generations until Milton Dance died intestate in 1904, and the property, the agricultural operations of which had ceased for lack of passion some decades previous, went to auction to be sold by the local sheriff. The winner of this auction, Gerald H. Ludac, purchased the entirety of the plot for $1,300. As an interesting aside, the auctioneer included a wealth of rumors about the land, including that it was believed to have been haunted by a group of rogue Union Army soldiers under the sway of an evil witch doctor. These stories were supported by the presence of several mysterious and dilapidated structures. Ludac was unfazed by the lore of common folk. His intention was to lease the premises to an industrialist who saw the benefit of the property's location on the edge of the outward expansion that side of Trams.

Hillocks Shoes, which specialized in various work boots, built an operational factory on the site that functioned well into the 1930s, when the company began to experience the economic woes of the nation's deep depression. In a Hail Mary maneuver to garner an influx of liquid assets and offset the encroaching bankruptcy, Mertus Hillocks, grandson of Hillocks Shoes founder, Robert Hillocks, sold the property, the factory, and all attachments, including the company's goodwill, wholesale in 1935. He sold to one Conor Barrett, who saw the possibility of holding the property for value and selling for profit further down the road. The purchase price was $16,200.

World War II allowed Barrett the opportunity to volunteer his purchased factory and property to aid in the war effort. The US government paid to retrofit the factory, and from 1941 to 1946, tank chassis, walling, and A-31 Vengeance dive bomber cockpits were manufactured therein, predominantly by women who were joining in the nationwide war effort on the home front. Conor, who was in his early thirties when he purchased the property and one of the few individuals that steadily increased his wealth during the Great Depression, volunteered for the war. He served as an officer and was killed by two German soldiers in Foy, Belgium.

The property passed, through trust via last will and testament, to Conor's only granddaughter, Lila Gorman. Lila realized her grandfather's original ambitions and sold the property to Desuchre Industrials, a bulldozer and forklift manufacturer, and for most of the 1960s and 1970s, Desuchre was one of the main positive economic catalysts for Trams, employing some eight thousand workers. The plant increased to nearly four times the size it had been during the war. Business was good for a long time, and many of Trams residents fastened their livelihoods to the health of Desuchre manufacturing.

Beginning in the early 1970s and stretching into the early 1980s, the business began to struggle as new competition from Asia and South America entered the marketplace. The struggles were compounded by intense market failures resulting in a brutal recession in the early 1980s. Desuchre began opening manufacturing plants abroad, where labor and materials could be secured more cheaply.

Eventually, Desuchre was faced with the disheartening proposition of closing the Trams location.

In May of 1983, a series of large town hall meetings took place in Trams's VFW hall. The number of attendees was so great that the crowd leaked outside and folks communicated what was being said down the line, like a giant game of telephone. In the face of quasi-nationalistic invective and drunken badgering, the Desuchre board of directors initiated gouging layoffs over a series of months. When, finally, it was apparent that the plant would die, they issued a stop work mandate and handed off the matter to their CFO and legal counsel to sell off the property.

In what would come to be considered a cowardly betrayal by most Trams citizens, especially those still embittered by Desuchre's folding under market pressures, Desuchre sold its entire operational business interests to Sati Motors, Inc., a Japanese concern that specialized in similar types of bulldozers. It is at this point that the main players involved in the question of present ownership came into play.

Sati Motors, at the time it purchased Desuchre, was experiencing an awkward transition of leadership. This was mostly because their CEO, Ibuki Iwate, resigned for personal reasons, which may or may not have involved perverted sex acts with family members, depending on which rumors you trusted in. The newly elected CEO, Kyo Hosami, and his regime decided to move their regional operation to the city of Benson, which offered more favorable tax incentives and had a much less complicated past with outsourcing.

During this power flux at Sati, the plant sat dormant. One evening in late 1984, a group of some thirty unemployed and inebriated former Desuchre workers formed a mob and decided to burn it down. The foment began at Danny's, before it was revitalized and came to be known as Danny's Bar & Grill. As the group moved up Hjelmstad, more joined in. The final number of participants was nearly one hundred folks.

The plant burned for some thirty minutes before the fire crew was able to manage any semblance of control over the situation. Their arrival and efforts were greeted by resounding booing. The fire left minimal damage, but it served to reinforce for the new Sati heads the greater appeal of Benson. They took their insurance settlement, stripped the plant of most of the manufacturing machinery, which they leased off, and decided to sell the plot to the first one who made an offer.

Daniel Denard offered to purchase the property for $468,000. Sati's new CFO, Sato Takahashi, granted him the deed. Interestingly, Sato made no mention of this sale to anyone else at Sati, and immediately thereafter forgot about the entire transaction. He was working eighty to ninety hours a week and was responsible for handling legal documents pertaining to over seventy locations. CEO Hosami had presigned three copies in anticipation of the sale being attended to without his involvement. One copy of the deed remained at the bottom of a stack in Takahashi's personal records.

Denard's attorney, Pat DuFollet, did not record the transfer of property in the Trams County records, as was required at that time by state statute. Sati, through a unanimous vote of board members as was customary in property transactions for the company, decided to sell the plot to Sumpter Capital, who offered $516,000. The company then, without any interaction with Hosami, assigned a young attorney to the task of handling the transfer of title. He signed the deed over to Joel Sumpter, who quickly had the transaction filed in the Trams County property records.

Pat DuFollet, having realized his failure to file the deed, which he had been delivered, fixed his error by visiting the property records office and filing it. At this point, both Denard and Sumpter believed they held sole marketable title to Plot 547. Neither made any plans for some time, content to sit on the appreciating value of the land as urban sprawl dug in to Trams and the area surrounding Plot 547, previously either industrial or rural lots, turned into condominium plazas, strip malls with upscale grocery stores, corporate campuses, and ritzy restaurants and gastro pubs. Some of the original warehouses and mills were converted to studio apartments.

Bastien Ebersold desired very much to invest some of his inherited wealth in property ventures. The geometrical aspect of property calmed him. It was the theoretically perfect lines cutting into the countryside. This, Bastien found erotic. And he had been approached innumerable times by young strangers, and also some sons of men in his social circles, with aspirations to put together mixed-use plots and populate them with leased-out spaces for businesses. All they needed was start-up capital that did not come from their daddies. They wished to be viewed as self-made, at least as much as one born with plenty can be seen that way.

Joel Sumpter had, in the time between purchase of the plot and Bastien's interest in it, switched gears in his business model. He now owned a small media and production company, which was doing quite well and demanded much of his time. Sumpter was happy to part with his investment, seeing the profit that would be his. The transfer was relatively quick. Ebersold bought the plot in fee simple for $1.4 million.

There was no escrow, as Ebersold was flush and required no loan. The deed was signed and delivered. Bastion himself took a copy to Trams filings. Two days later, a young intern named Trisha slinked down into the basement records room of Trams facilities to file the copy of the deed and transfer of title away. As all those before her assigned to a similar task, she could not possibly have anticipated the disarray she encountered. Bent on causing no commotion, nor increasing her responsibilities in a summer internship, which she was doing to appease disapproving parents, she slapped the copy down upon some leaning stack of papers. One among many in the chaos.

Bastien reached out to Wolfgang Glaubus, of Glaubus, Glaubus. Wolfgang was the son of Flavius Glaubus, a friend of Ebersold senior's. His business plan was the most complete, and he had a proven track record of intelligent choices. His idea was to develop the plot into a self-contained mixed-use community, with apartments, amenities, grocer, bars, and entertainment. They would market it to young professionals as a complete living experience. It would essentially be a whole city's worth of attractions within walking distance.

Bastien and Wolfgang, after securing their title and coming to terms on their collective vision, put several signs up along the edges of the plot and also at the corner where it abutted Boundary Road. The large plastic signs gave notice to all businesses interested in locating within the planned community. They included an architectural rendering of their intended result. Below, were Gluabus, Glaubus and Ebersold Equity logos surrounded by tiny, dense legalese, including phrases such as "subject to zoning approval," "contingent upon approved financing," and "mutual equity claims."

In the years immediately after Denard secured his deed and title in the property, Trams city planners, city commissioners, architects and prominent business owners came together to form a plan for the ultimate residential and commercial center. It was their response to the recession on the early 1980s, caused by the exodus of skilled labor and manufacturing jobs. The catalyst was contact from officers of Ziltban, a Fortune 20 pharmacology company. They expressed interest and a great deal of forethought in constructing a thirty-million-dollar research facility on the unrestricted lots along Boundary Road, adjacent to Plot 547.

Despite predominantly carrying on most of their research from other locations, the Ziltban facility would create a gold rush of employment. And on the tail of that gold rush would come all varieties of opportunities for thrifty development. Thus was born the Revitalization and Renewed Trams Industrial Sector Plan. The plan had phases. Each phase had chapters, with steps therein. The only problem was that Daniel Denard refused all of the investors' initial offers to purchase his property. Plot 547 remained the last and only piece of land necessary to be acquired in order to proceed with phase two of RRTISP.

It was then that the commissioners voted, upon the recommendations of several city attorneys, to forcibly acquire Plot 547 through the mechanism of eminent domain. This was the same meeting that put a zoning inlay in place for the adjacent properties, as commercial C-4. This rezoning would become a problem for many future establishments in the area, as they would have to seek out a variance or re-inlay prior to construction, and sometime prior to investment.

Denard contested the eminent domain action, which explained that the area was being condemned and reappropriated for public use. But, after consulting a lifelong friend who taught constitutional law at a state university law school on the other side of the continent, he backed down, realizing there was a series of legal precedents allowing a city municipality to transfer ownership of real estate from a private individual to another group of private individuals if the purpose benefited the public and the deprived owner received just compensation. Denard decided to deal with the situation amicably, in hopes of receiving a larger sum.

Because Denard brushed shoulders with several city officials and many more friends of theirs, Trams offered him the average of three estimates approximating market value. It was less than he would have obtained by putting the property on the market, but he made no stink because it was still far more than he had put in a few years earlier, and the money could be used later on with his newfound allies in the city's administration.

Seemingly moments after Trams received title to the land, Ziltban informed Trams that they would not be pursuing their state-of-the-art research facility. They were locating it instead in Northern Ireland, where tax havens and other business incentives made it virtually dimwitted not to partake. Thus, the influx of jobs and new money, upon which the entirety of the revitalization depended, was null and void. All of the private businesses backed out of RRTISP, seeing very clearly that without the Ziltban influence, development in the area was a decade, maybe two, away and so too remote for immediate investment.

So Plot 547, which the city had shelled out so much of its budgetary surplus to acquire, lay bare. Several of the surrounding plots were sold off here and there at discount rates as the grocery stores, gastro pubs, and condominiums began to trickle in with the arrival to Trams of other large corporate headquarters. RRTISP was hastily forgotten and, eventually, the plot was transferred into the Trams Land Bank, where most properties, usually smaller residential lots, go to be auctioned off years later for the price of a ten-year-old automobile.

Now, when both transfers of Plot 547 were made by Sati Motors, such transfers of real estate in Trams were governed by state statute sections T.R.C. 5301.47 through T.R.C. 5301.49. These sections contained the state recording act, which specified who would have priority of clear title in the event of competing claims. This particular statute was a variation of what is known as a race-notice statute, as pertains to marketable title of land. The race-notice act gave priority of title to the party that records first in the proper local property filing office but only if the party also lacked notice of prior unrecorded claims on the same property.

The probate court overseeing Bastien Ebersold's action to quiet title and declaration of ownership came to conclude, largely in part due to the efforts of employees of the Trams City Building & Zoning Services, that Ebersold held proper title to Plot 547. Though Mr. Daniel Denard did in fact receive conveyance of deed prior to Sumpter Capital, his attorney, Mr. DuFollet, failed to properly file the deed and transfer of ownership. Thus, Sumpter had no legitimate form of notice prior to his subsequent purchase and filing. True marketable title flowed to

Sumpter, who later conveyed clean title of the land in fee simple absolute to Bastien Ebersold.

There was some scuttlebutt about whether Ebersold and those involved at Glaubus, Glaubus should have known about the city's condemnation and eminent domain proceedings, as they were part of the official court record, widely published about and the subject of rumored. Although, in the end, the probate judge Thomas Masky decided that it was irrelevant for three reasons. First, Trams never acquired proper title to the plot since they levied their eminent domain specifically toward Denard, and not the plot in question. Sumpter was never informed, nor had any opportunity to make his case in court. Second, the city's purpose for acquiring the plot had vanished. It had fallen into the city land bank, where most properties end up due to failures in the real estate market or fungible development projects. Third, Ebersold's plan for the lot would essentially fulfill the vision that Trams originally harbored for the area. Thus, it was akin to them acquiring the land from Denard and transferring it over to Ebersold to enact the revitalization aspects. For all of these reasons, further deliberations were found to be unnecessary.

All of this was in line with the conclusions at which Sherry and Hans had arrived. Sherry had originally contacted Pollock, recalling his mention of the plot in question being relevant to his upcoming presentation for Mr. Freedman. Pollock was also Quentin's golden boy. She pondered the danger in providing him access to her task, which would eventually find its way to Quentin and allow him to counteract her gain in favor within the department. But then she figured that she could work it the other way around. She could turn him over. Put him to *her* use.

Her considerations were for naught; Pollock did not return any of her phone calls. It didn't surprise her. It was late Friday afternoon when she reached out and her query would involve many hours of weekend labor, within the confines of the dreaded basement records. It wasn't exactly a sweet deal. But she was miffed about receiving no response whatsoever. Her more paranoid aspects wondered if he were icing her to demonstrate allegiance to Quentin.

Then she thought of Hans. He was bright and enthusiastic and, perhaps most importantly, it was obvious that he had gained Mr. Freedman's favor. Having worked this out, she knew Hans should help with this, and she congratulated herself on the cohesion of it all, the unity of destination. She was exuberant and called immediately. Hans picked up after two rings, heard out her simple offer for extra worked and simply replied, "Absolutely. I'd love to be involved. I'll be over ASAP." Sherry left the conversation feeling confident and clever.

Hans placed his cell on the desktop and smirked. He looked out upon the flowing Rhatze, which ran underneath his apartment, thrashing around the concrete support beams. His palling around and pleasant general banter had gained him friendships with most of Trams staff, but this was the first actual work assignment that his efforts had garnered him. "Some men look upon their difficulties and say 'Woe is me.' Others say, 'Thank God for the opportunity.'" His smirk grew as he snapped shut his black laptop.

He had been listening to Rob Durci's latest EP, which was released on his website days earlier. Hans's Facebook stream had notified him of every new song post since he had flagged Rob's site as a favorite. Hans had initially been quite surprised to see Durci's social media presence after such a long period of reclusiveness.

The EP was comprised of three songs, all approximately ten minutes long. The music was electronic with waves of found-sound percussion littered in and out. It was moody and mournful but very rhythmic. Hans felt that the music, especially the third track entitled "Backward Slave," was persuading him to feel guilty. He didn't want to feel guilty. And yet he did feel some loyalty to keeping up with Rob's music, even so many years after their last personal interaction.

Rob's previous full album *Talking Lemon Wedge*, had become popular enough, mostly through online downloads, plays at parties and dancehalls, and personal interest from employees, to be incorporated into regular rotation at Independent Radio 104.5 The Dive. The radio station was favored among Hans's peer group. So, apart from Hans's personal investment in his old teammate's endeavors, it was inevitable that he would hear one of his songs every couple of weeks or so, whether at work or on the PA at a local establishment.

Hans was locking his bike outside the Trams brick building within fifteen minutes of Sherry's call. He swiftly walked inside and rushed down into the basement, where Sherry was sitting Indian style with a mess of manila folders and an old microfiche viewer against her back. The two of them spent the next forty-eight hours putting together the entire chain of title for the plot and preparing a brief explaining the City of Trams's position on ownership. This brief would become greatly influential in the city attorney's office. It very poorly advocated for the plot's inclusion into the land bank, thereby tacitly nudging Judge Masky to quiet title in Ebersold's favor.

Pollock and Quentin were equally caught of guard by the weekend of work when they returned Monday. Pollock had been reconnecting strings of memories from his drunken escapades with Cabe. The missed calls from Sherry had initially been alarming enough. But, knowing that he had lost out on an important opportunity to Hans because he was passed out drunk with Cabe nearly sent his anxieties into pandemonium. He still had the presentation though, which had essentially become critical to keeping his job.

And in the midst of all of the discord around his sobering return to work that Monday was the question of what had happened to Cabe. His belongings still remained at Pollock's but he did not. Pollock had tried him perhaps a dozen times both with voice messages and text messages saying "Emergency! Are you still alive???" But Cabe had been incommunicado. And Pollock had four thousand dollars in cash that he had won betting on cocks.

Everything about Monday was a mess. It was possibly the worst Monday of Pollock's life. He was still alarmingly hungover, even though he had not had a drink since Saturday evening. He was avoiding the inevitable apologies to Retta, who was responsible for many of the unanswered text messages he had found the previous afternoon. And he could see the coffin being assembled for his short-lived career in Trams. He wished he could tell someone what a rat bastard Hans Flowers was.

After a conversation with Quentin about how they were both essentially left in the dark concerning the brief, Pollock decided that he would hunker down and finish his presentation for Mr. Freedman, which he did with the focus and haste of one bailing water from a sinking lifeboat. He worked at his desk like a madman, paying no attention to the jokes and anecdotes Quentin occasionally shot out from his adjacent workspace, or the self-satisfied nod Hans directed to him from across the Trams main room. Everything around him was terrifying chaos, and the only thing that would calm it would be writing his report, putting to words his clearest belief about the future of property disputes in the Trams zoning department.

Chapter Nineteen

Their horses were barely visible to one another through the mist. They were made aware of their location by the clomping of hooves upon clods of frozen grass and the riders' sniffles. Orange flickering orbs in the encampment glowed through the forest. Max nodded over to Titius to indicate that this was the spot. But he was puzzled because there were no guards like before, and it was very quiet. The scene was altogether different than he had left it. Large billows of smoke wafted toward the men through the trees.

Mr. Bieler steered closer to Max and whispered, "Do you think that they moved on, perhaps?" Max shrugged his shoulders. The group of riders gathered together, guns at the ready. Titus cocked his Reiser pistol and followed its sights across the perimeter of the firelit region. Nothing moved and nothing made a sound except for the casual neighing and rein-tugging of the horses. The mist slowly grew thicker until, though only feet away, the members of the posse could no longer see one another at all.

Max looked down at his horse's mane. The hairs were much thicker and lighter than he had remembered. It wasn't straight black but instead made of several different colors dispersed throughout. There were reds, blonds, even whites. And the occasional grey. He thought of the horse's lineage and where all of the colors came from, how many generations to arrive at this array of color that lay before him. He then realized how little of the mane he could actually see while maintaining focus on the individual hairs. If he tried to gaze upon its entirety, the detail faded.

He looked up from his horse and found that he was completely entombed by mist and smoke. As he peered through the sheets of grey, his eyes played tricks on him. There seemed to appear strands of multicolored hair fluttering about, but he knew it couldn't be. An image of an oak tree then popped into his mind. It struck him that trees were the countryside's strands of hair. He pictured the whole world existing on an old man's head. Having done so, he wondered what color the entire forest of Earth would be from afar.

At this time, Max noticed he was thinking strangely. It was also unclear to him how long they had been looming at the edge of the encampment. His mind wandered again, mulling the definition of time. He held his gloved hand in front of his face. It seemed strange to be his. It seemed strange that anything outside of his head was his. The thought startled him. He began to get scared about his own mind and what it was doing.

A hand reached out from the fog and slapped his thigh. A face appeared above it. It belonged to Titius. His left eyebrow was raised in consternation. "Max, we are going to tie up the horses and go in on foot. Come on." He spoke as if convincing himself. But Max welcomed the break in his own thoughtfulness. He hopped down from the horse and waded through the smoke. Once the reins were wrapped around a tree, Max squatted down next to Titius and most of the others in a tight circle.

Mr. Teller was bent over, coughing. Mr. Sells was smiling and staring at Max. Max stared right back at him, contemplating the features of his face. They seemed absurd to him. All nose and chin. The smoke was pungent with a pine-like odor, and it was choking and stinging to the throat. Several of the men wrapped scarves over their mouths. Bieler had pulled his lapel over the bottom half of his face and was speaking through it. "We'll spread out and push inward," he said, looking around to see if the others registered understanding. The whole group nodded despite the perplexity sinking in.

The men did as planned. But the visibility was so slight that it had the effect of isolating each man. Max hunched along, using the orange glow of firelight as a goal. Occasionally he would hear the crunching or swearing of one of his mates who stepped wrong or ran into something. Laughing was coming from his far right. The proportions of Mr. Sells's face remained in Max's mind.

Max reached the closest fire pit in unison with Mr. Bieler. They knelt together next to it, scanning around with outstretched firearms. There was no one around and the fire itself had burned down to a pile of steady embers. "It could have been abandoned hours ago," Max said. The others could be heard scampering past on either side of them. Both Max and Mr. Bieler found themselves seduced by the flickering of the waning coals within the fire pit. The two of them hunched across from one another and watched the glowing orange logs as they hissed and spit.

Once the others could no longer be heard, far ahead by then, Mr. Bieler shook his head as if waking himself, stretching his eyelids. He waved Max forward with his gun and the two began moving again. The smoke was now thick enough that Max's rifle hand would fade from view when extended outward. He moved along with his knees bent and butt low. His mind returned to trickery, offering up visions of hair and Mr. Sells through the grey cloud.

Though the smoke warmed the area several degrees, it was still below freezing, and Max's hands and face were quite cold. Yet, he noted that he was covered in a thin layer of sweat from head to toe. His heart was pounding, so he dismissed it as nerves. He worked hard to pay attention to any sound and keep moving forward as swiftly as he could while keeping low. Wide tree trunks would emerge from the mist and he would swing around them. Four more fire circles passed hazily by his periphery before he came back upon Bieler.

Max startled at his presence but lowered his gun in time to avoid friendly fire. Bieler turned rapidly toward Max upon his approach, a twisting head from the void. His eyes were as large as fists and blood red. They seemed to be stretched forth and protruding from their sockets. He reached out and caressed Max's cheek with his gloved fingers. They slid along his wet skin with ease. "What on Earth is happening?" he asked Max.

"I haven't the slightest," Max said, short of breathe.

A twig snapped and Mr. Sells's face, its confounding proportion in full force, manifested to Max's left. "Good lord!" Bieler said. "I nearly fucking shot your head off!"

Sells settled on his knees, forming a triangle between the three gathered men. "What, should I have announced myself?" he asked. Max looked around, trying hard to detect any trace of the others. Sells said, "We are going to kill each other off if we keep at it like this. Where is everyone?"

Bieler took a deep breath and wiped his forehead with his coat sleeve. "Come on, we need to keep pushing in. We haven't shot one another yet, and we seem to have figured there isn't anyone else around, so hopefully the rest will have come to the same conclusion, no?" Sells and Max both nodded and rose again to their feet.

"Let's stay close, though, right?" Sells said. Max and Bieler nodded and the three continued on, Bieler in front and Sells and Max right behind, shoulder to shoulder. "We should have brought some damned lanterns along," Max heard Sells mutter.

The grey turned black as the trio hobbled deep into the interior of the encampment, leaving all of the fire pits behind. Bieler stopped abruptly, raising his arm to touch rotting wood. It was the barn wall. Max and Sells spread out to Bieler's sides. Sells lit a match, flashing a bright, flickering circle of light upward along the wall. "This is the center," Max said.

"It's not that big," Sells said, moving the circle further along the wall.

"Let's find the door," Bieler said. And with that, the three began moving left, Sells now ahead, lighting the way.

As they moved along, Max noticed flashes of red light shooting through the uneven chinks of wood. "Fire inside," Bieler noted in Max's ear. They quickly came to the barn door. It was ajar and the three peered in on enormous flames.

"All right, on one." Sells said.

Bieler said, "All right." He and Max moved to either side of the opening, holding out their pistols. "Three, two, one," Sells called, and then hastily pulled the door fully open.

Max jumped up and stepped inside, swinging his pistol left to right. Bieler followed suit on Max's right. Harsh heat and smoke poured from the large flames inside. The smog was too much and it overtook Max, causing him to fall down choking and coughing. He pulled his jacket up and submerged his head within the collar and, like an injured animal, scrambled backward along the ground on three limbs, retreating from the barn.

After reaching some thirty paces from the barn entrance, Max stopped and took a moment to catch his breath. The burning in his throat had dissipated, but his eyes and lips still itched. He finally pushed his head back through his collar and took a look around. His friends were not around and he was in complete darkness. The smog was growing thicker now that the barn door had been opened. He sat and listened but heard nothing. He wondered what had happened here.

"Hey!" he called out into the darkness. No response. "Bieler, Sells! God-damn it, hello?" Again, no response. He thought about heading back toward the barn but the stream of smoke was too thick. If anything he needed to retreat further back. He decided to try one more call before leaving. "Mr. Rombathe! Titius!"

A moment of silence followed, then, "Max, where are you?" It was Titius.

"Here, over here…" Max called out.

An arm grabbed his shoulder. "Max, thank God. I've lost the others," he said, hunching down.

"Me too. We need to get out of here." Max said.

"There are bails of marijuana burning in all of these fires. Either these folks moved on and burned what they couldn't take along, or I fear that we may have just walked right into a trap."

Max thought this over. "That explains all of the strange thoughts I've been having," he said.

"Yes, I don't quite seem myself," Titius said.

Max could hear Titius clearing his throat and spitting out mucus. "So what kind of trap, then?" he asked.

* * *

Pollock had brought his finished presentation to Mr. Freedman's office while Mr. Freedman was out. He tossed the plastic folder into the in-box on the desk. There was a certain degree of surrender involved in the action. He had, more or less, condemned the entire enterprise of private property and the adversarial nature by which zoning disputes were resolved.

Further, it severely contradicted the City of Trams's position regarding Plot 547. Prompted by Martin's request to Trams to cede the plot for a chartered tent city, the probate court made an ancillary ruling that resulted in a denial. Notice to vacate the premises was issued and served. They had twenty-one days or else the marshals would get involved. Pollock had advised that the city should make available spaces like these, for those whom the market had failed.

But even more than this, Pollock knew that in his paper, he was really condemning human beings altogether. He was lamenting the fractured society. So by tossing this content on Freedman's desk, he was making plain he could do without his job. The thought of Hans getting his mark occurred to him. But it didn't feel like he was losing. It felt like he was admitting something to himself that was necessary before moving forward. And so he walked with a lightness that had escaped him for some time. He even felt somewhat hopeful.

His winnings from the cockfights, an event still curious in his memory, had supplemented his savings enough that he could afford to be unemployed for some time while he figured out his next move. That very idea communicated to him that his whole life might be falling apart. And that made him feel very alive.

Quentin had looked over the proposal before Pollock turned it in. A proud grin was stamped across his face when he returned it. He said, "So you found your balls after all. It's a hand grenade. Freedman's going to hand your job over to his golden boy and they are going to get started on the University Corridor revitalization. But you already knew that, didn't you?"

Pollock, sitting at his desk, threw his hands up in submission. "Maybe city planning isn't my calling," he said, with calm introspection. It made Quentin erupt into laughter.

Though Quentin did sadden at the prospect of Pollock leaving the department, he couldn't ignore that the firm resolution in the presentation made him proud. He decided he wouldn't have it any other way. Having come to this understanding, he made his own resolution to become more involved with Pollock, personally, as friends. So when Pollock said that Retta had specifically mentioned he invite Quentin along to her dream catcher party, it delighted him and he accepted promptly.

Cabe finally made his way back to Pollock's house after an extra week of booze, drugs, and gambling. He was no worse for wear and quickly commenced cooking meals and cleaning the house. Over the next couple of weeks, he reached out to several wineries. Two were receptive and he was "undergoing the courting process" before committing to either.

Retta had only met Cabe in passing one night when she biked over to meet Pollock to go to the movie theater. In light of his and Pollock's troubled past and out of respect to their newly repaired friendship, Cabe remained aloof and reserved in her presence. He merely said, "It's good to meet you. Pollock has spoken very highly of you."

Retta was receptive and responded, "Likewise." They shook hands. Pollock quickly shuffled her out of the foyer before either had a chance to mingle.

Though Pollock was honest with himself about desiring limited time between Cabe and Retta, he had his own respect for the rekindled friendship and mentioned to Retta that Cabe should be invited along to the party. "The more the merrier," she responded, excitedly. She was thrilled by the increasing turnout. More than twenty people had RSVP'd on Facebook. And now more than five additional acquaintances were coming as well.

But what she was really excited about was that she could offer up something unusual to all of her older friends. It wasn't a drab potluck or routine bar night like the past dozen infrequent meetings had been. Her friends would have to work together to build something, something she thought would be great. She liked the idea of the fire, too. It put butterflies into her stomach. After turning it over in her head several times, she also began to see that it might be cheesy and forced. Her hosting anxiety started to grow as she battled thoughts of no one wanting to help with the dream catcher or everyone being bored. "Ah, buggers! It will be fine," she said aloud.

She also worried some about the permanence of Remy's upturn. But this worry was mostly quashed as she watched him finish fixing the back deck and then turn his attentions to other neglected portions of the house.

Pollock and Retta had grown close very quickly. They were spending the night at each other's, but mostly Retta's, place a few nights a week. They had fallen into a successful rhythm sexually. But there were several areas that concerned Retta. Pollock never talked about his family or his past. He made mention to her that he wasn't close with his parents, but that was about it. And he seemed to have an obsessive belief that his great-aunt was still inhabiting the house in which he lived. All attempts to find evidence to convince Retta of this failed, so Pollock stopped mentioning it to her. But Retta had caught Pollock reading the diary several times. She dismissed it because she understood that his great-aunt did mean a great deal to him, for whatever reason. And it seemed like maybe that was his way of holding on to her memory. Although, she had certain reservations about reading another's private writing.

Pollock had been irritated after having read one of Mary's entries toward the back of the journal:

> We are sleeping together now. I admit that it is not what I
> wanted but life is so many little disappointments. I'm too old to be
> lonely. I have started drinking again…

The entry seemed to affirm for Pollock that his great-aunt had given in before the end. She had abandoned her aspirations and taken up with a horny old bandit. It rang as a defeat. Pollock's thoughts returned to the entry several times a day.

Cabe and Pollock spent a Wednesday night drinking beers and reminiscing about their college days. Cabe cooked a complex borscht and served the two of them. And though Pollock did wish for his friend to move on to his own dwelling at some point, he couldn't help but note that his coresidency did have its perks. In fact, for a couple weeks, Pollock did no chores, and yet all the laundry was done, and he ate well-balanced, home-cooked meals.

He even found sack lunches for work with a sandwich, apple, and yogurt inside. The sardine cans remained stacked in the pantry, uneaten. They were, however, pushed to the side to make room for the bountiful whole foods that Cabe had picked up from the expensive co-op grocer. There, the aisles were supplied only with organic, pesticide-free, and locally grown products. He thought his friend was turning into a real granola cruncher. Though he never expected to see these items in his home, they suited his digestion.

Things were quiet around Trams City Offices after the initial wake from the whole Plot 547 determination. Pollock mainly kept himself occupied with ancillary busy work and esoteric conversations with Quentin, like exactly where the demarcation between science fiction and fantasy resided. It was a topic Quentin loved to corner people with. Pollock had managed to avoid the topic during their entire time working together. But, now that Pollock was essentially phoning it in while waiting to get fired, he succumbed to it.

The Thursday prior to Retta's party, Pollock was fired. He was called in to Mr. Freedman's office and sat calmly in the red recliner, which had no business being in an office building, while Mr. Freedman gently and tactfully laid out the many reasons why Trams zoning and Pollock were no longer a good fit. Because he knew that it was coming, Pollock entertained himself during this meeting by appreciating the euphemisms and allegories Mr. Freedman used. Pollock hadn't anticipated just how much Freedman would respect his feelings. He grew sentimental toward his boss in those final moments that the man retained that title.

"We have to maintain professionalism," Mr. Freedman said in his growling baritone. "Now, its not lost on me that you've been going through something here lately. If you'd like to talk about it, I'd be happy to make time for that. But as far as your position here in the department," he wrinkled his nose in an air of disgust, "well, that ship has sailed. I can't take this to the city commissioners, this plan of yours to donate land to the homeless and destitute." He leaned forward, his swivel chair creaking and snapping with protest. "You do realize that taxes are as good as paychecks around here?" he asked Pollock, tilting his head and swirling his finger around above his head.

Dozens of rebuttals and intelligent responses came in a flurry to Pollock's mind, but he did not employ them. It struck him as ironic that Freedman was discussing professionalism, when everyone knew he was eager to begin movement on the University Corridor project to stoke an ancient romantic flame. Pollock played it amiably brief. "Yes sir. I understand," he said, rising from the recliner and extending his hand.

Freedman was mildly insulted because he had more to say. And also because it appeared that Pollock cared so little that he would make no protest. Swallowing his pride, Freedman met Pollock's hand with his own fat palm and said, "Best of luck. You'll figure it out."

The words rattled around in Pollock's head. He stood blankly at the front of his desk with his messenger bag in hand and his good pen slid into place in his pants pocket. He could think of nothing of value to take with him. Quentin was absent, likely smoking up top. So Pollock turned and casually strolled out through the front entrance of Trams Facilities. He caught bits of rants by angry customers. "Three weeks, they told me it would be…I shouldn't need a variance and there is no…how in the hell is that considered signage? It's antique African artwork…"

Pollock stood barefoot, cracking his toe knuckles on the living room rug Friday morning before sunrise. Cabe was snoring madly, hanging off the edge of the couch. A mess of empty wine bottles sat scattered over the coffee table. It was just as it had been when he returned from Retta's the previous evening. Pollock slowly spun 360 degrees and took in the house. Moving boxes were still stacked in various corners. A whole season had passed and he had not unpacked. All of the decor and all of the furniture remained when he arrived. And here he was, unemployed, with his old mate, also unemployed, nursing the beginning of another hangover.

The scene made him ashamed, as if he had carelessly wrecked into the present. He couldn't remember why he had been interested in his job to begin with. Worse still, he was unsure what the world was about. And admitting such made him believe he had regressed greatly. Everyone else seemed to have figured these things out years ago. Not Pollock. In his midtwenties, he felt back at square one. "You'll figure it out," he remembered Freedman saying. "You'll figure it out," Pollock said.

Retta had been very supportive of Pollock's termination but had also insisted that he talk to someone about it. "I think I'll be okay," Pollock said a little defensively while they hung out in her bedroom.

"Job loss is one of those big life events. It's like death, separation from a loved one, job loss, and then a bunch of abuse situations," Retta said, face down on the comforter as Pollock pressed hard upon her spine and heard three, maybe four vertebrae pop. The bedframe rattled. Retta interrupted herself with a long moan of delight. "I saw someone when my mom passed. And I was young. It was kind of scary and upsetting at first. I hated her for a while. But in the end, it was just, so, so worth it. I can't explain. Just think about it will you?" Retta asked, twisting her neck to look up at Pollock. He was purposefully silent. "Pollock! Promise me you'll at least think about it."

Pollock overcame his defensiveness. It was humbling to look down at Retta, physically submissive and asking this of him only because she cared for him. He smirked like a caught cat. "Okay, I promise."

Now, standing in his living room, thinking himself a failure, he wondered if he might see someone after all. His health coverage did not expire for another three months. It was one of the few specifics he had remembered about his termination. Content to let the choice linger, he made his way into the kitchen and seated himself at the nook. He pulled down the binoculars and scanned the street. It was still too early, and he did not spot anything of note. The Ventillis' bedroom light was on. Mrs. Studebaker's car was parked with one wheel on the curb lawn.

Pollock replaced the binoculars in their case as Cabe arose and let out a pained groan. Bottles clattered to the floor. "Ah, fuck," Cabe said and entered the kitchen. He did not acknowledge Pollock, but plopped himself down into the free chair, lowered his forehead to the table and wrapped his face within his arms.

"Rough night or fun?" Pollock asked. Cabe flung his head up and slid the chair several inches backward. "Jesus fucking Christ. Where'd you come from?"

Retta was reflecting that she often idealized her friendships from afar, when she was alone, only to be acutely disappointed by the actuality of being around her friends. There seemed to be an inherent unhappiness abounding. Musing over whether these feelings were two sides of the same coin, she decided that it did not matter. The party was about putting in the effort to be better, to make things better.

The weather was perfect for an outdoor get-together. The high was forecast to be 77 and the low, 68. Pure sunshine and a slight breeze. The sky was already deep blue when Retta clothed herself and made her way to the back yard to begin assembling a fire pit. Within the clutter of their garage sat a stack of several dozen patio bricks of three varieties of grey and brown. They were surplus from an ancient yard-improvement project. Remy always overestimated quantities, as was often evidenced by the numerous Tupperware containers full of leftovers stacked throughout the refrigerator. He was also sentimental about objects. Thus, the garage had slowly turned into somewhat of a museum.

The grey bricks were twelve-inch-long rectangles, which could be stacked in such a manner that they interlinked at the corner, forming a curvature. Each stone was four inches thick and, when circled in this way six rows high, the result was a cylinder with air holes all around. Retta used a garden trowel to dig out the grass at the bottom of the ring. Inside the house, she had a computer paper box full of several weeks worth of newspaper and cardboard squares for the initial ignition. Pollock had arranged to bring bundles of split logs from the mill for the actual burning. Retta was struck by this detail. It relayed a certain domesticity between her and Pollock, as if they were cohosting the party, even practicing for future, further house-sharing activities. She filed the notion away into her subconscious competition with her friends and acquaintances. It was proof of some forward motion.

Stacey Ingram had been an in-again, out-again friend of Retta's since middle school. They used to trap boys in lies by three-way calling them. Recently, the two had been having prolonged Facebook conversations and met for lunch and booze at Cowlick's Pizza Saloon. She had agreed to come over early and help set up things with Retta. She arrived just as Retta was situating the paper box next to the fire ring. "Hey girl!" she said in her nasal soprano, tiptoeing through the grass in flip-flops. She had enormous yellow-rimmed sunglasses hanging low on her petite nose and was wearing a flower print bikini top and cut off jean shorts, the inside pocket fabric of which hung lower than the actual jean material. She was blonde and had the physique of a seasoned long distance runner.

"Hey, Stace," Retta said coolly, feeling quite unattractive by comparison in her aged black Crosby Stills Nash & Young T-shirt and stained sweatpants rolled knee high. Retta had always felt unattractive around Stacey, though. Most people did. The two hugged, asses out.

"I brought some chairs. We didn't talk about it or anything, but I figured it wouldn't hurt."

"Oh, good thinking. Thanks," Retta said, in earnest.

"Help me carry 'em?" Stacey asked, delighted that her contribution was well received. Retta nodded and the two walked out front to Stacey's Jeep.

It was parked along the curb with the top off. It was black and had neon green and pink stripes along the doors as if made by a brushstroke. It reminded Retta of a 1980s beach film, or maybe one with the Brat Pack. And since she loved the Brat Pack, it made her feel tremendous. The weather, the Jeep, and the party had her so excited, she said, "Things are good," to no one in particular.

Stacey, bent over the tailgate, heard her and said, "Just wait till you see what else I brought." After a bit of a struggle and some banging, Stacey yanked a red cooler out by the handle. She placed it on the curb lawn and opened it up. Inside, among clods and caverns of ice, were a dozen Seagram's Escapes hard fruit drinks.

These were the same drinks with which Retta and Stacey had together each gotten drunk for the first time in eighth grade. They had on several occasions since then, while drinking together, imbibed the iconic adult beverages as sort of an inside joke and a nod to their enduring friendship. Retta instantly recognized them and let out a lengthy squeal of excitement while running in place. Stacey mimicked her and joined in the squealing.

Once the lawn chairs had been combined with the Adirondacks and porch loungers from the garage and placed into a wide circle around the patio stone circle, the two each cracked open a Seagram's and commenced day drinking. Retta had battery-powered speakers sitting atop one of the chairs. She plugged her iPhone in to them and played *Pet Sounds* by the Beach Boys. "You and your oldies," Stacey said, playfully.

"We'll listen to this album and then you can choose what's next," Retta said.

"Who still listens to albums?" Stacey asked.

Stacey and Retta continued drinking and chatting idly until almost three o'clock, at which time Retta, despite the seducing pleasure of her buzzed relaxation, decided she better rise and assemble the rest of the supplies for the party, including beginning the dream catcher. She noted the sturdiness of the fresh pine deck planks beneath her feet as she pulled open the sliding glass door. Nothing was moving and nothing was soft. She thought her dad had done a good job. It was strange for her to think of him like that, as "Dad." She hadn't called him anything but Remy for some time. The change struck her as a good omen.

Retta had taken Remy's truck a few days earlier and parked along the shoulder of Boundary Road. There she scavenged for good twigs and felled branches. The smaller finds would serve well as tinder for the fire, and the larger branches would be bound together by twine and bark rope to form the circular frame of the dream catcher. She returned from the trip with enough for several fires and a dream catcher the size of a small house.

She carried them through the kitchen and living room and out onto the deck. This saved the distance of going around the outside of the house. Fox watched *Planet Earth* "Deserts" while she came through cradling a heap of wood in her arms and then trotting back out to the garage for the next bundle. The episode of the show was nearly finished by the time the truck bed was empty. It took her a dozen trips back and forth between the truck and the back yard to fully unload all of the sticks into two separate piles. They had left all sorts of little scrapes and tiny gashes along her forearms, which now itched as they healed.

As Retta emerged from the house with three spools of twine and metal sheers, Stacey shouted out, "The dream catcher idea is fantastic, by the way. I mean I love drinking…but there's always that balance, you know? Like, if you're just drinking and nothing else, then you kind of feel like an alcoholic, and well, depending on company, things can get pretty boring or you get sleepy. But, most times I don't want to pay attention to a movie, or if you go see a band, then you end up with a kink in your neck, and your knees hurt from standing too much. But crafts are perfect, you know? It keeps you…engaged. And I love dream catchers. Never made one…" She furrowed her brow in thought.

Her words made Retta smile to herself, content to know that at least one of the guests appreciated the task. "This one is going to be huge, too," Retta said. "I have so much wood for it, it's going to be ridiculous." The quick trip in to retrieve the twine had left her a little winded and she felt somewhat dizzy. She'd already had three drinks. She decided to hold off on the alcohol and have some water for an hour or two, instead. She didn't want to be drunk when people started showing up and embarrass herself.

Remy had taken Fox on a day hike. Over the past week, Fox had burned through every nature documentary on Netflix, paying particular attention to the segments pertaining to birds. "Cave swiftlets build their nests from threads of saliva," he said in distracted excitement. "Threads of saliva. It takes thirty days to complete. Threads of saliva. Thirty days to complete." And so, because Remy was beginning to feel better, he figured his boy would enjoy walking through the woods of Capper Hollow. It was an hour and a half northwest of Trams. Remy promised to return in time to participate in the festivities.

Retta was enjoying the quiet of having the house to herself without Fox loudly emulating bird songs. And she was enjoying the sun. She arched her neck over the lip of the plastic lawn chair and let the heat plaster her face. Some foot-stomping pop-folk band was playing through the speakers next to Stacey, who was nodding her head and taking long draws from her fifth or sixth Seagram's. The song sounded like so many other songs Retta had heard lately, but it was perfect for the moment. And because she was so relaxed and so contented, she almost wished there was no party, and that she and Stacey could just continue, exactly as they were, for the remainder of the day.

Stacey began prattling on about her failures with online dating and quickly restored Retta's excitement for additional company. "He was still living with his ex. Like, all of the furniture in the place was apparently hers. So we came back from—that was our third date at that point, we went for chili dogs—anyway, we came back, and she had taken all of her furniture and left a note saying she couldn't believe he had been cheating on her. Ugh, what typical guy." She paused and checked her phone. Replacing it back on the chair's arm, she continued. "Then there was Paul. Paul was great until we started getting…intimate."

"Uh oh…"

"Yeah," Stacey said, "he was so nice and smart. But he could not get, you know…hard. I tried to help with my mouth but nothing happened. He said he was just nervous, like performance anxiety. It wasn't a big deal, you know? I said we could just hang out and try another time. So we did. But like two more times he still couldn't. And he got like, snotty with me. He kept saying I should stop making fun of him. I was like 'Dude, I am being super understanding right now. Like you need to handle this entire situation differently because I am not the one that is having trouble functioning properly.'" She took a large swig of Seagram's and let out a stressed grunt. "Uh. What a little shit he turned out to be.

"Anyway, I'm starting to rethink this whole online dating scene. I thought it would be easier, you know? Like just sort out the weirdos and the losers, and then flirt from home before even putting any effort toward appearance or driving somewhere. But I think that there's just so much more that you can't get from guys until you've been around them several times. Like how do they act with their friends? You know? And what are their phone conversations like with their parents. I need to know these things." Stacey nodded to herself.

Against her more prudent analysis, Retta grabbed another Seagram's. "Fuck it," she said aloud as she cracked off the twist top and took in the cold, sweet drink.

"Thatta girl!" Stacey howled with her sugary soprano. The sun beat down perfectly, as if concerned with the girls' comfort and well being. Lawn mowers churned and sputtered farther down the long street. Paul Simon was now playing through the speakers, and it was nearly enough to put Retta to sleep. She was leaning far back in her chair, her feet atop another. She was almost horizontal.

Pollock had fallen asleep Friday night without knowing. After brief dreams involving mason jars that either doled out compliments or insults to a person depending upon their attraction to the contents they'd been filled with, Pollock found himself sitting on the train tracks outside of Trams. He recognized it was the Trams tracks by a yellow insignia spray-painted upon an electrical box just a few yards off. It read: "Peanut Butter Lover Used to Push Poor People into Bins." Pollock stood up and gazed over toward the city. It was gone. He rubbed his eyes and looked again. He was exactly where he thought he was, only the city was absent. There were no marble and steel buildings downtown, no dilapidated industrial parks on the far edge, no neighborhoods dotted throughout the web of highway viaducts. Instead of Trams, the entire fourteen-mile radius was one large, empty field of grass. His heart rose and seemed to indicate to him the coming of ruin.

From down the tracks, a dirty man approached. He walked bent forward, as though his lower back was pained. His outfit was something a nineteenth-century aristocrat might wear, with wool vest, matching knickers tucked into high button-sided socks, and plaid flat cap. But his clothes were all tattered and faded. "Good day my friend," he said as he came close to Pollock. He stopped square with him and extended his hand, "Name's DeSoto. Pleasure to make your acquaintance," he said in a gruff and almost British-sounding voice.

It was unclear to Pollock whether the man DeSoto was a threat or a friend. So, he conducted himself neutrally, coolly. "Hi. Pollock," he said, meeting the man's hand. They shook for a long time, DeSoto putting great vigor into the action. He then freed his hand and placed it upon Pollock's back, turning him so that, side by side, the two faced the large field below.

"You're probably wondering where your town went, yes?" DeSoto asked. Pollock nodded in agreement. DeSoto took a long breath. His exhale stunk of hard booze. Pollock wore his displeasure at this openly. DeSoto said, "You do not know where you are."

"What does that mean?" Pollock said, almost accusingly.

"It means that you thought you were living here but, perhaps you are not. Perhaps you are living elsewhere?"

The question swirled around Pollock's head for a moment. Finally, he asked, with a growing impatience, "What the fuck! Live where? Where is 'elsewhere'?"

"Tsk, tsk," DeSoto let out and then turned his back on Pollock and began making his way down the tracks in the direction he had come. In singsong words he said, "I've got time to do whatever I please. Just gotta save some time to make a warm loaf of bread…mix the dough and set the timer right…" Very quickly his singing was inaudible, and then the man himself was out of sight. Pollock stood swiveling his view between the disappeared city and down the tracks where DeSoto had merrily strolled.

Several dreams had occurred subsequently, but it was this dream that remained in his considerations after he had awoken Saturday morning. He even muttered the name to himself as he brushed his teeth. "DeSoto." He figured that the dream might mean he had a clean slate. There was nothing but opportunity ahead of him. And so he settled his uneasiness about it by pronouncing that it was, in fact, a harbinger of future happiness.

During the morning, while Cabe again slept off another night on his continued bender, Pollock logged in to Mingle and erased his profile. He smirked over all of the strange sexual requests he'd received during his time using the site. But he and Retta were solid, and he had a good feeling about where things were headed.

After brushing up his resume and perusing several public job-posting boards, he got into his car and headed over to Creighton Mill to acquire enough wood for the evening's consumption. It felt strange to have free time, now that this was all that he had. While at the mill, he fantasized about becoming a lumberjack, the opposite of an office job in a cubicle. The idea quickly subsided as he loaded the bundles of split logs and realized that he had neither the muscles nor the stamina for such intense labor.

Pollock paused once he had snapped shut the tailgate and leaned back against the side of his truck. He brushed his wiry hair from his sweaty forehead and aimed his eyes up to the sun. It was a beautiful day. The heaviness and the divisive perception he'd been carrying around felt strange now. He saw he had no real troubles. And yet he felt so "away," so far from anything. He mused for a while, in this position, wondering if he was so miserable because of his job, because of what he had glimpsed of how private property as a system worked in Trams. He didn't want to be naïve.

He'd remembered thinking in a way similar to this when he was very young. His palms would be held out in front of his face, opened wide and pinky to pinky. The evidence was there. And he understood plainly during those moments that he was not real. The hands held out in front of him proved that they were someone else's. And he wondered if maybe, despite its strain on credulity, someone else had been swapped into his body. And he, in turn, had been swapped into another. He imagined that's why he didn't recognize his own hands.

After all, there was a gulf between his earliest memories and what lay beyond them, earlier than them. And it was just on that precipice that the memories of not recognizing his hands occurred. He toyed with the idea that he was a time traveler after his return, arched over his truck in the gravel parking lot at Creighton Mill that Saturday morning. He couldn't recall for sure and, afterward, felt fairly silly for falling prey to such typical daydream.

He thought of Cabe, passed out on Pollock's great-aunt's couch, and it dawned on him that he'd spent so much time dwelling on past interactions that maybe he didn't know himself. Himself, as he currently existed. He wondered if he was still waiting to get to know himself, but disparaged that idea as New Agey, kumbaya shit. And with that, he slapped his hands back hard against the side of his truck bed and turned away from the sun.

The drive home was swift, as he managed to avoid almost all red lights. During long straightaways, he would peer down at his free right hand. While really staring at it, he found it striking how foreign it still seemed. He felt so removed from himself and imagined that hallucinogenic drugs, like LSD, might produce similar experiences.

After Pollock returned home, Cabe persuaded him to take him to a hardware store so that he could peruse through the tools and pick a new hatchet for splitting the wood that Pollock had purchased. "Even if it's been dry, the best wood is still that wood in the middle." In recent days, while both sober and inebriated, Cabe had been feverishly devouring YouTube videos of fire-building techniques. Littered throughout the living room was an array of trial and error attempts at various fire aids, including feather sticks, small scale replicas of log cabin fire structure and the reverse or self-sustaining fire structure, and two Altoid tins filled with natural fire starters, predominantly birch bark, old man's beard, and pine resin.

Aside from any qualms Pollock harbored regarding room organization and cleanliness, the display of Cabe's growing obsession was a direct and startling testament to the dark side of having too much free time. Pollock saw one of his potential futures in Cabe. And in so doing, the previous resentment and distrust he had held toward his friend faded even further and, instead, something like pity appeared.

However, the resentment, as remote or marginal as it may now have been, was still there. Pollock knew this because, when Cabe repeatedly announced his intention to prepare all of the tinder and fuel wood, start the fire, and keep it going beyond anyone's expectations, Pollock was a little jealous, thinking Cabe wanted to outshine him in front of Retta. It was a nasty sentiment underneath it all, and Pollock managed it well, but it was there.

Such a motive hadn't occurred to Cabe. He was merely fascinated by the mechanics and constructions of fires. It was something he had never closely considered. In all his years of camping and backpacking, which he fancied himself somewhat of a veteran, at least for someone of his few years, he'd always just lit paper on fire with matches, and then slowly piled snapped twigs over it in a tepee shape, adding larger branches until the fire needed no more attention. The notion that this process could be approached at different angles, and yield divergent results was frankly titillating. And, above all, Cabe was bored out of his mind. The Fire Chef Project, as Cabe began calling it, gave him purpose.

A hatchet and folding saw were quickly decided upon, and the two slumped back into Pollock's truck and headed over to Retta's. The sun had begun its initial descent and all of Trams became shady and, somehow, lazy. Pollock demonstrated his parallel parking skills behind Stacey's jeep and Cabe nodded in amused approval. Cabe opened the passenger door and hopped out onto the curb lawn. He arched his back and kinked his neck side to side. When he noticed that Pollock was still seated he said, "Yo, you coming?" through the open window. Acoustic folk music could be heard coming from behind the house.

Pollock closed his eyes and took a deep breath. His prework habit had now translated to the social arena. His nerves were amped and his heart rate elevated. It became instantly apparent to him that he was dreading this party. He didn't want to be there and wondered why he'd come, anticipating a disaster. After a second measured breath, he firmed his resolve and mustered some confidence. He knew he was among friends and he could make the party a good thing if he chose to. A phrase entered his head, but he couldn't recall where it came from. Regardless, he liked it. "The future is ours," he whispered.

He was on the verge of moving when, like a crashing wave of deafening clamor, the radio sliced through his meditative peace. "All I needed was the love you gave, all I needed for another day…only you." Pollock ripped the keys from the ignition and mumbled, "Fucking Yaz!" under his breathe.

Laughing, Cabe said, "What the fuck was that?"

Pollock didn't respond, but instead slammed the door shut with extra vigor and trotted around to the yard. "Let's go say our hellos, maybe enlist some helpers for all of this wood," he said.

They made their way around back, Cabe following behind Pollock, who was more marching than walking. The folk music grew louder as they approached the fire pit. It was growing darker by the minute, the stars overhead coming into focus, piercing through the pastel glow of dusk.

"Hello, hello," Cabe shouted out, catching up to Pollock. Retta, now in a floral print dress that ran to her ankles, some fashionably retro hippy remnant, sprang from her chair and skipped over toward them. She was still barefoot. Without a word, she wrapped her arms tightly around Pollock's neck and pressed her lips forcefully against his. "Beautiful day. You're just in time to get the fire going before dark." It was readily apparent to both Cabe and Pollock that Retta was already well on her way to heavy inebriation.

"Good results, baby!" Cabe responded. Pollock nodded reticently. Retta then hugged Cabe. "Thanks for coming!" she said, struggling a little to keep her stance. Pollock glanced past Retta and surveyed the fire pit. There were maybe ten people, all drinking and engaging in disparate conversations. Pollock prepared for introductions and small talk. A hand cracked down on his shoulder and fingers curled into the soft base of his neck.

"Hey buddy," Hans said, with a contented smirk.

Pollack was enraged. He said nothing to Hans but merely turned his head to acknowledge his presence, and then grabbed Retta by the forearm and led her away from the others, nearer to the house. "Hey!" she shouted, furiously, displeased with Pollock's hearty grip.

"What the fuck, Retta?" She looked at him with confusion. "What the fuck is he doing here?"

Retta exhaled in consternation. "Stacey, my friend that you haven't met, and I went on a booze run and ran into him at the grocery store. He didn't have anything going on, so I invited him along. Like, I think he's into Stacey. You really need to chill out." She pulled her wrist from his fingers, rubbing it with her other hand.

"He's not into your friend, he's into you. And just generally trying to humiliate me. If he stays here, I will ending up killing him. I will."

"I get a little jealousy," Retta said, "but this much insecurity isn't becoming. Just play nice, and if he's bothering you, then, like, hang out with any of the other dozen people here." She placed her palms on his elbows and implored him with a soft look. He looked past her and watched Hans and Cabe laughing and nodding at one another as if they were the closest of pals. "Look, things are really good right now," she said. "I don't want you to drag things down. It's been going really well between us. Just try to enjoy yourself, okay?"

The soft look was effective. Pollock nodded. "Fine. I need a drink." She smiled and led them back to the circle, where Cabe was kneeling and tinkering with the ground and the alignment of the brick stacks forming the rim of the fire pit. He looked up and addressed Retta.

"I like the design of the pit. The holes in the weave will let in some oxygen, but not too much."

Derek, who had arrived some thirty minutes earlier and had mostly kept to himself while nursing his Pabst Blue Ribbon tall boy, said, "So when are we gonna get this bad boy burnin'?"

Cabe hopped back up to his feet. "I like where your head's at," he said and turned to Pollock. "Shall we?"

"Indeed," Pollock responded and the two of them began unloading the wood. Derek and Hans helped, and it only took three trips. Once all of the logs were laid out on the lawn, Cabe commenced sawing the logs down to two-foot segments. He then split the segments into halves, and some into fourths. He worked hard and fast, and whenever anyone asked if they could help, he waved them off. "Fire Chefs only."

While Cabe processed the wood, Pollock made his introductions to Retta's friends. With a whisper in the ear, she would explain how little she knew most of them, but Stacey was different. "She's the best friend I've had. We don't see each other so often, but, like, we always pick up where we left off. It's important to me that you two get along, you know, like the Spice Girls song?" She laughed at this, and for all of his anxiety and frustration, Pollock smiled and nodded his head, admitting the hilarity of the reference.

Tony and Danielle were a married couple that happened to be wearing matching yellow T-shirts. In block white text, the shirts both read "biscuits." Nearly everyone present had inquired about the meaning of the word, and each time the couple merely responded with mirthful chuckles. It was no different when Pollock asked, and their raucous reaction annoyed him.

Retta explained to Pollock that, during college, Tony had been a hippy with long hair, who dumpster dived and organized protests of all sorts. In the years after graduation, he had joined a Presbyterian congregation where he was now employed as a youth minister. He and his wife lived in a community house with twelve fellow Presbyterian roommates. The clean-mouthed, well-manicured young man at the party was at odds with how she'd remembered him. And, before long, it was apparent that they had ulterior motives, of the proselytizing variety, for attending the party.

After organizing the logs into four piles by size, Cabe sprinkled some paper, twigs and two birch bark curls from his Altoid tin into the pit. This kindling caught right away and he began adding the pieces of split wood. Once those were burning, he moved on to the larger pieces. The whole group sort of instinctually quieted and focused on the infant fire. The wood was dry and cracked loudly.

Pollock saw that for all his research and preparation, the fire Cabe built was pretty simple. He figured that, perhaps, with a focused audience, Cabe felt the pressure and reverted to his more familiar fire-starting methods. That, in fact, was what had happened, and Cabe let out a massive exhale of relief once the fire was burning steadily, with a growing heap of smoldering coals underneath its teepee of halved logs. It hissed and kissed forth sporadic bouquets of glowing sparks.

The advent of the fire proper coincided with the onset of night and everyone's face and body became hues of flickering red and yellow. Hans sat himself nearest the iPod and speakers, which turned him into the de facto disc jockey. So, accordingly, a great many Jimi Hendrix, Lightnin' Hopkins, and Bo Diddley songs played. Tony and Danielle kept requesting U2. "Bono's lyrics are so powerful," Danielle explained to Hans. She then proceeded to sing along to every word of "Sunday Bloody Sunday" while it played, to the pleasure of Tony and chagrin of everyone else.

Derek mostly quietly nodded along to conversations, or stretched out one end of his bottom lip to express disagreement. But he got excited to request songs.

His choices were circling around the Smashing Pumpkins, Radiohead, Spiritual-ized, the Ramones and the Sex Pistols. He'd give a glib endorsement of his own request each time and then bob his head intently as it played. "'A Wolf at the Door' is the best song from *Hail to the Thief*. Totally underrated album."

Dikembe, who wore a buttoned-up black silk vest as a shirt, had brought a cooler full of beers from Zeitgeist Brewery where he worked as a hops specialist or brewmaster's assistant, depending on who asked him. There were sixty stouts, IPAs, and porters inside. In conjunction with the six-packs, cases, growlers of beer and mead, and bottles of wine that nearly everyone else brought and the other cooler that Retta and Stacey had fully stocked with Seagram's from their booze run, the party was equipped with enough alcohol for each person to imbibe until they were passed out drunk, and then some.

Wallace was Derek's life partner, though the two remained about as separate as any two other people at the party, and he kept interjecting political facts and opinions on which no one seemed interesting in commenting, except for Cheryl, who was a nursing student with Retta. "Increased taxes cost more, sure, but an-other way of looking at them is that they make more things free. For everyone," Wallace announced during the kindling stage of the fire.

Cheryl responded, "Right? Imagine never having to make a tuition pay-ment." Derek, from across the pit, stretched the end of his lip.

Jess, Jen, Abby and Carolyn all arrived together in high heels and glittered dresses. Somewhat entertainingly, Quentin arrived at the same moment. He strolled up the sidewalk with a bottle of sherry for Pollock under his arm. With his rigid plain black ball cap and stonewashed jeans, his appearance resembled that of an undercover federal agent. The four girls poured out of their Uber SUV, their heels clicking against the concrete, accompanied by their lithe giggles.

"I take it that this is where the party is?" Quentin said, with a sincere smile as he approached.

The girls, never having met this older man before were instantly alarmed by his introductory remarks. "Uh, can we help you?" Abby said with disgust, eyeing the stranger as if he were a creepy sex predator. The other girls all turned in unison, forming what Quentin perceived as a hostile formation akin to lionesses defending their territory. He guessed that made him the wayward chimp.

"Yes, you're right to be suspicious. My apologies, my name is Quentin. I am a friend of Retta's. She's invited me over to her soiree, to which, I assume, you are headed as well."

The SUV pulled away and the girls remained gathered in their defensive front. "You're friends with Retta?" Carolyn asked, more at a loss as to how this man figured out Retta's name than actually considering he might be telling the truth. The others stood stone-faced.

"Yes. Pollock introduced us. I used to be his—Well, I am sort of his professional mentor and personal friend. He's my protégé. Do you girls know Pollock as well?" he asked with an even larger smile, trying to warm the interaction.

"Who's Pollock?" Abby asked, still disgusted.

"Never mind. Pleasure to meet you..." He turned and made his way through the driveway.

Abby shrugged her shoulders and the others followed suit. Pollock, sitting in a chair beside Tony, and still perturbed about biscuits, looked out over the fire as Quentin rounded the house and entered the backyard. From Pollock's view, it appeared as though Quentin arrived with an entourage of scantily clad millennial females in tow. It made him happy and alleviated some aggravation with Hans and Cabe, and, well, biscuits.

Before Pollock could stand and greet his much welcomed former boss, the four girls, in piercing high-pitched screeches announced themselves. "Retta!" "Here we are, bitches!" "Hey girl!" The entire fire circle, even Cabe, who was hunched over the flames adjusting the placement of a midsized log, stopped what they were doing and watched the four shake their hands and scream and laugh as they washed around Quentin and began making their rounds of hugs and compliments.

Retta continued imbibing Seagram's with vigor. Her insides were dancing, and she was warm and happy. The skin on her forehead and above her toes burned from the earlier sun. By the time she had finished greetings with the girls, it occurred to her just how well the party had been going. Everyone had pitched in on the dream catcher. It was completed before Pollock and Cabe had even arrived. It sat in its ten-foot glory at the end of the yard.

Standing alone and to the side for a moment, Retta looked upon the crowd in the backyard. She couldn't make out what everyone was saying, but all of the faces had smiles, and many were laughing. She noted how diligently Cabe was keeping the fire going. Even Pollock was playing nice, jesting and joking with Quentin. It matched the hues of her emotional place. The momentum of the recent past was continuing. The good feelings were strong, and it made her happy that she could quell all of her previous hesitations.

"God, it feels so delightful to be drunk in the summertime," she said, loud enough for the whole bunch to hear it.

"Amen to that," Cabe said, pulling his warming beer bottle from the ledge of the brick circle, raising it high to the night sky, and tilting it up to quaff the contents. In doing so, he managed to smear black ash underneath one of his eyes and along his nondrinking forearm.

The party went along with a mix of to-be-remembered highlights amid a black wall of fuzziness. Cabe did an admirable job of keeping the fire blazing throughout. Pollock and Quentin mostly hung together, rehashing notable interactions they had shared with Trams citizens. Hans spent the majority of his time engaging the gaggle of scantily clad girls. Mostly he was interested in Jen, who had also run cross-county in high school. They regaled each other with tales of their respective successes and failures. And as the night went on, the alcohol set in.

Retta had drunk herself to the point of becoming aware she might pass out. It was an embarrassing prospect, being the one responsible for the party. So she started drinking water and laying low, alone in her plastic chair, doing as little as was required of a hostess. And for all her determination to stay awake, she did fall asleep. Everyone noticed at one point or another, but she looked so very comfortable and had extended such hospitality, that no one bothered her.

There came a point when the partygoers began rehearsing their parting scripts and then split, making their goodbyes to those they believed merited it. The biscuit couple departed with merely an amicable nod to those left. Cabe, contented with his performance, eventually lay down on a beach towel in the grass, which Stacey had set out hours earlier, and fell asleep. Wallace and Derek made a show of their departure, shaking hands with all present.

Dikembe sat cross-legged at the fire pit, aggressively swigging the Zeitgeist beer he had brought, almost as if intent on finishing that which all of the others had neglected to imbibe. The gaggle of girls, highly aware of the dying social event, saw themselves out front to wait for their Uber. They merely pursed their lips upon exiting the yard. Jen gave Hans her number before departing. She had hopes of moving forward with Hans. She had found him dashing and capable. Dikembe disappeared at some point.

Around the dying embers remained Pollock, Quentin and Hans. The mood was tired. Quentin felt far too old for his surroundings, yet honored to be welcomed in and somewhat proud to have survived and to be among those left at the end. Pollock had settled in to an insular attention to the pain in his ankles. He bent forward from his chair and removed his boots, and then his sweaty socks. The relief was great, and he couldn't believe he had been wearing pants and boots the entire time.

The quiet became quite pregnant. Conversation was coming. It was only a question of between whom and of what. The crackling and hissing of the scorched logs filled the backyard until the silence became unbearable. Pollock envisioned carrying Retta into bed and then cleaning up. Quentin was picturing his father on those weekend marches through the Acadia trails. He wondered whether he would follow his father's rainbows into the afterlife. The idea terrified him. It was a terribly boring view of things to come. And it scared him that he was already thinking of the end. He moved his eyes back and forth from Pollock to Hans.

It was Hans who finally broke the silence. "So what's the deal with you, bud?" he said to Pollock. The question made Quentin uncomfortable, seeing the impending battle. He straightened his back and directed his attention to Pollock, who had murder in his eyes. Quentin thought the "bud" was especially provoking and clearly meant to be received as disrespect or, at minimum, a challenge. The potency of the words hung in the air for a moment before Pollock responded.

"Can I help you with something?" Pollock said. His response was brilliant in how it dismissed the import of Hans's previous question. Quentin took a moment to admire this in an almost fatherlike way. Hans responded with a snort of appreciation, as if he had anticipated the antipathy. The silence returned for a moment until Pollock offered up more.

"All brilliant people know that the truth must be suffered," he said. Quentin squinted, a bit confounded by what the relevance of this response could be. Yet, he was eager to see how the conversation progressed. This was as close to live entertainment as he had come in some time. And, in any event, he had a proverbial horse in the race. His heart rate elevated and his eye flicked back and forth between his current and former colleague with accelerated frequency.

"Pollock, you carry yourself as if there is some veiled reality that only you can perceive. Why is that? What is it that you think gave you access to this secret nature of things? Are you the only one? The chosen one?" Hans asked, with a smirk of satisfaction. Pollock looked quickly at Hans, not keen on any of the knee-jerk responses that came to mind. Hans leaned over the dying embers. The plastic chair creaked under his weight. "Look, you take yourself too seriously. And you have too-thin skin. I don't know you all that well, but I believe that you are probably a great guy. You just weren't the best suited for that job. *You* lost. It's not *my* fault."

Pollock and Hans met eyes, Pollock's adrenaline surging madly. "What the fuck does that mean?" Pollock said.

Quentin's eyes leapt back and forth between the two like a cartoon cat watching a ping-pong match. Hans's smirk faded, with a visible air of pity overcoming his previous self-satisfaction. This only angered Pollock further, who was beginning to feel very cornered.

Hans took in a deep breath and said, "The environment allows those to thrive which are best suited, best adapted to it. It's not that complicated. Ecosystems weed out the tourists, the ill-equipped and—"

"Ha!" Pollock said. "You're explaining selection to me? You think that I don't understand how selection works? This doesn't have anything to do with selection. I had great plans for Trams, Hans. But at every turn it was you whispering fucking God knows what into Freedman's ears. You're not serious about this job. You're just a hustler."

"A hustler, hmm?" Hans said, amused. "Well, you say that you understand selection and that it played no part in our twirl of fate. Yet, I think if you really understood, you'd see that whispering in Freedman's ear, as you put it, well that's what was required. It was what the environment demanded. And if you cared, or rather, if you were the most fit for this position, you would have been doing the same. You didn't though. And so now I am a *hustler*? You can call me whatever you would like. The truth is you lost. You lost and it is not my fault." With this pronouncement, Hans became very serious. Images of Rob Durci flashed through his imagination.

"Bah!" Pollock howled, rising to his feet. It had become too much. "I may have lost, but at least I'm on the right side of things. You and Freedman are going to turn Trams into a freak show of cronyism development projects. Private-partnership strip malls with tax abatements as far the eye can see, right? Don't you want to change the environment? Not just abide by it at any cost?" He looked down upon Hans and felt somewhat righteous. It had all become clear to him, that he had a point of view, that he was taking a stand. And it was curious that he felt like he hadn't before. He knew now it had been there all along.

Hans remained serious. To him, the mood had shifted from uncomfortable to grave. He spoke quietly from beneath Pollock's aggressive posture. "Those partnerships create a lot of jobs. Look, I should probably take off. This isn't going to get us anywhere good. You can complain and lament on your own time."

The condescension, the belittling, it was all too much. Pollock couldn't bear it. He reached out and lashed his knuckles against Hans's cheek. The backhanded slap seemed to echo through the humid summer air.

Quentin's jaw dropped. At the precipice of violence, most humans fill with a rampage of nerves. The inner beast, usually somnambulant, peers out through its lashes. And a savagery of biological origin becomes sickeningly apparent. Quentin, Hans, and Pollock all experienced a flash of this sickness. And the conversation that had been unfolding at once was irrelevant and ancient. Hans slowly rose to his feet. He was much taller than Pollock, and because of this, the move itself shifted the power dynamic.

"Do it again," Hans said, calmly looking down at Pollock. There was no regret in Pollock; he was fully committed. This physical outburst was the conclusion, the topper of something that had been building for some time. Without reconsideration, he threw his elbow across his body and swung his hand back as

hard as he could. Instead of landing once again upon Hans's cheek, it was inter-
cepted by the hard grasp of Hans's left hand. It remained there a moment until
Hans pulled it sharply downward and kneed Pollock in the head.

The blow knocked him sideways into the grass. But his confidence in his aggression only doubled and he clambered to his feet. This time he swung a fist.
Hans ducked his head aside and the punch missed. He rebutted with a left hook of
his own, which landed squarely on Pollock's eye ridge. Again, he was flung to the
grass. Quentin, now on his feet, called out, "Enough, boys!"

But Pollock had just begun, and was about to triple down on his original
play. He hobbled to his feet, and through his pain and anger, dived into Hans's
midsection, wrapping his arms around his waist. He planted his feet and attempted
to lift Hans from the ground. But Hans merely grabbed Pollock's rear belt loop,
arched his back and flung him over his shoulders, like an expert wrestler. Once
again Pollock was in the grass, and it was becoming obvious to him that Hans was
going to get the best of this dust up. Nevertheless, he quickly rose to his feet.

"Goddamn it, enough, Pollock. Enough," Quentin said, stepping between
him and Hans. He recognized in Pollock his own deep hurt and disappointment. It
was so familiar and embarrassing. It was inconvenient and agonizing. Quentin
had learned long ago to cover up these failures with a distanced cynicism, using
wit and sarcasm. It was alarming to see someone struggling with it so viscerally.

He put his hand on Pollock's chest. Pollock shoved it off. "Go take a
breather. Go, now!" Quentin pleaded, pointing to Retta's house. Pollock looked
past Quentin at Hans, who was hunched over, hands on knees, huffing fiercely.
The rage was unbearable, but Pollock instinctively followed Quentin's command.
He opened the sliding glass door and thrust it shut harshly behind him as he paced
across the living room and entered the kitchen.

There, having just put Fox to bed and heading out back to gauge the state of
Retta's party, stood Remy. Pollock, propelled by his jittering adrenaline, almost

crashed into him. But he stopped in time, and the two strangers stood face to face. Pollock noticed that Remy had pockmarks all over the hollows of his cheeks. This was the first time that he had seen the man's face. The past few weeks, Remy's triumphant return, slipped completely from Pollock's memory. "What a worthless piece of shit," he said, "leaving Retta to take care of everything." And with that, Pollock launched into the man. Their entwined bodies cracked hard against the kitchen linoleum. Remy's head thudded into the metal of the oven frame. Pollock cocked his armed and clocked Remy directly in the forehead. The hit stung his fist, but did not dissuade him at all. He punched Remy in the head, again and again and again. The man was unable to put forth any resistance.

Noah Studebaker had left his overalls phase behind and now focused mostly on leather biker jackets. He was polishing his vintage black scooter in the driveway. Mr. Studebaker was smoking a cigarette at his workbench. Pollock saw him in his jean jacket through the garage window. It was strange because it was afternoon, and there was no air of secrecy. Perhaps Mrs. Studebaker was out of town, or Mr. Studebaker had made some sort of stand for his liberties.

The Ventillis' bedroom curtains had been drawn for the past several weeks and Pollock had observed a heated argument that ended in several objects being tossed about and broken. The next morning, a girl pulled into the drive in a red Ford Focus and Karen came out with luggage. She wasn't wearing her lab outfit. Pollock watched Benji's fingers spread open the first floor blinds as the two finished packing the car and then drove off down Nyqvist.

The Ne'er-do-wells had been quiet lately and their sightings sparse. Pollock still owed them a good braining for the little breaking and entering stunt they had pulled on him. But that seemed utterly irrelevant at this point. It didn't even anger him to think of it anymore. The binocular eyepieces were beginning to leave sore circles around his eyes so he replaced them on the kitchen nook. Surveillance had been Pollock's main daily activity for the past several weeks, aside from his meetings with Eddie Reinart.

After what had happened at Retta's and his earlier conversations with her about the positives of therapy, he contacted the offices of Trams Community Counseling and Therapeutic Solutions. He had been directed there by a representative from his insurance plan because they were in network. After emailing in a quick questionnaire, the TCCTS office administrator directed him to Eddie, who specialized in depression, anxiety, anger and stress management, and suicidal ideations.

In their initial meeting, Eddie referenced a section from the questionnaire in which Pollock had written that he believed he may be depressed. Eddie explained to him that depression was a mood disorder that caused a persistent feeling of sadness and loss of interest. Also called major depressive disorder or clinical depression, Eddie told him it affects how one feels, thinks and behaves and can lead to a variety of emotional and physical problems. "You may have trouble doing normal day-to-day activities, and sometimes you may feel as if life isn't worth living." Pollock nodded along, indicating that all the above applied to him and also that he knew all of this.

"So you do believe that you are depressed?" Eddie asked.

Pollock thought a moment and said, "I don't know if my being depressed is the problem, so much as a symptom of the real problem, which is that there is no way to live with other humans. Period. It's the truth and there's no escaping it."

Eddie nodded her head, adjusting her suit pant that had caught against the rough wool fabric of the chair. "Okay. Perhaps you are right." Pollock's eyes, which had been complacently wandering about her office, flicked back to her. He was expecting her to deny his premise, yet here she had agreed.

She continued, "I can see that, sure. People are mostly pretty nasty and cruel to one another. I struggle with depression myself, and quite frankly, a lot of it has to do with that very reason. That's a trigger. But…the depression itself is separate. One can be genetically predisposed for depression. And it manifests in a change of brain chemicals—low serotonin and dopamine, spiked cortisol and norepinephrine. These changes are what tracks with the feelings of sadness, the obsessive thoughts, and the stress about interactions. And sure, maybe we can't fix the whole of human drama tomorrow, but we can adjust how we react to it. We can lessen its burden so that it's not so pervasive and paralyzing."

Pollock wanted to fight with Eddie. He figured this stance was natural since she was trying to categorize him, and at heart, he thought of himself as special. He wanted to outfox her. So it was surprising to him how easily and maturely he agreed with what she had said. He arrived to their second meeting ready to cooperate and put some trust in her wisdom. By the third meeting, she had recommended that Pollock needed to imagine what he wanted next, what he wanted in his life. She sent him home that day with that sole objective as homework before their next meeting.

And so he had been meditating on what his move could possibly be. He knew he couldn't be a reclusive misanthrope the rest of his life. But he worried that every time he got mixed up with people, it all went sideways, fast. The recurring doubts and anger, the cyclical reflection on the night of the fire, kept him from conjuring any images of a better future. Feelings of futility and impossibility kept rushing back into him. Thus, he had spent his time watching the neighborhood.

And now, as he set the binoculars down he felt guilty that it was because of skin soreness from overuse and not because he was doing his homework assignment for Eddie. He slouched down onto the couch. The couch where he had slept for months and where Cabe had lived for weeks. He sat there motionless for two hours until he heard a curious sound. It reminded him of the football stadium heard from across town on Friday nights. But it wasn't Friday, or even autumn.

And what he could now make out as different voices were getting louder and louder.

He rose to his feet and trotted back over to the window. Spilling out from the woods into Klum Court were hundreds of people. They were all yelling and hollering and shaking fists to the sky. Pollock rushed out onto the porch. As he watched the crowd march through the court and onto Nyqvist, it dawned on him that these were tent city folks. He then noticed that they were all wearing something that covered their heads and faces.

Once they were near his house, he saw that they all had strapped mirrors to their faces, each a different size and shape. Some appeared to have been stripped from cars, others were broken pieces from a larger whole. They looked over at him as they passed, and he could see odd reflections of the front lawn and his porch where their eyes should be. He caught himself in a large oval affixed to one of the taller walkers. Their chants were indistinct screams, guttural, primal, and haunting.

His phone buzzed in his pocket and, like a programmed zombie, he pulled it out and read his newsfeed notification. It read: "Strange Homeless Protest Shocks Three Cities: Benson, Elam, Dowd."

"Three other cities…" he said, perplexed. There were no reporters or cameras around. But people were starting to come out of their houses. The ancient lady Sheffield stood inside of her Plexiglas with a look of mortification plastered across her grey wrinkles. The Ne'er-do-wells assembled in hierarchical order between the Ventillis' house, fresh from who knew what secret orneriness.

As Pollock stood contemplating how many other cities and towns had exactly the same flood of tent city evictees spilling out into its streets, one of the mirrored walkers made his way up the steps and pulled off the mirrored mask. The dark skin and kind eyes were familiar to Pollock. It was Martin. He reached into his windbreaker and pulled out an extra mirrored mask. He held it out and Pollock's heart pounded.

Epilogue

Retta's lower back and ankles ached from so much dancing. The flashes of green and red lights spreading over the dark crowd still glared through her retinas, and she could still feel the awkward jabs and embraces of sweaty strangers on her shoulders and ass. It was a quarter mile walk through the sand between the concert pavilion and the hotel lobby. She reached it just as the dawning sun began leaving its orange shimmer on the Tasman Sea. The leather seat in the patio diner comforted her exhausted body. She peeled the rank bandanna from her sunburnt forehead and tossed it atop the ceramic table.

"Morning madam. Might I start you off with some coffee or juice?" a smartly dressed waitress asked her with a cordial smile. Retta had been up for nearly twenty-four hours, most of which was spent standing or walking from one stage to another to catch as many sets in the EDM music festival as possible. She couldn't imagine staying up much longer, but also didn't warm to the idea of sleeping through her last day in Sydney.

"Coffee, please. Black with a shot of espresso if you would," she said.

"Certainly. I'll be right back with that," the waitress said and darted off dutifully.

The city was still quiet. It was Sunday morning, and most of its inhabitants had not yet awoken. In the distance were faint howls, screams, and laughs from the festivalgoers, many of whom had elected to camp directly on the beach. But the year had been very good for Retta, financially. She had settled in at Clifton Memorial Hospital. And Remy had transferred a rather large portion of the profits from the house to her. So she had paid $950 Australian dollars to rent a proper room at the Marriott for the week. The king-size bed with memory foam mattress and plush blankets had, itself, been worth the money. Stacey had tagged along, so the bed was shared, as well as the expense. But it was still divine to Retta.

"And here you are," the waitress said, setting down the large white mug upon the tabletop. "Will you be needing anything else, any breakfast?" Retta shook her head, and the waitress disappeared without a word. She cupped her palms around the mug and took in the hot liquid. It was still cool enough outside that the warmth was welcomed. Remy and Fox popped back into her head as they had done throughout the week, ganging up to make her feel guilty.

She had not seen either of them as often as she would have liked these past few months. But when she did visit with them, it was clear that they were happy and well cared for at Aunt Myra's house. Fox got on well with the cousins, Freddy and Vinnie, and Remy had taken to the three-car garage. Myra's husband, Mario, had been a mechanic for many years before starting his own garage. That garage had turned into a chain of garages, and Mario now mostly handled the business side. He gave Remy a part time position working engine rebuilds. It kept Remy busy enough, and having him around the house was exciting for Mario because the two could bond over cars, an interest that appeared to completely skip over both of his offspring.

Retta visited with these thoughts of them and then quickly dispelled them, returning to the present. She wanted to be in the moment. She had dreamed for so long of visiting this country, and now that she was here, she could hardly believe it. There was a solemn pride about her as she pondered her achievement. It had all passed by so quickly, and now she was leaving. But there was a sturdy hope within that realization. She reflected on the previous week and all of the delightful little surprises it had held.

Her phone was pressing against her hipbone within her shorts' pocket. She arched her back against the chair back and slid it out. Stacey had texted her two hours ago.

> Heading back to room with Steven.
> If you come back, just give me a warning and we will get decent.
> Wink Wink!
> Great night!
> Awesomeeeee

She snorted and shook her head thinking of Stacey and Steven fucking in the king-sized bed. "Good thing I decided not to go to sleep," she said, and took another warm pull of coffee from the impossibly large mug. Through the lattice-work over the patio eating area, she could begin to see the occasional office light flickering on inside the jumble of downtown skyscrapers. The sparse rumblings of starting car engines echoed around from unknown directions. Seagulls chirped and cawed. And behind it all, the ocean gently heaved.

It was a monumental moment and one that Retta knew she would carry with her for the rest of her life. She turned around to fully absorb the scene, to perfect the memory so that she could carry the truth of it within. She tapped the iPhone camera and set it to panorama. Then, trying to keep her arms from shaking, she swept the camera across her field of vision. She looked at the result. "Perfect," she said.

She turned, balancing her knees on the chair and captured a panoramic shot of the area behind her, leading back to the beach she had just hiked across. Having decided she was pleased with this result as well, she tucked the camera back into her pocket and took one last swig of the cooling coffee, wondering where to go on her next trip.

* * *

The red curves of the new lawnmower reflected the sun directly into Hans's eyes while he mowed. It was one of the few things that displeased him about his purchase. It cut more evenly and pushed with a great deal less effort than his previous model. It edged and turned more easily, as well. He had found that he was now able to cross hatch angled rows of mowing, allowing the lines from the wheels to form a nice argyle pattern. Manicuring the yard had reached its next level.

Hans had never before taken much interest in landscaping. But now that he was a homeowner, he found himself devoting more and more of his Saturday and Sunday mornings to lawn care activities. The trunk of his Honda sedan was gritty from transporting two-cubic-foot bags of brown mulch, peat moss, and potting soil. Throughout the spring and summer, Hans had transformed the back lot from an unruly field into a pleasing display of shapes and colors.

The edges of his beds were lined with uniformly sized sedimentary stones from the quarry. Along the long left bed, there extended a straight line of intermixed perennial wildflowers and dwarf pine shrubs. The shorter right bed was punctuated by rhododendron and fern varietals. At the back of the yard, in the middle, was a circular bed centering on an eight-foot Japanese magnolia. It was just now approaching full bloom, sprouting haunting white and pink flowers. The wind had been carrying the petals over the back fence and into the Graysons' yard. It was an issue that would have to be addressed at some point in the future.

But Hans's most prized section of his new obsession was situated in the back right corner. It was a rock garden filled with all sorts of rocks he had hauled back from the Rahtze's banks. Above the rocks hung a hammock for after-work breaks, and behind the hammock was a small two-door shed which Hans had constructed himself following internet instructions. Inside the shed, he stored his growing collection of tools: a chainsaw, now two lawnmowers, hedge clippers, shovel, trowel, solar powered Weedwacker, pole pruner, and a smorgasbord of pots, seed packets, gardening gloves, and insect-repellent citronella candles.

His new weekend yard fascination had cut into his running regimen. Saturdays and Sundays had previously been his long days, where he really dug in and paced himself for distance. But once he began working for Ebersold and making good money, the running seemed less pertinent, less vital. Having a beautiful home and well-tended back yard in which to entertain guests had become the dominant calling for him. And so, over the span of a few months, he settled into running only during the week so that he could devote his weekend mornings, and often afternoons as well, to his landscaping visions.

The change in schedule amounted to approximately thirty miles less running each week. And his body had responded. He could feel the mounting softness over his abdomen. The accruing jiggles. He could also tell that his metabolism wasn't what it had used to be. Just two years previous, he could eat whatever he pleased, including sugary cookie treats, and there would be no physical consequences. Nowadays, he had to be cognizant of how many calories were in the blueberry muffins he more and more loved to consume during breakfast. He also began drinking.

It seemed he was right at the beginning of what would inevitably be a losing battle. He knew he could return to strict running form and his old dietary restrictions, perhaps even imposing further caloric strictures. But then he would miss out on all of his newfound joys. For example, Hans had discovered Indian cuisine. Palak paneer had proven to be the most delicious meal he could ever have fathomed. But one plate of the stuff was 1400 calories. And he also now had a routine ritual of drinking cold beers after he was done with the lawn work for the day. One cold beer quickly turned into three, and then four and a two-hour hammock nap afterward.

Or he could give in wholeheartedly to his new desires and leave his physical prowess and the highly meditative features of his long runs behind. He fondly reminisced about his Willerly Hills days, but he felt he was facing a new frontier of careers, mortgages, and lawn care. Those days seemed such a long time ago to him, now. Every time he thought about Willerly Hills, he ended up thinking about Robert Durci.

To the surprise of most but not at all Hans, Durci had become a successful musician. He was playing sets on the music festival circuits all across the US and Europe. He wasn't the headliner, but he was usually third or fourth down on the marquee. The name "Robert Durci" was always printed much larger than dozens of other smaller, lesser-known acts. His music had become the go-to brand for ravers, tweakers, partiers, and all variety of EDM fanatics. Retta was always listening to and going on about Durci. There was still an uncomfortable twinge in Hans when thinking of Robbie. His recent success made it much more bearable. He was proud of his old competitor and considered him a friend.

Hans finished mowing the yard and moved the mower into the shed, wiping the sweat on his brow with his sleeve. His tongue was already salivating in anticipation of the taste of ice-cold hops washing over his tongue and then sliding down, cooling his throat and stomach. He clicked the metal latch shut and headed for the garage fridge. He walked through the long mulch bed so as to avoid disturbing the crisp green argyle design.

These days, when thinking of Robbie, he had to think about Pollock. It only seemed appropriate. Hans considered Pollock a friend as much as he did Robbie, but Robbie and Hans had squared off when they were both still children, really. Pollock had been Hans's first adult adversary. Pollock was older than Hans, and

Hans's victory had had been so sweet, but also so taxing. His mind was forever tattooed with Pollock's existence. The tattoo wasn't exactly regretted, but it was large and permanent.

Hans wondered where Pollock was. No one had seen or heard from him since the fire. He had fallen hard. Hans thought it possible Pollock had fallen even harder than Robbie. But since he held Pollock and Robbie in the same category, he maintained a twinkle in his eye, a hope deep in his being that Pollock would rise again, stronger. Hans figured it would take some time, but he had no doubt Pollock would be a success yet.

The cap snapped as he twisted it off and poured it past his teeth. It was delightful and refreshing. The garage fridge wasn't quite as cold as the one in the kitchen, but Hans had learned that entering the air-conditioned kitchen to retrieve the beer ruined the impact of the cold liquid. The juxtaposition of the soggy summer heat in the garage and the cold beer far outweighed the slightly cooler temperature of the kitchen fridge when compared to the cool kitchen air. "Ahhh," Hans let out in delight after finishing off a Belgian ale in one long pull.

He snagged the cardboard handle of the six-pack container and brought the remaining five beers out to the hammock, once again treading carefully through the flowerbed to get there. Several vertebrae cracked with relief as he collapsed into the hemp netting. The sun assaulted him furiously, so he placed the bottom of the next bottle against his forehead. The effect was successful.

Each subsequent swig was a bit warmer, but it didn't matter, because Hans was becoming more and more tired. His neck and shoulder hurt from the awkward logistics of drinking horizontally. The Graysons' corgi, Gerard, was digging at the fence again. He speculated on whether the dog wanted to escape or if it was after something, and wondered how far it would get before the Graysons stopped it. A scary prospect presented itself; it would be a disaster if Hans came out back one day to discover Gerard burrowing up into the magnolia bed. It was a problem that he would have to prevent, at some point. For now, he didn't care. Hans was exhausted and it was naptime.

* * *

"Bastien Ebersold," he answered, setting the pencil down on the easel's ridge.

"It's a huge fucking problem!" the caller blurted. "Not even sure how fucking huge it is yet. Everyone who knows is losing their shit! We need you to get over here, boss,"

"Okay Keith, what's huge?" Bastion said calmly, masking his concern.

"Hold on a second, let me get away…" The receiver filled with hisses and scrapes and the sounds of jostling and rubbing.

"Keith? What's going on?" Bastion asked, his mask slimming.

"Okay, bodies man. Skeletons. Buried everywhere…er, all around the south courtyard. Its going to punch a hole in everything…I mean, I'm pretty positive that we gotta report this. I haven't checked yet, but I'm pretty damn positive! Huge fucking mess!"

Bastien stood up from his stool and switched his cell over to his right ear. "Whoa. Keith, don't do anything. I'm on my way over. Okay? Just sit tight until I get there." There was a moment of silence. "Keith?"

"Yeah, okay. Just hurry. Like I said, people are losing their shit about this." Bastien slipped his cell back into the chest pocket of his dress shirt and took a critical glance at the drawing as it stood. The image was a woman's upper back. The skin had been cut and opened up so that the spine was exposed. A wrench was affixed to an upper thoracic vertebra, twisting it clockwise. Bastion wasn't that pleased with how it had turned out.

He ripped the paper from the easel, crumpled it harshly in his hands, and tossed it to the floor. "Bodies," he said aloud. The plan for Courtyard Communities Living Space had gone so smoothly that Bastien had anticipated a hang-up would be soon arriving. But he did not anticipate there would be bodies. Although, this wasn't an entirely unusual issue. He'd encountered small graveyards, often Native Americans, in many of his development projects. In most cases, it was possible to continue on with the project and leave only a small area behind schedule while officials and local anthropologists examined the site.

But the on-site workers usually took issue with such a situation. Bastien thought most people had seen too many scary movies like *Poltergeist* and, at the first mention of a native American burial ground, firmly stand opposed to any further involvement. So, while the impediment was usually a relatively small fix, it did always involve replacing a number of workers, which was hard if word spread. He knew extra pay helped, but Ebersold had a reputation for completing his development projects at or below budget.

So the additional pay, whether to retain current superstitious workers, or entice others to begin, would have to come from his personal accounts. Bastion mulled this over on his ride to the site. But, more present in his mind was the failure of his latest sadist drawing. Initially, it had seemed to him that wrenching one's vertebrae would produce such sweet pain. It now seemed very bland. And it all played into Bastien's fear of diminishing returns. He worried that he had already had the greatest kicks of his life, that his greatest torments were behind him. Thinking about what life could possibly come after this one disturbed him something gargantuan.

Once at the site, Keith rushed Bastien up to an observation scaffold overlooking the dig site where the southern fourth of apartments and stores were to be erected. It was a large expanse of disturbed dirt, some several dozen feet deep.

Therein, scattered, yet in consistent rows and columns, were hundreds of human skeletons. The scale overwhelmed Bastien as he focused on what he was seeing.

"My God," Bastien said quietly, terrified and also wholly thrilled by the sight.

"Yeah," Keith said. "I let the workers take the rest of the day. It only makes sense. This isn't a Native American family buried at the edge of a quarter acre plot. It's a big fucking mess. Huge, like historical. And we gotta report it." Bastion was absorbed in his contemplation of what had occurred there and wasn't paying much attention to the foreman. Keith noticed put a hand on Bastien's arm. "Hey, boss. We gotta report this, yeah?"

A week later, at the recommendation of the Trams Community College anthropology department, a private laboratory, Trace Labs, arrived to take samples and conduct a series of contextualizing experiments. Another week and they had results. Using radiocarbon dating and sampling the surrounding soils, the bodies were determined to be just over 150 years old. The initial report, circulated among Ebersold's partners, indicated that most of the skeletons had traumatic indentations to their fingers, feet, eye sockets, and the back of the skull. All appearances led to the implication of some form of ritualized or sacrificial violence.

* * *

Several evenings later, Canby squeezed his plump midsection through the gaping split in the house's back door and furtively scurried across the laminated kitchen tiles. The lawn was still unmowed and reaching heights that provided him full coverage. No lights in the house had been on for years. But the occasional coyote or bobcat could wander inside. It was an attractive locale for all wandering beasts. And, the Ne'er-do-wells occasionally snuck in to engage in their latest fad: smoking pot.

He peeked around the corner of the vestibule and out into the living room. The moonlight poured through the back dining room windows and made everything on the first floor a pale blue. All was quiet and safe. He hopped up onto the sagging couch and burrowed into the nest he had made in the rear of the back cushion. It was going to be morning soon and Canby was tired. The night had been rewarding. And the night had been exhausting.

Earlier, he'd met with his brothers and several other male friends in the Cappis's Barn to share with them tales of scavenging. Life as an adult raccoon was more solitary and Canby appreciated these social events dearly. He'd raised his brothers for almost a year before they went their separate ways, and his heart constantly reminded him of their absence. The dark sky above proved much more ominous when looking upon it by oneself.

It was likely that Canby would not live much longer. Many other raccoons his age had already moved on. He'd come across their lifeless bodies all over the edges of his nightly routes. Between cars, coyotes, illness, miscellaneous accidents involving humans, and diabetes, a short life expectancy was a harsh reality for their kind. At least in Trams. But his new home in the abandoned house on Nyqvist Boulevard offered him a better opportunity for longevity. He wished the same for his brothers.

THE END